Hired Luck

TWISTED LUCK BOOK 2
TERNION UNIVERSE

MEL TODD

BAD ASH PUBLISHING

Copyright © 2020 Melisa Todd

All rights reserved. No part of this publication may be reproduced, distributed or transmitted in any form or by any means, without prior written permission.

Publishers Note: This is a work of fiction. Names, characters, places, and incidents are a product of the author's imagination. Locales and public names are sometimes used for atmospheric purposes. Any resemblance to actual people, living or dead, or to businesses, companies, events, institutions, or locales is completely coincidental.

Hired Luck | Mel Todd – 1st ed.
ISBN 978-1-950287-18-5
Book Design by ArtisticWhispers

Roll with the punches, or the punches will crush you.

CHAPTER 1

The job outlook for those who chose not to give in to the seduction of magic is poor. While people were once discriminated against because of their skin color, now it is your ability to use magic. Stop the bias now. Treat all people equal.
~Freedom from Magic

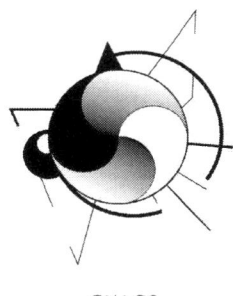

CHAOS

I really miss the Rockway 911 operators.
My thought turned wry as I leaned against the faded brick wall, the heat of the day soaking into my skin, and gazed at the scene in front of me. Even after so many dead and almost dead bodies, this one made my skin crawl and I didn't want to get any closer. Normally I wanted to investigate, figure out how they were killed, make sure there was nothing I could have done to help. But this one, I didn't even want to be as close as I was. I swallowed again, really wishing I had a soda. Carbonation might scour the fear out of my throat.

"You're reporting a dead body?" The person, woman I thought, asked on the other end.

"Yes."

"Location?"

I rattled that off, even as I tried to shake off the chills washing through my body. It was ninety-five with eighty-three percent humidity. Chills should not have even been part of my being. Instead I wanted to back up further into the sunshine and bake the cold out of my soul. I pressed back harder against the wall, a lizard seeking heat.

"Is the death by natural causes?"

"Not even remotely," my tone bleak as I said that. Part of me wanted to run away, but I stayed, my mind projecting the image of the young woman nailed to a White Pine with strange circles surrounding her. I couldn't get it to go away even if now I looked at the park from an angle where you couldn't see anything.

The way she had been killed screamed ritual magic, but that was all I knew. Ritual magic, possible. I didn't know another damn thing. I really needed more hours in the day to learn more but right now medical stuff was still my focus. If I didn't get a job soon, my savings would start dwindling and every day that passed caused my stress to ramp up a bit more.

"Have you performed lifesaving activities?" The operator had no personality, but right now my uneasiness didn't even allow for snark. Though I suspected I'd be lashing out when the cops showed up and treated me like an idiot.

"No." My voice flat. "And I will not. You don't want an ambulance. You need investigators, forensics, and a coroner."

And maybe the FBI or some other group. OMO?

The operator's voice got frostier. "And who are you to say what is needed?"

That got through my apathy, and shock and I snapped back. "The person looking at a twenty something year old young woman nailed to a tree with her heart and eyes missing. Her face cut up and peeled off, and I'm pretty sure her fingerprints were removed from the amount of blood that dripped from the tips of her hands. So yes, I'm sure an ambulance won't help her."

There was a long pause on the other end, then in a much nicer voice. "Please provide your name and contact number for the officers that are arriving."

I could hear the sirens in the distance as I provided that. Over her protests, I hung up. I needed a few minutes to gather myself before dealing with the circus that was about to begin. It felt like the sightless face stared at me, but I knew it wasn't. She couldn't see me on the other side of the tree. Right?

I'd been out walking around the area of our apartment and got a bit lost. I wasn't that worried about it, figuring getting lost now and then was part of the fun. I'd gone down an alley, and it opened up into a tiny park that reminded me of the ones I'd seen in Savannah when I visited a long time ago.

Smiling, I'd headed in when the scent of blood hit me - that coppery sweet scent that etches across your soul, or at least had across mine. I'd frozen, then turned and saw her on the tree not twenty feet from me. You would never see

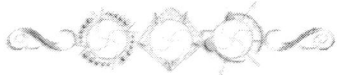

her until you walked into the park. From the outside, nothing gave away what the trees hid. Nothing to let you know a woman had died there.

Her hands were lifted above her head and nailed to the tree, holding her body in place. The killer had peeled her skin away from her face, leaving torn and bleeding flesh, plus two holes where her eyes should have been. Her button-up shirt was open, revealing the hole in her chest. Her hands were a bloody mess, as if they had been peeled also. She looked like something out of a horror movie, but I was the one looking at her.

I'd backed out to the safety of the walls of the buildings, leaning against them for a long time until I could hold the phone without my hand shaking. With the other deaths I'd seen none of them had this level of darkness, of horror to them.

And here I thought that part of my life was done. Stupid for thinking that I guess.

I didn't have time for much more as sirens, the squeal of tires and slamming of doors occurred behind me.

They don't know you: be calm, no attitude. Getting thrown in jail your second week in Atlanta would not be a good thing.

"Did you call in the report? There's a dead body?" A youngish cop asked and I saw his partner - older, black, with a definite Danny Glover in Lethal Weapon vibe. He wasn't doing anything to risk his retirement.

The idea made my lips twitch; I needed the humor but I kept my hands at my side and nodded. "Yes. In there, against the tree."

The young man looked around, jumping at the rustle of the leaves in the trees. I don't know if my being so calm helped or hurt. "Stay right there," he snapped out the order, moving sideways into the small park, his gun aimed low. I knew the second he saw her. He started to retch and sprinted back towards me, hitting the opposite wall and losing everything he'd eaten. Unfortunately, I now knew he'd had a sandwich for lunch. What little appetite I'd had fled completely.

After he managed to stand up, his partner, who must have gone back to the car while the younger cop avoided contaminating the evidence, handed him a bottle of water. After rinsing his mouth he looked at me, eyes hard.

"Why don't I see your stomach contents anywhere?" His voice accusatory. I wanted to sigh. If I'd killed her, I would not have called it in nor would I have left the body anyplace so obvious, or at least so public.

"I've seen worse," I said, my voice noncommittal. Going into my weird life, not to mention I wasn't sure if this was body fourteen or eighteen, it depended on if you counted the dead people I'd seen while working, would not make them feel any better. Though I hadn't seen worse, not really, but death didn't make me throw up. So I left it at that. Besides, the guy with his bones turned to mush really had been worse. He'd still been alive.

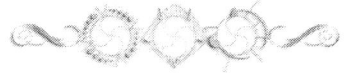

"Oh? And how's that?" His hand had tightened on his gun, and his partner, who still hadn't said a damn word was looking around the scene but hadn't stepped in far enough get the full the impact of her presentation. That word surprised me. It was a presentation, but to who or what? The people that found her or did it mean something for whatever ritual she'd been used in.

Again, this isn't something I want to get in the middle of.

The glare of the officer reminded me I hadn't answered him, so I told him the truth. "I'm a paramedic."

Something flickered in his face, but he relaxed. "Okay. You got ID?" That started the whole ball rolling. Two hours later after answering what seemed like a million questions, all my personal information taken, they let me go

I headed back to the apartment and glad Jo was out doing orientation today. She might not notice I'd been gone all day. Even though the thought of food made my stomach churn, I swung by the Kroger, a local grocery store, to grab something for a simple dinner. While cooking quesadillas insured I would burn them to a crisp or they would not cook at all, Jo could get them perfect in a few minutes. Loaded down with bags I climbed the three flights to our apartment. Maybe by this evening I'd be able to eat. I really didn't need to lose any more weight.

"Well, hello there," a voice drawled. I'd been focusing on trying to get the door open, without letting any of the bags slip, so his words startled me. By some miracle the door popped open and I stumbled in not backwards. Straightening up, I turned to see a man, probably about five ten as he looked taller than Jo, leaning against the doorframe of the apartment opposite of us.

"Uh hi." Both hands were full, I had to pee, and I wanted to get some caffeine. The questioning had worn me out but I still wasn't used to wasting money on drinks when I could make my own, better, iced coffee at home.

"So, you must be my new neighbors? I'd heard there were two sexy women who had moved into our little building. Nice to see my options are looking up."

I felt like an idiot. Whatever I was into, he wasn't it. "Thanks, I think. Look, I have to get these put away. I'll see you around?"

I felt rude as all get out but my bladder was threatening to rupture right there. I shut the door on his surprised look. I dumped the grocery bags on the table and all but sprinted to the bathroom. Ten minutes later, feeling mostly human and with all the groceries put away without spilling or breaking anything, I looked around the apartment.

It still felt odd and like I was visiting but the two bath, two-bedroom apartment was nice. Marisol and Henri had helped us move. There were two desks in the living room and a tv against one wall with a futon couch. Jo's idea. She enjoyed cuddling and I loved being held by her. Besides, it made falling

asleep on the couch easier. Each bedroom was small but with decent closets, and the bathroom had a tub and a separate shower, which had been major selling points for both of us. Long baths were a major luxury and one I hadn't been able to indulge in for years.

But I still felt like I needed to keep it neat. Henri, knowing my life, had double secured everything we put in. Bookcases, pictures, the desks, and made sure there were anti-static mats under the chairs. All in all they had Cori proofed it as much as possible.

The desire to go research ritual magic and try to figure out what that poor girl died for dragged me to the computer, but I realized I needed to check my current job applications, and then apply for more, ranked higher on my must do list.

I was trying very hard not to let my lack of a job get to me. It was July 24th. School started August 5th and I really didn't want to destroy what savings I had before I got started. Granted, it had only been two weeks. After graduating with honors, acing the paramedics exam, and getting my certification to drive ambulances, I didn't know what else to do to make myself employable. I started considering getting a job at the local coffee chain but it felt too much like accepting defeat. The court date with my parents had been anti-climatic. They hadn't shown, just sent a lawyer. I agreed I would not instigate communication with them until Kris was over eighteen but I didn't say I wouldn't communicate. It gave me an opening, and someday I'd hear from him again.

With a deep breath and a forced positive attitude, I logged onto my email and started going through it. One of them was from Ruby EMS. I clicked on it, figuring another form rejection letter. I'd seen enough of those lately that it was becoming depression. I was about to click the delete button when the words on the email registered.

"We would like you to come in for an interview about the open position we have at Ruby EMS for a paramedic on July 26th at 9:00 am. Please confirm if you will make this interview."

Merlin's balls, yes!

I leaned back and tried to center myself. Then I slowly responded, indicating my acceptance and that I would enjoy meeting with them on Friday. Hitting sending had me up and dancing across the room, then flopping backwards on the couch with a grin.

I gave myself a whole ten minutes of glee. Then I reminded myself an interview was not a job offer. With a groan, and pushing down a spurt of worry, I got back up and went through the rest of my email. There were no other interview requests, but no rejections either. I'd take that as a win. The next hour I applied to three more jobs, carefully attaching my scores, my internship, and my letters of recommendation to all of them. It had only been a week, but I'd find something. I had to.

The blast of chimes from my phone startled me and at the same time I saw the lock to the door turning. I smiled at Jo as she walked in, looking pumped and tired, as I answered the phone.

"Hello?" I didn't recognize the number, but when you were job hunting, you answered every call and checked your voice mail obsessively.

"Cori Munroe?" It was a male voice, officious with nothing about it to imply anything. I suspected it was a cop.

"Yes?"

"This is Detective Leon Stone. We would like for you come down to the station tomorrow and give us an official statement. Are you available at nine-thirty in the morning?"

Tomorrow I could do. Friday would have been problematic.

"Yes, I came come in then. Address?"

A minute later I hung up to see Jo looking at me with a funny expression on her face.

"Why do I think that was the police?"

A wave of guilt hit me and I pushed it down. I didn't exactly ask for weird stuff to happen to me. It just did, and I dealt with it the best I could.

"Because it was?" I responded, unsure. Her expression had me worried.

"Yes!" A huge grin split her face. "I knew you'd find trouble in a place like Atlanta." She settled onto the futon, looking at me expectantly. "You tell me your story and I'll tell you about the campus."

I laughed. Leaning back, we exchanged stories of the day. It felt good and when she heard about my job interview, I'm pretty sure the whoop she gave out would have gotten people complaining at us if they weren't all still at work.

While it didn't wash away what I'd seen that day, I felt myself center, with her as one half of the grounding force. I had this. I just knew it.

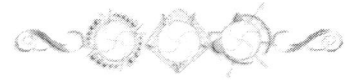

Chapter 2

The OMO announced today it would petition in front of the UN to remove sanctions against Mages Serving at the highest levels in many governments. They point out that mages are some of the most educated people in the world. Why hurt your own country by preventing their service?
~ Magicial Politics

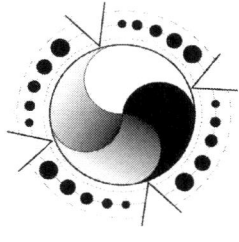

ORDER

Why do they keep asking me the same questions?
I had shown up willing to help and answer what I could, not that I knew anything. However, by this point I wanted to beat my head on the table, wishing I could just call Laurel or Sam and have them talk to the cops.

Detective Stone, an older man with dark coffee-colored skin but a slim nose which implied multiple genotypes, met me as soon as I gave them my name. I had a sinking feeling when he just sneered at me. But the girl deserved my best, so I worked toon keep my smart mouth to myself, . At least that was my intention. After two hours I struggled to keep that idea in mind. It didn't matter what I said. He kept insinuating that I had some ulterior purpose for being there and surely I had something to do with the body.

He annoyed me so much if I'd been a mage I would have done something creative, like turned his clothes into paper. Besides, how stupid would you have to be to commit such a gruesome murder and then just call the police? I thought it would take longer than I'd been alive to grow balls that size. But they had managed to make my desire to be helpful and polite crumble into ashes by this point. And I needed more coffee.

"What I don't understand is why you were in that park. It is all but abandoned. Why would a pretty girl like you be walking around such a place?" His voice carried an innuendo that I'd been there for illicit activities. I'd tried to be polite but at this point I just wanted to stab him. With that last comment my temper snapped with an audible sound. That or I had started to crack. Could have been either one.

"Officer Stone. At this point if you don't understand what I mean by the words 'walk around' and 'explore' then I can't help you."

"It's Detective Stone, and you look here, young lady..." I cut him off. It turns out spending five weeks with cops that like you and make sure you understand exactly what the law does and doesn't allow can be extremely useful.

"No. You have my statement. I have been here for three hours. I've answered every variation of question you could ask. You have my statement about where I bought coffee not an hour before I made the call. You know where I live. So, unless I am under arrest I am leaving. Now." I gave him a level stare, my hands flat on the table so he couldn't see them tremble. "Am I under arrest?"

"No," he admitted slowly, glancing up at the clock. "You aren't. But you haven't answered the question about ritual magic."

"What question about ritual magic? I'm not a mage. You checked with the OMO." I didn't have to even ask to know they had done that. The OMO connected to every law agency. They ran your OMO status just like they ran your license looking for warrants.

"Technically you don't need to be a mage to do ritual magic. You can use it if you know the forms and how to channel it."

I'm sure I had a stupid look on my face. I hadn't heard that, and now I wanted to ask more questions. Normal people could do magic? Then the image of the girl flashed in front of me again and I fought a shudder. No. I had no desire to do anything with ritual magic if it required that sort of thing.

"That may be. However I had nothing to do with her. I didn't lay her out all presented for her photos. So while you keep wasting time with me, the person behind this is getting farther away."

I couldn't get it out of my head: her shirt, flowing yellow with green flowers on the edge, new jeans that were still bright with blue dye, long curly hair that looked like she'd taken time to style it. It had to have been styled or the humidity would have frizzed it out. But mostly it was her face: no make-up, blood dripping from both eyes, the skin peeled to reveal muscle and bone, and

a mouth open in a silent scream. The perfect image. I could almost visualize the movie poster it was for, and I wanted to scream. I wanted to cry.

"What do you mean 'lay her out' for her photo?" His voice sharp as he leaned forward, pinning me with eyes that looked like buckeyes.

Crap, I said that. I really didn't mean to. At least not out loud.

I blinked rapidly to get my emotions back under control and let a sigh escape. "Even the cops on the scene would have been able to see how she was laid out. The pine tree's lower branches draping to frame her with no obstructions. She was there to be found and photographed. Do you know why?" That question slipped out and I tensed, waiting for the next attack, but the detective didn't jump on it.

"What do you know about the symbols used?"

I blinked at him. "Again, I'm not a mage, so nothing. I wouldn't know the difference between magical symbols, Norse runes, or Tolkein's elvish."

He glared at me. "This isn't a joke or something outa book."

"No, but you sure are acting like the stereotypical cop, too stupid to not know the person in front of you is just the red herring to distract the audience while the real bad guy is getting away. Heck, now that I think of it, I can think of at least three episodes on Law and Order: Magical Investigation Unit that had this same story line." He flushed red, which was interesting under his dark skin, and opened his mouth. I spoke first. "So, as I believe you said, I'm not under arrest. Unless you have something to charge me with?"

He growled looked at his watch, then back at me. I sensed another stall, but I was done.

"Are you charging me?"

"No," the word sounded like I had dragged it out of him.

"Wonderful. Then I am leaving." I pushed up from the table, turned, and headed towards the door. My hand was wrapped around the handle when he spoke behind me.

"Don't leave town. We might have more questions."

"Considering I just moved here, I hadn't planned on it. But if this is the level of professional courtesy I can expect, I might change my mind." I pushed the door open and strode out, amazed that my knees didn't buckle from stress. They made being brave and telling authority to suck it look so easy on TV and in stories. I kept expecting someone to grab me and make me stay, tell me they had evidence linking me to the crime. Or something. Right now, I just wanted away from here, and the way it felt like everyone was staring at me.

I headed out, not waiting for anyone to show me out. My habit of mapping out places as I entered helped, that and the fact that most police stations seemed to have similar layouts. The exit was up ahead and I heard people mutter as I walked through. My temper and frustration were boiling over, and I couldn't help but smirk as one of the coffeepots cracked in a snap

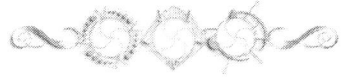

of electricity and smoke started rising from it. That got everyone's attention away from me. This time I just was glad for the weird stuff and I headed for the exit.

The lobby was full of people. No one paid attention to me and that was all that mattered. The clear glass doors from the entry area beckoned me and I felt a spring in my step as escape stood just a short distance away. I pushed out the doors to the muggy Atlanta air and stepped out. The wave of thick wet air mixed with exhaust and sewer smells almost made me miss the icy air conditioning and vague stale smoke smell of the station. Almost. I stood there for a moment, getting my bearings. A man approached from the opposite direction I needed to go caught my attention. He stalked, not walked or strolled, and his intent look was so focused I expected the cement sidewalk to melt as he came my way. I didn't think he was cute or sexy, but he had a face that promised character. Good or bad character I didn't know. Something about him made me think he'd be a formidable enemy.

He glanced up at me, his eyes focused on my temple, and I waited for the normal dismissal, but this time he frowned at me. His stare was more confused than intense as he kept moving forward. I'd had enough drama for one day. Shaking my head and trying to rid myself of the frustration that coated me like ash, I headed down the steps and down the street the other direction. I wanted to walk the area around Ruby and prep for the interview tomorrow.

I dismissed him and the other cops from my mind as I walked. The streets were starting to look familiar and after watching the Atlanta traffic, I was just as glad that I didn't have a car. The drivers were all kamikaze mages, acting like they could survive everything and anything.

That is how I spent the rest of the afternoon. The areas I walked through were much creepier than I was used to. In the middle of the day I didn't feel unsafe just out of place though, partially because of my skin color, my gender, and just the fact that I still didn't feel at home here. However, from a few of the glances from the men loitering on the streets I thought maybe a self-defense or a martial arts class for both Jo and me might not be a bad idea. I had no desire to be a victim and not acting like one was the best choice. I could punch decently, Stinky had taught both of us. The best way to stop a guy and how to throw a decent punch, but I had no illusions that most men weighed double what I did and were stronger.

I really need to join a gym. Or at least start using the one at apartment complex.

I beat Jo home by a whole five minutes. She walked in the door, an odd look on her face. She'd spent the day doing placement tests, seeing where she rated and what classes she needed to get caught up on.

"Hey. Tests over?" I was still a bit out of sorts from the police station. She glanced up at me and for a moment I thought she would say something. She had a look of something on her face: Worry? Fear? Sorrow? Stress? Then it

disappeared and she smiled.

"Meh, tests. They always suck. I mean really, who remembers who shot who to start World War Two? And if I need to know what time a train will get here, I pull it up online."

"Gavros fried the Archduke Ferdinand with lightning, and that was World War One, not Two. Two is a lot harder to nail down. And I completely agree with you about trains and using an app. Besides, since when has a train ever kept a constant rate of speed. Idiots keep laying on the tracks." That had been a call that was up there with falling guy. Having your legs severed because you laid down on the track had to be way up there in the stupidity levels. No, the train won't stop.

"Show off. I swear, don't you forget anything? I can never keep that stuff straight and how does knowing it make me a good or bad mage? I'm a math person, not a words person." There was something odd about how she said it and I frowned looking at her. "Ignore me. Grumpy. I hate tests. Taco's for dinner?"

"As long as you don't make them super hot. I have the interview tomorrow. I don't need to emit toxic fumes."

"Spoilsport. If they all die as they talk to you, doesn't that mean you have the job?"

"I don't think it works that way. Though I'm not sure they could charge me with murder for that." I sighed glaring at her. "Now I have to go look that up. Thanks. Not."

Jo snickered and headed for the kitchen. "Go look it up and let me know. I'll get tacos going."

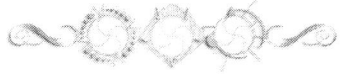

Chapter 3

After the Civil War the US barely held together. The government looked at what was going on all over the world. Mages were battling each other. They had become almost currency between nations, and their lives were very short as learning to control offerings and make sure they only gave what they could afford to had yet to become the science it is now. Then Rudyard Kipling wrote a story that sent shock waves through the political world and started the idea of the draft.
~History of Magic

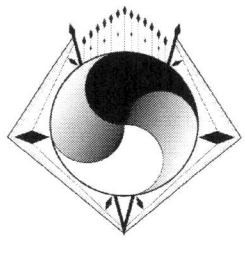

SPIRIT

THE next morning I called a rideshare. My bank account was good so I needed to quit stressing every expense. Showing up to an interview hot and sweaty would not make a good first impression.

I got there at least fifteen minutes early. At least I knew I looked decent. For my birthday present, Marisol had bought me an interview outfit. Nice black slacks, two different blouses, and a suit jacket. The shirts were silk, and I was super paranoid about getting anything on them, so there was no coffee after I put them on. Which mean I spent all morning walking around the apartment in my bra and slacks. Jo found it amusing. I just flipped her off and inhaled my coffee, then went to pee twice before leaving.

"Please wait in here. Your interviewer will be in shortly." A young man, obviously with better things to do than deal with job applicants, ushered me into a room that had seen better days. I had hoped for a document to read or something. The room was almost sterile and ugly, with scraped up beige walls and chairs that had seen better days.

My tension, worry, and every other emotion in my mind twisted together until I felt like a cat on a live wire. I had to keep doing breathing exercises. My first interview. I could do this.

A brisk knock on the door pulled me out of my swirl and an older woman walked in. At nine thirty on a Friday morning she had circles under her eyes. Her hair was coming out of its bun, the streaks of gray ugly against her sallow complexion. If I had to guess, not enough sleep and too much stress.

"You Corisande Munroe?"

"Yes, ma'am," I responded in a bright affirmative tone. I tried very hard to project pep and energy, not worry and nervousness.

She arched one brow as she sat down on the chair across from me. "You're applying for the paramedic position. Did you bring your certifications?"

I slide the originals across with a pang of worry. Those were the proof of everything I'd done. Not that I thought she'd do anything to them, and it wasn't like I couldn't pay to get a new one, but still.

"Letters of reference?"

This time I slide across copies. The originals were safe in the fire box Henri had given us. Along with all the important paperwork.

She spent some time going through them, which confused me as I'd attached everything to the application, but the last time I had been on a job interview was for the Grind Down.

"Everything looks in order. Your references are glowing. I called and talked to Sally Chang earlier today."

That surprised me as she had acted like she'd never seen this before. My face must have betrayed my surprise because she gave me a half shrug. "I like to see who comes in prepared. If you prepare for the little things, the odds are you're prepared for the important stuff."

She slid the documents back to me and opened up another folder, counting paperwork. I waited for questions, for something, but she just nodded after a minute then looked up at me.

"Can you start on August 5th? There are two days of orientation, paperwork, and training. Then you will be on rotating twelves. The current opening is for the twelve-hour shift, though with seniority you can apply to the ten or eight hours as positions come up. This opening is from seven am to seven pm. Is that acceptable?"

Dear gods. Mornings again. Why me?

I let the idea of sleeping until eight or nine, drinking my coffee at a leisurely pace, fade into a fantasy. Instead, I fought to keep my snark under control.

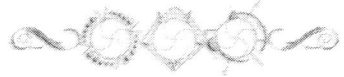

"That's it? You don't want to ask me any questions? See if I will fit in?" No matter what, I didn't think interviews went like this. There was no way the premier hospital in Atlanta would hire me, not without testing me to make sure I could handle it. This had to be a joke or another test.

She just looked at me, seeming older than what I suspected she was. "Cori, not to be mean or dash your hopes because I know you're young, but no one cares if you fit in. If you show up, do the job, and don't wash out in the first month, everyone will regard it as a win. Our turnover rate is so high that if you don't suck, you'll move through the ranks quickly. We get the worst calls, the ones where the death rate is over 25%. We gave up trying to select only the best of the best; they don't last any longer than the ones that are just competent. There is a world of difference between being able to do the technical aspects of the job and deal with the day-to-day emotions. To know people call sometimes because they were too lazy to go get more insulin and would rather go to the ER for diabetic reasons, then pry dead bodies out of a car, and still be ready to go to the next call is what we need." The images of the boy in the back seat of the car, Bobby, flashed through my mind.

"At the end of the day, you have the skills. If you can make it in this job, which Sally seems to think you will, then we'll be happy to have you. The question is, do you want the job?"

Her question hung in the air, and I blinked. Of course I wanted the job. This was my dream.

"Yes. I want the job."

The hint of a smile softened here face. "Excellent. Then the starting salary is 17.80 an hour. Performance reviews and raises every ninety days until you are at 18.50 an hour. Then reviews go to twice a year. Here is the list of infractions and how you should deal with them." She gave me a look to imply I could ask questions now if I wanted.

I'm starting at over 17.80 an hour. Holy moly, I'm rich. Even with the max of everything taken out, I will have money. Like lots of money.

At Grind Down I was the highest paid at 9.50 an hour. On good weeks I'd get another fifty or so in tips. But to make this much money, even before taxes? I locked my jaw so my shock wouldn't show. I shook my head mutely at her questioning look, still shell shocked, and resisting the desire to jump up and down in excitement.

She pulled a sheet out of the stack. "Here's where to be. The first day is mostly the bullshit stuff. The second is all the mandatory training for Ruby Medical. You'll be told where to get a uniform." Her eyes ran up and down my body, but there was nothing personal in them. "Your size is average enough, the location listed on your sheet should have some in stock without a need for a special order. Shoe requirements, hygiene requirements, and other dress

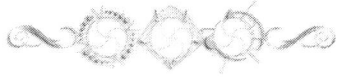

codes are all listed. Good luck." With a huff of effort she pushed herself up from the table and headed out the door without a backwards glance.

I sat there, looking at everything she'd shoved at me, and frowned. Weren't you supposed to be excited when you got a job? Your first job as a real adult. I didn't know how I felt. Shaking my head, I got up, gathered all the paper, and put it neatly back in my bag. I headed out and winced as the door behind me popped off the hinges.

"Dammit. Someone call maintenance to fix that damn door. This is the third time this month it's done that." A voice in the office called out behind me and I sagged in relief. At least maybe that weird thing was not weird, it was just a thing. I could live with that. I ignored the desire to scratch my head.

I got another ride home. No way was I about to mess up my good clothes. I walked into an empty apartment, changed and then just sat there, strangely off kilter. I had my first job. I started in a week. Now what.

For the first time in a very long time I had nothing to do for more than a week. What a weird feeling.

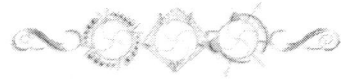

Chapter 4

While no one has captured a unicorn, it is widely agreed they do exist. And the only know dragon is not available for study. However, knowing something exists and KNOWING are two different things. Which means most magical creatures reside as something mythical and rare.
~History of Magic

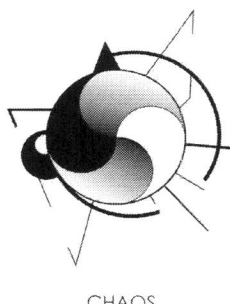

CHAOS

*T*oday . I start my new job, my new life, today.
The thought kept running through my mind and it took everything I had not to skip, which at six in the morning had to be something approaching a miracle. I figured it'd wear off fast, so I might as well enjoy it while I could.

Jo didn't talk about her tests, and I didn't push her. Who enjoyed taking tests? We spent our week exploring the neighborhood, going to all the touristy things we'd never done, and even splurged on a day at Six Flags. I cringed as I spent the money, but we had a blast. We took the time to get a few more things for the apartment, run back up to see her family, and get me four sets of jumpsuits and better socks. I'd learned quickly that thick socks were a must when you were in the boots all day. They made life much more pleasant. Even if paying almost twenty dollars a pair hurt, Sally had convinced me it was money well spent.

While Jo and I spent a lot of time together, she never mentioned how she did on the placement tests, but I didn't worry about it. Jo was a whiz at so many things, though I seemed to remember only average grades in any class not focused on math.

Jo started school on Monday but she, unlike me, didn't have to be there until nine am. The first two days I showed up at eight and did paperwork and training. I don't know what I expected, but mounds of disclaimers, acknowledgments, watching videos about harassment, reporting, diversity, ergonomics, and other things that made no sense at all given my job were not it, though the hazardous chemicals one at least made me think.

It was a waste of sixteen hours, but I got paid. My nerves were in such a state I couldn't even drink my coffee that morning as I reached the station. I'd spent part of the prior week learning the bus routes and getting a Marta Pass.

Standing outside, I looked up at Ruby Hospital. They had three teams running the twelve shifts, then two each on the ten and eight-hour ones, but that meant most of the time you had five teams, a number that seemed huge to me compared to Rockway. But this was Atlanta. I stood looking at all the bays with their doors down, and then the door that said staff.

I double checked the badge in my hand, verifying it said my name and had my picture. Then I took a deep breath and walked in. My jumpsuit was in my bag though my boots were on. I'd been considering letting my hair grow just so I could do ponytails. They seemed easier, and my lack of mage status would be very obvious at that point.

Stepping in I looked around, this place would be my home, for a while at least. At least that was my intent. I had entered a narrow hallway, or at least it felt narrow. One side was all lockers and benches, the other side had two doors leading to what looked like offices. One of them read Shift Supervisor, the other read Department manager.

I checked my paperwork again, verifying it said to present myself to the Department Manager, one Donald Smith. I swallowed and knocked on the closed door. The frosted window prevented me from seeing if anyone sat inside.

"It's open," a voice called, and I blew out a sigh of relief. At least someone was here. I turned the knob and stepped in. It was a smallish office, about the size of Laurel Amosen's, and set up about the same, except for the addition of a bookcase full of binders. The man sitting next to the desk had looked up as I stepped in. He was older, at least fifty, with pasty skin and with the florid nose I'd learned to associate with someone who drank way too much, way too often. He also had reddish blond hair that was thinning rapidly and dark brown eyes that speared into me like a weapon.

"Who're you?" His voice had the mushy southern drawl that my parents had prevented in me, at least when they paid attention. It didn't help that he seemed to be missing at least two of his front teeth, maybe three.

"Cori Munroe. I'm starting today?"

Wouldn't you be expecting a new employee? Please tell me he knew I was coming.

My nerves stretched as he just stared at me, not saying anything. I kept myself from shifting uncomfortably, but I could feel my skin starting to burn with nerves.

"Great. Another complete newbie. How old are you?"

I was surprised and confused. Didn't he have my birth date on the paperwork? I answered. "Twenty-one, sir."

"Merlin save me. At least you can drink. Might keep you alive. Got your badge?" He asked as he pushed himself to his feet, revealing a belly that strained the buttons of his light blue oxford shirt.

Wordlessly I held up my badge, thrown off balance again.

He grunted. "Follow me. I'm Don Smith. I make sure your timesheets are completed, reports filed, and competencies kept up to date. My favorite type of employee is the one I never need to talk to. Do what I ask you to do the first time and I don't give a damn about anything else, as long as you don't kill anyone. You got your stuff?"

This time I raised my bag, swallowing. I felt like I was walking through a minefield. All my experience with Molly had not prepared me for this. I took a deep breath. I had this. First days at any job were always tricky.

"Here's your locker." He pointed to one without a name or a lock on it. I memorized the number, 13. Did that mean good or bad things? "Get a lock, make sure it isn't more than a quarter-inch thick so when you quit, cutting it off isn't an issue."

I glanced at him but he just stated it the way you'd state to remember to fill up the ambulance before going off shift.

"Be here at least ten minutes early. Listen to your senior partner. If in doubt, do what he tells you and argue with your shift supervisor after the fact. You'll get your schedule before you leave today. You may rotate partners depending on multiple things you don't need to worry about. For your first month or so, it's Jorge Roland." He pronounced it the Mexican way, with an h.

"Jorge, your new partner is here," Don called out as we walked into an open area. At one end was a kitchen with a large table in the middle, with more lockers and storage against the wall between here and the bays. The main area looked like a large living room, with a table against the back wall. There were two doors to what I figured were bathrooms, but I made a note to myself to double check. To my right was more lockers and a bench in front of them. Most of them had boots or bags in front of them, waiting to go. There were three people in the room. The one that rose and headed my way was a man with skin the color of an americano; pale but rich, with shocking white hair and eyes so pale blue, the combination confused me.

"Great. I get a newbie? Not even a low mage? What did I do to make you hate me Smith?" The man, Jorge I figured, didn't whine, but it didn't sound like a joke either. If anything, it sounded the way I felt when I found grounds in my cup of coffee. He had a lyrical tone to his voice, and it might have been pleasant, except for the look on his face as he looked at me.

"Don't look at me. You're short and this is what HR sent over. You know how they feel about us. Have fun. Don't break her on the first shift. I need at least a week for them to go through other applicants."

"Have fun, Munroe. If you break, please don't leave body fluids everywhere. I hate having to get this place cleaned." With that he turned and walked back to his office, leaving me standing there feeling about three inches tall. My scalp burned and there was a click and a rattle and about two cups of ice spit out of the fridge door in the kitchen.

"Well, hells. What is up with this blasted fridge?" A woman, tall with dark brown hair in a horse mane style said as she pulled herself up from where she was reading and stalked over to pick it up.

"Whatever. "So, name? Munroe?" Jorge asked, looking at me as if I was the worst thing he'd ever seen.

"Cori Munroe. Hi." I put on my best smile but I could feel it shake.

"Whatever. Do your job, don't get in my way, don't toss your cookies on patients or in the rig. Don't drink or do drugs in a way that I notice. And don't ask to drive. That isn't happening." He scanned me up and down and shook his head. "Get dressed, we're on in five minutes." He turned and walked away, leaving me standing there. The other two people, one of them was the woman cleaning up ice. The other was a man with lightly tanned skin and tight curly black hair who glanced at me then away, focusing back on what he was doing.

I will not slink. I will not let them see I give a damn what they think.

The pep talked helped a bit, and I walked back to my locker, I'd brought a lock. It had been on the list of things I'd probably need. I pulled on my jumpsuit, though I left it mostly unzipped. I wouldn't roast in the current temperature, but it wasn't cool, and I knew how quickly the jumpsuits got hot. No need to get myself worn out before I started. I slipped my phone in a pocket and clipped my badge on. I had brought little besides a few pieces of jerky and a granola bar. Enough that I could get by if we didn't have time to eat.

Now that I was here, and my nerves were about to explode. I needed caffeine. I headed to the kitchen, seeing an old coffee maker. And by old I meant it was a percolator, in poor condition.

"Is it okay if I make coffee?" I asked the room in general, though I was rapidly learning that around here, asking might not be the best way to go. Just doing it and waiting for someone to yell at me might be better.

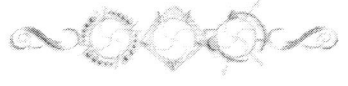

"Whatever. We don't rate a real coffee pot. What I want is a pod coffee maker, but these jerks keep breaking them." It was the woman, and I just nodded. I dug and found a decent amount of ground coffee. It was stale, but it would do, especially as I found cinnamon. I scrubbed out the percolator as the bottom looked like sludge from the last decade, then started it brewing. It had just started as a bell ran and I flinched.

"Shift notification. Don't worry about it," the man said. I needed to be introduced to people but right then I didn't care. I was watching the coffee, my mug waiting for its life-giving effects. As the aroma of fresh-brewed coffee with hints of cinnamon filled the air, I heard another vehicle enter the bay. A minute later the door banged open behind me then there was another loud crash.

"What by the planes?" A voice yelled, at the same time another yelled, "Shit."

I whirled, surprised, and looked as two people - men, dark hair, and exhausted was all I could get the impression of, stood staring at the door laying on the floor.

"Someone, go get Smith. I swear this place will fall down around us someday. How hard would it be to get decent maintenance?" one man muttered as he stalked in. He froze and tilted his head, sniffing. "Is that honest to god coffee I smell?"

I paused, my better nature warring with my need for caffeine. My selfish nature won, and I really didn't care. "Yes," I said as I filled my mug. It was a big pot, there should be enough, but I wasn't about to risk going without. "I made it. Help yourself." Part of me wanted to offer to serve them, but Marisol had counseled me against it. She'd told me if I started out serving, I'd never break that image or that role.

"Start as you want to continue, Cori. Don't let anyone treat you like a servant."

Her words rang in my head and I stepped back, taking a sip. Not perfect, but damn decent. I needed to bring better grinds, but not yet. I'd wait more and see how this place worked out. I could always bring a small French press to make my own coffee if I needed to.

"Me first. My newbie, I get to taste it first." Jorge appeared as if teleported and poured a huge mug. He took a tentative sip, then another one. "Not bad. Nice to see you're good for something."

Jorge's words, crankiness, and nerves drove my response. "Be nice. Or I'll only make enough for what I pour in my mug. I'll help out, but I'm no one's servant, or their newbie."

"Ooh, puppy's got bite," the woman who'd cleaned up the ice said mockingly. Before she could continue, a voice rang out over the speakers.

"Call Bus Red-Four. Car accident, Andrew Young and Courtland."

"That's us, newbie. Let's see if we can set a new record," Jorge mocked as he headed into the bay.

I scurried after him, glad I'd been ready. Here I'd use the supplies in the ambulance, though not having time to go over it made me nervous, I'd figure it out.

"New record?" I asked as I climbed into the passenger side of the ambulance and strapped in.

"See if I can break you in two days or less." His smile had no teasing it in.

Mine was just as humorless. "You're welcome to try, but I don't break."

"We'll see. Welcome to Hotlanta, newbie."

CHAPTER 5

The draft has affected this country in profound ways. While some people end up in the military, the majority take the degrees they earned and end up in labs, engineering, medicine, or even working with consumer companies. They are often the gateway to permanent careers, but not all magicians are so lucky.
~History of Magic

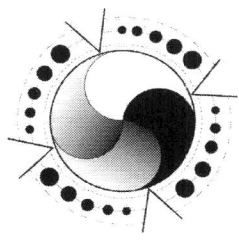

ORDER

I like the work, but maybe I made a major mistake accepting this job.
That thought, that idea, haunted me all three of my twelve-hour shifts. Rotating twelves meant three days on, two off, two on, and three off. I had started on the three on. So by Friday, adding in the two eight-hour days of training and paperwork, I'd worked well over forty hours. Which left me exhausted and unhappy. I didn't mind the work but feeling like an unwanted guest was getting old. And even for me, that was a lot of hours.

In theory, you only worked thirty-six hours, reality was you worked a bit more. You didn't get to leave in the middle of a call, though you tried to get back to the bay at least thirty minutes before the end of shift so you had time to fill out paperwork and turn everything in. That didn't always happen. Sometimes calls were three or four hours long. Which screwed everything up.

I eventually figured out a few names. Lisa, Mike, Raul, John. Our shift manager should usually be Kelly, though since I hadn't met that person, I still didn't know who that was. All of them treated me with that strange not contempt, but no unfriendliness either. They answered questions but didn't talk to me. The only thing they seemed to agree on was my coffee. They also didn't pull any shit on me, which meant I couldn't complain about being mistreated. I just felt like a foster kid - tolerated, but not really wanted. It was not the work environment I had dreamed of.

The shifts hadn't been too bad, but my strangeness followed me even here. The first day it was only minor things. As we went on a call that first day, three different cupboards in the back of the bus popped open when we hit a pothole, scattering supplies everywhere. Jorge cussed up a storm, swearing he'd locked them. Luckily that first call just required on-site treatment and we took fifteen to clean it up. I took it as a chance to learn where at least some of the stuff was. Finding the silver lining in weird things had become second nature.

The next day was a call where a car had hit a power pole. It snapped, leaving live lines all around the car. The victim was awake and aware, and miracle of miracles not panicking. But no matter which direction we approached the lines would move and block us. It took an hour for the power company to get that area shut off. It was strange enough the Jorge was almost social on the way to the next call, but I hadn't pushed my luck.

Overall it wasn't horrible but as I walked out Friday night, I missed with an almost physical pang the camaraderie of Kadia, Carl, even Molly and her social panic. It hurt to not have anyone to talk to. I worked with strangers all day long and none of them seemed to want to be more than that. Jo was focusing on her schoolwork as both of us wanted tomorrow to go back to Rockway with nothing hanging over us. I let her be and read another couple of chapters on diseases that were almost impossible to diagnose, either before or after death. I didn't find any answers, leading me back to mages again. I gave up about ten, exhausted from a day of trying to pretend I didn't care about how my co-workers treated me, and went to bed. Dreams of a girl screaming as her eyes were cut out followed me all night.

Saturday morning Jo and I were both ready to go by seven am, needing to get back to familiar territory with a passion I don't believe either us had expected. On the back of her bike I tried to let the wind tear away my fears and worries. Neither of us talked, we just enjoyed the speed and the feeling of home awaiting us.

When we were approaching town, I activated the radio between us. "Can you drop me off at the police station? Then I'll walk to Grind Down? Dinner at your parents?"

"Sounds good. Yell if you need me."

We both needed some time alone, and I figured she wanted to go to the shop and see her dad and brothers. Me? I wanted to talk to Laurel. I didn't

know if she'd be around on a Saturday, but I got the feeling she usually dropped in on Saturday's paperwork from what I'd heard, so I figured I could try. Either way, I knew that Grind Down would be open.

I climbed off the bike and tucked the helmet back into the storage bag. Jo took off, driving faster than she had with me. That incident with the deer had made her a bit more cautious, at least when I was on the bike.

Should I feel good or sad about that?

I entered the station, cataloging all the differences between our small police station and the bigger one I'd visited in Atlanta. This one won the battle, hands down, for comfort and safety. While they both smelled of stale smoke and coffee, this one didn't have that aura of hopelessness Atlanta did. Or the feeling of guilt. Or maybe that was me.

"Hey, Cori. Thought you were living down in Atlanta now?" The desk sergeant asked, giving me a sharp look.

"I am. Just off this weekend so I'm up visiting. You really think I'd miss any chance to have Marisol's cooking?"

"Probably not. I won a casserole of hers once," he closed his eyes a look of pleasure so intense, I almost felt like I was intruding by witnessing it. "Still the best thing I've ever eaten. So whatcha need?"

I think I needed this. To not be treated like the enemy.

"Any chance the Chief is in? Wanted to talk to her for a minute."

He glanced down at his logbook. "Yep, sure looks like it. Go on back." He buzzed me in, and I headed on back. I couldn't pinpoint the minute Laurel became someone to talk to, someone to trust, but it had happened. And while it confused me, it was also kinda nice.

Her door stood open, as usual. I'd only seen it closed when someone was getting chewed out, or the occasional discussion about sensitive matters. I didn't know if she was a great police chief, but I had the feeling she was a pretty good one.

I knocked on her door, watching her as I did so. Dressed in jeans and a tank top, I suspected she had other plans after a quick stop at the office. Her hair, as always, was a neat cap of dark espresso above her cafe au lait skin. She'd become my measure of all other cops, and Detective Stone was failing badly in comparison.

Her head lifted. When she saw me, she smiled setting down the papers she'd been looking at and waved at the chair. "Hey, Cori. Come on in. What brings you to the backwoods so soon?"

"Weekend, off work, and Marisol's food, of course." I settled myself into the chair as I tried to think about the two topics I wanted to ask her.

"Always a valid reason to visit the Guzman's, but I notice you're sitting in my office." She leaned back, looking at me, but where I had once seen annoyance in her gaze, I now saw the patient humor.

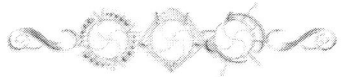

Maybe this is a side effect of growing up? Ugh, who wants to be more reasonable?

I fought a smirk at my own mental rambling. "Had you heard anything about a body being discovered in Atlanta with ritual magic involved?"

Her amused look dropped off her face as she snapped up straight in her chair, now completely focused on me. It was still intimidating.

"Let me guess, you found her."

"Of course. The cops don't believe that I just happened to stumble across her, but that part doesn't matter. What I am curious about is, have you heard about it? The death was gory, bad. And I haven't heard anything. Have you?"

Laurel turned and typed on her computer for three long minutes but I just waited. The software to go through open cases wasn't the newest thing in the world. Honestly, some days I suspected it was older than I was.

"No, there is nothing here. Do you have a name?"

"I have nothing. Heck, I don't even know when she is being buried. I figured I would at least go, but I kept expecting to see something on the news and I haven't. Isn't that odd?"

Laurel looked at me, settling in. "Describe it to me."

Taking a deep breath, I did. The images still too vivid, too real in my head. Part of me wished I could erase them, so I didn't need to hold that my mind. I already saw it in my dreams. When I finished, she shook her head.

"No. And that is worrisome. I'm not saying Atlanta shares everything, but anything regarding magic should be sent out, especially ritual magic. So there is your answer. Does that tell you anything?"

"Not really, but it points back to my needing to ask." I shrugged, trying to seem unaffected. I don't think she bought it, but crying wouldn't change anything. "I've never not learned the name before. It feels wrong, disrespectful in some way." And it was driving me crazy.

She nodded. "If I hear anything I can share, I'll let you know."

I got the subtext, some things she couldn't pass on and wouldn't.

"Thanks. The other one is a weird question, partially because of this girl. Have you ever pulled someone in for testing, someone without mage symbols?"

She arched a brow, frowning, then laughed a little. "Ah, that law. The short answer is no. Basically no one does it. Oh, a merlin or a high-ranking mage might, law enforcement or other first responders? We don't."

I blinked at her, cold shock washing through my body. "But the consequences of not turning them in are really bad."

"Oh true, but if I remember correctly the last time they charged anyone was the late 1800s. The issue is we don't have time, and most of the time it isn't as obvious as they want you to think. If you see someone vaporize all their hair or something like that, sure feel free. You'll never see it and if you do and they are helping, you'll pretend you didn't see. If they are hurting someone, you'll

stop them. In the second case, you let the police take over but it is one of those things on the books just in case they need it. It's not one they actually expect people to use or do. Magic tends to be much more subtle. And the average person, especially one not a magic user, would never risk it. Mages can be deadly if they want. I know you read what Scott Randolph did." I swallowed and nodded. Laurel just shrugged. "Besides, very few high-rank mages aren't registered. Those that aren't often have a family history of it."

I must have frowned at her because she laughed. "Go look up one of the *yakuza* families or the magical Russian mobs. The Gregories and the Rasputians. They rarely got tested because that meant they had a harder time staying in the shadows, but since they were outed in, oh the mid 1900s, the OMO will show up and require testing of everyone under fifty. And they show up *en masse*. Now? Just test. The benefits outweigh the penalties." She tapped her temple. "Besides, it's always better to be on the more powerful side." Her tone had a touch of bitterness as she said that, but she just shook her head when I gave her a look. "You'll see."

We chatted for a few more minutes, then she chased me out so she could finish her paperwork and then meet Martin for lunch.

I walked up the street thinking about what she'd said. So someone might have seen this person kill the girl and walk away? The idea didn't register with me. How could you do that? But I got the fear. I did, I just couldn't think of being more scared than wanting to help.

The welcome smells of coffee, pastries, and steamed melt pulled me into Grind Down as I pushed open the door. It was busy, as it was still early Saturday morning - not even ten yet. Kadia was at the bar while Carl was busing tables without a cast.

Kadia saw me first and I winced as her "SQUEE," cut through the air worse than the tornado sirens. Next thing I knew I had an arm full of bubbly girl, braids bouncing around enough to make me dizzy.

"Oh, I've missed you. This place is so boring! Nothing ever happens! Why are you back? Are you okay? Did you get a job? Tell me you're coming back here and can work weekends?" her questions tumbled over each other a babble brook of words.

"I'm here to visit. Yes, I got a job. No, I'm not coming back." I was laughing the entire time and watching her face go from excited, to depressed, to excited, amused me. But still, I had missed all of them.

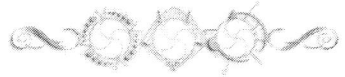

Chapter 6

Order magic is reputed to be one of the most powerful, at least when it comes to its use. By utilizing the spell Pattern or Transform, those with the ability can focus on the tiny images visible only under some of the most powerful microscopes, thereby becoming invaluable. Those with those doctorates often spend their draft in the R&D sections of the government, and then benefit from a bidding war afterward. Those not so blessed get the more menial jobs.
~Freedom from Magic

SPIRIT

They made me coffee on the house, Molly stuck her head out and said hello, then disappeared. I spent time talking to Kadia and a few regulars, but I'd also texted Sally. When she showed up, I grabbed her a coffee and pulled her into a chair. She was someone I wanted to catch up with and ask some questions. She'd promised me an hour, then she had a date.

"I am so glad you could come. I need to talk to you." She was laughing as I corralled her into the chair.

"Not that I mind free drinks," she said sipping her iced blended coffee drink. " What's up? You didn't kill anyone, did you?"

"No," I gasped, my mind breaking on that and completely kicking me off my flow. "No. I just, I got a job at Ruby in their EMS department."

"Oh that is great! They are a good company. Lots of excitement."

I slumped. "Yeah, if I can stick it out."

"Oh please. You handle everything and never blink. The work won't chase you away, so what is it?" She leaned in, looking at me sharply. After the bus incident where she'd offered up so much hair, it was almost in a bob that hit her chin. It was relatively close to how I wore mine and I noted she actually had nails - not long but not down to the quick.

"They hate me. They just say they don't want to waste time getting invested when I won't make it. Heck the HR lady said the same thing. I had credentials. I was hired. If I washed out, well then oh well, they'd just hire another someone else. Why?" I'm pretty sure I seemed pretty pathetic. I'm not saying people always loved me, they didn't, just look at the Munroes. They'd done everything possible to get away from me.

"Ah," She signed and leaned back, looking and playing with her cup instead of looking at me.

"What?" I sat there feeling like bees were buzzing under my skin. Did she have an answer for me? A way to make them at least not hate me?

"Cori, this job is hard and strange. You'd be amazed at the number of people that don't make it a month, much less a year. Then you have certain subset in it strictly for the amount of sex they can get."

"Huh?" The comment made no sense and I couldn't figure out what she meant.

Sally grinned but there was an aspect of sadness to it. "Most of the people we meet are patients and a lot of them are very grateful for our help. There's an entire section of first responders who use that gratitude to get laid. In Atlanta I'd suspect you have those people. Plus there are people who don't deal well with the constant violence, and the high cost of living. So while I hate to say it, I get their attitude. Hire you, if you last, great. If you don't, oh well. They didn't waste any time screening you."

I stared down into my coffee, looking for answers. "Fine. I guess I can understand that. But why is everyone there so," I struggled for the right word, "standoffish."

"Why start to care about someone who's going to be gone in a week or two? Stick it out and they'll warm up. Really. It was about three months before I even bother to talked to Jeff. I was sure with his laid-back attitude he'd bail after the first bad call. Well he didn't, and he got me through that call with calm poise. But yeah, you need to give people time to see that you can handle the job."

I sighed. It wasn't the answer I wanted, but it was probably the best I would get. We chatted a bit more, then she took off and I stared out the window wondering about how to stick it out.

About noon Jo came and got me and we went to her house. She talked the entire ride about how much she missed the shop, the doing things with

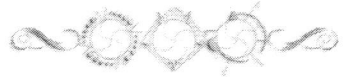

her hands, things that made sense. I didn't say anything, but her first day of school had only been Monday. If she was already jonesing for mechanics work, school would drive her crazy.

"My girls are home!" Marisol grabbed both of us in a bone-crushing hug. "It's about time. Have you lost more weight?" She glared at me, and I just shrugged. Not owning a scale kept me ignorant. I preferred not knowing.

"*Mami*, we've only been gone two weeks. We're fine." Jo hugged her mother as she continued to fret. I wondered if it was Jo being the youngest, a girl, or just the whole college thing that brought out the fretting in Marisol. Either way it was a new facet to her.

"We'll see about that." She dragged us in. "Now tell me what your classes are because I just know you'll do great. You're the smartest of all of us."

I only noticed because I was sitting next to her and the couch sagged like a sway back horse causing me to lean against her, but when her mom said that, I felt her stiffen and flinch at the same time. It was a weird feeling. I pulled away to look at her, but she just smiled and pulled out a piece of paper from her bag.

"I figured you'd ask, so here you go. My class list."

I'd seen it already, so I knew what was on it, Marisol grabbed it so fast I was surprise Jo didn't get a paper cut. She just snickered and leaned back.

Did I imagine the stress? That's odd. She and her parents rarely had secrets. Did they?

We spent the afternoon chatting with her mom and going over the classes. Jo had comments on the teachers and the campus, but she didn't say much about the coursework, using the excuse it was only the first week.

Marisol put us to work getting dinner ready. Even Marco and Paulo were coming over this evening to grill Jo. She just nodded but pointed out we needed to leave by seven as she didn't want to drive in the dark.

That made me hide a smile. It was the perfect way to get out early, cause her mother would never disagree with that statement.

Henri just grinned as he pulled dinner out of the oven. It was a Mexican casserole that should have fed them for a week but might give them leftovers tomorrow. If we didn't leave with most of it in Jo's saddlebags.

Either way, it was a nice day, though I still worried about work and my place in the EMS department. But I couldn't do anything about it right now.

We escaped about seven-fifteen with enough food for tomorrow in her bags and started the drive home.

"Hey. You okay?"

I'd chosen now to ask. The helmets and her inability to turn and look at me might get her to talk where if I cornered her, she'd avoid.

She stayed silent long enough that I thought she wouldn't answer.

"What if I don't succeed?"

"What do you mean?" That idea had never occurred to me. Jo succeeded at everything. A decent B student in high school, sports star, and so good with engines.

"I mean everyone keeps talking about how good I'll be, and they are on me to choose my major. Talking about all the options I have. And well what if I don't? What if I don't manage to graduate?"

It was probably a good thing she couldn't see my face. I'm sure the surprise and amusement I felt would have been obvious.

"Jo-Jo, I've never known you to fail at anything. Besides, they are paying for the degree, remember. I'm very sure the government will do anything reasonable to make sure you pass and so they can use your magic fully."

"You ever think about that?"

"About what?"

"What they do to people who don't succeed, who can't handle college and never learn to use their magic the right way. Do they treat them as ronin and kill them?"

I flinched and the bike wobbled. She got it back under control but my mind was racing down that idea. What do they do? Did they kill people? I wanted to lie and tell her they would never do that, but I couldn't fake that much trust in any government agency.

"I don't think you need to worry about it Jo. You'll do fine. It's just the first week. You'll get back into the swing of things."

"Yeah, I'm sure I will. Just first week jitters." Her voice was bright and cheery, and I knew all the way down to the bottom of my soul, she was lying. But I didn't push it. I'd watch and make sure she was okay. As her BFF I couldn't do anything less.

We got home late Saturday and both crashed. The drive and the socializing turning us in to zombies.

Sunday I cleaned since she'd cooked all week. I needed to get a feel for paychecks. Most of the medics just bought food when they were out. I still packed mine, but way too often I didn't get to eat as we were never back at the bay to grab it. That meant by the time I got off shift I was shaking with hunger, which wasn't good. I couldn't afford to get that hungry. It was yet another problem to overcome.

"So how's your homework going?" I finally broached the subject again Sunday night. After the discussion on the way home, I hadn't wanted to push too hard but I'd watched her fighting with it most of the afternoon. I knew she was avoiding it when she offered to do dishes. Jo hated doing dishes. "Learning anything interesting?"

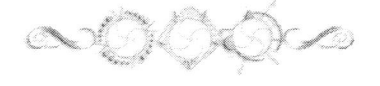

Jo groaned. "I swear I wish I'd never emerged this high. This first quarter just might kill me. I don't have to do to many of the stupid courses so that is at least a help, but I need to take basic English. I mean who cares who Beowulf was? I'm not studying to be a historian." She'd slumped backwards in her chair, looking like a woman with all the weight of the world on her.

This, at least, felt real. The fear of failure wasn't as strong, but I still felt like there was something I was missing. But what?

"Oh, it can't be that bad, can it?"

"Nah, yes, no? I don't know. There is a lot of reading and you know I've never been a fast reader." Something about her tone felt off, but I just nodded. Jo had been the tomboy: more interested in playing sports than doing anything resembling schoolwork. "But the lectures are cool. I have two classes on magic, one the history of it. You should read this textbook. What they taught in high school is like telling us an iceberg is mostly underwater, and nothing else. I like the practical applications stuff, though really the more I get into it, I'm starting to see why mom and dad rarely use it. You have to get super fine control to do anything that isn't going to make you go bald." Her face had brightened, and she sat up. "Here watch."

Jo picked up a piece of her notebook paper and hung it upside down. "This will cost me about a strand of hair." She frowned and the paper waved up as if a sudden wind had hit it, then back down. "That is me learning the cost of things, super basic things, but it will take me about three months to grow back the hair I blew to do that, when I could have just done this." With a wry smile she wiggled the paper. "Yeah, magic seems like a lot of work. I mean moving molecules and stuff takes almost nothing, but you need to learn a ton to be able to," she paused then in the tone of repeating something that was a mantra, "visualize, verify, and actuate. Otherwise you're just making offerings that could have been done easier with a calorie expenditure." A wry look on her face. "They promise next semester we'll learn how to use the fat stored in our body to power it. It's one reason so many mages are skinny, if not in good shape. It would be nice if we could build muscle, but I'll take burning fat."

As she talked, she'd brightened up, with her normal excitement present. My worry faded as I listened to her. I'm sure I sounded more depressed talking about work. New situations were hard. Exhaustion set in as I thought about tomorrow. I was trying so hard not to dread it, but I did. The more I thought about it the more I wanted to sleep. Maybe I would think about my lunch issues as I fell asleep.

"That sounds neat. Kinda sad I'm missing it." A yawn split my words and I laughed. "But I'm headed to bed. I can't express how exhausted I am, though some of it might be dread about tomorrow.'"

Jo nodded. "Being the new person is hard, but I have faith. Well faith in you. Go to bed. I have another chapter to read, then I need to start writing a paper on the various cell matter we can use as offerings, as well as ethical considerations for at least one unusual one. That is due at the end of next week and if I don't start it now, I'll never get it done."

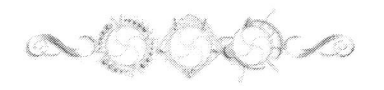

"Ova, semen, or uterine lining," I responded without thinking about it much. They were all cells that either regenerated or not all of them were used. They should have the same weight as blood cells power wise, and most people would never miss them.

Jo blinked at me, then a slow grin spread across her face. "Those are great ideas. Thanks, Cori. We have plans for the next weekend you're off. I figure we'll enjoy exploring when you're off and I'll double down on schoolwork the weekends you work."

"Sounds good to me, but remember we are still on a major tight budget until I figure out how much I'm actually getting. Since I'm working, this weekend should give you a chance to be ahead in everything."

Jo made a funny face then waved her hand. "I'm broke too. What about wandering around Centennial Park and just making sure we know all the cheapest places to get food?"

"That sounds good to me." I waved night and stumbled back to my bedroom. After a shower I crawled into bed, planning on thinking about my lunch and how to carry it with me. I seemed to be back to the starving thing again. But instead, my mind drifted to the girl in the park. I'd watched the news and checked online occasionally, but I couldn't find anything about her. I didn't know what that meant. Did it mean I hadn't seen a dead body?

The scent of her blood, the sight of her face with empty holes where eyes should have been, and the terror carved into her expression slammed back into me and I flinched. No, there was no way that was fake. I knew what death looked like. She'd been dead.

Then why? Why nothing? The cops hadn't called again but still, I would have thought there would have been a news story. The fact that it there wasn't a story made my skin crawl even more. I read too many true crime books and it pointed towards a cover up. The idea of covering up a murder made me want to call the news station immediately but that I knew would be the height of stupidity.

You're used to small town life. This is the big city, maybe it isn't that big of a deal.

The idea made me vaguely nauseous, that a death like that wouldn't be treated as important. I pushed the thought away; the cops had been too upset. Even Detective Stone had been on edge, though I didn't know about what.

The question was, what now? Not my business, but I'd found her. I'd been the first person to see her death and try to do something, not that there was much I could do by that point.

I gave a bitter laugh. I had to know. To get her name and send flowers to her grave if nothing else. I was off on Wednesday. Maybe I could swing by the police station and ask. While I doubted that they would give me much information, surely her name and where she was buried would be information they could share.

I nodded, even knowing that wouldn't be enough to satisfy me but I'd learned a long time ago, not all needs were satisfied. With that thought, I snuggled deeper and focused on lunch options. I'd probably have to give up and ask someone. Oh well, friendly they weren't, but hopefully they would answer this.

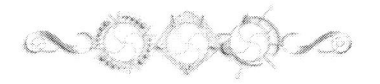

CHAPTER 7

There are always hierarchies in everything, be it jobs, society, or social groups. Merlins are often regarded with respect by other mages and fear by non-mages. But while they can do great things at a fraction of the cost that a magician or wizard would pay, they still have limits. No matter what TV or movies shows us the magic of a merlin is just as subtle and small as that of a hedgemage.
~Magic Explained

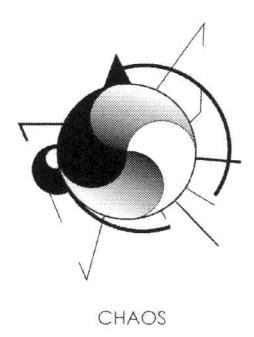

CHAOS

I'll give it a month. If it isn't better in a month, I'll go find another job.
At that moment, I didn't know if I hated the shift or if I hated the people I worked with. I would never be a morning person.
Screw it. I'll treat them like Sam treated everyone he pulled over. Polite but ready to shoot them if they started trouble.
That I could do. Moving slow that morning, I'd made coffee just as shift started and we were hit with a call as I filled my cup, which meant I was stuck with Jorge before I could ask Lisa any questions. While Lisa wasn't friendly, she at least half smiled at me occasionally. I'd figured I could ask her more than the others.

"Huh. Figured after last week you wouldn't show up today," Jorge said as he slid into the other side of the bus. "Thought for sure that drunk driver throwing up on you would have made you run for the hills. All you pretty little things can never handle it when it gets truly messy."

"I guess I'll take it as a compliment that I'm a pretty young thing," I said it in a Southern drawl, putting a twang on the last word and making it "thang." But then I dropped it and gave him a look. "You did know I graduated from the internship program and was involved in the mass casualty in Rome, right?"

His head jerked to look at me as the blush from my earlier words started to fade from his cheeks.

"Wait, the band bus incident?"

"Yes. I'm from that area so they called me up. I did my internship working as an EMT II for the Rockway Fire Department. I'm not going to say I've dealt with everything, but I've been exposed to a variety of things. And I'm still here." A bit of a challenge came out in that last statement and I lifted my chin a bit.

"Hmmm," he said, glancing at me, but he didn't say anything else as we were pulling up to the call.

As always, a moment of trepidation hit me as I stepped out of the bus but they were getting shorter and shorter. I knew I wouldn't always succeed but my exposure to situations grew every day. So far nothing topped the guy who fell from the sky and pulverized pretty much every bone in his body. And the girl. Her picture flashed in my head again. Wednesday I'd go see about her, or at least ask if they had any info.

 Person stuck in a tree was a new call for me. Which meant as I slid out of the cab and looked around, I expected to see lots of tall trees. Maybe someone wedged in one, or at least someone stuck up a telephone pole. Instead we were in an area of apartment buildings and strip malls. The area was mostly small apartment complexes, and while there were a few trees, they looked like mostly Magnolias, the young small ones, not the giants. Those could impale a herd of cows if they wanted.

We looked around and Jorge hit his radio. "Dispatch, we're at the address. Can we get details?"

"The caller sounds more than a bit inebriated and drunk, but I would head to the back. I think that is where they said they were. They aren't responding to questions anymore, though the operator says he can still hear them."

I tilted my head, listening and trying to trace something or anything down. "I think I hear something from back here." I heft the bag up on my shoulder, and headed around the back of the apartment. As soon as I turned the corner, the sound of men and women yelling and shouting became clearer.

"I thought you said you called 911? Where they hell are they?" A woman's voice all but screeching in panic. "He's going to die up there."

I picked up my pace a bit. I had to find time to get to the gym. Skinny was one thing but these big bags were heavy. I pushed my way past a wall of hedges and slowed, looking at the throng of people all looking up. I cataloged it all in a snap glance. A grill in one corner, coolers full of beer, and a trash can that looked like it was working hard on being filled with beer cans. Then I followed their gaze up and blinked.

"Well, that's different," I murmured.

"Blasted drunk idiots," Jorge muttered and clicked his radio. "Dispatch you need to get a ladder truck out here asap and someone to figure out who owns the tower at this location. They're going to need to do repair work."

Still shaking my head I took a deep breath and moved forward, taking the lead. While Jorge was senior, there wasn't any need to wait for him, this one was obvious. "You called for assistance?" I pitched my voice to be heard over the chatter. Mrs. MacDowell's drama lessons came in helpful occasionally.

"Oh finally. You've got to help him," a woman said, rushing over to meet them.

"What's his name?" I asked still trying to get a better view of the man stuck up the cell phone tower.

"Oh that's Charlie. Well Charles, but we call him Charlie. He's hurt." The woman kept babbling as I set down bag. I glanced at Jorge quickly to make sure he'd watch it. He nodded still talking on the radio. People raided bags if they weren't watched. I moved over toward the base of the cell tower. It was on one of those fake trees towers with large metal spikes off of it. I peered up closer and saw he had a climbing loop on him. It was probably what kept him up there instead of laying dead at the base.

"He work some place that he climbs a lot?" I asked looking up at the limp body. Too far away to see details.

"No. Damn fool bought it at a garage sale and wanted to prove how easy they were to use. He got his ass up there all right but then decided that was too easy and he was going to skip from one branchy thing to another. And well, he slipped and," she sighed and waved her hand.

"Cori, I'm headed out to wave down the truck. They should be here in a minute." I nodded at him and moved closer to the pole. Red caught my attention and I crouched down to inspect the significant amount of blood on the pole near the base. I looked closely and while it wasn't a huge amount, it was enough that it indicated either bleeding for a long time, or a short serious bleed.

"How long has he been up there?"

"About twenty minutes. But if you mean hurt and not responding," she paused to shout up the pole, "you're a stupid idiot Charlie Booth!" She signed and looked back at me. "About eight? Ten maybe? When he fell and quit responding I think someone called you. I mean, you're here right?"

"How do you know him?" I kept my voice neutral but nothing I saw made me feel good about his chances if we didn't get up there fast.

"I married the idiot," her voice was exasperated but I could hear the worry in it. "He's a good man, but I swear when he and his friends start drinking... It's like watching people do stupid things on videos, but they do it for real. At thirty-one you would have thought he had learned better by now." She chewed on her lip, her dirty blond hair escaping the ponytail and falling into her eyes. "He going to be okay?

The sound of a motor coming through the opposite side prevented me from needing to answer. While the side we came through had a hedge of bushes, they came through the thin trees on the other side as there was only an empty lot.

Jorge came through the way we did, dragging the gurney with him. I watched them get the ladder set up with a basket attached. One of the fireman, the name Statton on his chest, walked over to me.

"We need one of you to go up, but we've got an issue. That ladder is only rated for about three-fifty, four hundred if we push it. My smallest guy on this rig is pushing one-eighty, and the victim has to weight close to two hundred."

I looked up at the man. I could see the beer belly from here and grunted, doing the math in my head.

Jorge is easily one-ninety or more. There is no way he can go up.

"I'll go. Even with my suit on I'm not breaking one thirty. But I'll need your guy's help. At two hundred he's going to be too heavy for me to move by myself." I forced myself not to cringe as I said that physical strength was one of the major issues people had with female first responders.

"I could move him by myself if I went up." Jorge said making me feel better. "But you really don't want me up there. Anything much over three feet off the ground and I get vertigo. You'd be rescuing two people."

Statton nodded. "Come on then, Munroe?"

I looked at him, confused for a second, then remembered that was my name on my chest. "Yeah, give me a second. I need to get a portable bag."

For all the standoffishness at the station, Jorge worked with me quickly to create a light bag I could take with me, one that would hopefully let me stabilize Charlie until we got him down. Once I had that strapped around me, I headed over to the truck with Statton. Another man, helmet and jacket off, nodded at me.

"Call me Matt. You ready? I'll climb first and you follow. I'll brace and we have a basket to slip him into that we can then lower down."

What is it with me and baskets lately?

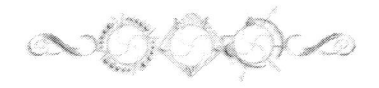

I glanced at the contraption that hooked onto the ladder and nodded. They put in in a harness, and showed me how to hook it, so when we got to the top, I could hook it. If I slipped, I wouldn't get killed. In theory. I didn't mention how often things went wrong. Why tempt fate?

"Lay on MacDuff."

He laughed and flashed me a smile of bright white teeth. "And damn'd be him that first cries, 'Hold, enough!'"

The correct response made me laugh and he smiled again. "English minor. Don't ask me why."

I shook my head and let them help me up onto the truck. They had braced it and the ladder looked like it was at full extension to reach just beneath where Charlie hung.

With one last check that I was following him, Matt started climbing. I let him get a few rungs above me and then followed. Going up the ladder was a mix of climbing and crawling with the ground getting further and further away.

Huh, it doesn't bug me when on rollercoasters, why is this so different?

That little question kept me occupied and moving on automatic until my hand hit Matt's boot.

"Up here. I'll move to the side. I've got a hold of one of the arrays and they are relatively sturdy, but he looks in bad shape. You'd better move fast." His voice had lost the good humor., I let myself move my gaze from the ladder that represented safety and my only way down, to the person I was there to help. Charlie looked his age. His hair was a bit thinner than it had probably been at twenty; he had a belly that needed less beer and more walking, and face with lines of pain. I reached over to check his pulse-thready but beating.

"Move down a bit, I need to be higher up so I can get a good look."

Matt nodded and in a move that would have seen me dead on the ground oh so far away from us, moved over me and down, leaving me up at the tip of the ladder with my patient.

Okay, show time Munroe. Time to step up, this person is depending on you.

I moved up and over and inspected Charlie. The woman on the ground said he'd been trying to skip between the things, antenna arrays maybe, and fell. The climbing loop had saved his life, but also made him fall. He fallen in between two of them, wedged hard. One leg had a bad break, as I could see the white of bone. He'd been in shorts and tennis shoes. A severe laceration on his scalp and if his shoulder wasn't dislocated, it was damn close from how it bulged outward.

Leg first, that is where the blood is coming from. Then address the rest.

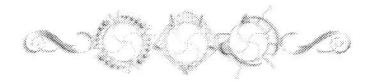

I shifted, feeling the ladder move as I leaned in a bit more. Getting a good look at the leg I cringed. It looked like when he fell his leg twisted and caught. The fibula had fractured and stuck out the side of his leg, tearing a lot of muscle and veins. It hadn't been up high enough to get the femoral artery though, so blood loss but no bleed out. This we could deal with. It took a bit of twisting and precarious balancing but I got the inflatable brace on his leg. It would take a surgeon to get it aligned properly, but it shouldn't move or tear anymore. The laceration on his head was bleeding but other than surface damage I didn't see anything that worried me. Both of his eyes reacted, though he was still out, which for right now was a very good thing. If he woke up and struggled, we'd have an issue.

I turned and looked down at the firefighter. "I've stabilized the biggest injury, but now we need to get him down. I can't lift him, but I think if we unhook him and pull on his shoulders, we can slide him into the basket." It would be tricky, and I kept having to breathe to keep myself from freaking out at the height, precarious position, and the craziness of what we were about to do.

"Got it. Give me one minute." Matt reached and pulled the basket, hooking it to the cable that ran up it as part of the retraction mechanism. He then locked it in place so it wouldn't move. "Let's do this." His encouraging smile back and I tried to take some strength from it.

With my harness hooked, I braced one leg on the tower and one on the ladder, trying so very hard not to think, just do it. Matt braced in a similar manner, looked at me and we lifted and got Charlie half into the basket as opposed to laying across the arrays. But the arrays still took most of his weight, with the climbing loop still fastened.

Step one done. Now to step two.

I reached out and unhooked his climbing loop. Charlie shifted, and slide down. His whole weight slammed into the ladder and it dropped downward knocking the basket at an angle and Charlie's unsecured body started to slip out.

Chapter 8

Time, one of the branches of Spirit that is often misunderstood. Time mages can not go back in time, nor can they travel like a superhero through time. Instead they can control how they move through time, and in small area rewind time, seeing what happened. Now Time mages are rare, but they excel at research and forensics. Though the cost to rewind time grow exponentially for how long it has been.
~ Magic Explained

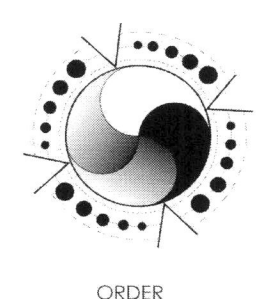

ORDER

Oh by Merlin, no!
The world stopped. I felt a chunk of my hair vaporize as Charlie hung suspended in midair. I reached to pull him back into the basket. How could I move when all around me everything froze? Even the leaves had quit moving. With a surge of effort I heaved, trying to pull him back to the basket. It felt like I pulled him through thick sludgy oatmeal but he moved and I got him back in and time snapped back into motion. I almost felt sick as Matt spun looking at me.

"Thank Merlin, you're fast. Let's get him secured." Together we worked to get Charlie strapped in and began the process of getting him back down to the ground. The world moved around me, but I was operating on automatic.

I stopped time.

The thought bounced and rattled around, breaking everything I thought I knew. A hedgie couldn't do that. Oh, you could be strong in time, but a hedge might be able to slow how fast a cup fell. Not stop everything around them. At least that was my understanding. The moment of time being suspended was still crystal clear in my mind.

"Huh, you just might make it, Cori," Jorge said as we got Charlie strapped into the gurney. "I've never seen anyone react like that, and you kept your cool without blinking. Takes a certain type of people to do this job. You might make it after all."

"Thanks," I manage to reply, but I had caught a glimpse of myself in the side view mirror. I could see the chunk missing in my normally smooth bob. The bob that almost never needed trimming.

I'm a mage. But I can't be a mage.

Even as Jorge talked the rest of the shift, telling people about my quick save, I couldn't get myself to believe or understand what had happened. I knew I needed to get tested. This was so wrong. But if I tested out high? How could I test out high? But a low rank couldn't have done that.

The conflict between what I knew and what had happened kept me quiet and confused all day. I couldn't wait to get home to talk to Jo. See what she thought. Tomorrow I had to work, but I was off Monday, I could go and get tested then. Then I would know for sure.

The idea of testing out high and starting over again made me want to cry. I didn't want to give up everything. I'd just finally gotten it. I huddled in the back corner of the bus, doing nothing but staring out the window. How could I be a mage? Especially an archmage. Maybe I had imagined it all.

But the chunk of missing hair couldn't be denied. I kept touching it, feeling it. But is that what happened?

The harder I tried to remember, the more doubts I had. Maybe I really reacted that fast and the rush of adrenaline made it seem like time stopped. Something could have caught the chunk of hair and I didn't notice it getting cut off. Or heck, when was the last time I had paid any attention to my hair.? Maybe it had been like that for a while. Jorge hadn't seemed to notice.

My thoughts bounced between two extremes, leaving me even more exhausted by the time I got off the bus. The single flight of stairs to our apartment seemed like a mile. By the time I'd gotten to the top, I just wanted to crawl into bed and hide - hide from everything. I swallowed and pushed open the door, trying to look forward to Jo and the smell of food. I stood there, the door open and one foot inside.

The apartment was dark and no scent of food. Confused, I stepped all the way in and shut the door behind me. "Jo?" I knew she wasn't here, but I called anyhow. As I expected, there was no answer.

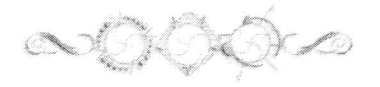

Standing in the middle of the living room I wracked my mind to remember if she had said anything. When we'd talked, before I went to bed, she'd indicated studying and papers.

Oh, maybe I should check my phone.

We had it on silent so calls didn't come in when we were with patients and with the turmoil of the day I'd completely forgotten to look at it. A text from Jo popped up as soon as I pulled open the app.

`Cor going out with peeps for study and talk. Be back late. Dinner in fridge. Ta!`

I sagged in relief. No one to pester me, no one to make me face something I wasn't ready to face. But I had wanted to get her opinion, see if what I thought was right. If maybe I really was a mage.

So what am I trying to avoid, the knowledge I'm a mage? Or the fear of losing everything again?

I couldn't answer that question, so I grabbed the burrito waiting for me. Jo knew my penchant for easily consumed food. I heated it up while I stripped into something comfortable to sleep in. Somehow, I managed to eat without even being aware of what was in the burrito. I didn't realize I'd eaten it all until I went to take another bite, and nothing was there.

Shaking my head, I went to bed after checking four times that I had the alarms set for tomorrow morning. At this point I wanted to stay long enough to get to the daily eight hour shifts. I hated twelves and the moving days was a pain, though being off Monday would make things easier.

I fell into sleep but it wasn't restful. Instead, I went back to the weird dream of those moments between me rushing to Stevie's side and him dying in my arms. The fight with darkness, the pulling at my very being, and the weird double snap that came into me.

The wail of the alarm came as a relief. I pulled myself up and staggered into the shower. It was only there that the rest of my brain caught up with thoughts and ideas.

Am I a mage? Should I get tested? Did Jo make it home? Will the cops talk to me?

The list of questions seemed never ending and I tried to order what I needed to do. But first and foremost, always, was Jo. Stepping out, I wrapped a towel around me and padded over to her bedroom. She kept her door open a crack always, saying she liked to have fair warning of other noises in the house. Today was no different. I pushed it open wide enough to stick my head in and checked. Sure enough, she lay face down on the bed, one arm hanging off, and a gentle snore rattling her nose.

The scent of beer and cigarette smoke hit my nose and I fought a sneeze. Where in the world had she gone? Most study groups didn't involve those two things. I paused and shrugged. Maybe they did. What did I know?

With a shake of my head I backed out and continued to get ready for work. I needed to be out at the bus stop by five-thirty to make it to work before seven. I left water and pain killers waiting for her on her nightstand before I left, her snoring still audible. Oh well, I'd talk to her tonight. Maybe by then I'd have a plan.

I'd taken the time in the morning to cover up the chunk of missing hair so it looked less obvious. I still didn't know what it meant, but either way I'd have to deal with it soonish.

Walking into the bay I headed for the coffee pot, having finished my first mug on the way here.

"Morning, Cori. So I did some research on you," a friendly voice chirped at me and I almost tripped as I spun. This was my fifth day and the first time anyone had talked to me in a friendly voice, much less greeted me. Lisa stood there with a smile on her face, though a smirk hovered at the edges.

"Morning," I replied, my tone wary. "And did you find anything?"

"Well, after Jorge told us about your adventure yesterday, and your coolness under pressure–which, by the way, I don't know if I could have done." There was honest admiration in her tone but the barely hidden smirk worried me.

"Thanks?"

"No, you did good. Though what I find interesting is what I got through the rumor mill." Her smirk had blossomed to a full-blown one and mentally I braced myself for whatever was coming. Even though my brain scrambled, I couldn't think of anything. My grades had been good, my performance at all the internships had received high scores. So what could she be smirking about?

"And that is?"

"A nickname? Cori Catastrophe?" Her grin was wide and everyone paid attention to us at this point. For my part my knees almost buckled.

That is it? That's what she has? Oh, who cares.

The relief that washed through me made me giddy. While I hadn't wanted to talk about my weird life, after yesterday I didn't think it mattered. "Yeah. Lots of weird things happen around me. Or I find them."

"If nothing else, having you here will be interested. Welcome aboard, Cori."

Jorge walked in about then and grinned. "I think I'm calling you Catastrophe from now on."

I turned to see the group of them grinning at me, and for the first time I didn't feel like an intruder in their space. But the joy I would have felt at that not two days ago didn't emerge. Instead, the idea that I would lose all of this, lose a place I might have belonged, spiked even harder. I swallowed back tears and turned around, lifting my voice as I did so.

"I assume you would like me to make coffee?"

A chorus of "yes, please" filled the area. I focused on the coffee until I had control of myself again. The lunch box idea seemed an even stupider thing to worry about but I was tired of being hungry. But rather than bugging Jorge, I took my mug and went out to the bay.

The Atlanta heat hadn't settled in yet, but at seven-thirty it was already muggy and thick. Yet another reason to someday live in the mountains. Pulling open the passenger side door, I started looking. While I had the training to drive the rigs, for the most part I didn't like to drive and was more than willing to let anyone else drive for me. I did need to grab the rig once a month just to practice. Not knowing how wasn't the same as not liking to drive. Though public transportation was annoying, it was cheaper and less scary.

Fifteen minutes later I still didn't see a good place to stick a lunch and sighed with frustration.

"Whatcha looking for?"

Where a day ago his voice would have been uninterested, maybe even cool, today Jorge sounded almost curious. Almost.

"I'm trying to figure out if there is some place I can put a lunch bag or cooler or something," I admitted, straightening up.

"Why?" He had a frown on his face, and I had to laugh. Some people didn't get either being broke or being frugal. Either way, at least he wasn't contemptuous. I'd take that.

"I'm broke. I don't even own a car. I really can't afford to eat out every day and we aren't back here consistently for me to keep my lunch here." I shrugged. "So I was trying to find an option that might work."

"Oh. Huh." He frowned, looking at the rig. "Never thought about it. I like eating out. Only chance I get to eat things my wife would strangle me for eating." He got in the other side and looked. "You know there really isn't BUT most of the crap in the glove box can be tossed or shouldn't take up much space. You could easily get a sandwich or slim container in there." He leaned down and popped open the glove box, pulling out stuff and separating it into two piles. The keep pile comprised of registration and the manual. That left a nice space for me to shove food. The burritos Jo made, a few PB&J's, nothing that would go bad, but stuff that would keep me fed.

"That will work great!" I managed not to gush, then felt guilty. They thought I would stay. I wanted to stay. But what if?

I shut down that line of thought. Monday go to the police station. Ask my question. Then decide. Maybe put it off another week. A week wouldn't make that much of a difference. Next week I would have Wednesday, Thursday, and Friday off. That might be better. Go in Wednesday morning to give myself a few days to deal with the outcome. I didn't want to be a mage. I wanted the life I'd been struggling to have.

"Great and sorry. That just didn't occur to me. Most of us just eat on the run or here. But yeah, I get being broke." He looked like he was going to say something else, but the speaker went off.

"Unit needed at Peachtree Center NE and Ellis St. Car versus Pedestrian."

"Let's go. And if we're out today, I'll buy lunch," Jorge said as we both jumped into the rig. I started to protest but he waved me away. "You earned it. If I had gone up that ladder the patient and I would both be dead. So you earned lunch." I nodded, putting my mug in the cup holder and buckled in.

"Sounds good, and thanks."

"Yeah, we're a group of jerks, but most people think this is an easy gig and bail after the first few days. Not worth the effort."

"Bailing isn't on my plan," I said, forcing a smile.

But some things might be out of my control.

Chapter 9

Hedgemages are the forgotten magic users among use. While it is estimated more people are hedgemages than the official 35% of all tested, in reality the numbers may be as high as 75% of all people. This implies that many people are doing magic all the time, but it is so intrinsic to their very being they never realize it. It also suggests that treating anyone poorly might be a fatal mistake.
~ History of Magic

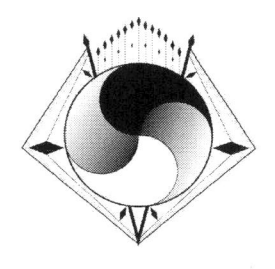

SPIRIT

I really hope this isn't a mistake, but I need to know.
I stood outside the police station, the same one I'd been questioned at a few days ago. I'd spent Sunday avoiding talking to Jo, which oddly wasn't hard. Apparently, she had both drank too much and let someone try to make her sober, which resulted in giving her the hangover to beat all hangovers. When I got home, she was curled up on the couch, sipping water, and begged me not to talk too loud as she studied.

I had softly laughed and rubbed the top of her head which elicited a whine.

"Remember, you have class tomorrow."

"If I die today, I don't. So just let me die."

"Hmm, you know what Marisol would do right now, don't you?"

"Oh, please Cori. For the love of magic, please don't." I swear she whimpered as she said that.

I laughed, refilled her water, and went to bed. I had my own drama to deal with. Jo learned fast, I doubted she'd ever do that again and if she did, I would pull a Marisol. That would involve cranking music as loud as I could and finding the worst tasting stuff to eat. But for now, I was just as happy to slip into bed and sleep in.

Sleeping in felt great and let me avoid Jo, who left for a nine am class, which found me back here, staring at the police station.

The worst they can do is question me again and I don't have anything else going on today.

I took a deep breath and promptly coughed as I got a mouth full of car exhaust. There were days when I really missed Rockway. Still coughing, I pushed my way in and enjoyed the cooler and much cleaner air inside.

"May I help you?" It was a question. At least the words should have been one, but the grumpy woman manning the desk made them sound like an accusation. Her hair looked like she'd been in a tornado, streaked with grey and piled on her head. A style that looked cute on Jo, but this one had more lines on her face than I had eyelashes and smelled like she lived in an ashtray.

It took me off my stride a bit and I stammered. "De-Detective Stone? I mean, I, uh, I wanted to talk to Detective Stone?"

She glared at me. "About what?"

The attitude made it even harder, but I pushed through. No matter what, I needed to put flowers at that woman's grave. Let her know her death mattered to me. Nothing else had eaten at me as much. I only rarely went to the funerals of those I found but I always followed, knew their name, kept them in my thoughts. This woman, this girl, I knew nothing of, and I needed to give her that much. A name and a goodbye.

"The girl in the park," I hedged. I would not blurt out things in this public area. Already more than one person had walked by giving me a weird look.

Her face tightened, but she nodded at some wore and defaced chairs. "Sit. I'll see if he's available."

I backed away but didn't sit. The chairs looked like they might carry a laboratory's worth of diseases. I had a sudden desire to start spraying the disinfectant we used to clean the ambulance on them. Sitting on those might kill me.

"What? Decided to tell me what you refused to tell me last time?" Detective Stone's voice sounded right behind me and I jumped, bumping into the chairs. They fell apart like a house of cards. We both stared at them and I just closed my eyes for a moment, wondering how much of the disaster that shadowed me really was my fault. Pushing it away, and my scratchy skull, I looked up at him.

He had a slack-jawed look of surprise on his face that made him look stupid, and it helped.

"There wasn't anything I didn't tell you, as I'm sure you are well aware of."

He crossed his arms across his chest, creating man boobs which I'm pretty sure wasn't the effect he was going for. "Then why are you here? You must have some more information to give us."

I fought not to roll my eyes. "What else could I have told you? If you've been doing your job, you know I just moved here. I'm the roommate of a new mage at GA MageTech. You should know that I'm a newly hired paramedic at Ruby. Anything else doesn't have anything else to bear on this case. Or did you have another question?" My tone challenged him, and I noted more than a few people, both cops and others, were watching us with a variety of reactions.

"No. That's what I found out. But that doesn't explain why you're here." His voice was just as challenging, and my teeth ground together. I was going to have dental issues if I kept this up.

"I'm here because there has been nothing in the news: no mention of her, no asking questions. No 'can you identify' this girl messages." I was about to continue, but he cut me off.

"What? Is that your fix? You're looking for attention, a bit of glory hound. Want to be known as the person who found the victim? Sell your story to the tabloids? What? Has our keeping this under wraps messed up your plans? You were sure you'd be famous for finding her?"

"Are all cops here in Atlanta this blasted stupid?" I spat the words out, we were both almost yelling now, but while I was aware of the audience, I didn't really care. "I don't give a damn about anyone knowing who I am. I'd be happier if no one ever knew I existed. But she did. I just wanted to know her name and when and where she was going to be buried. I thought she deserved to have flowers and me knowing her name. Forgive me if I thought that by seeing her in death, I at least owed her the courtesy of laying flowers on her grave."

His mouth dropped open to let loose what I was sure was about to be another attack on my stupidity and involvement in her death. Coming here had been a waste of my time.

"Is there an issue?" This voice was arctic cold without a trace of Southern accent. Stone went white and turned slowly to toward the man who had spoken. He was older, maybe fifty, with gray streaking the sides of his head. His suit, while not screaming money, fit well and went with his cold blue eyes and dark brown hair.

"Captain Jessup, sir, we were having a discussion."

"At the top of your voices, in the lobby, where at least twenty people are now listening and I'm sure someone has recorded it. All about a case that we wanted to keep under the radar until we had a better lead."

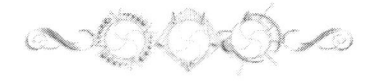

"She, well, I," Stone sighed and his shoulders slumped. "My behavior was unacceptable, sir. I know better."

"Yes, it was. And yes you do." He shifted his attention to me, and I wished he hadn't. He had no mage symbols on his temples but from the way his eyes pierced me, I would have believed he had the ability to read my thoughts and my soul. "I take it you are our only lead in this case."

Only lead? Are they serious? I know nothing. How in the world can I be their lead?

Worry and annoyance caused my mouth to run off again. "If I'm the only thing you have as a lead, your case is going nowhere, and that girl will never find justice. Because I don't know a damn thing and don't have any ideas for you."

Stone clenched his fists, but the captain nodded.

"That is a true statement. I have gone over all the statements you gave, and I believe you are correct in your avowal that you know nothing of the young woman's demise." He kept his voice cool and quiet and already people started drifting away, though one or two seemed a bit disappointed at that. "At this time we still do not know her identity." That comment rocked me back. They didn't know who she was? But she was a mage, or was she? Wracking my brain I tried to remember if she had a tattoo.

"Wasn't she registered with OMO?" The words slipped out and they both looked at me.

"She had no tattoos. Why would you think she was a mage?" Captain Jessup asked, still in that smooth voice, but this time his attention didn't waver from me at all.

"I don't know. The symbols. They seemed mage like. They made me think of," I struggled to find words from what I had sensed. The symbols, obscured by dirt and detritus, had just seemed like twisted magic, something to do something, but they also felt fake. "I just thought with the magical symbols she must have been a mage. But that was just the impression I got. I don't know anything."

"Stone, did you run her through OMO?"

Stone shook his head. "No mage tats why bother?"

I looked at both of them. "Didn't you get the same training as I did?" At their clueless stares I elaborated. "Anyone who is tested gets logged into the OMO system. You're only required to get the tattoos if you're a magician or higher. But to get access to the classes, you need to be tested and registered. Lots of hedges go to be tested just for the access. Even if they never actually use their magic."

Stone blinked at me, but Jessup nodded slowly. "You know I did get that information, but it was so long ago I'd completely forgotten. I need to institute a new policy to always run via OMO. No matter what. Stone?"

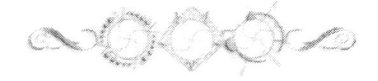

"On it, sir. I'll run that ASAP."

Jessup nodded. "I assume we have your contact information?" Looking at me as he asked.

"Well, I gave it to him, so probably?"

"Then, I promise: If we figure out who she is and have a time of her interment, I will make sure you are notified. If there is anything else?"

I sagged. I hadn't wanted to fight with them. Why couldn't some people just be nice?

"No. Really, that was all I wanted. I just wanted to know her name. It seemed wrong I'd seen her dead and didn't know her name." I shoved my hands in my pockets and avoided his gaze.

He allowed a slight tilt of his head. "Admirable attitude." With that he turned and started back behind the secure doors, Stone following him.

"Dammit, I was trying to keep her here a little longer. He wanted to see her," Stone muttered, but I heard him as I turned away.

"And you work for him since when?" The captain's cool voice made me feel better as I headed out.

The conversation was silenced with the door closing behind them. A cold shiver went down my spine and I headed out. If they were talking about me, and I knew they were, I didn't want to meet whoever Stone had been waiting for. In fact, leaving right this moment sounded very good. Turning on my heels I headed for the door at a quick pace. The frustration of the entire conversation wore on me and adding in the confusing last few comments meant it was time to go. I stepped out into the heat, then turned down the street with the chill still trickling down my back. I headed away from the police station, not running, but closer than I liked for a reason I didn't understand.

A crash, honk of horns, and the cessation of the cold caused me to turn around. One of the big banners announcing DragonWorldCon, a convention held every year about everything involving magic, both real and imagined, had broken loose and collapsed on someone. The fabric moved and even from here I could hear the words they were saying - absolutely not things acceptable for mixed company. With a half snicker I turned and headed away. I had cleaning to do, stuff to buy, and I needed to look at what continuing education course I could take.

I didn't think about taking the mage test. Not today. I had enough to consider.

CHAPTER 10

With the rise of magic, there was a matching decline in Christianity, Islam, and Judaism. There had been a rise in Wicca, Druidic Sects, Buddhism. Most people now identify as non-secular, though some worship gods they say reside on the other planes.
~History of Magic

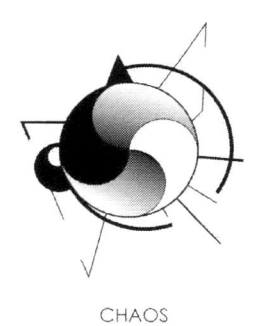

CHAOS

Now what do I do? A day off and nothing to study? At this rate I'm going to need to find something else to do to keep me busy.

The apartment was empty when I got home. I checked the schedule and saw that Jo had classes until three that afternoon. That meant she'd probably get home about four.

Good. Plenty of time to clean and get laundry done.

That was the exciting way I spent the next two hours. But by the time I was done the apartment was clean, the last load of laundry was in the machine, and my legs were killing me from running up and down the stairs with full baskets of clothes.

Just more proof I need to join a gym.

That idea caught me. I'd have time to go with this schedule. Once I got a few paychecks in, that was something I could do. I still avoided the OMO thoughts, I just wasn't ready. Or I was avoiding it, or a bit of both but either way, I'd mentally braced myself to go in soon. I wanted it to be a weekday while Jo was working; I didn't want anyone to know until I had the results.

The lock rattling in the door pulled me away from the laundry folding and I looked up to see Jo walk in, lugging a backpack and looking tired. Something else lurked behind her eyes but it vanished as soon as she saw me.

"Yo, how goes your weekend?"

"I hate rotating twelves, hate, hate, hate, but it lets me get chores done without everyone else in my way." I nodded at the piles of clean clothes. She was much more of a clothes horse than I was and my clothing was pretty simple under the jumpsuits, though in winter it'd probably be more substantial.

"Ooh, yes, my favorite tank top." She grinned and set her bag down, flopping on the couch next to me and started matching socks. "You have any plans tonight?"

I blinked at her, my brain not tracking. "Tonight?"

"Well it is your Saturday, right?" Her smile sly and teasing, and I went on alert. I knew that smile.

"I guess so." I hadn't really thought about it like that, but she was right. This was like a Saturday. "But it's your Monday. Shouldn't you be studying?"

"Meh, is classes, all the boring stuff right now. Besides, I got invited out with a bunch of students. We're going to the Varsity. You want to come? I mean, it means I don't have to cook," she wheedled a bit.

That caused a flash of guilt. She did get the brunt of the cooking. I had no issue doing it but I swear, nothing ever went right. Even her mother, who believed everyone could cook, had kicked me out of the kitchen. It was that bad.

One night out, the Varsity is like hamburgers and hot dogs, I can afford that. It's a night out.

"Sure. But won't I be intruding?"

Jo gave me a funny look. "You're my best friend, and my roommate, of course not. Besides it is kinda an open get together. Show up, eat, bitch about school. You know, normal stuff."

I couldn't think of a time I'd ever done that, just hung out with anyone that wasn't Jo and her family. Maybe this is what I needed, to actually have a life and have fun.

"Sure. When do we leave?"

Jo glanced at her watch. "Eh, probably about two hours or so. It will take us about twenty minutes to walk there."

"Sounds good." I fell silent, finishing the last of the laundry.

"Fine, fine, your silence it speaks volumes. I shall get up and study until then." She dragged herself off the couch, acting like the force of gravity pulled her back down.

I blew a raspberry at her. "It really feels odd not to have something to study for. I was thinking maybe taking a class or joining a gym. Lugging that stuff around and then climbing a ladder yesterday proves how out of shape I am."

"Wait? What? Ladder?" She plopped herself back down, staring at me. "Spill!"

I laughed and told her about the adventure but I said nothing about time stopping or my missing hair, or anything relating to magic. That would be after I tested. At least, I thought I would test.

Make up your mind. You can't keep going back and forth about this.

Telling her the story and answering all her questions, she was more interested in my job than I thought, or she was avoiding homework. I figured the odds were running about fifty/fifty on that. But she settled down and stared at her books for a bit then and started in on something on the computer. I read for a bit, for fun. The idea still astonished me but I wasn't reading fiction. Instead, I was working on a library book I'd gotten about deaths in children. Looking for something that would account for Stevie dying in my arms.

And if it was a mage? If he died by magic?

I couldn't answer that question, so for now I pushed it to the back. The library had a huge section on magic and mages. It would be next on my list.

"Hey, you ready to go?" Jo yelled from her bedroom. I looked around, confused. I'd been so wrapped up in the book, it was fascinating and creepy how many ways you could die, that I hadn't realized she'd gotten up.

"Ummm, I guess. Is what I'm wearing okay?" It was the same jeans and clean shirt, a t-shirt style but in a solid dark red color. It brought out the red in my hair.

"Sure," she said as she came out. I rolled my eyes. Gone were her jeans and t-shirt for Guzman's Repair Shop. Now she had a form fitting tank top and her hair was up in a ponytail.

"Someone there you're trying to impress?" I recognized Jo on the prowl. This should prove amusing.

"Maybe," she said, looking away from me. I smirked at that. Watching her flirt was something between a prancing horse and a bulldozer. Jo didn't do subtle well.

I got up, slipped my shoes back on and ran a brush through my hair. Jo had said nothing or hadn't noticed my alteration, so I was not about to bring any attention to it. We headed out, enjoying the air that had cooled a few degrees from that afternoon. We talked about nothing important, just enjoyed the walk to the varsity. The city buzzed around us, and I smirked at the DragonWorldCon banners appearing everywhere. I had a soft spot in my heart for them after the day I'd had.

The noise and excitement outside the Varsity became apparent even a block away. Students, mostly in their early twenties, milled around and clogging the parking lot and sidewalks. It made me glad we weren't even trying to park her bike. It would have been a challenge.

"Hey, there they are," Jo said, her voice rising in excitement. I saw a group of people and followed her there, watching the morphing groups around me. Almost all of them had tats on their faces, in fact, I saw very few that didn't.

A group of four, three guys and another girl - from the slump of Jo's shoulders, I figured her current interest wasn't here.

"Hey everyone, this is my best friend, Cori. Cori, this is Joey, Linc, Mark, and Shelia," she introduced in a wave of gestures and a blur of faces. They all glanced at my temple and a flicker of something then flashed over their faces. Jo didn't notice, but I felt it those flickers as blows and it took everything I had not to make an excuse and leave. I put up with enough shit at the job, I would not let them chase me away.

I regretted that decision in the first fifteen minutes. Being at home in the empty apartment would have been preferable to having them treat me as a mix between a pet and a piece of furniture. I tried not to seethe because the conversation was fascinating, but people talked over me, ignored any comment I made, and even Jo didn't seem to notice, too busy sparkling in the social buzz. The worst part was knowing beyond a shadow of a doubt, that if my face was tattooed, they would have pulled me in and welcomed me.

The long ago conversation with Kadia rang more true than it ever had. But how in the world would I get past it? Could I?

The real question is, do I care enough to try?

When the waitress brought our food, I prepared to be ignored even more. I'd already realized my stomach was churning too much to eat a hamburger. I'd just ordered a large vanilla milkshake, figuring the bland sweet milk would help settle my stomach. Besides, it was cheap enough that I didn't stress the much money.

I was already smarting from just how they talked, but worse was Jo not seeing it. She didn't catch the subtle put downs and how they talked about people without magic. That hurt more than anything, and I was ready to ask for my food to go. I turned my head to watch the waitress. I wanted that shake more to give me something to do than anything else. She was two steps away when her shoe caught on a sticky part on the floor. I saw the tray flip and head towards the table - not in that magical slow motion but more just like normal accidents. They had stuck me on the edge, mainly to make it easier to ignore me.

This arrogance gave me the time I needed. I stepped out and to the side, and moved just in time to avoid the platter of food, drinks, and unfortunately my milkshake hit the table with a resounding crash that brought the whole restaurant to a standstill, and looking at the table with five students all coated in what would have been their dinner.

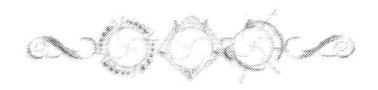

"And I believe that is my cue to leave. Have a nice evening peeps." I dug in my pocket and pulled out a five tossing it on the table and turned and walked out.

"Cori! Wait!" I could hear Jo yelling but I didn't slow down. I just kept walking, torn between annoyed and pissed off, and blessing my karma for once. I couldn't think of a more fitting end for a bunch of jerks. But Jo was in much better shape than me, or at least she could move when she wanted to, and she caught me before I got to the apartment.

"Cori, what was all that about? Why did you leave?" Her voice confused and a hint of anger to it.

I turned and stared at her, arms across my chest. She still had a few fries sticking to her and from the sticky wet brown substance, it looked like she'd been hit with Coke mostly.

"I left because I wasn't wanted. Your friends," I put a sneer into the word, "didn't even bother to notice me. Much less take any time at all to talk to me. And worse, and what really hurts," my control slipped because it had hurt, "you didn't notice or do anything to stop it."

"I did-" she started to protest, and I just looked at her, my arms crossed, hugging myself. Jo blinked, her eyes tilting up as we stood there, the apartment building lights a beacon of safety. But right then I didn't want to be comforted. My skin crawled with annoyance and hurt, of all the people I never expected this from her..

"I," she started again, but her shoulders slumped. "You're right. I am so sorry. I just," she swallowed and looked away from me. "I wanted them to like me and I assumed they'd like you too, cause you're Cori."

Her misery colored her words, and I wanted to put my arms around her and hold her, tell her it was okay. I didn't.

"You know even if everyone says there are no prejudices; there are. And not saying something is how it starts. Now," I held up my hand before she could say anything. "I could have said something also, but I didn't. And that's on me. But if those are your friends," I stressed the word again, "are they the people you really want to hang around?"

She looked away and I got the feeling she was hiding something else but I didn't push it. She'd tell me in time, when she was ready. Besides, I was still annoyed at the whole situation.

"Okay. And I'm sorry, Cori."

"Me too." I looked at her again. "But I'm not touching you until you shower. You look sticky and I don't need that on my clothes."

Jo glanced down and laughed a little. "I feel sticky. If I don't shower soon, I might turn into a statue. It feels awful on my skin."

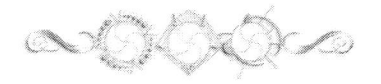

I laughed, shaking my head. "Come on, I'll open all the doors, so you don't need to touch anything. Personally, I'd strip in the shower. Leave your shoes at the front door and I'll clean them."

"Thanks. You're the bestest."

"Maybe. Next time, let people know I'm the bestest?"

"Deal." We headed up into the apartment. It still hurt but I had faith in her. She'd always be there, but no one was perfect. Right? I ignored the niggling worm of worry. Between the mage stuff and work, I didn't have time to worry about anything else.

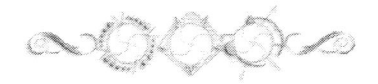

Chapter 11

While making testing mandatory has been thrown around in Washington DC for years, there are only a few countries that make it mandatory for all citizens, interestingly two are Asian and one is tiny. Japan and North Korea both require it three times. Once upon turning 21, then again at 25, and a final time prior to marriage or 30, which ever is later. The other country is Lichtenstein. They require it at age 27 if not already tested and all immigrants into their country are required to test if they are not mages registered with the OMO.
~Magical Politics

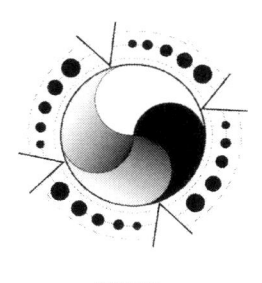

ORDER

Just one more day. I can do this and then I'll figure out the mage thing.

I'd spent Tuesday exploring, getting more books from the library, and trying to figure out how to set up a savings plan that would pay for more schooling someday. I didn't even look at the OMO, though I kept rolling it around in my head. I also slept in. That was the best part of the day.

I showed up Wednesday morning and it felt like I'd walked into a different world. Jorge waved and smiled at me. Lisa came over to talk to me as I made coffee and everyone teased me about Catastrophe Cori. It felt normal. Heck, I didn't even mind the teasing. It was the best day of work I'd had in ages.

Our calls were random, but routine: accidents, overdoses, people being stupid as Labor Day weekend approached. I kept it together, and life was good. Jo was more serious in the evenings. It seemed like she always had a book in front of her, muttering to herself, but I didn't pry. I did plan on seeing if I could get her to take me to the college library this weekend. There were some books that looked fascinating.

Friday morning dawned hot, humid, and with thunderclouds and lightning threating to break at any moment.

"I really hope we don't get more people up trees or cellphone towers today." I said looking out the bay to the heavy dark clouds like cotton balls saturated with blue black ink.

"Yeah, 'cause you would be the one going up there, not me. I have no desire to die by lightning."

I grinned at him. "You never know. You might get mutant powers and become a superhero." The comic book characters from Marvel were all the rage right now, and who wouldn't want to be Wolverine, always healing and immortal.

If I was immortal, that might give me enough time to learn everything.

The thought was wistful as I sipped my coffee. The heat had been enough that I gave in and made the coffee iced. Of course that lowered the caffeine level, so I had warned everyone I was using the super caffeinated mix and made iced coffee for the entire crew. That might have been a mistake from the looks of ecstasy on their faces as they sipped on that brew. I grinned to myself as I sipped. I fit in here. I could be a valuable member of the team.

That caused my smile to fade. I'd already decided to get up early Saturday. Jo rarely crawled out of bed before ten on the weekends, and I thought she had something today which would make her really late home. If I got up at eight, I could test and be home before she got up.

"All units, report of multiple bodies at Centennial Olympic Park. Repeat multiple bodies. All units respond." My head jerked up and looked at Jorge the same expression on his face that I knew was on mine.

Oh shit!

I turned and sprinted for the rig. Slipping into the passenger side, I dropped my coffee in the cup holder, buckled in, and grabbed the radio. "Unit Ruby 3 responding," I said, even as I saw everyone else headed toward their rigs. We pulled out first, mainly because we'd been in the bay, already dressed and ready to go. I glanced at the clock in the ambulance as we pulled out, twelve-fifteen, the start of lunch.

Ruby wasn't too far from Centennial but it was surface streets, and that meant people. It took an agonizing ten minutes, even with sirens and lights blaring, to get there. What really set my nerves aflame was all the other sirens I heard. As we approached, I saw ambulances from various companies and hospitals, along with police and fire all headed toward the park.

"Dear Merlin, what happened?" I whispered. Even at the bus crash there had only been a tenth of what I saw approaching here. I clenched my jaw, hoping it was all just an over-reaction, but deep down, that part of me that knew when bad things had happened pulled up into a tight, hard ball. We screeched to a halt at the border of the park and jumped out. We grabbed our bags from the back. We didn't want to get the gurney until we knew what we were dealing with. I swallowed hard as Jorge grabbed SMART tags and we headed to where police were waving. It was a stream of jumpsuits, uniforms, and people running towards the center of the park.

We came to a halt, along with just about everyone else, at the fountain of rings. The fountain was the center of the park. Five Olympic rings were embedded into the ground as part of a huge fountain. In the summer it was popular and lots of people used the area, which made what lay in front of me even more confusing.

At least fifty people, maybe more, lay crumpled on the surface of the fountain. They all lay unmoving with blood leaking from them into the water. The air around felt weird and thin, as if the sky itself was about to rip in two. The clouds above looked like they were seconds from dumping, and even with the heat, I felt cold seeping into me. We stood, frozen, as we looked at the enormity of the situation.

Where do we start? Which direction?

A man with a police uniform jumped up on one of the two walls surrounding the fountain with a bullhorn. "Everyone, listen up. We don't know what happened or how. Start triage, tag if you need to. We have enough ambulances that if you get a red, get them to the hospital and move on. Ruby gets reds first, then Piedmont, then we'll move to Emory. VA said they can take some if we need them, after that..." he looked around, his face white. "After that we'll figure it out. If you see something that might give us clues as to who did this, try to preserve it but the people are the first priority. Go."

His command cut the string that had been holding us and as one we moved forward. Jorge and I headed to the first victim directly ahead of us. Young male, Hispanic, maybe early twenties, I dropped to my knees, but I knew even as I touched his throat what the answer would be. His neck had been slit, and the blood ran into the fountain, creating patterns of red in the flowing water.

"Black, tag and move." I pushed my worries and doubts to the side even as I rose and headed to the next a few steps away. I saw the symbols carved into her skin, but what registered more was the sluggish pulse under my skin.

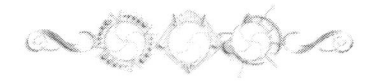

"Red!" I yelled as Jorge finished tying the tag. He dove over to me as I was ripping open the woman's shirt. I realized most of them were young, though there were a few that looked older - by that I meant in their thirties or forties. None of them were obviously older than that. That struck me as weird in the part of my brain that watched for this. Mostly I focused on her and not the two areas in the sky that felt raw and torn and the odd feeling that there should be three.

There was a lump on the back of her head that worried me, especially as one of her eyes bulged out, implying pressure behind it. But her pupils reacted, and she had a pulse in all her extremities. Under her shirt I found the real wounds. Her light green tank top had been pulled up and then back down, which also seemed off. It meant she hadn't fought when she someone cut her. That same someone carved, or cut, a pattern into her chest. It looked vaguely familiar, but off. A circle with small circles surrounding it. At each small circle a deep wound went straight into her abdomen made with something like an ice pick I thought. None of them were gushing blood, but her belly had already distended.

"Abdominal wounds, probable perforated spleen, liver, possibly her intestines." That last part depended on the angel of the weapon, and if she had been lying down or standing. If her intestines had been perforated, she probably wouldn't make it. If they hadn't, she had a better chance but either way, it didn't matter.

"I'll get the gurney, stabilize her and call it in."

I nodded, already starting to brace her, wanting to make sure she didn't move as we got her onto the gurney. By the time I had her ready to transport, IV installed, and all her vitals recorded, Jorge was back. In a quick move we lifted her onto the gurney and strapped her down. We headed back to our rig moving as fast as we could without risking her. All around me I saw other people doing the same, and all too many black tags around the wrists of others.

"Did you hear anything?" I asked as we jumped in. Me staying in the back to watch her as he sped to Ruby. At this point they had blocked off the streets to give us quick, clear access, so the drive there should be much faster.

"Not really. All they said was one minute the fountain was fenced off as if it was under repair, the next, there were bodies everywhere and people started screaming."

He drove through the street like he was in a race car. Normal hand off procedures would be truncated today. We didn't have time and even seconds might make the difference between someone being a red or a black tag.

Magic. Someone used magic to kill these people, or at least they used it hide their deaths.

I knew illusions were possible for an Air mage. You could make people see or not see something by bending the air to reflect light, or something like that. Another thing I didn't know enough about.

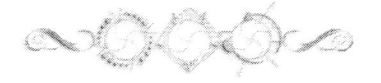

We slammed to a halt in the emergency bay just as another bus pulled out. We jumped out and handed over the woman to the people running out to greet us. In five minutes, we transferred her vitals and we were back racing towards the scene. And scene it was. By this time the place swarmed with people. We headed out to an area no one had hit yet, or else they were all dead. From a distance sometimes it was hard to tell. Again, I glanced up at the areas of the sky, but the raw tears didn't seem as bad. No one else looked up at them, so maybe it was just me and being weird.

"There," Jorge said. A young man, his skin was so dark in the gloomy light that I worried about being able to see his wounds. I dropped next to him, my fingers searching for a pulse.

"Got one, he's alive," I said, my voice was purposefully loud over the noise of sirens, people, radios, and just the sound of the city. It surrounded us like a dense wall, and I pushed it all away to focus.

A hand grabbed my arm as I was about to slide in the IV for saline, shattering my concentration. Whoever had grabbed me, lifted me up, and dragged me away from my patient.

"You! You fucking did this. What the hell did you do? And where, by Merlins' balls are your tattoos? And why in the world did you cut off your hair? You need that and you're going to need do more to answer for your part in all this."

A man that looked vaguely familiar had my upper left arm raised up above my head, almost pulling it out of the socket as he had to be at least six foot three inches of imposing mass. The dark shock of hair and aquiline features in a suit worth more than my monthly salary glared at me. His merlin tattoo gleamed in the light made of blues, reds, and greens that seemed to be more than just tattoo ink.

"Let me go!" I ripped my arm away. "I don't have time for you." Jorge had stood and looked at the man with alarm and anger.

"You did this, and you're coming with me now!" He growled.

"I had nothing to do with this. Get out of my way, you're risking my patient."

"No. You're coming with me now and I'll damn well figure out why you aren't marked." He reached for my arm and I reacted. I knew we were lucky the young man was still alive and this yahoo was taking up time my patient didn't have. I pulled away, rotated and put all of my weight in the punch into his jaw. He didn't see it coming and I hit him hard, with a buzz of static electricity rattling down my arm.

Blasted clouds have everything all electricky.

He fell to the ground in a heap and I spun back to the boy, getting the IV in this time. His blood pressure was too low due to blood loss. He, like the others I'd seen so far, had things carved into his body, though this pattern was different. But the deep puncture marks were similar. The symbols clicked into my mind as we got him onto the gurney and blood seeped through the bandages.

"By Merlin, the person doing this is carving the magic symbols into their bodies. Look!" With Jorge looking at me, and the idiot on the ground, I traced the symbol, realizing this one was spirit, while the other had been order. The deep marks at the points of the design that made a weird sort of sense.

"What about him?" He asked, nodding at the idiot.

"Leave him. He's just unconscious."

"Do you know him?" Jorge looked worried as we headed back to the ambulance.

"Never met him before," I said, but at the back of my mind something niggled. The patient moaned and I cast it aside. Later, when I had time to process this, I would. This day would live in my mind, and I couldn't help but feel that it was connected to the girl I found.

Chapter 12

While mages are often described as Time or Air or Earth - this only indicates their strength in a specific branch. It doesn't always indicate that they can use everything in that branch. For example, there are usually six or seven spells or areas of magic within each branch. And at least one of them are only available to someone strong in that branch. But that doesn't mean that any mage can use all of them expertly. College teaches you how to use them and tips and tricks about using the spells, however it takes decades of practice to be able to use them the way most people think. It is one reason why many mages rarely use magic.

~ Magic Explained

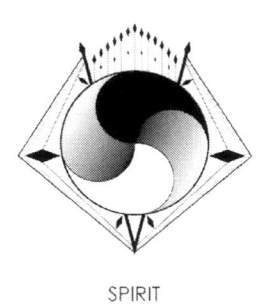

SPIRIT

By four-thirty, all that were left were the black tags. That meant we had to stand back and let the forensic teams do their best. Jorge and I were one of the groups that stayed. We couldn't take them to the morgue until after they had been examined, but it felt wrong to just walk away and leave them there like so much garbage. We stood silently, near our rig, watching the techs swarm the scene. By the time we got back, the man I'd decked had left. I couldn't find it in myself to care.

There were three groups of us and none of us spoke, just watched. The last count had been twelve dead, a total of twenty-seven victims. Even the police had stopped their chatter and the GBI, the Georgia Bureau of Investigation, had taken over the scene. They had order mages out there, trying to reconstruct what had happened.

It reminds me so much of that girl. But why didn't they know this was coming?

I had no illusions as to the omnipotence of the police, but how did you hide planning to killing twenty-seven people? And why twenty-seven? So many questions, and for a long bleak moment I regretted not going for the police academy. I wanted to be out there trying to figure out the answer to what happened. But I couldn't. So I stood and watched and waited.

A stir of motion on the other side of the fountain drew my attention. Five people, all men from the way they walked though at this distance it was hard to tell, were storming into the area. They were arguing with the GBI, or at least that was who I thought they were. I could have been wrong, but it looked for all the world like a territorial dispute. I amused myself, imagining this as a gang war and almost laughed at the idea of them wearing stuff from West Side Story. After all, the love of a Merlin for a norm was always good story fodder.

"Hey, Cori?" I looked at Jorge, my mind pulled from my weird musings. "Isn't that the dude you decked earlier today?" He pointed over at the people I'd been being imagining as modern-day gang bangers. His comment made me focus on the people, not just the general actions of all of them. Sure enough, the lead man had the dark hair I remembered and the pale skin. Even from here the colors of his tattoo were shocking.

"I think so. Ugh. So how much trouble am I going to get in for decking him?"

Great. First month on the job and I'm going to get arrested. With my luck he's with the GBI or something.

I fought back a groan. I really didn't need this in my life. At this point, I just wanted to go test tomorrow morning and then go from there.

"Eh. He was interfering with your efforts and I'm pretty sure that is illegal. Besides all his rambling made no sense. I know where you were all morning. I don't think you had time to dart out, kill or try to kill twenty-seven people, and get back here before I noticed you were gone." His amused sarcasm made me feel better. But still, what had he been going on about?

"Well if I get arrested, I'm going to be pissed."

Jorge shrugged. "It happens, but don't worry about it until they file charges." He grins. "Aren't you glad you have the next two days off?"

We had kept our voices low but even the spurt of amusement felt wrong, looking at this grizzly scene.

"Yeah, think I need to decompress after today." There was a bit of fear in admitting that, like I was failing. But Jorge nodded.

"I agree. This is not normal. If this didn't affect you, I might be even more worried about you than I am by anyone that does well in this job." He trailed off as we watched the order mage create a replica of the body at his feet. It stood and looked blankly out at the world, and then flinched as blood appeared on his torso, but the created image didn't move or react.

"Okay that is creepy as hell," one of the other techs muttered. I agreed, but what bugged me was the lack of reaction, not the recreation. I hadn't realized there was a way to control people like that magically. The idea made my skin crawl. That you could control anyone to the point they would let you do that, much less so many, was scary. I swallowed hard as bile churned at the back of my throat.

"Oh fuck," another tech said, and the tone in her voice had all of us turning to look at her. She was a pretty black woman, strength in her stance with long hair in elaborate braids in a thick single braid down her back. She had brown eyes that I suspected normally sparked with joy. Now she looked washed out and her mouth had lines around it as she swallowed hard, trying to speak.

"Marjorie? What's wrong?" We had all turned towards her, even the cops had drifted over. Her skin had gone gray and for a moment I thought she'd be sick or pass out. Her partner put his hand on her shoulder and to my surprise, she leaned into it; she had come across as tough and no nonsense all day, but now she looked like she might shatter. "Marj?"

"One of my friends is an OR nurse at Piedmont. She said they just got out of surgery on one of the vics," Marj's voice shook, but I didn't know why. We knew a lot of them wouldn't survive. "She said they figured out why they didn't fight or do anything." A sob caught and she swallowed. The sound made a lump form in my own throat as my skin tightened, preparing for something I knew I would not like.

"Well?" Someone else asked impatient and her hands shook as she tried to put her phone away, her eyes staring at the park not seeing anything.

"Marj? What did they find out?"

Her eyes focused in on us, and I wanted to take a step back at the grief and hollow look in them. "They have an archmage on staff as a neurosurgeon. He wanted to watch the operation and was checking her pain stimulus response, as they couldn't get her to respond to anything. He realized the patient didn't have any brain activity outside of low autonomous activity. Her brain looks like someone let loose lightning in it. The brain stem is untouched, but her brain is fried. There is no one there to save. They're all walking corpses."

Her words fell with a power I'd never felt, and I locked my jaw to prevent myself from crying. A few people gasped and at least one person made a retching sound. I turned and looked at the bodies still left. With the brain stem untouched, they would breath and pump blood, but only for a while longer. With most everything else fried, they were organ donors, nothing more.

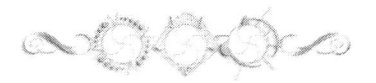

Looking at the scene, I filled in the bodies we had removed, and the symbols carved into their chests. All of it pointed to a mage and the deaths must be some sort of ritual. But what? Why?

"So we didn't save anyone. They were all dead. We just preserved organs." My words echoed in the strange heavy atmosphere and people turned to look at me.

"Pretty much," Jorge muttered. He didn't look at me, still watching the group of people arguing.

"Is it just me? Or do you want to go over there and tell them to be more respectful? All these people just died, and they are over there arguing about what? Who is in charge? Who cares?"

"Welcome to big city politics but I don't know who that guy is." It was one of the cops that had stayed near us. "And why does he have grass and water on his suit coat?"

"That would be because Cori punched him. It was a beautiful sight, and he went right down." Jorge said with way too much glee, in my opinion.

"Ouch. That's not going to make him happy. He's got to be from the GBI, or something, from how they are kowtowing to him."

"He's a merlin. He's arrogant," I muttered.

I really shouldn't have punched him. It isn't like it made any difference. I'll hold on to the thought that maybe some people will get the transplants they needed because of this. It's the only thing I have. The thought didn't help but maybe it would later.

"Great, here they come. Maybe they'll tell us they're releasing the bodies and we can get them to the morgue?" one of the other paramedics said. At this point it was a forgone conclusion the GBI would be doing autopsies on all the bodies. I'd have to see about grabbing the report when it was all done.

I focused on the men storming towards us. That finally got my memory to click. The guy was outside the police station both times. That was why he looked familiar. But this time, rather than glaring at the sidewalk, he focused on me. Belatedly I realized Detective Stone was with them too and I almost groaned. This wasn't something I wanted to deal with right now or here.

"Well, this will be a pain," I muttered crossing my arms and feeling myself hunch inward. "Two people with grudges against me."

"So you decked him, he was interfering in your job. I'll back you up. He needs to learn just cause he's a merlin doesn't mean he gets to do whatever he wants." Jorge stood up straighter, glaring at the men coming our way.

My skin itched and I wanted to scratch my scalp, but not here. Right now I just wanted to deal with the idiots, take these poor souls to their final place, and get back to the EMS department. Maybe take a call about a baby on the way or something. I could use a happy reason to end the day. As it was, I knew these victims would join the tree girl as regular visitors to my nightmares, which I didn't need any more additions to.

They got closer and my nerves flared, the same feeling of danger as that day outside the police station. I didn't understand that feeling. That sensation the other day had been freaky enough. To feel it again made no sense. I forced a long, slow breath as I watched the approaching men.

All of them were at least thirty, with Stone having the cheapest suit of all of them. The merlin had on something elegant that probably cost more than what I'd make this month. Two others struck me as junior agents, though they had mage tats on their temples, they weren't merlin's. It was obvious from how they trailed behind the guy that they reported to him, or at least he had more power than they did.

"There she is." Stone was speaking as they walked up to us. I felt the others shuffle away from me as Stone pointed at me. "That's Cori Munroe. She's the one that found the other girl, but I couldn't find anything linking her to the murder."

"The what?" I heard Jorge mutter, I felt his gaze on me, and heard the confusion in his voice.

"That's because I didn't have anything to do with it. And you know it. I'm just here as part of my job. Nothing else. I'm not involved."

I pulled my gaze away from Stone, enjoying his annoyance at me not cowering in fear, but I got caught by the other man's look. A red inflamed spot on his cheekbone where I'd decked him clashed with his pale skin and dark hair. This time I saw his eyes, a steel gray with no give, no warmth. If you could cast magic like in the old stories and the way movies made it look, I'm sure beams of energy from his eyes would have punctured me. I fought not to back up or quail. Okay, I'd decked him, but he'd deserved it.

Hadn't he?

"Cori Munroe, you are under arrest for conspiracy to commit murder, violation of the plane stability act, being an unregistered mage, and assaulting a federal agent."

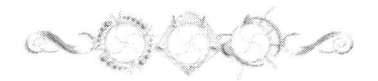

Chapter 13

Ritual magic as a vehicle to power is talked about rarely for good reason, it doesn't work. Or it might work, but those that get it to work have paid a price that most don't regard as worth it. But then the mage getting the power wasn't the one to pay the price. And any ethical human would never do that.
~History of Magic

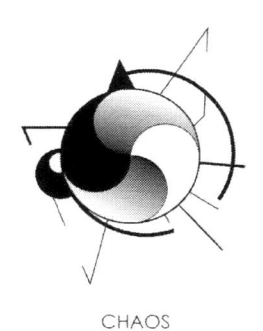

CHAOS

The words fell like boulders in a still pond and everyone erupted with exclamations around me. Even the people I had just met this day were demanding to know what he was talking about.

Me?

I was in so much shock I just stood there, gaping at him.

The plane stability act? An unregistered mage? What in the world?

Even Detective Stone was gaping at him, but the two junior agents had cuffs out and had my hands handcuffed tightly behind my back before it registered to me what they were doing.

"Hey! You can't arrest her for assault. You grabbed her first," Jorge protested.

"She shouldn't have walked away while I was talking to her."

They started to drag me away and my brain finally kicked out of neutral. Maybe I hung around Jo too much. I was even starting to think in car terms.

"I've never emerged. Or if I have, I'm so low I didn't realize it. And besides, you can't arrest me on that as I'm not over the age limit requiring registration. And since I don't know what the plane stability act is, I can't have violated it."

"Ignorance of the law is no excuse," his voice was flat and almost inhuman.

"No, but since you assaulted me first, I'm not over twenty-six, I'm not involved in any murder, and there are people here who KNOW where I was all day, you have no reason to arrest me."

The jerk smirked at me. "I'm a federal agent for the FBI Magical enforcement division and I have the right to arrest anyone until they prove they aren't a mage and all mages are subject to my authority. If nothing else, you're arrested because I said so. And I don't give a damn what you think, you're a mage and there is no way you can't know it. Take her to the OMO testing facility, I want her marked and drafted so I can press the proper charges."

They dragged me away to the surprised exclamations of the people left behind. I didn't bother to struggle. The two men were at least fifty pounds heavier than me, and obviously trained in how to subdue people from the painful hold they had on my arms. I went with them.

Look on the bright side. I was planning on getting tested tomorrow anyhow, so this isn't anything I didn't want. And this way I won't have the guilt of Jo asking why I didn't get tested when she asked me to. See, this actually makes it easier. I'll prove that I'm at best a weak hedgie and it will be over.

I relaxed into the back seat of the stereotypical black sedan they shoved me into. I didn't bother trying to talk to them or to get on their good side. I didn't care. I just wanted this over with, all of it.

The ride didn't take too long. The streets were still closed and they had a major OMO site near Ruby. I really wanted to hide as people looked at them pulling up to the door and dragging me out in handcuffs. How much more embarrassing could this get?

Treat it as a learning experience. You wanted to know what testing was like and you'll never see any of these people again.

I kept repeating that to myself, trying to not feel embarrassed. It didn't work, but I tried.

The doors slid open and I looked around, almost expecting unicorns or something. Instead, it looked like the reception area of the urgent care clinic. Boring. A small waiting room, with no one there, and a window in the wall with a woman sitting there. She was a little older than me with a tattoo of chaos on her temple. An Entropy mage, marked with swirls of color in fire and time. She arched a dark, perfectly plucked, eyebrow.

"And this is?"

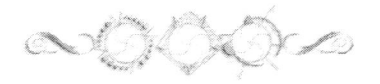

"Unregistered mage. Forced testing and registration with charges pending under the Ronin Act," the agent with sandy brown hair said, with a northerner's clipped accent.

"Unless she has the best skin care regime in the world, she isn't old enough to charge under the Ronin Act."

"Alixant said she has to test."

"Sorry, has to be willing until after the age limit. Do you have any proof she's a mage?"

I liked her. She wasn't intimidated by these bozos or whoever Alixant was. The guy I punched? It sounded like the name he'd have.

Before they could get into it, I spoke up. "It's okay. I'll register and test. I just want it over so I can go back to work."

"Up to you." I felt the tension fade from the two junior agents and I wondered if I had refused how much trouble it would have caused.

Oh well. Not worth it. Let me do the damn test, prove I don't have any magic to speak of, and maybe get back to work before I get fired. I wonder if I can get fired for this.

After they unlocked the handcuffs, they stood there as I signed the forms that she gave me.

"Okay, ready?" She asked, once I'd signed my life away. Her name tag said Rachel.

"I guess." She stepped out around and opened the door. "This way." The two agents moved to come in.

"I don't think so. This is her time. You can wait here."

"What if she runs?" One of them protested.

"You are free to go stand by the back door. Unless she creates another opening, she has to leave by one of those two methods." Her voice was so dry and cutting I wanted to applaud her. Instead, I kept my mouth shut and watched them.

"Go to the back, I'll stay here." The northern said and I just sighed. The other one, who had his blond hair in a short crew cut and had probably done military for part of his draft, headed to the back.

Once the door closed behind her, she took me over to a small area with a height chart. There, I let her take my picture, my fingerprints, and a retinal scan. The DNA swab surprised me, but it made sense. They wanted to know for sure who you were. It took forever to get everything into the computer, but she entered it and I verified everything.

"Okay, the next step is the power level monitor. Most people who come in are either very low and just want to know, or they are suffering from an emergence and tend to be disoriented, so what we put them through happens in bits and pieces. But for you it should be easy." Her tone was friendly, but impersonal. Just another day at work for her.

I followed her out of what was obviously the intake area into the back. Three people stood there, all mages, and one with a merlin tattoo. Someone that screamed tech sat looking at computer monitors, and he didn't even glance my way. The merlin looked up and paled, then frowned.

"You just emerge?"

"Not that I know of. I'm here to prove that I'm not a mage, or at least a very minor hedgemage." He frowned even more as I spoke. The other mage didn't seem to notice or care. She was older, her graying hair pulled back into a bun.

"Fine. Step inside. The door will close, and you may feel waves of pressure or something like wind. Don't panic, it's just testing your magical field. After that, if you are a mage, we'll decide your affinities."

She pointed at something that really did look like the fully body scanners at the airport but tech kept looking at his monitors. There was another door out of the place, but the older mage, the merlin had a funny look on his face.

"Why do you think you're not a mage or a hedgemage?"

I tilted my head looking at the weird contraption. "Never emerged, no family history of magic, no reason to think I am. Only here cause some idiot arrested me citing the Ronin act." I felt a bit of guilt. I did have reason to suspect but still, did it matter? I had nothing to do with any of those deaths.

His eyes narrowed but he didn't say anything, just nodded towards the machine.

I shrugged and stepped into the chamber. The door slid shut and I tensed waiting for something, for anything, to happen. Nothing happened. I stood there bored as I waited. No waves of pressure, no feeling of wind - just glass walls that were frosted, steel gray bars that reminded me of Alixant's eyes, and a gray floor. I sighed and started counting in my head. I reached two-hundred thirty-three before the door slid open.

Finally. Maybe I can leave now. Or at least get those idiots to leave me alone.

I stepped out of the chamber to just Rachel standing there. The others had gone. I looked around, but all the fancy monitors were dark.

"Did the test break?"

She had a smile on her face, but it seemed tense, a bit forced. "No. They needed to go check something. They asked me to take you to the affinity room and get that sorted before they tell you your rank."

"Why? I'm so low the test barely registered? It won't hurt my feelings that I barely qualify as a hedge." I resisted rolling my eyes. Why did people make it out to be such a big deal? I was fine not being a mage. My life was good. I didn't need any complications to it. I just wanted to get back to work and try to have a normal life.

Rachel said nothing, just ushered me into the next room. It resembled what Jo had said and there was a mage there. Her boredom was so absolute she had a magazine in front of her face. All I could see was a puffy haircut and long nails painted a pale pink that matched her skin tone perfectly.

"There are twelve objects on the table. Which ones do you like the best? Place them in order of priority to your own feelings on the other table." Her voice sounded odd, muffled behind the magazine, but I barely noticed. A blank marble table stood on the opposite side of me, the empty white space ached to be filled. The various objects on the table held my attention and I didn't understand why.

Jo had told me there would be objects, but she made it seem so mundane, so basic, that the idea of a yard sale table sat in my head. This table was a heavy, dark wood, with the objects scattered across in no grouping that made sense to me. I had expected the same ones Jo mentioned, but none of this looked like what she said. Maybe every office did it slightly differently, depending on who ran it?

In front of me was a silver hourglass, the crystals in it drifting through at a rate that just annoyed me, but I couldn't have said why. I started to reach, then stopped, looking at the other eleven objects. They all seemed odd and strange, yet mundane. A Rubix cube, all in a jumble of colors, a candle with a flame, a water fountain giving the room a gentle tinkle, and a pile of what looked like raw silk yarn.

I stood frozen, trying to decide.

"Just pick as many or as few as you feel drawn to. Don't over think it." The monitor's voice was vague and distant, I noted her comments, but didn't give them any weight. There was a hole in the table, and it bugged me. Oh, the hourglass called to me, but the hole ate at me like an itch. I couldn't see a pattern in the objects on the table, but there should have been something over there. I reached out, without conscious thought. I wanted to reach for three or four other things but I moved, and my hand wrapped around something. As soon as I wrapped my hand around it, something shimmered into existence. It was tiny; a bauble for a necklace of the spirit symbol. I moved it to the other table, though it hurt to lay it down. Then I turned back, reaching and grabbing without conscious thought.

A white disk with the word black, marring its surface; I that picked up, and tried to rub the black off with my thumb as I transferred it to the table. A glass bulb was next, pretty with purples and greens swirling it, but when I picked it up my knees almost buckled with the need to cry. This had happened twice before in my life. It was one reason I always steeled myself before handing people back things they had left. I set it down on the other table with a shudder, trying not to cry.

That was three, I should be done now right?

But I couldn't stop; there were things I needed to touch. The need to reach for a few more built inside me, to correct things that were wrong. The hourglass with its crystals going through at the wrong speed - I held it, wanting to fix. They needed to be whole, to be consistent, but one would be five seconds, the next fifteen, then three. I didn't know if I wanted to break it or pull it apart. Instead I set it on the table and tipped it over so the sand quit flowing.

I passed over the mineral that was mixed with at least three substances, the candle, the water, and the shredded ribbon; none of them called to me. But the earth in a vial, with a lone avocado seed in a pot next to it hurt. I poured the dirt over it, swirling it together, then set it on my table. As I set the last object on the table, the need snapped and I turned to look at what I'd done, even as cold worry swirled in my belly.

The amulet, hourglass, glass bulb, white chip with the word almost erased, and the pot of earth with an avocado seed in it.

What in the hell is all this?

I felt like I'd come out of a dream or something. I reached back for the amulet, needing it in my hands. A sense of something being seriously wrong seeped into my skull, but before I could focus on it, the other door in the room opened. I turned and only then realized the woman who had been manning the test was gone as Rachel looked at me.

"This way. You're all done."

I walked towards her with the amulet still in my hand. I forced myself to hand to her, but she just shook her head.

"You can keep it. They would like to talk to you."

That made no sense as I walked into another room down a short hallway. She pushed open a door. That caught me. Why was there no handle just a swinging door? It opened to reveal a room with four people.

Voices were talking as the door swung open and I focused on the sounds, before scanning the rest of the room.

"Damnit, if she was over twenty-four, I'd own her lying ass for the next two decades, and I'd make damn sure she paid for every death in blood and in sweat. I can command drafted mages to pay heavier prices."

"Well, she isn't, and I don't think she's lying. Let's talk to her first." The woman quit speaking as they turned to look at me.

Chapter 14

Where there is fire, there is smoke. Where there is fire without cause, there is a mage.
~Qin Lin Proverb

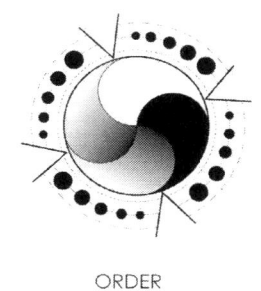

ORDER

I swallowed. Their gaze riveted me to the floor. To give myself some time, I let myself inspect the rest of the room and what looked like a dentist's chair.

I couldn't move. My entire attention fixated on the chair, the young woman that stood next to it, and the tray that stood next to her. A tray with ink, a tattoo gun, and templates.

"I don't understand," my voice shook as I dragged my attention away from the chair and to the other people in the room. One of them was the jerk from the park, Alixant. The other was the man who had spoken to me before I tested along with the woman from the room with the objects. I only recognized her from her puffy hair and the nails on her hands that were laid out flat on a table.

"What in the hell are you playing at thinking you can hide your power? Why weren't you dragged in before? Anyone as powerful as you without training is dangerous as all get out. I knew you were lying. So how did you know about the rips?" His voice tore at me like a whip seeking a target.

I looked at him completely off balance. "What are you talking about?" My voice quavered even more, and I found myself pressed against the wall, as far as possible from all of them.

"Oh, quit lying. We don't have time. If those rips form, the possible death toll will be in the thousands." He had stood up and was stalking over to me. "So get your ass in that damn chair, get marked, and I'm drafting you now."

"Steven," it was the puffy hair woman, but the name still made me flinch. "She has no idea what you're talking about and she doesn't remember emerging. She isn't lying."

The man turned, looking for a minute like he would hit me. His glare remained so fierce I couldn't help but press back further into the wall, wanting it to hide me.

"Fran, you can't be serious. She had to know. With her rank, her emergence should have made waves. Hell, why didn't we know? It should have been sensed by other Merlins in her sphere." He stalked back and forth, and my gaze kept going from him to the puffy blond, to the older man.

"What are you talking about? What don't I know?" I forced the words past vocal cords that were frozen, either with fear or nerves. I didn't know which.

He smiled at me, and nothing about it was friendly. "Welcome to the draft. You're a merlin."

I swear my knees went weak for a moment and I staggered a bit. "Are you insane? I can't be a merlin. I've never emerged. Merlins are incredibly powerful, I'm just weird."

He turned and looked at Fran again, and she nodded at him. With a snarl he whirled back to face me. "Did you have anything to do with the ritual murders in the park today? Do you know anything about them?"

"No!" I all but shouted the word, frustration and fear eroding the shock that had put me in a state of numbness. "How many times do I have to tell people I just found her? I always find weird things, or they find me. But I had, have, nothing to do with any of them."

"You know, I think that is why she is driving you crazy, Steven." The older man who had been looking at me with his head tilted. "She has wrapped both a Murphy's Curse and a Lady Luck around her. If anyone else had cast it, it would have worn off by now. But she renews it constantly without realizing."

"What?" I don't know if I said it, or if everyone else did at the same time. But I followed up with more questions. "What do you mean I keep those two things around me? What are they? How can you tell?"

He shrugged. "This is all stuff you'd learn in the Merlin courses your senior year, but long story short, almost all Merlins can sense magic. Some to a better or lesser degree. You reek of it but until I watched you for a while, I didn't realize it was you and not just your cloak of curses and luck. I can't imagine how exhausting it must be for you to keep that up. But either way, I'd stop it."

"Stop what? How?" I didn't know if I should panic, or just run away from these insane people. There was no way I was a merlin. "How can I be a merlin? I've never emerged. That isn't possible."

"Well you are, and I need your help. This makes you the second Spirit Merlin in the US since James Wells died," he broke off talking to me. Then, not moving his eyes from me, Alixant tilted his head to one side, as if looking at me from a different perspective. "Fran, is it possible? Is she the one?"

Fran frowned and flipped through the pile of papers in front of her. I just knew it was my file, that it was everything they had on me. "Corisande Munroe. Born April 15th. Twin brother died April 12th," she paused and arched a brow. "Huh, you know there was that paper on Merlins that came out about a year or two ago."

The agent released me from his gaze and looked back at her. "Which one?"

"Puberty onset emergence. If she emerged because of the stress of her brother's death, it might mean she's been a merlin for the last decade and she's the one James felt emerge. Which means she probably doesn't realize." She smirked at him. "After all, everyone knows you don't emerge until after puberty."

"Merlin's balls, I hate common knowledge. The more common it is, the less likely it is to be accurate." Alixant sighed and sank down in the empty chair, looking like a weight had just collapsed on him. "So she doesn't know how to use her abilities, is a walking time bomb, and had nothing to do with any of the deaths or the ritual trying to be created?"

"No," Fran sounded almost disappointed as she spoke. "And at this point she needs to get training. She will have a hell of a lot of habits to unlearn. Huh. I guess the teachers will have fun teaching her how to use her abilities correctly. You know she's probably the first natural taught mage we've had in a century?"

"If you are all quite done talking about me like I'm not here." I probably shouldn't have been so snappish, but they were telling me all this stuff and it made no sense. How could I have emerged when Steven died?

"Come on. Sit down," Fran said, pointing at the tattoo chair.

I couldn't help but look at it like it was a device of torture. A soft snicker ran through the room.

"Yes, the tattoo is a shackle, but you don't have a choice. Don't worry, you get some say so in it, but sit and we'll talk about it a bit. I get the feeling this isn't a good thing for you?" Her voice almost tender.

Crying won't help anything.

I told myself that over and over as I perched in the chair. I got the feeling my avoidance of the chair amused everyone, but they didn't laugh at me, at least not where I could hear.

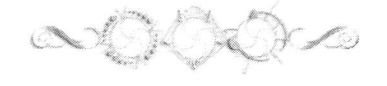

"My name is Francine Calamadar. I'm a Psychic archmage. I do truth spells like most people breathe." She moved her hair, exposing the entirety of her tattoo, a blue and pink mix that fit her. "Drives people crazy as you can't never tell me anything approaching a white lie. Or you can and I'll just know it's a lie."

I stared at her, not sure where all this was going.

"This is Steven Alixant. He's the primary for the FBI Magic Enforcement division. As you know, he's a Pattern Merlin but he's also the highest mage in public service right now. They can't promote him because that is the back up to an elected position."

I caught the subtext. I wasn't stupid. He was basically a director in the FBI, and if they promoted him, he would be in line for higher-ranked government positions where mages couldn't be. But what she was really telling me was he was powerful. Not just magic, but power and position. In other words, don't piss him off.

I didn't know how much I cared. He was an ass and I had no desire to work for him. I kept my mouth shut, mostly because I still thought this was a huge hoax but I couldn't work out what they wanted. Why in the world would anyone be trying to convince me I was a merlin? Because I liked some objects and their wind machine was broken?

My hand hurt and I looked down to realize I was gripping the chair arms so tightly that my nails were bending backwards. With a force of effort I relaxed them and set them in my lap, trying to pay attention to what she was saying.

".. Dr. Lawrence Rendol. He's an Air archmage with one of the best magic senses around. Most OMO rating centers have someone with strong magic sense to help with the diagnosis."

"What diagnosis? Nothing happened. So I stood in your broken machine and nothing happened. There were pretty objects I liked." I forced myself to hold out the amulet and Dr. Rendol sighed.

"I keep telling people we need to make the test have more bells and whistles, it just seems so boring and bland that people don't believe, unless they want to believe. Really, why can't we have something more obvious?"

It sounded like an old, well-worn argument, so I watched Fran and Alixant, both wary and curious. At some point Rachel had slipped back out.

"Lawrence, now isn't the time," Fran admonished gently and the older man heaved a sigh, turning his attention back to me.

"You didn't feel anything because the machine focuses waves of power starting at a hedgemage power level and going up to the max of the machine, which we thought was a merlin. Archmages will feel a bit of pressure near the end, and some merlins will feel their hair move, but that is it. You felt nothing. Your magical field and your own power is so high, most merlins won't match you."

"Great, so she has insanely high powers and is untrained. I'm still using her. This idiot can't keep killing people," Alixant groused looking for all the world like a child denied a treat.

"So I have power because I didn't feel anything? That makes no sense." I folded my arms, glaring at them. "If I was a mage, wouldn't I have been doing something?"

"I suspect you have a constant drain between Murphy and Luck, the energy to keep both up constantly must be massive." Dr. Rendol titled his head looking at me, squinting as if looking into a bright light. "I'd say you need to shut them off ASAP, especially before you start classes."

I wanted to scream. What drugs were they on? Why would I have a whatever these were on me? I didn't enjoy finding bodies, not to mention how it had driven my life and my choices.

"You're all crazy. You're trying to prove I'm magic because nothing happens. That makes no sense." I fought tooth and nail being a hedge, or heck even a magician, or whatever. I would have just gone on with my life. But a merlin? Just how much I would lose made my stomach churn.

The three mages all exchanged looks. "I don't believe I've ever encountered this before. I should make a note of it. Is there a way to cancel her shrouds and show her?" Fran said all this with the air of a woman making mental notes in her head.

"I don't give a familiar's ass if she believes or not. She's a merlin and I need her. If I don't get her now, this damned mage might succeed in ripping open the walls between the planes and then we're going to have a major problem on our hands," Alixant snarled, exploding to his feet with such force his chair fell backward.

The flinch was automatic. I wasn't scared, but fighting wasn't in my nature. Pestering, probing, looking for answers, yes. But violence? Not so much. I'd seen too many bodies from violence to be comfortable with or around it but he did nothing more than pace back and forth. I imagined I could almost see anger and frustration radiating out of him in waves.

"Stop being a prima donna," Rendol snapped and Alixant flushed and sat back down. "As for you, young lady. I'm more practiced than you, and I can stop the relativity twists you have going around your body. Then..." he paused thinking, then brightened. "Fran do we still have the redrum ball in back?"

"Really? Huh. You know that might work. I never use it in diagnosis anymore. I got tired of the reactions. Yes, I'll go get it." She spoke as if having another conversation and I was missing part of it. But whatever it was, it didn't sound good.

I watched all three of them, feeling like a squirrel trying to dart across a busy road. The only difference was I knew I was going to get hit by a car. The question was which one would hit me first.

The doctor rose and moved over to me and I pulled back, which had the side effect of pulling me further into the chair, which did nothing for my nerves. I caught the young woman with the tattoo gun watching all of this with wide eyes. I couldn't blame her. Watching a merlin, two high ranking mages, and a supposed merlin argue about if the merlin was a real merlin had to be something she'd never seen before.

Heck, I didn't believe it and I was in the middle of it but everything in me rebelled at that idea. Even if the idea of Stevie's death caused it, wouldn't someone have noticed before?

"This shouldn't hurt, if anything you should feel more energetic," he commented, his eyes distant. I froze torn between running and hiding but he didn't do anything. I'd been expecting his hand to reach out, to grab me, or for sparks to fly off his hands, something. "There. That should do it." His eyes snapped back into focus, and he smiled at me.

"What did you do?" I frantically groped around myself with my senses trying to feel or see if there was a difference. Not that I had a clue, but I still seemed to be me. I was still freaked out, worried, saw my life disintegrating, and…

I stopped and blinked, feeling almost dizzy. I felt light-headed and over-caffeinated like I'd been drinking Stinky's Mexican coffee nonstop. I shook my head, trying to chase the feeling way, instead I almost fell off the chair.

"What did you do to me?" I couldn't explain how odd I felt. Not drugged, that I linked with my wisdom teeth and the fun drugs they put me on then. Not drunk, not that I'd been drunk before. But still, I just feel light, unbearably light.

He leaned back against the chair, watching me. "I broke all the strands of probability and relativity that were chained to you. Those strands are normally fragile and fade fast but yours had been reinforced, over and over through years I suspect, and it took me a minute to snap them. I've removed curses and lucks before, but this was different. I would say your body is reacting to the excess energy and the lack of stress from no longer keeping up two major spells, which it has for years. Figure a mix of super high blood sugar and being drunk and over-exhausted all at once."

I didn't know if I believed him but I felt like I could sprint up stairs, wrestle bears, and even cook. Before I could ask anything else, Fran came back in holding a ball. Well, that wasn't exactly accurate. She held a coffee mug that had what looked like a billiard ball, the eight, sitting in it.

"Here you go." She shuddered as she handed it to him, stepping back as soon as he took it. "I understand why we keep it but that doesn't mean I like having to be anywhere near it."

He held the cup not as gingerly as she did, though he still treated it with respect. "One of your many abilities that I am perfectly fine not having." He took a deep breath and turned back to me. "Cori, I'd like you to get comfortable and then I'm going to put this ball in your hand. Once you have a good grip on it, I want you to reach towards it mentally. You'll feel a tug deep in you, asking a question, asking for an offering, but you've plenty to spare now that the cloaks are gone. Besides, this offering is often tiny compared to what is provided."

He probably meant his smile to be encouraging, but it gave me the willies. Still, I scooted backwards until I was mostly comfortable and then held out my hand.

With a rewarding smile, he dumped the ball into my hand. I had been right; it was an eight ball from any pool table I'd ever seen. They all leaned forward, watching me with intent eyes, which made it worse. I closed my eyes for a minute, searching myself. I still felt odd - light, unburdened. I put the amulet in my pocket, the symbol of spirit called to me and since they said I could keep it, I would. But for now I needed my hands free.

This makes no sense, but whatever.

Still unsure of what I was doing, I reached, using that weird tingle I sometimes got before something weird happened and poked at the ball.

Images exploded in my mind, and I started screaming.

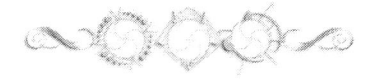

Chapter 15

OMO testing and power levels are still highly secretive. The OMO refuses to admit how their machines work, and if the few that have been taken and reverse engineered haven't provided any answers. The way to measure abilities remains as shrouded in mystery as magic itself.
~Magic Explained

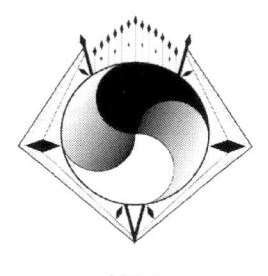

SPIRIT

I could feel wet blood splattering my hand, the ball, and my face. I was the person holding the ball. I was the ball. I could hear the scream shut off so abruptly, with the continuing thunk, thunk, thunk of the ball slamming into bloody flesh. The joy of the man holding it. I knew it was a man, hard, heated, thrilling in the death he caused with his own hands. Then another one, the ball impacting multiple places, then the sudden squish of a skull giving way and I sank into the squishy matter of the brain. I could feel it coating me as I hit again and again. The feeling changed to cold and empty: then the thuds, the need to slam into something, the need to feel someone die.

The images shut off and the creepy feelings of someone else, of me in an object that had no feelings. A sound filled the air as I became aware of reality around me. It took me a moment to realize the sound was me screaming. I managed to stop but my throat felt raw and scoured, like I'd been swallowing coffee grounds. More and more things registered. I was sweating and shaking, so wired that I could barely breathe. Everyone in the room was pale and staring at me, a few with looks of horror - the tattoo artist and Dr. Rendol. But Alixant and Fran stared at me with astonished and almost fearful looks on their faces.

"What the hell was that? What just happened?" My voice sounded raw and torn, and it hurt to say what I did. Fran picked up her phone, texting on it, while the doctor took that horror object disguised as a ball away and put it back into the cup.

"I think I owe you an apology Miss Munroe," Lawrence said, his body was stiff and he had a weird note in his voice I couldn't translate. "Most people, even merlins, get a few creepy sensations, a feeling of blood and thrill. But in all my years, I've never seen anyone react like that. I assume that is not what happened?"

"A creepy sensation? A feeling of blood?" My voice broke on those words as my stress spiked and I felt my body heating. I wanted to rage and scream and try to express the depths of horror I just experienced, but instead I started coughing. The pain in my throat made me unable to talk.

"Here," Rachel was suddenly at my side with a bottle of water. I took it gratefully, the coldness evident as I held it. I cracked open the seal and poured heaven down my throat. The icy cold wave soothed my throat but it still took me a minute to get to the point I could talk.

"It felt like I was there. I felt the blood, heard the screams, experienced the joy of the man as he killed people with that thing. I went through the deaths of at least five people, but from his joy I know that wasn't all of the people he killed. How many did he kill? How long was I in there?"

The doctor and Fran blanched, while Alixant just looked more intrigued. That reaction worried me more than anything else.

Lawrence cleared his throat. "He was convicted of the deaths of three people. All using that ball. Are you saying there was more?"

My laugh had no humor and I cut it short as my vocal cords spasmed again. I finished the bottle of water, already needing more. Rachel handed me another one, that same icy cold enveloping my hand.

Huh, must be a water mage. I'm not complaining.

I sipped this time, trying to slow how fast it went down my throat and wished I had a popsicle.

"At least ten. I got the feeling the first death with the ball was an experiment. He wanted to see if the sensation of blood on his hands was worth the mess. He loved it," even saying the words made me nauseous, and I desperately needed something else to clear the bile from my throat. "Can I get a Coke please?" There might have been a bit of desperation in that request but no one seemed offended.

"Sure. One minute," Rachel said before spinning away and out the door. She'd been pale too. Just how loud had my screams been?

"Well since he was killed in prison, I'm not sure it is worth reopening the case, but I'll make a note of what you said. I suspect you don't want to touch the ball again?"

My whole body flinched in an atavistic reaction. "You will need to kill me first." My tone was flat, uncompromising. There was nothing they could do to make me willingly go back into that nightmare. But on the bright side, something would now replace the nightmares of the ritual murderers. They had nothing on the sensation of blood running over my skin. I shuddered again, rubbing my shoulders. I needed a shower to try to clean feelings off of me.

"You know you'll probably experience worse as a Merlin," Alixant said, almost leering at me, but there wasn't really anything sexual about it.

"If so, you'll probably have a dead Merlin because if I go through that too often, I'll suicide." It was a statement. Already I could feel the evilness of that coating my soul and I wanted to cry. But how much of that was from what I had experienced, and how much was from being unable to deny what I was? A mage. A merlin.

Lawrence looked at me, his head tilted. "You know, I bet if she hadn't kept up those two cloaks for so long, she would have been strong in psychic instead of pale," his comment was abstract, his eyes unfocused.

"If that was pale, I'd hate to see what she could have done as a strong." Fran kept her voice soft but I still heard it and I looked at her. She was pale and looked at me with an expression she didn't have before. She must have noticed my gaze because she looked directly at me. "You're powerful. Even for a merlin, you are so strong. What you'll be able to do with training is, frankly, scary."

I blinked. She feared me. That idea, that concept made me sick again. I'd never wanted people to fear me. I just wanted a family. I looked around for Rachel now, even more desperate for carbonation to cleanse my throat. The burn now seemed attractive. She came back in the door, three bottles in her hand, regular and the two types of diet.

"Here. I didn't know which one you wanted."

"Regular please. I need the calories."

She nodded and handed it to me, and I could see it getting cold as she did. I twisted and poured, the sweet burn chasing away the bile and other things that had settled into my soul.

"So why didn't someone get rid of this curse thing, with all the stuff that happened around me?"

Alixant blinked at me, a furrow crossing his face, then it cleared. "Ah yes. I read your history. Really, I can't believe no merlin ever saw you. I know we're rare, but we aren't that rare."

"Shay saw me all the time, but he just muttered weird things."

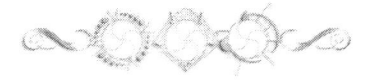

He paused and looked at me, a frown I suspected I would see a lot on his face. "Who's Shay?"

"Sato O'Shaugnessy. He always glared at me, and muttered about probability lines, but never said I was magic. Even Sloan Steward said nothing."

"Oh figures. The one Merlin in regular contact with you and it has to be Shay." He snorted what could only be extreme disgust paced back and forth in the room.

Huh? What in the world does that mean?

"You know Shay?"

"Oh, most merlins tend to be aware of each other, at least in the same country. But yeah. Shay has the worst magic sense of anyone I've ever met. Personally, I suspect it's because his earth magic is so strong, everything he sees is tainted by the earth's fields. But no, he might have sensed magic around you but unless someone really looked, I doubt they would have realized you were creating your own cloak. Most Murphys only last long enough to be annoying. Yours was damn near permanent. I'm surprised it wasn't getting worse but I suspect those two spells, once you figure out the mechanics, will be things you can use like whips with very little offering required," he said in an off handed manner, as if my world hadn't just being going through whiplash reorientations.

"Well, I saw him pretty much almost daily for a while, then Sloan a few times. Neither of them said anything."

Alixant threw his head back and groaned. "Those two. They both have almost non-existent magic sense. No wonder they never sparked to you. Anything they sensed, they would have thought someone just really hated you and had put the cloaks on. I'm not sure if you being in this entire situation is because of the Murphy, or the Lady. Hell, once Siab gets a hold of you and realizes what you did without knowing, she might try to use you as the basis for her PhD. It's more interesting than most of the random ideas she comes up with."

"What are you going to do about her power? You know she's an emotional time bomb right now. And with her magic not being drained constantly she'll be very powerful. I bet she has subconsciously learned to power everything down to a molecule unlike most of us. We tend to rounds to the nearest hundreds or thousands," Fran watched me as we talked but I had no clue what that meant. I suspected I would learn all of this one way or the other.

"I don't care. I need her. I don't care that she's untrained, I'll put in a waiver. She's working with me until we catch this maniac. With her skills she'll be a natural for this."

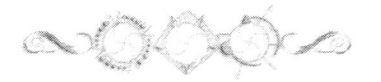

"A natural? You realize she is going to over offer, probably make more mistakes, and possibly corrupt evidence. You should wait until she gets trained and then ask for her," Fran protested, but I could tell her heart wasn't really in it.

"And how many people will be dead? If this idiot really is trying to rip open the planes, we might all be dead. No one is really sure what is on the other side. Just because so far it has only been familiars that come through doesn't mean that is all there is. Most rips are small, so nothing much larger than the size of a large dog has managed to get through. If it's ripped wide open, who knows what might come through. A dragon?"

I stared at him. "A dragon? Really?" the idea that he wasn't kidding made my blood chill and I took another swallow of Coke.

"Who knows? I know someone with a flying serpent, so that idea isn't so out of the realm."

"Elsba?" I spoke without thinking and he looked at me with a sharp hungry look.

"How do you know her?"

"I, uh, I met her when Sloan came into the coffee shop I worked at. He was talking to Shay."

"Of course. If you met Sloan you would have met Elsba, one of the rarest familiars I've ever seen. Your luck acting again."

"So, now what?" I didn't want the answer to that but I didn't see any other way to avoid it.

"Now you get marked. I take you to my team, get you embedded, and you help us track down this killer."

That sounded like so much that I wanted to sob.

"No." Fran spoke up, and I turned to look at her, she glared at Alixant, her face hard. "She gets her tattoo. That will take a while. Then she'll need to contact her work and let them know she's been drafted. We have specific forms for that," she said that more as an aside to me than anything. "Then she will go home and rest and try to adjust. You have her address. I doubt she'll run, but she needs some time to address all these changes."

"Fine, but I'll be there at seven-thirty tomorrow morning. You need to help us before this gets worse."

"But it's Saturday," the protest slipped out. I was exhausted and had been looking forward to just a weekend with Jo, having some fun. Granted, I also thought I'd be dealing with the realization I was a hedgemage. Now I had a lot more to deal with.

He gave a look that should have made me quiver. But after that ball, I'm not sure anything could scare me as much as having to reach into that again.

"What? And you think that this rogue mage is just going to take the next few days off? Twiddle his thumbs and give us time to catch up with whatever the hell he is planning?"

I just shrugged and curled up a bit tighter. All of this made me want to go home and just cry.

"Steven, enough. Finding out you're a merlin after you've emerged and been a little prepared is overwhelming enough. You dump everything else she's had today, I'd be in the corner sucking my thumb." Fran glared at him. "Go back to your team. Get them ready. They're going to have a hard-enough time adjusting to a new person, much less a merlin with zero training. Think about it, Steven. She doesn't know anything. How to do offerings, what spells there are, how to use, and how to even sense the magic in her own body and you know how grumpy they are about starting people late. The odds are she won't get in until the winter term."

"Oh gods. I'm going to have to train her. She isn't going to know even the basics," he groaned and sank into the chair holding his head. "This is going to kill me. I'll be bald by the time this is all over."

"Even worse," Fran had a sweet maliciousness to her comment that made me feel better. "You'll have to help her unlearn everything she's being doing unconsciously all this time. All those internal things she doesn't' even realize she is doing. You'd better brush up on the basics because she's going to need them if you want her to be any good at all to you."

"Merlin's ass, really?" He stood and glared at me. "Hell, I find the missing Spirit Merlin damn near a decade after the emergence was felt, and rather than having a solitary intelligent, educated mage, I get a powerful idiot that doesn't know a damn thing. I swear, if this maniac kills anymore people because you didn't bother to get yourself tested a decade ago, I'll see you're in service the rest of your life." He growled out the final words and stalked to the door. "Be ready tomorrow. I don't have any more time to spare on idiots."

The walls shook he slammed the door so hard. I blinked rapidly trying not to cry. I still felt bruised and raw from that blasted ball. I couldn't understand how I could have emerged as a pre-teen and I still wasn't sure what all the consequences were.

"Ignore him. He takes his job a little too seriously sometimes," Lawrence said. "We need to get you tattooed and then finish with the paperwork. It will be okay. People have been emerging for almost two hundred years, and the first six or seven decades everyone was self-taught. I'm sure you'll do fine."

He didn't sound sure. He sounded wary and worried, and that didn't help my sense of stability at all.

"I have to?" I knew I did, but the second that tattoo was on my skin, it was all over.

"Yep. I'm afraid so. You can't leave without the mark. Settle back. It doesn't hurt that much. We spread lidocaine into the skin and Tracy here is damn good." Jose gestured at the woman-older than me, maybe mid-thirties

I guessed. She looked more than a bit freaked out at everything that had happened.

But she stepped forward, a reassuring smile on her face. "Obviously Spirit will be the top tattoo, but do you have any preference as to how they are laid out?" I shook my head, having never thought about it. I couldn't even begin to figure out what the options were or how it should look.

"Okay, want me to do it in a way that is flattering and fits your face?" I nodded. Words were too much effort. I didn't think I'd ever been as lonely and scared as I was right at that moment. "It'll look great. Any color preferences. Since you have three you can have up to six colors." She looked down at the paper that Fran had handed him, listing my strong and pale affinities.

That much I could answer easily. "Dark burgundy or ruby red, emerald green, royal blue, and gold."

Tracy pulled the hair back from my face, clipping it back so it wouldn't be in the way. "I think I can work with that. I'm a pretty good artist, if you let me have a bit of freedom with it."

I knew I should challenge her, ask to see a portfolio, go back and forth about something that would be on my face for the rest of my life. Instead, I just nodded wearily.

"Whatever. Do what you want."

Conscious of everyone still looking at me and the questions in their eyes, I ran away the only way I could. I closed my eyes and watched my dreams burn in my mind's eye.

Chapter 16

Ronin. Taken from the Japanese tradition of a samurai without a master, they have reached urban legend status in modern American. Most of Europe refers to these mages who haven't registered with the OMO as Hoods, though whether they are referencing Robin Hood or meaning they often wear hoods to disguise themselves is unknown. They are often portrayed as misunderstood heroes, those with powers too great to trust others with, or damaged in some way. The truth? Every person is different, and every story has a different truth. But being hunted for not registering is rarely the thing of stories for the mage who is hunted down.

~History of Magic

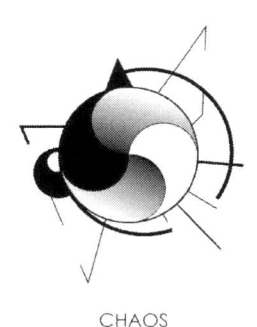

CHAOS

The tattoo didn't really hurt, but it did sting. A tattoo on your face was much more difficult than on your hip. But when she finished and I looked in the mirror, I couldn't complain. Well I could, but not about her work or artistry. All mage tattoos are the same three symbols, Spirit, Chaos, Pattern. Merlins got all three, but they can place them how they want. In school, kids would have contests about where to place them on their faces and the color combinations they'd use.

I never bothered to even think about it because I knew I wouldn't be a mage. Silly me.

She'd taken the colors I'd provided and used them to great effect on my pale skin. I usually kept red highlights in my hair and washed with a henna to give it my dark brown hair a tint of red. I could tan, but I rarely did. I never had time to seek out the sun, even in Georgia. The artist had gone with that, placing the Spirit symbol, with dark burgundy outlines, right above the corner of my right brow. The Relativity section she had filled in with bright emerald green that looked festive next to the burgundy. The two weak sections for Psychic and Soul she'd done in a shading of green that started with the vivid emerald but as the section spiraled to the center, it faded to almost nothing. My next symbol, Chaos, sat on my temple and the edge of my cheekbone. This one she'd interlaced with the spirit, making it look like a part of it with the same dark burgundy but the filling for Time she'd done in royal blue, dark and vibrant - a spark of joy on my cheekbone. The final one for Pattern curved down a bit, landing on the edge of my jaw. This one was subtler with the outline being in a softer shade of the burgundy, closer to a rose, and she did a pretty hash pattern of the blue and green overlapping, but softening and fading towards the center. Then, outlining each of the symbols was a tracery of gold that sparkled as I moved my head.

Staring in the mirror, I admitted it was stunning and I would have admired it on anyone else. On me, I didn't recognize myself and even touching the red skin. It seared more with emotions than physical pain.

"Here's your balm for this. It will heal fast and the gold is processed to be hypoallergenic, so you shouldn't have any issues. While you keep normal tats covered, these are too annoying to try, so smear heavily and don't sleep on that side for the next couple nights."

I took the heavy jar she handed me, still staring at my reflection. "Is that real gold?"

"Yes. We have the top end stuff available for all mages, and the metals help pull people's attention. If your health records indicate metal allergies, we even have gemstone ink."

I blinked, almost interested. She saw my reaction and smiled kindly. That kind smile meant a lot. "Later, if you want, you can get it enhanced with gems, even insets. I left it so putting a few emeralds, sapphires, or diamond chips along here would make it stunning." Tracy lifted her hand tracing out the designs of the tattoos but not touching my skin. "Always leave your options open."

That got a bitter laugh out of me. "I tried. I really did. It seems to have been wasted effort." I sagged and turned back to Fran, the only one still left. She was reading a book this time but I could tell she was paying more attention to me than anything she read. "Is there a way I can get a ride back to Ruby EMS? I need to get my stuff and talk to my coworkers." I looked at my phone, just going on nine p.m., so odds were most of the people I worked with would be gone. I didn't know if that made me happy, or not.

"Sure. My shift is about over, so give me a minute and I'll give you a ride."

I nodded and hesitantly headed towards the door Rachel had popped in and out of, half expecting someone to scream 'She's Escaping!' No one did and I walked down a short hallway towards the door marked 'Exit' and found myself the little area where Rachel had taken all my info. It seemed like eternity ago. She still sat there at the desk and looked up as I walked in.

"Hey, how you doing?"

I shrugged, no idea how to answer that, much less to a stranger. "Any chance I can get another one of those icy cold Cokes?"

She smiled a sympathetic smile and nodded. "Sure." She got up and pulled one from the cupboard. They had all manner of sodas, waters, even some beer and wine in there. As she handed it to me, I could see the condensation appearing on it.

"Isn't that a waste of offering?" I didn't mean to pry, but now stuff like this mattered.

"Nah. Doesn't even take half a single strand of hair. I've been doing that trick for a long time and it barely costs anything." She shrugged as I took it. "You learn how to manage and use your skills. But really," she paused and glanced at my hair, "let your hair grow. You'll need it as you learn."

"It doesn't grow," I whined, glad for something more normal to talk about. "I've had it this length for three years, and I've barely trimmed." I saw Fran walk in out of the corner of my eye as I spoke.

"You know, you're probably the reason why," she remarked looking at me with an expression that was becoming all too familiar. I really wasn't a fan of the "ooh interesting science experiment" look, but they all seemed to have it.

"What? Like I decided I didn't want long hair?" I mean, I didn't really want hair like Jo's, but being able to get different hair styles would have been nice.

"No. That came out wrong. I bet your cloaks were eating every bit of extra hair and that made it look like it didn't grow. But you had to put in new highlights?"

"Yeah about twice a year, but it never got longer. I just assumed it faded towards the top as that was the least processed part." Now that I said it out loud, it sounded stupid and was one more proof of how I'd been lying to myself the whole time.

"I'd expect it to grow really fast over the next few weeks. Now that you have all that spare energy back, though I am curious as to what your normal offerings were. Who knows?" She shook her head, acting like she was biting her tongue.

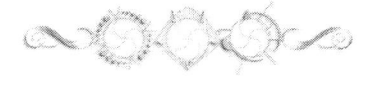

I didn't say anything and just walked out of the building with her. The hot humid city air smelled of smog and was so thick it hurt to breathe. I'd never been so glad to feel it hit my face before, but the stinging on my face reminded me I was shackled now. I tried to move my hair to cover it but it was mostly too short, and the heavy balm glued any stray hair to it, making it bug me. I look around and then felt like an idiot.

"Fran, thanks for the offer, but where I need to go is only two blocks away. I'd rather walk."

"You sure? You have a car there?"

"I don't drive. I'll take the bus."

She got a funny look on her face. "Why don't you let me give you a ride to both places. I don't mind."

I looked at her funny. While I wasn't looking forward walking into work after I'd been all but kidnapped, I didn't need the dubious support of someone I barely knew. Heck, I wasn't even sure what her last name was, Calamari? No, that was squid.

"I ride public transportation all the time. I got it. And I could use the alone time to deal with some things. Thanks anyhow."

She crossed her arms, hugging herself. "Okay but be careful. Being a merlin isn't what you expect."

I gave a laugh that sounded harsher than I had intended, but it felt right. "Being a mage wasn't anything I ever expected. I have no expectations of merlins. Don't worry about it." The only thing I had with me were what was in my pockets. I was starving but I didn't want to be around strangers anymore, especially those who acted nice but had their own plans about me.

I gave her a brusque nod, turned, and headed down the block. As I turned the corner, I caught her staring after me, still with that worried look on her face.

Whatever. Like after all that, I'm supposed to believe she cares about me besides as an example of what else they need to be aware of?

Righteous annoyance fueled the start of my two-block walk. It had mostly faded by the time I reached my destination. The humidity was worse than usual this evening and in my jumpsuit I felt sweat running down my back. I was more than ready for fall to get here. Maybe I could move to Alaska where at least it was not this hot.

The random thoughts distracted me as I pushed open the door to the main area and walked in. I stumbled to a halt as everyone turned and looked at me. Jorge, Lisa, Raul, they were all still there, everyone looking exhausted and worried. Then they saw me.

"Cori! You're back. We were about to call the police for illegal kidnapping," Jorge said as he jumped up and strode to me. He got about five feet from me when I saw, as if in slow motion, his eyes glance to my temple and he froze like someone had just melted his boots to the floor. "Cori, are those tattoos a joke?" His voice thin with emotions I wasn't sure of.

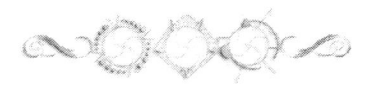

In response, my hand drifted up to my face. They didn't hurt, but they radiated heat and I couldn't help but be very aware of them. "No. It turns out I'm a merlin." This time I didn't bother to disguise my bitterness. "Apparently I'm an anomaly." They hadn't called me that but I could read the subtext of what they said. I'd probably end up being the subject of several theses.

Others had joined him. Half of the normal people there, then the next crew that I'd only met in passing. They all stared at my tattoo with odd expressions.

"What type of anomaly?" Lisa asked, her voice distant, and I felt part of my life crumbling around me. All that work to get them to like and respect me, and some ink would ruin it all.

"You know how you don't emerge until after puberty?" I stood in the entryway, their presence forming a barrier between me and my locker, one I wasn't willing to brave. But I needed my keys and my belongings.

They all nodded, still looking at me. Their bodies screamed wariness and worry, I just didn't know about which fact.

"Well, I, per them," a bit of bile might have coated that word, "I emerged at right before my twelfth birthday."

The shock was clear on their faces, but Jorge had an unmoved one. "So just like I thought, you're quitting." His voice was a slap of accusation across my face.

I wanted to scream that it wasn't my choice, that I wanted to work in my chosen profession, that I wanted my life back. Instead, I bit the inside of my mouth to stop from letting any of this leak out, and replied, my voice calm. "I don't know. The lead investigator says he requires my help as I'm the only Spirit Merlin on the east coast. I don't know what help I'll be but from everything they've said I don't have a choice. And no matter what, I'll have to go back to college. They say I've learned way too many bad habits. I'm hoping I can stay here until then. I'll try."

As I said the words, I decided I would. This could count towards my draft, right? Part of working with the city? I'd worked so hard for this and feeling it slip out of my fingers like grains of hourglass time sliced at me.

"Don't bother. I knew you'd leave." He turned and headed towards the door. "I'm off. See you in two." He didn't look back as he slammed the door behind him. The others shifted uncomfortably but they filtered away, leaving only Lisa looking at me with sharp eyes.

"Not what you wanted?"

"No," I growled the word. Why did everyone think being a mage was what I wanted? I had no desire to serve for a decade or to get a degree in something I had no interest in - to not be able to help people. It chafed at my soul.

"I get that. Had a cousin who emerged. Just a wizard, but he wasn't happy. He had wanted to continue his parents' business as a plumber but they made him do his service in the Army." Her eyes were bleak. "He didn't come back."

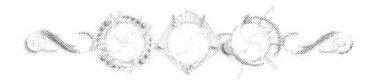

That threw cold water on my attitude. "I'm sorry."

"So am I. Good luck." She turned and walked away, leaving me standing there in what, once again, felt like enemy territory.

Chapter 17

Rage against the OMO, for they create chains to limit humanity to what it thinks you should be. Rage and fight, Ronin forever.
~Underground Mages Forever

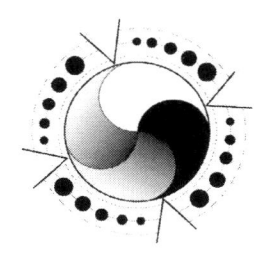

ORDER

Acting on a hunch that I hated, I cleaned out my locker. I'd fight to come back but part of me suspected I wouldn't be welcome and that I wouldn't win. But that didn't mean I couldn't try. Packing everything in my bag, I walked the block to the bus stop. A buzz in my pocket jolted me out of my haze.

Yo - Cor where are you? Got home late after library. You aren't here. Everything cool?

Oh Jo-jo, how the hell am I going to explain this to you?

I didn't even address the worry about her bailing or being unable to handle the next step in Catastrophe Cori.

Crazy day. Headed back now. Talk when home?

Her response was immediate, which helped a bit.

K. Need food? I forgot to eat. I hate history.

Yes, please. Starved, haven't eaten since bfast

Ugh, not good. You know that. Am cooking now. Everything nachos?

My mouth watered at that. Everything meant beef, mushrooms, black refried beans, cheese, sour cream, and salsa. Sounded like the solution to my abused taste buds and empty hole in my stomach.

Yes!

lol - see you at home.

I slid my phone away and my smiled faded. I could only hope she'd be as cool with my appearance as she was with my long absence. The bus pulled up and I dug out my pass. The bored driver glanced at me as I tapped my Breeze card to the little machine. He paled as his eyes latched onto my temple and he swallowed, watching me walk back.

What in the world? Ugh, I don't need that today.

I moved through the bus but made sure I sat down in an empty row behind the driver, mostly to avoid his wide-eyed stare.

Yeesh, you'd think he'd never seen a mage before.

I stared out the windows, trying to figure out how I had ended up here. The day had been a blur and it didn't make sense to me that I had started the day as a no one and ended up as a merlin at the end. It didn't fit into my worldview and that threw me off balance even more.

"Hey, lady you got change to sp–" the aggressive, whiny words cut off as I turned to look at the speaker. Young, scrawny, with a tough guy look and a cap on backward covering his dirty blond hair, but nothing disguised the look of fear as his eyes snagged on my tattoos. "Sorry, ma'am didn't mean to bother you." He babbled, backing up and pulling the stop requested cord.

Others on the bus, not that it was packed with riders but still a Friday night meant it wasn't empty, started to turn and look at me. Their eyes wide as they saw the rawness of the tattoo and it felt like a physical reaction as they pulled back from me. I saw at least two get up and dive out the door with the thug as soon as the bus stopped. I realized the driver keep nervously glancing up at me.

I just want to go home.

I inhaled sharply through my mouth, fighting back tears of exhaustion and just emotional overload.

I've survived everything else, I will survive this too. I will not break.

A few deep breaths and I felt calmer. Everyone gave me a wide birth, and I didn't care, counting the stops. Part of me wanted to get off earlier to avoid the looks and the low level of panic in the bus. I'd kinda thought Shay was weird, but I'd never feared him. What was their issue? I just shook my head and glanced around. People avoided my gaze and ducked their heads but I realized as I looked around, I didn't see any mages.

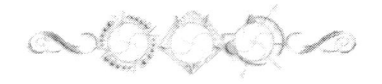

Blinking, I thought back about all my bus rides both here and in Rockway. Other than Shay that one time, and he usually kept a cap on, I couldn't remember seeing very many mages. Maybe one or two the entire time, and they too had worn caps. That surprised me, and I looked again. Mages were a smaller portion of the population, but surely they weren't that rare or that well off.

But I didn't see any. I also refused to get off to avoid the stares, though I thought about it. Bottom line, I was too exhausted to walk another few blocks just because my presence made them uncomfortable but I realized how oblivious I had been. Kadia's comments sank in further now than they had.

Great, so I'm biased on top of everything else.

I scrubbed my face with my hands and winced as I hit the fresh tattoo, smearing goop everywhere. I sighed and tried to smooth the goo back over the abused skin. Getting an infection was the last thing I needed. I pulled on the next stop and I swear the driver had the doors open before he even stopped. With a shake of my head I got out and felt the doors snap closed behind me, abnormally fast. I glanced back as the bus actually burned rubber getting away from.

Oh, good grief. What? Like I'll melt them in their seats? People are idiots.

I headed up the way to the apartment, glad for the darkness that had finally fallen. It made it easier to avoid people. With it being mostly students and the weekend, there were people everywhere but I just kept my head down and walked the stairs to the apartment, my beacon of hope.

I headed up the stairs and paused outside the door, worried and stressed. I don't know how long I would have stood there if I hadn't heard another door unlock and start to open. Nathan was the last person I wanted to deal with tonight. With speed born of avoidance, I unlocked the door and stepped in, shutting it firmly behind me.

"Finally!" Jo all but shouted, springing from the couch, textbook in hand. "I was waiting for you. I wanted to go get dinner out and maybe we can catch that new movie. It's supposed to be great. Also, I wanted to ask about Dragonworl-" she stopped looking at me.

I knew she couldn't see the tattoos, I stood with my right side to the door not looking at her.

"Cor? What's wrong? Did something happen?" She set down her book moving towards me. "Cori? What happened?" All humor and excitement had faded from her voice. Now worry replaced it as she moved close. "Cori, look at me."

She's your best friend, she's never going to leave you. Get over this stupid fear.

With that sharp reminder to myself, I dropped my bag, ignoring the thunk as it hit the floor, and turned to face her.

Jo sucked in a sharp breath and moved towards me. Her hand reached up and ghosted over the tattoos, not touching me but I could feel the heat from her skin. "Cori?" Her voice held so many questions that I didn't know the answers to.

"I guess I should have gotten tested when you suggested," I managed before Jo pulled me into a hug and I lost it. All the confusion, the horrible bodies, the way people treated me like a criminal, then like an interesting specimen, feeling all my dreams die, then that horrid, horrid ball! It all came out and I bawled there in her arms on our entry floor.

I don't know how long I cried. At some point we moved to the couch, and she got up to get me water and Kleenex. She gave me time to weep and held me or let me go as I needed, no talking, just being there while I let it all get out of my system. But finally, my tears dried up, and I felt more than a bit stupid.

"I texted Mami. She'll be here soon."

"What?" I couldn't stop the protestation that burst out. "No."

"Cori, hush. I'll lay money she walks in any moment laden with food and more than willing to talk to you." Jo paused and swallowed. "We talked a lot the day after I emerged. You'll see. She has a way of putting everything in perspective."

"But, that's mom stuff. She's not my mom, she shouldn't have to –" I bit off the words as Jo glared at me.

"It is also *Tia* stuff, and she is your Tia by love. So deal. You have a family that cares, and nothing you do, or are, will chase us away." She paused and gave me a long considering look. "But if you steal my girlfriend, we'll have serious words."

I blinked at her, the non sequitur derailing me. "You have a girlfriend?" Maybe I had missed something? Was she dating someone? I scrambled through my memories trying to figure out if I'd forgotten something.

Jo burst out in laughter. "No. But when I do, if you ever steal her, I'll be very pissed at you." Her smile made me groan. She'd pulled me out of my mope expertly.

"I'm pretty sure I can guarantee I won't steal your girlfriend. But if I do, I'll let you be the best man at our wedding."

"Ouch. Burn. Wench." She was laughing as she got up. "Where is the jar of goop they gave you? You're wincing, which means you're hurting. Then when mom gets here, you can tell us everything." She pulled two Cokes out of the fridge and handed one to me as a rap sounded on the door. How a rap could sound imperious and worried, I didn't know. But it did. "There's mom."

Jo answered the door and Marisol stood there. "You said you two needed me. I'm here, what's wrong?"

I stood, still shaky from emotions and stress facing her. "Hi, Tia."

"Oh my," the words a soft gasp. She came over and lay her hand on my left cheek. "*Mia hija*, it looks like you have much to tell us."

"Yes, she does, and I haven't heard any of it yet. Let me take your stuff and we can eat while you talk. I'm starving."

Her saying those words made me realize that was probably half of my issue. I hadn't eaten since that morning. Jo set the table: all the fixing for nachos had been ready to go. We sat down and with their loving eyes on me I started with the bodies and I didn't avoid any of it. Not the Murphy's Curse, the Lady Luck cloak, the ball, the tattoos, their weird reactions to me, and especially when they thought I had emerged.

"That does explain much," Marisol said leaning back. She'd only nibbled on chips as Jo and I ate. "But there are bright sides to this."

I gave her a bleak look. "Not everyone wants to go to college. You know they'll want me to get a doctorate. I don't even know what I want to study. And I'm in the draft now."

Jo reached out, putting her hand on mine. "Hey, it's not so bad. And you like school way better than I ever did."

"True, but still, I don't start until January and they are going to drive me to major in certain things. I don't know what I want," I didn't manage to keep the whine out of my voice, and I sagged a bit. "Sorry. I'm being selfish."

"Of course you are. It's your life, you're allowed to be selfish about it. All you can do with life is take what has happened and deal with it. But as for things about this, that are good?" she paused and gave me a grin that had me worried. "Now you can properly learn to cook since disasters won't keep happening, and maybe you can get a car. A lot of your valid fear was apparently due to these cloaks. Now you can step out and do more stuff."

"Oh," I said, stunned. I hadn't even thought of those things. I ran through a few little other things that had not occurred to me. Maybe now I could find out why Stevie had died. I could become anything.

"And," she said mildly, interrupting my thoughts. "I get to get you an emergence gift." Jo and she exchanged smiles and once again I thought running might have been the better option.

"Fine. Then I want this." I pulled out the amulet with the spirit symbol on it. "Can you get me a real necklace? One that won't tarnish and wear out? Something I'd be proud of."

Jo took it from me, looking at me then it. I could see emotions and thoughts running across her face, but they were so fast I couldn't figure them out. "Deal. But might take me a while. Okay?"

I froze, horrified. "Jo - I never got you anything."

She leaned over and kissed my forehead. "I know. You were so wrapped up in everything that you didn't even think about it. Being my friend is all that matters Cori."

Shame flushed through me and I vowed to find her the best gift ever. No matter what it took.

Chapter 18

The spells that mages can do are well defined and well researched. Those few who dare to reach beyond are either specialty researchers for the OMO or shortly very dead.
~Magic Explained

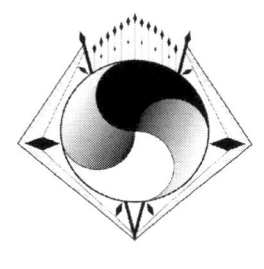

SPIRIT

That night I slept deeper than I could ever remember sleeping. No dreams haunted me. When my alarm went off at six, I lay there disoriented and tried to remember why I was getting up. Then everything flooded back into me and I jerked upright, feeling my pulse hammering, but nothing fell, nothing broke, the power didn't go out, nothing.

Huh. Okay, maybe I can get used to this.

I sat there waiting, but nothing happened. A strange light feeling filled my mind and I headed to the bathroom, not excited about today, but maybe all of this wouldn't be as bad as I thought. I made sure to stay quiet as Marisol was asleep on the futon. She said she'd head back to Rockway tonight, after she made sure I was okay. She wanted to leave me some ideas about careers and go get me an emergence present. I still didn't know how I felt about it, but her excitement made it so I couldn't refuse the offer.

I pulled out my best jeans. New ones I'd bought that first weekend down here, and a light tank top and a loose shirt. While I had a dress, this really was the nicest of clothes I had. And, of course, my tennis shoes. Other than sandals and work boots they were my only other shoes. I made my coffee and headed out, phone in my pocket, filled coffee mug in my hand.

I reached the parking lot and looked around. The air was still cool, but already I could sense the humidity waiting to mug me. I sipped my coffee, rolling the taste around in my mouth. I was playing with adding spices to the grounds, but I still thought the flavor was better when roasted with them. Oh well, something to consider.

A black sedan came into the parking lot at seven-thirty on the dot, with tinted windows and nothing to give it any personality. I just sat and watched it. I wasn't happy about any of this, but even I could see there might be some long-term benefits. Short term I was annoyed and at this point I didn't see how my life could get any more complicated.

It only took three minutes before the driver's side door flew open and Alixant half stood out of the door. "Well, aren't you going to get in the car?"

"Oh. Hi. Sorry. Didn't know it was you. Not like I have any way to know what car is yours," I said as I slowly rose and stretched a bit, then moved his way.

"And you didn't come over to look?" He demanded, glaring at me.

"I don't know what they teach people where you come from, but around here we don't approach strange cars. Especially ones with tinted windows." I'd finally meandered over to the passenger side and he pulled off his sunglasses and stared at me.

"Go change," his voice was flat, and I blinked and glanced down at what I was wearing, then back up to him in his suit. "Into what?"

"A suit, professional wear. You're acting on behalf of the FBI, on behalf of my division I expect you to look respectable."

That cause me to bristle. I looked decent. Maybe not like an agent or anything but I didn't look like riff-raff.

I forced a nonchalant shrug. Something told me if I let him start running roughshod over me now, I'd set a very bad precedent, and he'd already arrested me once. "I'm afraid this is what you get."

"You will go and put on more suitable clothing," he almost roared.

"And that would be defined as?"

"A suit, or at the least black slacks and a blouse."

I gave him a long look. I'd dumped all my slacks the weekend we'd moved along with most of my badly worn clothes. The only blouse I owned was the one Jo had transformed and Atlanta would freeze in July before I wore that for him.

"Okay." I turned and started walking away from him towards the bus stop. I counted in my head. I made it to eight.

"Where in the hell are you going?" He slammed the door to his car as he stormed after me.

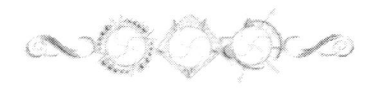

"Well, if you want me wearing something at tacky as that," I ran a dismissive look up and down his very expensive and very nice suit, "I need to go shopping."

"Argh," he ground out, actually clenching his hair. I stared at him, cataloging everything. He had dashing dark looks that would have set most women I'd known into raptures of delight. His features were even, and his body seemed to meet the standards most women talked about. To me, he just represented frustration and the shattering of dreams. He took a deep breath and let his hands drop, staring at me. After another moment he closed his eyes, breathing in and out. I watched him sipping my coffee.

I'd thought about this in the shower. There really wasn't anything they could do to me. They couldn't fire me or anything for being a pain in the ass and I refused to lose who I was just because I'd become a mage. They would take me as I was, and I enjoyed having the money to buy clothes I liked, as opposed to clothes I tolerated. When they got me an actual employment contract maybe I'd get a suit, but overall, I preferred my jeans. They made me feel comfortable and safe.

"We started out on the wrong foot. Let's get past that. I need you. I need you badly enough that I don't care if you wear a bikini and feathers. You're the only Spirit Merlin in the area and even better, you know the South. I'm only down here for this case, and this place is worse than being in another country. I need your help. We still don't know for sure what this idiot is trying to do but I'm worried that it's going to get worse if we don't stop him."

"Or her," I said, mostly to be a pain in the ass.

He froze. "You think the perp is female?"

I sighed and headed towards him and the car. That speech was probably the closest I'd get to an apology. "I don't think anything but assuming it the person is male is short-sighted don't you think?"

He looked thoughtful as I slid into the car. It was clean, almost new smelling, and I looked around. Outside of a fancy dash, it just seemed to be a regular car.

"Were you expecting lots of sci-fi gadgets?" He asked, his voice dry as he buckled in.

"Yes, but I guess the government is too cheap to spring for them." I buckled also, my mug firmly in my hand.

"Tell me everything you know about the murders." It wasn't a question, but a demand and I wanted to sigh. I knew, absolutely knew, that every statement I'd given had been uploaded into the system, and if he didn't know how to get them, he didn't deserve this job. Which mean he'd probably read them ten times and wanted me to spontaneously come up with some glaring clue I never noticed before.

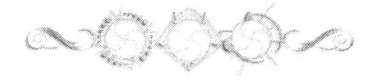

I'll never make it through today. I'm already tired of him and it hasn't even been thirty minutes.

"Assuming you're not a moron, I figure you've already read everything I've said multiple times. So why don't we start with what questions you think I didn't answer." I took a drink to stop myself from saying anything more. This would be hard enough.

He didn't look at me but I saw his hands clench on the steering wheel. I knew I was playing with fire, but I got a perverse sense of enjoyment out of antagonizing him. The best part was everything I said was true.

"Fine. What drew you there?"

"First or second scene?" I countered. He needed to be very, very specific. "And if you say second, I'll quit talking."

That glare almost heated up my coffee. I looked out the window. We were headed away from downtown, so a new area to me. The idea of being able to drive without worrying about something going haywire was an idea I still played with. I'd give it six months first, make sure the disasters were really over.

"The first," he ground out. And I might have heard him grind his teeth. If he billed me for dental costs I wasn't paying.

"As I said in my reports, nothing. I was learning the area. We'd just moved here, and I was trying to get a feel for the local area."

"That area is more than ten blocks from your apartment."

I shot him a glance then looked back out the window. I didn't want to miss scenery or deal with his glares. I didn't know where he was going with this line of questioning.

"And?"

"And college students don't walk, they drive everywhere. Why were you walking in that area?" He said it the same way I would have said Marisol is an excellent cook. An immutable fact of existence. Too bad he was incorrect.

"Well, since I don't have a car and I wanted to know what was in the area, I walked. Which means maybe you should stop making assumptions."

I didn't look at him but I heard his teeth grinding. I drank coffee so I wouldn't laugh.

We rode in silence, and I was fine with that, but no good things last forever. "Did you smell anything odd?"

Hmm... interesting question. Did I?

I closed my eyes and thought back but other than blood and trash and urine, nothing jumped out at me.

"Not that registered. Blood, yes. But otherwise it was the same stuff, trash and city smells."

"What about your magic sense, what did you sense?" he demanded.

This time my attempt to be good failed and I turned to stare at him. "Really? If you are this stupid, how in the world are you in charge of this? Until yesterday, I didn't know I was a mage. I didn't know there was such a thing as magic sense and I can guarantee you that I didn't know how to use it." He tried to interrupt me, but I kept right on talking. "If you're asking, did I sense or feel something I couldn't explain, the answer is no. The only thing that stands out to me is the look of pain on that girl's face. Now are you through asking stupid questions?" That last part came out a bit snappish.

Alixant yanked the wheel, pulling into a parking lot that had quite a few cars in it for a Saturday. He slammed on the brakes, throwing me forward and I sloshed out coffee, which was impressive given the coffee mug I had and how little was in it.

"I will have you up in charges if you don't cooperate and give your all in this investigation. That means not being obstinate and helping us find the killer."

"I don't KNOW ANYTHING!" I shouted the words and felt my skin tingle, this time I recognized it for what it was, magic. My magic. I'd always pushed it down and tried to ignore it but this time I embraced it, pulling it towards me like the last chocolate pastry. I had no idea what I was doing but my anger took over, doing things by instinct. This time I could almost see it, the Murphy's Curse settling around him and his car, the strands of probability twisting and shattering, and the offering of the top layer of skin easily paid.

Between one breath and the next, all the alarms on the dash went off, two tires ruptured with enough force I was glad he'd stopped, his watch fell off his arm, smoke started to rise from his pocket and all the buttons on his suit fell off.

I looked at all of this and then at the fine powder of dust on my arms. "Well, that was different. Now if I could do that on purpose and not only when I'm ready to beat someone to death."

The wave must have shocked him because he looked around, sniffed, and reached down pulling a phone out of his pocket that was leaking smoke.

He looked at me, then back at the car and took a long breath, holding it in at each point. I didn't know if what I did was allowed or not, but I didn't care. Sitting in jail would be better than dealing with this jerk.

"I think," he paused and looked around and heaved a sigh. "I suspect I deserved that. Treating you like a suspect is not going to work."

"Not if you want me to actually work with you. Otherwise, I'm just going to sit in a corner and read." I didn't mention that would drive me crazy. Some things I wasn't about to tell anyone.

"I'll try, but don't expect a miracle. That isn't who I am." He pushed open the door and climbed out.

I followed, but this time I tried to see if what I'd done was visible. But I didn't see anything, though my head itched.

Huh, all this time that must have been offerings.

I bent over and scratched my head, then dusted off my arms.

"Is it still around, the magic? I mean the Murphy's thing. I never really did anything active before. At least not consciously."

He glanced the car and shook his head. "No, but I'm not driving it again until a mechanic has gone over it with a fine-tooth comb." He turned and started walking. We were in a quiet office complex off Lennox, but there were a lot of cars, all with government tags.

I followed, but said nothing, guilt starting to set in about the magic lash out.

"I've never had to deal with anyone using magic on an instinctual and emotional level. Most mages are in college learning the basics before they ever have a chance to more than play with it. You'll need to try to break that habit. It will either get you killed or arrested, because you did hurt something. I do find it interesting that I didn't get hurt."

I stumbled to a halt and must have made a sound because he turned and looked at me.

"Are you okay? Your face is pale, and you look like you might throw up."

Throwing up sounded like a very good idea.

"Did I? I mean my magic," I swallowed, coffee churning in my stomach. "Did I cause the deaths of the people I stumbled across?"

Chapter 19

> To a large extent magic is like the stories told and is intent centered. While that mostly is verified via anecdotal evidence, it seems to hold. The few deaths caused by emergence, Murphy's Cloak, or even young mages playing with their abilities is less than what any statistics would predict.
> ~Magic Explained

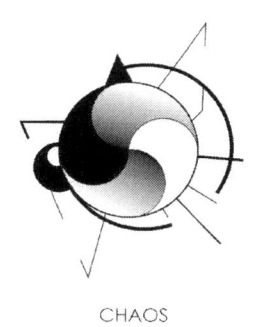

CHAOS

He didn't even look back at me, just waved at his outfit. "If you could have killed me with that, I would be dead, not just looking like a hobo, though I probably should be glad I wasn't eating anything at the time. I might have choked. But no, Murphy's Curse doesn't work like that, though I suppose if you directed it, maybe. I think it more worked to give you reasons to walk towards them or to be there. But you would probably make a fascinating case study if anyone had realized what you were doing before it was dismissed."

So much I didn't know. His calm dismissal of my worries and his vague apology went a long way to soothing my ruffled feelings, but at the same time I still fought my own resentment.

Waste of energy. Like caring about the Munroes. Accept it, adapt, move on. Becoming Ronin really isn't a good option.

The made me laugh at myself. Me, as a Ronin? That would be a failure before it even started. I followed, looking around the area. It looked like a typical office complex. Wherever I had thought he was taking me, this wasn't it.

He walked into a building, pulling out a badge and waving it at the card reader.

"This place only has basic security. I'll get you a badge on Monday but for now I want to explain why I need you so badly and what we know." He talked as he walked, assuming I followed, and I did. Still disappointed. It looked like an average office building. I'd been in enough buildings the few weeks of working on the ambulance, both here and in Rockway, to recognize the blandness. What I'd seen convinced me I never wanted to work in one, yet here I was. My spirit shrank down even more. How did I get myself into these messes?

He went through one more sealed door and stepped into a large area that had a long white counter and drawers against the left wall from the door with a bunch of fancy machines on it. Five cubicles were on the wall straight ahead from us, and to the left were rolling white boards, the hugest computer screen I'd ever seen and a conference table with six chairs and power outlets everywhere.

The expensive electronics everywhere gave me hives. If I fried one of these, they'd never forgive me.

"Come on. We don't have any more time to waste. I can feel the killer getting ready for the next attempt."

I swallowed and followed him in, feeling more and more out of place with every step.

One of the two agents that had arrested me, the one with an accent that sounded like the ones I'd heard on TV when talking to people in New York, stuck his head out and blinked.

"Merlin, Steven, what happened to you?" The accent was there, and it brought others out. The other agent looked way too fit to be real with his blond hair and dark blue eyes; he had to have won the genetic lottery.

Alixant glanced down at himself and I paid attention to what he focused on. Mostly I had avoided looking at him. I didn't want to make him think I cared, but even I blinked when I really looked.

His jacket looked like half the threads had snapped, the buttons were gone, his belt had broken, his shoes were frayed, his tie had shredded at the tie bar, and his shirt collar was all wonky.

"Oops." I wasn't that sorry but still, he looked ridiculous. Others had stuck their heads out of their cubicles and they all gaped at him.

He heaved a sigh and pulled the jacket off. It almost fell apart in his hands. "Take this as a lesson to not get a Spirit merlin truly pissed off at you." His voice had a wry tone to it, so at least I didn't think he was about to try and kill me. "I liked this jacket," he muttered as he dropped it on the table. "Okay, listen up—this is Corisande Munroe. She is officially drafted and while she can't start her mandatory college until next semester, we need her now. Here is where we stand on everything." He turned and headed to the board, looking rumpled and vaguely wrong.

"Umm, and who are these people?" I didn't even try to not be snide, looking at the two familiar strangers and the one unfamiliar one.

He groaned and turned around and looked at all of us, treating social niceties an obvious waste of time. "They have badges. Read them." I put one hand on my hip and stared at him. I hated first days anywhere and this was already the worst first day ever. I didn't really think I could make it worse.

"Fine. Niall McLachan, FBI Agent, he's my evidence person. An Earth archmage. He is excellent at seeing what isn't obvious or doesn't match or even what has been added to the scene." Niall looked at me his eyes lingering on my temple.

My instinctive reaction was to wipe, thinking something was stuck there, but the simple act of creasing my brows reminded me of what he was staring at.

"Not a mage, huh? What were you trying? To go Ronin, learn without oversight and strike out on your own?" The sneer in his voice could have been used as a weapon and I glared at him.

"I didn't know I was a mage but I did know you were a jerk. Nice to know I was right about you," I snapped back. This whole situation would never work.

"Chill, Niall." The other guy, the one with blue eyes, crew-cut blond hair, and a smile that I suspected should make me swoon. He stepped forward, holding out his hand. Before he could say anything else, Alixant spoke.

"And the agent acting all charming is Chris Jones. Pattern archmage. My database specialist and he's the one that will reconstruct things, at least normally." Alixant's voice had a sour note to it but rather than get offended or upset, Chris shrugged.

"I can only work with what I have and the perp in this situation isn't giving me much. Nice to meet you, Cori." He smiled, completely relaxed and almost zen like. It was both attractive and repelling, considering how wired I was.

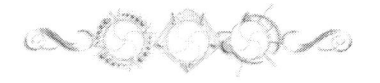

This time I shook his hand, but still wasn't sure about any of this. But the last agent grinning at me was not what I expected. Yes, she had on dark slacks, and a white shirt - but that was the extent of any agenty thing about her. Her slacks looked like yoga slacks and they hugged her tight. The white shirt was open and revealed a blood red camisole and tattoos along the top of her breasts, or at least the hints of tattoos. Her long black hair was twisted on top held by a pencil, while the piercings in her eyebrow, lip, and ears were all titanium and reflected back the rainbow at me. But her grin and wild make up, cat eyes, emerald eyeshadow, and lips painted bruise purple, ensured she was the only one I even found anything in common with. At barely five feet tall, all the men towered over her. Asian features didn't tell me anything, but while Atlanta had a large Korean population, I didn't think she was Korean, but who knew.

"And this is Non-organic wizard Kajsiab Siong, my forensics specialist, currently becoming an expert in ritual magic. And who needs to pay attention to the dress code."

The woman all but bounced up and down on the balls of her feet. "Ignore him. I'm Siab, Kajsiab. It means peace but trust me, I'm not peaceful. And before you ask, no I'm not Chinese, I'm Hmong, and don't ever tell my mom anything. That woman makes tiger mom's look like sloths. So, I need to ask you questions about all the scenes and try to add them into the database I'm creating. We don't really understand ritual magic yet and I'm thinking the information we are gathering here will be enough for my PhD. But you never can tell when something more interesting might come along. Or maybe I'll get two. That might make mom slow down for a minute. So, how are you? Are you a full agent or what?"

"Merlin's balls, Siab. How much caffeine did you have today?" Alixant's voice was a growl but I noted other than his snide comment about her clothes, he didn't say much. That meant I could wear whatever I wanted. Score. I'd take what victories I could get.

"Ooh, yes. More caffeine. What a good idea." She sprung away from us heading to a pod coffeemaker on the counter. I almost protested the horror of having such a thing but managed to bite off the protest. But if I stayed here long, I'd have to bring in a French press or something decent. Pod coffee was colored water as far as I was concerned.

"Steven, she hasn't gone home. As far as we can tell she's been here since yesterday morning," Niall said, his voice expressing annoyance and maybe if I listened carefully, a touch of concern.

I followed her with my eyes and scanned her again. But if that was what she looked like after a day of working, I was always going to be the frump in the group.

Oh well. At least I don't have to worry about being the only caffeine addict here. She'll probably love me for my coffee alone.

Making the best of a bad situation I turned to Alixant. There was no way I would ever call him his first name. Even thinking it hurt, so I avoided it.

"Agent Alixant. You want to tell them the rest? And maybe convince New York boy here that I'm not a Ronin about to go on a rampage, or at least convince him I'm not a draft dodger?"

He sat down at the conference table and glared at all of us. "We have a killer to catch. You want to deal with all these non-essentials? We don't have time."

"If you want us to actually be able to work together, I'd think it's worth the time. Don't they teach you anything about teams and interpersonal relationships in the FBI?"

I'd had two entire sessions in my various courses, one focusing on teamwork, and how important it is to connect with people on the human level. Without it you tended to dismiss or overlook others. In situations where lives were on the line, it was as important as anything. While this wasn't triage, it mattered. It was one of the reasons I'd been so frustrated at Ruby. Besides, if it annoyed him, it added an extra layer of attraction to it.

"Fine. Take seats people. Let's get this over with so we can move onto important stuff."

I gave him a look at the implication this wasn't important but he didn't notice, already typing on a laptop and bringing up things on the wall screen. Siab came on over, holding a cup of something hot. I refused to give it the appellation of coffee. The other two sat on the other end of the table from where I had taken a seat. Looking at all the shiny equipment and tech, I wondered how much of it would go up in smoke. Then I remembered about my lack of a Murphy's curse.

Huh, maybe phones and computers won't be as fragile as they have been. It would be nice to get a new one.

That idea got filed, pay would be an issue again and I didn't want to spend anything until things stabilized. Even thinking about another four years, or more, of school made me want to cry. None of that mattered now, I would just focus on the present and then move on. Nothing else I could do.

"As far as we can tell, Cori emerged a few days before her twelfth birthday. Most likely triggered by the death of her brother, so she had no idea she emerged. What is fascinating though, other than the fact it steered her into being involved with both of the cases so far, is she had a self-created and fueled Murphy's Curse and Lady Luck cloaked around her all the time. It seemed to have been an unconscious creation and was then managed the same way. While it is evident she had no involvement with the murders, she is still the only Spirit Merlin on this coast and I expect her to assist in finding this madman," he nodded giving me a sardonic smile, "or madwoman and stopping them."

All three of the agents looked at me and I fought not to shrink back. I channeled it into a smirk and looked at Niall. "So, no I didn't think I was a mage and I had no desire or intent to draft dodge. I just didn't realize I had emerged, much less that I was doing magic at all." I kept the rescue of the patient to myself. No need to confuse the issue.

"Huh. We'll see," he muttered, crossing his arms, but at least the glare had dialed back a notch. Siab looked like she was about to explode with questions, but Alixant cut her off.

"Now to the stuff that matters." The images on the screen stabilized and I looked at the girl I'd found and one of the other victims from the Olympic Park. They still looked like nightmare fodder but after the redrum ball, they couldn't even faze me. At least I hadn't killed these, vicariously at least.

"I know what you have been working on, but right now we are still nowhere. Victim one. Jane Tanner, and apparently we have Cori to thank for getting her identified also." Something heavy was in his voice I didn't understand.

He must have seen my funny look, because he continued. "It was your suggestion." My face must have still shown something, because I didn't know what he was talking about. Alixant heaved a sigh of exasperation as if he was dealing with morons. Whatever my look had been, it changed to a glare as I moved over and took the seat farthest from him. He pretended not to notice, but he did expand. "You suggested they check the OMO databases since even hedgemages are registered if they test. They found her. One Jane Tanner. Pattern hedgemage. Enough so that she'd doing well playing solitaire and putting together puzzles. I've received word that so far, all victims found at the Olympic Park were also mages." He turned and pointed to an image on the screen, a picture of where all the bodies were found.

Before he could start talking, I interrupted. "How many of the victims lived?" This froze the room and he looked back at me. "Eight are still alive, but it has been verified all of them are in a vegetative state. Next of kin are being contacted and they will most likely be harvested."

If possible, an even greater pall settled over the room, but my mind raced. That comment set off a lot of other ideas. "Are you sure ritual magic is being performed?"

I remembered the weird waves in the sky, but that didn't mean anything. I'd also seen one, I thought, when Elsba was hunting.

Siab piped up, "Oh, ye-"

"Stop." Alixant's voice cut her off and she stopped like someone had hit the pause button. She didn't look intimidated, more resigned. With a quirk of her mouth, she leaned back and waited. Alixant turned to look at me. "What are you thinking?"

I resisted the urge to shift in my seat as his gray eyes locked on me. "The manner in which they were controlled. I haven't seen the med reports or anything, but from what I heard before I was so rudely dragged off," I paused to glare at Niall and Chris. They both just shrugged and seemed unaffected. I needed to ramp up my glare ferocity. "They were all disabled in a way that preserved body functions for a decent amount of time but destroyed upper cognitive abilities, I THINK," I stressed that. "I don't know, but if that is the case, what if this is all a massive cover up to get someone an organ that they are on the transplant list for?"

Alixant whistled and leaned back. "That is quite a theory. Got anything more to go on?"

I shrugged. "I don't know that it is anything to go on. I don't know if the puncture wounds damaged organs or how many were donors. Just that one thought struck me because of a comment. Some specific organs are always hard to get and it's darn near impossible to game the system. But if you flood it with organs even someone low on the list might get one."

"Chris, put it on your list. I want blood types, donor status, and who all the organs go to."

I expected protestations. The donor list was supposed to be confidential information, but he just nodded and started typing on the computer in front of him. All of them seemed to have, or have brought, a laptop with them and were clicking as we talked. Once more I felt like a complete outsider and I fiddled with my coffee mug. At this rate I'd need more just to give myself something to do.

"Then if we're ready to pay attention." He pointed to the screen. It was a high shot, maybe from a chopper or from a nearby building, showing all the black-covered bodies or outlines of the ones we had taken. The five Olympic rings were obvious, but I couldn't not see the bodies. It kept distracting me. I had no idea what he thought we would see. "At this time there isn't an obvious layout. Ritual magic, contrary to folklore, seems to be more on what the person doing the ritual regards as important. Numbers, patterns, all of it can vary from person to person, but for the most part you have to get university training to get the basics."

"No, you don't." The words slipped out of my mouth and they all looked at me again.

At this rate I'm going to get burned to a crisp by all the people staring at me.

"Yes you do," Alixant said slowly. "To get access to training and ritual magic, much less how to use it, you must be enrolled in a university program and be in your senior year or your graduate program."

"Okay, maybe. But all the books are in the university library. While you aren't allowed to buy most of them online, they ask for your Mage registration id if you try, you can easily read them at the library or you can just check them out." There were some things that were considered restricted information, like with porn you had to be eighteen. Well, for magic texts you needed to provide a mage but no one looked that carefully.

"That requires you to be registered at the university."

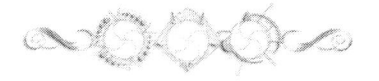

I wanted to roll my eyes. I'm not sure how I didn't. "For anything. You can be taking classes part-time and get a library card, or you know, borrow your roommates? Most of the time you're using the self-checkout anyhow. I'm just saying if you wanted to learn ritual magic, it wouldn't be that hard to learn yourself. Or if you had a mage friend or relative, get them to buy you the books."

"There are days when I over think things too much." Alixant actually sounded exasperated with himself. I didn't know if that was good or bad. "I was so sure it had to be a trained mage that it never occurred to me they could have taught themselves. That makes our job a hell of a lot harder."

Because I was curious, I asked my questions about the marks. "Did you verify the symbols being carved into their chests?"

"Yes. They were the three main mage symbols, but done roughly, with no detail to them. Of the twenty-seven people, they all had the symbols." He replied as he started bringing up the images of all the victims. It hurt to see them there. One image of them alive and happy, the other right next to them their dead, or as good as dead face.

"What about Jane? What did she have on her?" I rolled the girl's name around in my mind. So simple and short, just like her life.

"Chaos. We still don't know why as we didn't find any other symbols anywhere else," Niall answered, still snarky. "Unless you destroyed them when you found the body."

"I don't touch crime scenes and I never went closer than five feet. Either they weren't there, or you missed them." I snapped back, annoyed already. I took another mouthful of coffee to try to keep myself from doing something truly stupid, like braining him with it.

"Enough. Niall. Give it a break. Even the Psychic mage said she had no idea she'd emerged, much less at twelve. Cori, I believe you. We are all just a bit on edge and the pressure we are getting is high to solve this."

"What about the other murders?" I don't know why I asked that, but once again everyone looked at me.

"What other murders?" Alixant asked the question slowly, almost like he was scared of what I might say.

I shrank back a bit, but pushed on. Laurel had told me I had a good instinct for this work. Since I was now in it, why ignore what I felt or thought. "Look, numbers in ritual mean patterns. You can't go from one to twenty-seven, it doesn't make sense. There should be a three or a nine or something. That jump makes no sense. If one wasn't powerful enough, why would you instantly jump to twenty-seven?"

It seemed reasonable to me, but they just looked at me and I wondered how much of an idiot I'd just proved myself as.

"She's right. It's what's been bugging me. There has to be more," Chris said slowly. "There is no pattern. That's why I can't put it together."

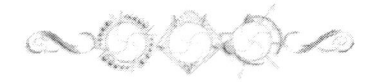

"And one to three to nine to twenty-seven would make sense. Lots of ritual on threes jive with human understanding," Siab put in, her eyes sparking as she leaned forward. "But the bad thing is the next number would be eighty–one."

Alixant growled looking at them. "We should have come up with this. Why is this newbie the one seeing the obvious?"

"Oh, that I can answer. Our heads are so full of patterns and previous cases, we have it all cluttered with everything that has happened before. Right now, on the surface this looks like that Zodiac case from the seventies, where the archmage wanted to ascend to Merlin, so he was draining high ranking mages. Doing them in patterns in the golden gate park. It didn't work, so no one ever repeated it."

"Or even the Strangler in New York, killing any mage higher than he due to jealousy issues until he was caught," Niall said. "We're seeing stuff from other cases in this one, and she isn't." He half smirked at me. "I'm assuming you aren't a serial killer junkie?"

"Umm, no. Ask me about weird disease or strange ways to die, exotic poisons, I'll probably know. But serial killers, not so much."

Alixant looked at us and shrugged. "Okay, Cori—what do you see?" He enlarged the scene of the Olympic park, so it took up the wall in horrific detail.

Chapter 20

Ritual magic is still regarded as something crones or herbies use, not real mages. While no one can deny some of the crones who've spent a lifetime with herbs and using their magic in the small ways can use their rituals to heal or aid, their ability to teach has been limited as every mage needs to create their own, and the success of ritual magic is low.
~Magic Explained

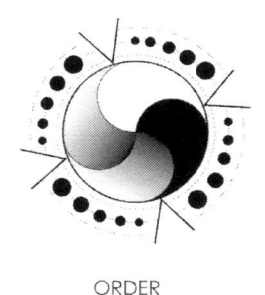

ORDER

I really wanted to say nothing because that was the answer but something niggled at the back of my mind. The image of us carting away a victim the red seeping through, and the two angry ripples in the air, like bulges almost about to tear but not quite. There was something about the bodies.

"Did you move any of the bodies before we, the medical responders, showed up?" I turned and looked Alixant.

"A few were turned over to check for life, but that is about it." He had focused on me again and I wanted to squirm.

"The positions they are in are odd. Most bodies I've seen, where the person drops dead, are more straight, often on their backs. These? The people all crumpled on the ground, like puppets with their strings cut. They weren't even all on their backs. Were the cuts done while they lay down or while they were standing?" I went over the wounds in my head again. I'd have to talk to a doctor to be sure but most of them that I'd treated seemed to have an upward tilt to them, like someone driving the blade up.

"Do you have the ME reports yet?" I wasn't a doctor but the medical examiner's report would tell me a lot about the wounds.

Alixant arched a brow at me and I realized I'd interrupted a discussion between him and Niall. I fought back embarrassment. I really hadn't noticed they were talking, caught up in my own little world.

"No. Should get it by Tuesday."

I nodded and sank back. I couldn't think of anything else. There had to be other murders, and I knew some medical stuff. My so-called Merlin status didn't seem to do me any good but I didn't know what else to do. I closed my eyes and wanted to be back at Ruby, no matter how they treated me. At least I knew I could be useful there. Here, I had no idea what I was.

Learn, you can always learn. Maybe something will lead you to Stevie's death.

I turned to Siab, forcing a smile, but when she saw me her smile made mine real. "Can you tell me about ritual magic? I mean, I was going to check some books out on it but I don't know anything."

Her smile changed her from interesting to vibrant. "I warn you, once I start talking, it's hard to get me to shut up. And since you're a Merlin, you'll get all this when you get to those classes, so I'll skip the basics?"

"I just don't know the basics, but I figure focusing on what is going on with these murders is the important part. But I think I'm here because I decked him and it pissed him off."

"You decked Steven Alixant? I mean, really? With your fists?" Her eyes widened and I couldn't tell if her astonishment was horror, or amusement, or shock.

"He tried to stop me from helping someone. Besides, it's not like I knew who he was then. Or now, for that matter. I mean he's a merlin doing his draft service."

Her mouth opened, paused, then she snapped it shut shaking her head. "That is one conversation that needs drinks, and no listening ears. Back to ritual magic." She paused as she brought something up on her computer but I got the feeling she was more trying to organize her thoughts than anything else.

After a minute she nodded and brought up the image of the first girl, Jane. I didn't cringe, though it took me a moment to recognize her. Lying flat and nude, and the wounds on her chest were visible. There were things I hadn't seen when I found her. The eyes, peeled away face, and her missing heart had taken all of my attention. While there was still a gaping hole right below her sternum, this time I could see the cuts her clothes had covered.

"He dressed her after she was dead?"

"Yes, but almost immediately after. I think he is an Air mage and is creating illusions, so no one sees him as he is working. Then he drops it and walks away. I think, and this is all supposition, the heart and eyes were the offering-"

I cut her off, eyes wide. "Wait, you can do offerings of other people?"

She ducked her head. "Bad choice of words. Let's say it was what the unsub thought would be a good gift or something for whomever he was trying to summon. But that is what doesn't make any sense."

"Wait, back up. I'm lost." I hated to admit that but at this point I was confused and felt like I was missing pieces. Okay, I knew I was missing pieces, but none of this made sense.

"I'll explain, starting at the beginning might be good for all of us." Alixant's voice interrupted and I looked at him. I'd been unaware he was following our conversation. But rather than looking at me, he put the picture of Jane and the park up on the display.

"The body was found on July 24th, but they suspect she was killed at least twenty-four hours earlier. Forensics examined the scene but found no markings outside the ones drawn on the tree. After taking the body to the morgue and doing and examination, the following was discovered." He clicked and the picture zoomed in to focus on the cuts on her stomach. "The drawing of the chaos symbol was done while she was alive and breathing, the blood tells us that, but there were no indications of struggle or pulling away. She is currently being checked for the same brain damage as found in the Olympic park victims. The eyes were taken next and then the heart. There is no information as to what the heart or the eyes could be used for but there was no trace of them found at the scene. At that time the police considered it a simple murder and the prevalent theory was that the symbols and posing of the body were to cover up some sort of mugging gone wrong or domestic dispute."

I gave him a look at that, but he ignored it. Detective Stone had not made it seem like that. He made it seem as if something had gone on with her death.

"I got Fran out to the park after the Olympic deaths and she verified some magic was done there but the traces were too subtle for her to track. With the running water and the number of people over that area, most traces were obliterated."

"Can't you just not leave traces? Or not use magic?" I felt stupid for asking but as that ball had showed, it was easy enough to kill something with brute force and malice.

"But the entire point is magic, they are doing a ritual," Siab piped in and I wanted to scream. None of this made any sense. Why in the world was I here?

"Which means what? What is ritual magic? I mean, I've seen a movie or two, but they always show it as a way to channel and amplify or maybe summon something. I don't know what is or isn't real."

"God, you wanted the Ritual Witch series, didn't you?" Niall sounded totally dismissive. "That was just young adult drivel. It wasn't worth the time to watch it."

"I was a young adult when it came out. The young woman was caught between a Merlin and a non-magical, unsure if she would emerge and she had to decide whom to love. It was amusing. And the special effects were incredible," it came out as a protest, almost a plea, to understand and I growled at myself silently.

Why in the world am I justifying a movie and book series I loved a few years ago? Not like it didn't make billions, so I wasn't the only one that watched it.

"Yes, you can use ritual to amplify some spells, but it takes time to set up and the effectiveness is debatable. Some herbies use them to intensify the remedies they use. And I know of one merlin who uses it for his planar research. But most people find it too much effort as what works for one person won't work for another. While summoning something from the other planes is possible, the only successful ones I've heard of have summoned familiars and without fail, they never went to the summoner. So that hasn't been popular for a few decades. Movies not withstanding, there are no documented successes of summoning demons or angels from the other planes."

"Are there demons or angels?" Everyone just shrugged, which didn't make me feel any better. "So if familiars won't choose you, why or what are they summoning."

"That is what we need to figure out and stop them before they succeed. It looks like they are playing, and since ritual magic is so much about intent, what they may or could do, worries me."

I sat back and looked at them and it finally clicked. Alixant had grabbed me because he didn't have a clue. No idea who or why, and he felt there was something about me being a Spirit merlin that might give him the edge they needed. I still thought there were at least two murders we didn't know about. None of this made sense, but that didn't mean anything. I'd studied how to heal people, not why people hurt others. Just because I'd been a pretty good with the Rockway police didn't mean I had even the slightest clue what I was doing.

"Why do you think I can help? What is it about me being a spirit merlin that has you excited?" The blunt question felt like I'd just announced we only had decaf coffee left.

All the agents turned to look at Alixant, the same question obvious on their faces.

He groaned. "Why can't I just get people that do their job and don't ask questions? Or throw fits with their magic?" He gave the cuff of his shirt that had almost fallen off a morose look.

"Because you'd rather get the job done right than deal with yes agents?" Siab said, leaning forward to watch him, her tiny frame dwarfed by the table and office chair. From the side view the many braids she had caught my attention, and I wondered if I could do that. If my hair started to grow that was.

"Yes agents, that I should be so lucky." He rubbed at his face, then turned to me. I itched for a notebook or something. Since I didn't have one, I leaned back and paid very close attention. "For reasons we don't understand, Spirit Mages have an affinity to Planar rips. We believe it is these rips that allowed magic to seep into our work. I'm sure you know the history, so I'm not going over that. But merlins seem to be able to control or even heal these rips, if they can get to them in time. I rather wish you were strong in Soul, because that class has the best chance to deal with them, but pale is better than nothing. If I can get you near a rip and you believe you have magic, there's a chance you might sense where the rip leads and maybe heal it. Hopefully, before anything bad comes out."

I choked on a laugh. "You want me to heal something I've never heard of? With magic I've never used? And figure out how to do it with no training and no idea what it might cost?"

He leveled dead gray eyes on me. "Yes. Or all of Atlanta might pay the price."

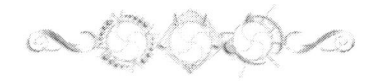

Chapter 21

Remember, a well-educated mage is a long-lived mage. Get your degree and survive to see your grandchildren.
~OMO Slogan.

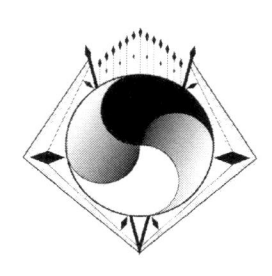

SPIRIT

Nothing else was accomplished the rest of the afternoon and I escaped by three. There wasn't much I could do and I didn't know anything to help and not just ask annoying questions. Refusing Siab's offer to drive me home, I walked to the bus stop, lost in thought.

I couldn't deny I was a mage, though I now understood why Shay wore hats all the time. The looks on the bus weren't as bad this time but I sensed more hoodies in my future.

Settling in, I stewed all the way home. This was a waste of my time and energy. Sure, if they had something happen, I'd help, but until college started, and I still needed to apply and everything, I'd work at Ruby. There at least, I could be useful. If my coworkers would even accept me back. That worry scraped across raw edges, but even if they didn't talk to me, I'd be able to help people. At least for a while.

By the time I got to my stop, I almost felt calm. Climbing up the stairs I opened the door to the apartment and smiled as the welcoming smell of con carne wrapped around me. I walked in, dropped my bag on the table and smiled into the kitchen.

"You're spoiling us, Tia."

Marisol beamed at that moniker, but then she looked at me and her smile took on a sly edge. "Welcome back, Cori. And since you are no longer a walking disaster personified, you can come help."

I hesitated. A lifetime of learning that anything I did in the kitchen was a recipe for disaster made me over think, but it had been a full day since anything had happened. That struck me then. I'd been in that office with all those computers and nothing had fritzed or gone haywire. Well, outside of my attack on Alixant. I couldn't even lie to myself that it had been an attack.

"I'd like that." Five minutes later, hands washed and my stuff put away, I was in there helping. I'd always loved the magical science of cooking but for the first time that I could remember, nothing went wrong as I helped. We had con carne, refried beans, tortillas and her secret rice, though we all knew the secret: saffron, cilantro, peppers, and just enough orange juice to make it sing.

We had everything mostly done when it dawned on me this was Saturday. Not a weekday. "Where's Jo?"

"Oh, I sent her on an errand. She should be back soon. Help me set the table."

Her voice was too light, too casual, but I had no illusions I'd be able to pry anything out of her, so I dropped it, content to wait. With Marisol here the table was getting a workout, even if the three of us were crowded using it.

"You do know it is driving me crazy not to ask about your day," she said we she filled water glasses.

"I had wondered, but honestly there is not much to tell other than me asking stupid questions. I really think I'm there just because I pissed people off so much."

"Are you going to stay?" Her tone was too casual, and I frowned.

"I have a choice?"

"Of course. Granted someone else has to lobby for you, but you aren't ever required to take the first government agency that offers you a job. Think of it like getting your degree and getting job offers. It is up to you." She shrugged. "While this man may have immediate precedence due to the deaths, you still have a degree to complete before you really need to worry about that."

I opened my mouth but the door opened, and Jo came sailing in, all bounce and joy. More joy than I'd seen a while. Once again that niggle of worry ate at me, but I couldn't place it.

"Did you get everything?" Marisol asked and headed over to her daughter.

"Of course." Jo handed her a bag.

"Excellent. Come on Cori. Sit. Jo, go clean up."

"Mami, I'm not exactly dirty. I went to the store, not the shop." Jo said, her tone amused.

Marisol shook her head. "Sorry, habit. You're usually covered with grease and other stuff when it is dinner time. Then wash your hands and sit down."

Jo was already at the sink, still snickering. Marisol flushed a bit but waved me to my chair. "Sit, both or you."

I did, but I had no idea what was going on. They were both grinning and almost giddy, so I wasn't worried, just wary. Jo in that good of a mood often spelled mischief.

They both settled down, and Marisol handed me two items. One a set of three books wrapped in brown paper and a ribbon, the other just looked like a card.

"What? Why?" I just stared at them until Jo shoved them into my hands.

"Your emergence gift, silly."

"But, I, I mean-"

"Cori, I couldn't get you what I wanted as this wasn't something we'd planned, for, but we love you and you deserve an emergence gift as much as anyone did."

I wanted to protest, but all I could do was hold them fiercely too myself.

"Open them. Maybe they aren't quite as cool as a new motorcycle, but I don't think you would have enjoyed that gift, much less getting it up and running," Jo teased, nudging me with her hip as she started dishing food on all our plates.

I moved over to the side, paranoid about getting food on them. My hands shook and I didn't know if they shook from excitement or nerves. I opened the envelope first. I pulled out the card and the piece of paper in it. It took me a full minute to try and understand what I saw.

"A certificate for a spa here in Atlanta?"

Marisol shrugged. "I know you've been so focused on school and now it is going to start over again. I just thought you might like to go get a massage, maybe have one of them show you things to do with your hair. Since I'm pretty sure it will start growing. You could get it colored or use it if you want to get fancy for a date?" She sounded hopeful and I ducked my head.

For everything I had talked to Marisol about I'd never talked to her about my lack of sexual attraction to anyone, male or female. Since I still didn't know how I felt or why, I wasn't going to discuss it.

And what does that have to do with getting a massage and a facial? This a treat and will probably be fun.

"Thank you. I've never been. Are massages nice?"

"Oh, they are addictive. Maybe every month or so we can set up a girls' weekend and go?" It was an offer, tentative but a real offer.

Jo's face lit up. "I'd like that. A break from the every day, like once every three months. We can schedule it?"

"That would be great," Marisol grinned and it occurred to me she might miss having girls at home.

Everyone sounded enthused and I thought I might be too, but first I'd go get a massage and see what I liked or didn't like.

That led to the next package, and I unwrapped this a bit faster, then gaped. "How?" In my hands lay the four book set of the definitive magic skills, used as reference only, because they were too expensive to let out into regular hands. You had to be a Merlin to even get access to them, but in them lay all the information about magic I could ask for. Oh, lots of practical stuff was missing, like how to do offerings, the basics of using magic, and any laws surrounding them. But this, this would answer any question I had, or could think of before starting classes.

Magic of Chaos

Magic of Pattern

Magic of Spirit

I wanted to cry. I would learn so much, get so many questions answered, maybe find out something about both myself and the killer.

"Well, I might have snuck a look at your ID and your registration number. When I called, I said I wanted to get it as an emergence gift for a new merlin and provided your ID. You'll need to register the receipt of the books online in the next day or so." Marisol nodded at the slip of paper in the first book. "But I thought it might be what you needed. A car is a bit out of our league, and I couldn't see you driving a motorcycle by yourself."

"Oh yeah, no. Riding with her is bad enough."

"Well, maybe weird things won't happen anymore now that your cloaks of good and bad luck are gone," Jo fired back. "Now eat. I'm starving, and *mami* needs to leave to go back home tonight, preferably before it gets full dark."

Marsiol cast her a thoughtful look "Do I want an example of weird things?"

"No," both of us responded at the same time. I got up and put my books over by my desk, planning on reading tonight.

"Very well. So, have either of you decided about your major? Or at least thought about it?" This look was mostly aimed at her daughter.

Jo groaned, and she focused on her plate. "Just let me get through this first year. Everything is basics anyhow, nothing that I need to focus on. Then I'll go over the options and decide."

All of us were eating but Marisol focused on her daughter, a frown on her face. Did she notice the same thing I did? The odd discomfort you never expected to see on the "live life to the fullest" Jo.

"Fair enough. What about you, Cori? You think of anything?"

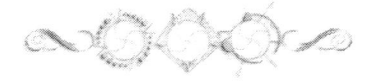

I started laughing with my mouth full and choked. A few minutes of coughing finally made it so I could talk, even though my eyes watered. I gave her an incredulous look. "I'm still struggling with the idea I'm a mage, much less a merlin. Heck, that means they are going to want me to get a PhD. I don't even know what I want to study." Though saying it made my mind sit down and start thinking. I shut off that process. I needed to get through the next month, then I'd figure it out.

Marisol sighed. "The two of you. Fine. I'll give you until next summer, but then I will be nagging both of you to lock down what you need to study, with concrete plans as to your future. Neither of you are teenagers and you need to plan."

"Yes, M*ami*," Jo said dutifully, her joy diminished in a way that hurt to see. Marisol frowned at her, biting her lip but she dropped it. "I've got to head back soon. Henri says he misses me."

We spent the rest of the dinner with me looking longingly at the books and enjoying Marisol. Jo perked back up, teasing me about needing to do my share of the cooking.

"Fine, but that means you need to do your share of the cleaning."

"Huh, I think I'll stay with cooking. It's easier."

When Marisol left Jo dug out her books and started on homework, while I reverently cracked open Magic of Spirit and started reading the first chapter.

Chapter 22

Knowing how to do something is one thing. Knowing if you should do something is what takes time to learn.
~Merlin Arthur Conan Doyle

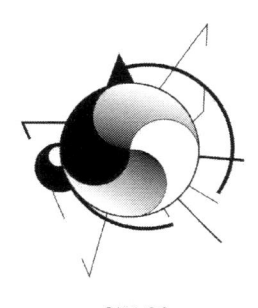

CHAOS

WHOEVER had written the Magic Of books, knew their stuff, and had managed to write in the world's most boring manner. But either way I persevered until ten. Then I started getting ready for bed. Jo had given up an hour earlier and was watching a TV show on her laptop and headphones.

My phone went off with a jangle and I frowned at it. Usually Jo was the only person to contact me. I picked up the phone not sure who it could be, probably spam.

`You do not need to come in tomorrow.  A package will be delivered to you tomorrow.  Read it and study what is in there.  Be ready to leave by 7:00.  Siab will be picking you up.`

I suspected I knew who it was, but that had nothing to do with not wanting to pull his chain.

`Who is this?` I texted back, waiting.

`Steven Alixant.  Don't be late.  Dress professionally.`

How in the world did he get my number?

I managed outrage for a whole thirty seconds, before remembering all the interminable forms I'd filled out which included my address and phone number. I wrinkled my nose in a glare at my phone, even though it hadn't annoyed me. I refused to respond, instead I threw a pillow at Jo to get her attention. "Jo, you have any plans tomorrow?"

She tossed it back to me as she pulled off her headphones. "Nah. I'd like to get out of the apartment for a while. I'm getting a bit stir crazy."

She did seem a bit wired. "School not going well?"

"Just boring and too much sitting. At least at high school I had sports to distract me," she said, shutting down her computer, and not looking at me.

"So join one of the sports teams. You were incredible in high school." It wasn't a lie, she had been. Soccer, lacrosse, and basketball had been her sports, and she'd usually been one of the most valuable players.

That got a smile from her as she stretched, doing that silly pose again. "That would be nice, but mages aren't allowed to play. Risk of your magic helping even unconsciously is too great."

"Ah, I guess I could see that. But hey, I know I need to join a gym; want to do that with me? As well as find a coat? Or something. The FBI jerk says I need to look more professional. And I really need to exercise more."

"Oh, that would be great. I might not get fat with the magic stuff, but that doesn't mean I'm staying in shape and already I'm missing the work at the shop. I didn't realize it was almost a full body workout each day."

"Good. I'm off tomorrow and except for reading a book the jerk is sending me, I just need to shop, and we can join a gym."

Jo tilted her head at me. "What about money?"

I froze, then sighed. "I hadn't thought about that. Dang it. I'd just gotten used to having a regular paycheck."

With extreme reluctance, I picked up my phone and texted him. `What about a paycheck? Otherwise I'm going back to work. I have bills to pay`. I didn't need to be nice, cause he wasn't. At least that was the excuse I would use.

`Paperwork Monday. Already have full rent waived for your housing. Salary to be determined.`

I looked and shrugged. "Well apparently we don't need to pay rent anymore. So unless we join a super fancy gym, I think I can handle it."

"Yay. I'm going to get you in the best shape of your life now that we don't need to worry about treadmills exploding when you walk by."

A feeling of dread settled into my soul and I suddenly regretted this idea very much.

We crawled into bed and I set an alarm for nine. I might as well enjoy sleeping in. Who knew when I'd get to do it again.

My dreams that night were distracted by someone's cat crying, a soft plaintive mew. It was loud enough it that almost woke me up, but not quite and just enough that I muttered about people and crying cats that morning in the shower. We headed out and Jo was bright and cheerful. We found a coat, signed up for a gym a block from our apartment, and had lunch out. I'd also, much to Jo's amusement, found a floppy fedora-like hat. It was a burgundy color I loved and flopped enough that with my hair brushed forward most of the merlin symbol was not obvious. It made me feel better to not have it on display. I'd have to get used to it but for right now, I could avoid.

Part of me hated every minute out in public, people glancing at our temples. I was so used to the dismissal that the double take and the wary step back caught me off guard every time. Going back to the FBI office seemed like an escape by the time we got back to the apartment. I was exhausted and just wanted to hide from everyone and everything. A package waited at the doorstep.

"What's that?"

"Oh, this must be what the jerk said he was sending to me." I picked it up and frowned. It wasn't the normal sender I mean, who didn't get things from Amazing but instead, from Quantico? The desire to set it back down and back away slowly washed through me. Instead, I picked it up and started to unlock the door.

"Well, hello neighbors." We both turned to see Nathan leaning against the door jam. I'd turned in a such a way my left side faced him, not the side with the tattoos.

I'd seen him a few times, each time I was rushing somewhere, so other than a "Hi," I'd been too busy to worry. But from the sigh Jo heaved and the way she stiffened, I guess she hadn't been so lucky.

"Hey, Nathan."

"I don't understand why two good-looking women aren't having guys beat down their door every day. You should let me take you out and show you the best places in Atlanta." While his words were friendly, the leer made me wrinkle my nose. He didn't scare me but there was nothing about his invitation that made even interested in knowing him as a friend.

"Again, I'm a lesbian. Your dangly bits don't interest me at all," Jo said, boredom obvious.

"How would you know that? You haven't' seen what I'm packing or experienced how I could make you feel." His response was instant, and I looked at him, stunned. While in high school Jo had dated the occasional guy, after her first kiss with a girl, she'd spent weeks in rapture over it. How great the kiss had been, the softness, the full breasts, all the things she'd never cared much about in a guy she loved on a girl: stomach, ass, shoulders, back. You'd have thought she'd discovered a new chocolate.

"Are you really that much of an idiot?" The words slipped out without conscious thought. Me and my stupid smart mouth.

He bristled, straightening from the slouch he'd held just a minute before. Jo stiffened and I wondered what else he'd said to her.

"Are you calling me stupid?" He demanded, looming suddenly.

"Well, you just implied that by looking at your genitals Jo would suddenly become delirious and decide, after almost a decade," I might have added a few years to get that, but it sounded better than six years, "She would decide that women didn't do it for her anymore and become hetero or at least bi. I would think anyone getting a college degree would have more than enough intelligence to know it doesn't work like that. You can't turn on or off what you like, what makes you happy."

He sputtered and had his face flushing.

"Though maybe that's why you are still here. You haven't figured out how the world works yet. Much less how to interact with people. What is this, year five, or six?" I tapped my chin thoughtfully to make it look like I was pondering. He was one of the mage students, but from his reaction I figured I was right, though it had been a complete shot in the dark. He just seemed like the type to always stay a student and avoid having to work.

"You know nothing. You're just a hanger-on riding your friends coat tails while you get cheap rent. Does she know you're using her for her mage benies? Or did I misunderstand and you're paying on your back?" The cruelty in his voice slapped me.

I was stunned to realize a week ago I might have flinched at that and worried it was true. But now, a feeling of cold dread at this is how power abuse started flashed through me. It didn't prevent me from turning and looking at him fully, my merlin tattoo bright in the sun.

His eyes went wide, and he paled. "Wow, um, sorry. I didn't realize. I was just being friendly you know. I won't bother you. Please ask if you need something." He was backing up as he spoke. "Sorry to bug you." And he slammed the door shut. You could hear the lock sliding home from the other side.

"What in the four planes was that?" Jo sounded bewildered. Me, I wanted to be sick. Disgust coated my tongue and I needed to brush my teeth, badly.

"That was power abuse," I muttered as we headed in. I dropped the book on the table and all but ran to the restroom. A few minutes later, the bile had mostly ebbed but I still felt raw, somehow dirty. I'd just threatened him. And I hadn't needed to say a word.

"Explain." Jo had her arms crossed glaring at me. I sighed.

"What have you done outside of college since we got here?"

The question threw her off balance and she dropped into her desk chair, turning it to look at me. "Not much. Lunch out, shopping with you. That week off we had at Six Flags, but everything else has been school."

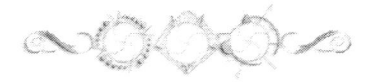

"School where most everyone is mages. Or with me? A normie?" The decision was still out if that was an insult or not, but it fit, or at least it had.

Jo frowned at me. "You know I don't care..." She trailed off and looked at the closed door. "Oh."

"Yeah. That was me abusing power because everyone fears a merlin. That was something I didn't know until lately. And I don't like it."

Jo sighed and pulled me into a hug. I almost resisted. I felt dirty, like a million showers could never get me clean. It sunk in, just how most people viewed mages. We were dangerous, and if you were a merlin, then you were the most dangerous one around. But I sank into her hug for a few minutes as I mourned one more thing this unwelcome event had cost me. Another chip in my rose-colored glasses.

After a muted dinner, I opened the package sent from the FBI office in Quantico. That was strangely cool I couldn't even get up the energy to care but the book drew some interest. Magical Rituals. It was a slim novel, especially compared to what Marisol had gotten me. Suspecting he'd probably quiz me in the morning, I opened it and started reading. In a few minutes, reality disappeared and I was deep in the magic of ritual making.

Chapter 23

By controlling knowledge, you control people. When you are dealing with people capable of destroying lives, buildings, governments with a flick of a finger, control becomes very important.
~Vladimir Ilyich Ulyanov

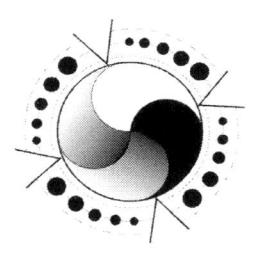

ORDER

Getting up Monday wasn't any different than any other day, but once again I was on the morning shift. Figured. The bonus to the day was the email from Ruby EMS terminating my employee and saying they would deposit my final check that afternoon. It didn't make me feel better, but at least I still had a bit of money. I dug through what I'd brought from my apartment and found a French press and some decent coffee. If I had to do this, it would not be in an under caffeinated state. They slipped in my small backpack and I headed out the door as I heard Jo start her shower.

I walked to the bus stop, having made a note of where I needed to go, and caught the bus there. This time I wore my hat, and I didn't care that it probably looked ridiculous. With my hair brushed forward, while you might see the edge of one of my marks, you didn't see all of them. I felt better but had already decided on hoodies as soon as it cooled down at all.

I spent the ride reviewing what I'd learned, which I figured everyone else already knew, so it would just help me not ask the obvious. But I couldn't figure out how learning about ritual magic would help. From everything I read, it was personal; no two mages would do the same thing to achieve the same result. So while we might suspect they were using ritual magic, we wouldn't be able to replicate it because we weren't focusing on the same thing. And even if we were, the symbols used wouldn't mean the same thing to us.

Then you add in the fact that the author had referenced a study saying their current breakdown of magic was wrong, and everyone had access to at least 1%, figure a weak hedgemage. It was something so small no machine could test it. But that meant even the most magic free human could use ritual magic if they focused and were very specific and careful. It made it scary, yet also rare that it succeeded.

Then why is this person even trying?

I thought about it as I headed in, trying to figure out what they wanted badly enough to do that. Or, maybe it wasn't want. Why did I do things? Fear, Need, Desire. I couldn't come up with anymore.

This is stupid, this isn't my job. I have no training for this.

At this point I hadn't even thought about what I might like to study for. That was yet another stack of paperwork I was waiting to get. All the suggestions and ways various skills could be used. I'd think about that later. I had some time, and I wanted to make the right choice, though the idea of testing out of a few classes ripped across my head. I stopped mid step. I had my degrees, I should be able to start as a junior or at least a sophomore, maybe higher.

That realization buoyed me until I got to the door. The card key access door. I peered through the window, but there was no helpful security guard to let me in. Reluctantly, I pulled out my phone and scrolled through my text messages.

`I can't get in.`

I stared at the phone. Five minutes I was leaving.

`Siab will be there shortly.`

I started counting in my head but it being the lone other woman made me reluctant to just walk away. Either way it didn't matter. Before I reached ninety, which would have been a minute and a half, the door pushed open and her smiling face greeted me. "Morning, Cori. Come on it, Chris has been here since six. He says he thinks he has something."

I followed her in, wondering how anyone could be so cheerful at not even seven in the morning. It was unnatural.

"I researched more this weekend, but I don't see anything that points to what they are doing using ritual magic. It doesn't make much sense."

"Yeah. I read some this weekend but I'm not sure looking at ritual is the way to go."

And why am I talking? My plan was to nod and not say anything.

I stifled a groan as she shot me a glance, unlocking the last door.

"That sounds interesting. What do you mean?"

I shrugged as we went through the door, not sure I wanted to voice the weird ideas I had in my head.

"Everyone gather at the table. Cori, sit there." He pointed at a chair with a pile of papers and a laptop and a cellphone in front of it. "Chris, show us what you have."

"It took me a bit. I started the queries Saturday, worked on cleaning up and validating the data yesterday, and today I got a hit." He had been typing furiously on his laptop as he spoke, and the wall screen sprang to life. "Valdosta, three dead. Signs of incisions in the stomach and traces of candles found at the scene."

"Why weren't we called?" Alixant's voice was a growl and I couldn't help scooting my chair further away. I had no desire to be the focus of his anger.

"Because until I worked through the ME's report, it had been reported as either arson, suicide pact, or kids playing with magic. The official cause of these was smoke inhalation and most of them were covered in third degree burns which means they still haven't been identified. I've sent a note to the coroners to run them through the OMO first. They keep the DNA on file forever as far as I can tell."

Instinctively I ran my tongue around the inside of my cheek, remembering the swab. Knowing I was in the system, that every mage was, created an odd dichotomy of support and revulsion, but it was one I didn't really have time to explore.

"We think this mage did it?" Alixant didn't take his eyes off the information on the screen as Chris typed.

"I think it matches the MO we are looking for, and it matches the next number I found," Chris replied evenly. It impressed me he didn't respond to the aggression in Alixant's question, but then that man rubbed me wrong. It was becoming a pattern. First Chief Amosen, now this guy. Maybe eventually I'd learn to like him to. Miracles could happen.

It took me a second to translate MO to *modus operandi*. All those crime shows were coming in handy.

"Very well then," Alixant all but growled, glaring at Chris. I almost felt sorry for the man, but he didn't seem to even notice the grouch glaring at him.

"The next was only found two days ago, which is why it didn't show up earlier and the location is Savannah. The victims were all found on a boat that had been docked at the end of the marina. It wasn't until scavengers started landing on the boat in large numbers that anyone noticed anything."

My mind instantly conjured the image of birds pecking at a body taking out eyes and soft bellies. I swallowed and took another sip of my coffee. Almost out. I'd need to make some in a few minutes. Anything to distract me.

"The only thing I have is that the owner of the boat was a known hedge and there were nine bodies found. There are no signs of a struggle. One of the windows and a door was left open so the damage to the bodies by local scavengers is severe. Until the autopsies are finished, we won't know for sure if they have similar wounds but best guess it went from one victim to three to nine to twenty-seven. It follows a logical progression."

Alixant nodded, settling back in his chair. Today he looked much more sartorial, his jacket neat, his shirt and tie in place, the black matching his hair. "When do they expect the results?"

"Right now their preliminary guess is the end of next week."

"That is not acceptable, tell them I want it to tomorrow," Alixant snapped, sitting up straight in his chair. I just watched a bit amazed. If this was how most merlins acted no wonder everyone thought that we were assholes.

"Yeah, we can tell them that all we want. This what they are dealing with." He clicked something on his keyboard and a picture popped up. I hadn't thought I was squeamish. I'd seen a lot after all. I got the impression of crabs, bugs, birds and what might have been a human body. I slammed my eyes shut and stood. I didn't open my eyes until my back was to the screen and I was headed to the small kitchen area.

"Where are you going?"

I didn't care about the demand in his voice, the annoyance or anything. I kept walking, but I did speak.

"I am going to make myself some more coffee."

"We are doing things here, you need to see this," his voice sounded like he was so furious that he was about to start spitting lightening. I still didn't care.

"The only way I am going to look at that is if you want me to empty the contents of my stomach all over your nice clean suit. So I'll listen and make myself some more coffee over here."

There was a long moment of silence and a noisy swallow. I dug out my French press, put water in the electric kettle and ignored them.

"Ah, yes. Um, well. Yes, proceed." He sounded almost apologetic and his voice almost had a note of regret. "I forgot that you haven't been through training. Your insights yesterday were excellent. But why would that upset you? You've seen dead bodies."

The water boiled and I poured it over the grounds I'd already put in the press. "Yes. But there is a world of difference between a body with wounds and injuries, even in death, and a body being eaten by crabs," I spit that word out. Crabs just gave me the creeps.

"Ah." He cleared his throat. "Ask them if they can at least verify if there were puncture marks, or wounds, on the body in an abstract version of the mage symbols that would be helpful. If they can tell if these people were immobilized the same way as our other victims, that would also be helpful."

"Will do. They don't have any leads but both sites were so badly contaminated, the odds of finding anything that we can link to our crime scenes are low. But they will try." Chris paused then said quietly. "The picture is gone."

"Thanks." I carried my press and cup back to the table. It still needed to brew for a few more minutes and I'd already doctored up my cup. They all glanced at me curiously but they sniffed the air appreciatively. I hid a smirk. The secret to so many people's hearts, caffeine.

"Niall, any leads?"

Niall snorted. "No. The rips faded by the time we got back there. The area was so trampled if there was anything, we missed it."

"How did no one see anything? I mean that was a lot of bodies," I asked checking the color of my coffee, another minute.

"Either the unsub, or someone working with them, was an air mage and created an illusion so that no one walked through. But still, they must have worked really fast because that was a relatively busy park. Someone might have stepped into it."

I shrugged. "Did you ask people what they saw?"

"We're still tracking down anyone there, the person who called it in was hysterical and has blanked out most of it."

"No cameras? Aren't there cameras there?" That sounded weird to me. Most of Atlanta had traffic cams and didn't all the crimes shows always have a camera pointed that way?

"Not in that area of the park. It's usually filmed but that day there wasn't anything going on." Niall had a sour sound to his voice, and I didn't blame him.

"So we have a mage able to kill quickly and easily, prevent people from seeing him or her, and has a ritual to rip the planes open?" I summarized as I poured. The coffee scent soothed me, and I suspected I'd be needing a lot of soothing. Glancing at the pile of paperwork I needed to go through, it was guaranteed.

"Basically," Alixant admitted.

"So with the next group being eighty-one people, it will be messy. How are you going to prevent it?" I was curious. I had no idea how to even find this person, much less stop them.

"Yeah, that was what I had figured," Chris said. "Eighty-one is the next logical number."

Alixant sighed and rubbed his face. For the first time I paid attention to the circles under his eyes and drawn face.

Hmm, maybe I should cut him a little slack.

"So based on the two sets murders we know were linked what do we know about the victims?" He asked, standing and staring at the wall but there wasn't anything there.

Chapter 24

The Son of Sam and the Zodiac Killer were both believed to have been practicing ritual magic on their kills, though of a type no one could or would identify. Experts from all over the world were brought in and they would never say what they thought it would do. The Son of Sam said he just liked to draw pretty pictures and enjoyed freaking out the police. The Zodiac Killer was never caught, so it is still unknown if his symbols were actual rituals or just another way to play with the police.
~History of Magic

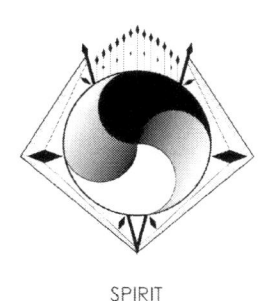

SPIRIT

Niall took that one. "All under forty, most were hedgemages, a couple magicians, all registered. Only a few of them had tattoos and only a few wore any markers, just jewelry or emblems. All were local and worked in the area. We are still trying to decipher how they were all drawn there. The Illusion the mage used was interesting. We got a glimpse from a few people who provided images they took at the park that day. There were saw horses around the water feature and a warning that the water was contaminated. No one asked and while they didn't see anyone, they didn't think anything of it." Niall paused and frowned at the report on his computer in front of him.

"What?" Alixant didn't snap it, but still made it clear he didn't want any delay. I had to learn his tricks. They were impressive.

"What I can't figure out is how the unsub got them all there. Yes it was lunch, but how do you get so many people to show up at one place? I mean the girl, and even the others, I can figure out how to lure three or nine people somewhere, but twenty-seven? That all meet his criteria?"

"I've started looking at their social media, but we are still getting id's and until I have them all, I can't lock in all the accounts." Chris chewed on his stylus while he talked, his eyes distant. "There has to be something that would get them there at once with different backgrounds."

"Flip it around," Siab said. "If you want to get a bunch of people in one place, willing to do something, how would you do it."

"Flash mob, contest, celebrity, give away, or meetup," I rattled off as I started going through and signing papers. The paper stressed not telling anyone about anything over and over, and I put those to the side. I wasn't about to give up my ability to talk to Jo. She was the only person who would keep me sane. The basic W-2s I filled out, though I still wanted to know what the salary was and the job description. So far, I had a big stack of not signed, and a small stack of signed.

There was silence in the room, and I looked up to find them all looking at me. "What? If I wanted to get that many people in one place, I'd do that. Granted, I think you'll find the real answer in their social media, but I'd bet on something like that."

Chris nodded. "Probably. Just time. Time we might not have. I can't get the bodies identified any faster, and we have no clues as to the person who did it."

Now interested, I looked at him. "I thought you were a Pattern mage. Can't you reconstruct the pattern?"

He growled and sighed at the same time. "Normally yes. I'd be able to get rough shapes to outline, get a few clues. But because he did the murders over running water, I run out of available offering before I can get a clear picture. I can get the knife marks, but the movement between victims was over the water and that requires too much to move back to where it was."

I shook my head. "I don't understand."

Alixant was frowning. "I understand, but I'd never really thought about it before. I wonder what else you could cover up with running water."

"A lot. Look," Chris spoke to me. "I'll show you." He grabbed a piece of paper and tore it into pieces and tossed it on the table. "this is simple and straight forward, but what I usually do with cases. I make an offering," a wisp of something rose from his head and I leaned in, staring.

"What was that?"

"My offering. This is simple, so only a few millimeters of hair are needed."

I stared at his crewcut and then the other two men, it registered they all had short hair, or shortish. Alixant's was at his shoulders, while Chris had a crewcut, and Niall had it only past his ears. Only Siab had long hair you normally associated with mages. "Why is all your hair short?"

Niall grimaced. "Fire mage. Last case. He fried our hair to make it harder for us to do magic and stop him."

"A serial arsonist, but even fire doesn't make things as hard to reconstruct as water," Chris said with a grin. I got the impression he kinda enjoyed explaining to me, and even Alixant looked interested. "Now watch." He waved a hand at the paper and an image of it falling into pieces reversed until the whole sheet stood there, readable, but immaterial. "Now I could take a picture or something. With water it moves constantly so every version of it is somewhere else the next second, same with air. So I struggle to get anything. Materials are easier to reconstruct."

I settled back, looking at the magic floating in the air. Being a mage sounded much more interesting now.

"All of this is fine. We know we still need to figure out who they were and why they were there. But the bigger question is how is, he going to get eighty-one people the same way, and what is the ultimate purpose?"

That didn't matter so much to me, but something else pinged me. "You know there is no way this can be a hedge or magician. To do this, they'd have to be high rank and maybe have a familiar to cut the costs. Right?"

Siab shook her head twisting a braid around and around. "Maybe yes, maybe no. If you knew exactly what to rupture in their brain, you could probably do it with less than 2-3 strands of hair."

"But what about the illusion?" I countered.

"Now that, I don't know," she trailed off. "We need to ask an Air mage how hard it would be. I've never explored illusions."

"No, Cori's right. The illusion would be at least a wizard or archmage. That would have taken a lot of work to pull off. Could we be looking at two mages?" Alixant's voice dropped a pall over the room.

"I still don't have all the bodies identified but I suddenly have a bad feeling that one of them is going to be a high rank Air mage." Chris said in a somber voice that caused spasms to run up my spine. Why in the world was I involved with this? I wanted to help people, not chase killers.

My gorge rose and I got up to put the French press away, my mind spinning.

"That adds a new twist if that is true. Why would a mage help with that? Blackmail? Threat? Can you lobotomize that carefully?" Alixant sound more intrigued than horrified. That bugged me too. Was becoming immune to human emotion part of this job? I could joke about wounds and horrible things, so how was this different?

I puzzled over it as I cleaned, needing to keep my hands active. I settled on the fact that I joked over things that were done, things I couldn't control and used it to hide my horror. They joked over what might happen. The same thing, just a different side. It made me ashamed and I resolved to be better. Just because he was an ass, didn't mean he was a monster.

I walked back over, they were going over the ME reports and I went back to paperwork. Even as I sorted forms and acknowledged health insurance, the idea of how to get that many people to do something, to do another ritual tugged at me. How would I pull that off?

A beep of my phone, barely audible made me blink and I pulled it out, already knowing it was Jo. *Hey, hope today isn't sucking too much. But wanted to ask, friend won four passes to DragonWorldCon. You wanna go?*

I looked at that and shrugged. *Sure, if I can.*

Kay-kay.

I sat there then opened the new computer, suddenly curious. It took me fifteen minutes to get it running. I had to type in all the passwords on the papers, validate my information and convince the computer that I had the rights to log in. Then connect to the wifi, and *viola*, I had internet. The lack of worry about it shorting out was nice, but then it wasn't my computer and that also relieved a bit of stress.

It took another minute to get the DragonWorldCon to come up but once I did, I blinked at how many people would be attending. Up to eighty-five thousand over a four-day weekend. It looked fun and there was so much to do. It might be would be a fun break, assuming I wasn't still stuck in this disaster.

I glanced up to see images flicking on the screen with Niall and Chris discussing something. Alixant was busy over in his cube and Siab was in hers. I could have moved to the one that had a piece of paper with my name scrawled across it, but it seemed unnecessary. Instead, I played over the weird sequence of events that got me here. Everything started with the first murder.

I jotted down what I knew. Four sets of murders. All in a one month time period. Out of curiosity, I checked the phases of the moon. I'd had a friend in high school who swore everything could be done by the phases of the moon but nothing obvious jumped out at me.

This is silly. I have no training; I know nothing.

I grumbled and kept digging through papers. The ads and images of all the stuff you could do at DragonWorldCon played on my screen as I read, and signed. Every so often the brightly colored images would catch my eye and I smiled. It really did look like fun. The science and skeptic tracks already had my attention.

After what felt like signing reams of paper, I finally hit the stuff that mattered, pay rates. I started reading the document, cringing at all the warning about this being a temporary status equivalent to a student intern and as such I was subject to hourly wage laws, legal bullshit, and more legal bullshit. Every paper I turned made me cringe, though the fact that if he made me work over forty hours a week, I would get double time and triple time on Sundays or holidays was kinda nice. By the time I hit the pay rate I was expecting minimum wage. My heart stopped when I saw the rate. I went back twice to make sure I read it correctly.

"I changed my mind. I'll work for you. You're still an ass, but I'll deal." My voice was loud enough to override the other conversations and they stopped, with Alixant sticking his head out to look at me.

He had a confused look on his face until he saw that I had was staring at the paperwork file. With a short laugh he got up and came over. "Saw the reimbursement rate, did you?"

"I'm not complaining, really, but you are paying me thirty-six dollars an hour. Why?"

"While you are working for the FBI under the waiver, you're basically treated like a contractor. So that cost is supposed to cover medical insurance, travel expenses, etc. Just government bureaucracy. Enjoy it. Your actual rate after you graduate will be higher but there will be a lot more coming out of it. Just make sure you fill out the time sheets."

I nodded fervently. That would be the next thing I did. "I wanted to ask about these." I tapped all the non-disclosure forms. "I need to talk to Jo about this stuff. If I don't, I'll go crazy because no one else will be able to talk to me."

"Let me see." He picked them up and rifled through them, then scribbled something on the bottom of the form. "Sign it here. This is a waiver for you to discuss stuff with Jo as long as you agree not to get into specific details with her, and she promises not to talk to others about it. She's a Transformation archmage in her first semester, right?"

"Yes. Though she doesn't know what she wants to do yet."

"Well, this will let you talk to her. Most of us have waivers for partners. She your girlfriend?" There was nothing in his tone that indicated he cared, just curious.

"No. Best friend since I was a kid."

"Just make sure she knows how serious this is. Anything else?"

I shook my head and handed him the papers. He wandered away and I wondered when I'd get my first check. I had a desire to go shopping, just to go shopping. The images kept cycling through, and I clicked on one. My blood went cold as the ramifications of what I read registered.

"I think I just figured out how the mage might do the next ritual," I said my throat dry with fear.

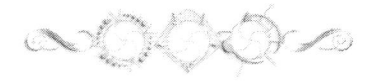

Chapter 25

Once you emerge you become a slave. A slave to the government, a slave to what has infected you. Resist. Ignore your emergence. Never use your magic. Set yourself Free.
~Freedom from Magic Group

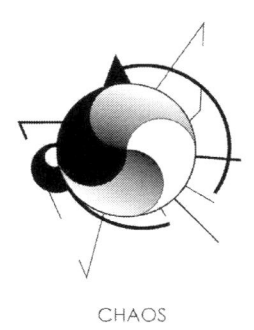

CHAOS

"WHAT are you talking about?" Alixant was up and over next to me before the words had faded away. The other two had stopped and Siab stuck her head out.

"How do I put it up on that big screen?" Alixant showed me and I flipped it up. That was neat.

"I think he'll do it at DragonWorldCon," my voice triumphant. All I got was blank stares from everyone. "Umm, none of you are local?"

They all shook their heads. "Technically we all live in Virginia now, but none of us grew up down here," Chris offered.

"My family all lives in Northern California, and I stay as far away as possible," Siab put in, sliding into the chair next to me.

"Oh." I leaned back and tried to figure out how to explain DragonWorldCon. I'd never gone, but Stinky had a few times and everyone knew about it, even if you weren't a huge geek. The convention took over downtown Atlanta once a year for the entire weekend. I'd never thought much about it, no time or money, but we were now close enough we could walk, and I could feel myself getting excited about the idea. At Ruby I'd already been warned all shifts doubled up that weekend, so I hadn't worried about it.

"Okay, this is a convention held downtown. The expected turn out is about eighty-five K over the Labor Day weekend. Entire streets are shut down. There are so many people moving around that some shops make their entire year off this weekend."

Whatever excitement they had faded. "That is just why he won't do it. Too many people." Niall said the words like I was a moron.

"Guys, you don't understand. This involves five hotels twenty-four hours a day. You can get private rooms. They have areas shut off for special events. They do everything. From concerts to shows, and people are eager to do it. How hard would it be to convince eighty-one people that they should participate in something special?" I put air quotes around the words. They fell silent looking at me.

"I've been to one convention a few years ago," Siab said, her voice thoughtful. "She's right. They had people lining up to do stuff, half the time with no idea what they were going to do."

Alixant groaned. "And if you are right? How the hell do we find it in that mess, with all those people?"

"Well, they have the schedule up, and most events or things should be on the list."

"Where is it?" The demand made me glare at him and he changed his voice a bit. "Can you show me?"

I pulled it up, and he showed me which printer to connect to. I started printing. The schedule itself was about twenty pages long. Niall grabbed it and made five copies, putting the original to the side.

"Okay everyone, grab highlighters and look at all the things you think it could be and highlight it. We'll compare in an hour." Alixant nodded at Niall to hand out the copies and they all got to work.

So much for going, looks like I'll be working.

I shrugged to myself and started going through the papers. Looking up what the different events were kept sidetracking me and the more I looked, the more I figured I wanted to go next year.

"Times up. What do you have?" Alixant called out.

"Steve, there have to be at least twenty things that it could be. Concerts where they are offering free face painting, special early workshops on everything from writing to costuming, I've got costume contests, after hours programming, all night video marathons. Frankly, I can think of about twenty ways if I was interested to kill eighty-one people." Nial stared at his paper in frustration.

"Same," said Siab and Chris. Everyone turned to look at me and I shrugged.

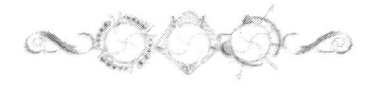

"All that plus gaming, the dealers' floor, heck people give you alcohol in squirt guns." Stinky had been very enthused with that experience. "There are private room parties that are open to everyone and some that are closed only to invitees. Some are scavenger hunts and quests that you pick up from random people. The possibilities are endless."

Alixant groaned, rubbing his temples. "Okay. Niall will you call and get us tickets, and I want rooms in one of the main hotels. I don't care what you have to promise. If this is twenty-four hours a day, we need to be instantly reachable. Chris, can you get her paperwork to HR. I want to make sure she gets paid. Not being paid means she can protest more."

It did? I'll have to remember that. And make sure every hour is recorded.

"Try for rooms on the lower floors, so you can use the stairs," I advised. Stinky had talked about having to climb twenty-three flights of stairs to hang out with a friend, carrying a case of beer because the elevators were all packed.

"Got it." Niall nodded and grabbed the paperwork and headed back to his cube. Chris followed him, his laptop in hand and the convention website up on it.

"What do you need me working on Steve?" Siab asked as she stood, stretching and causing braids to slither down her back like snakes.

"Please keep on your research about the purpose of the ritual. I've asked Cori here to read up on it and hopefully in a day or two you'll be able to bounce ideas off each other." Alixant said, standing and looking at the clock. "Cori, you're with me. I know it's almost lunch, but I want you to learn how to use a skill and look at the bodies in the morgue for me. Can you handle that?" His gaze was direct and I shrugged.

"As long as there aren't any crabs crawling on them, probably."

His lips tilted and I watched him, pretending I was someone else. He had striking looks and a nice body. Most women probably would flirt with him non-stop. As for me, I didn't trust him enough to even want to work with him. But he had made some headway on that so far. "I'll make sure they remove the crabs."

"That would be best. I've had enough coffee I'm pretty sure the vomit I could come up with would stain everything you're wearing permanently." I talked as I grabbed my coat and bag. I did, however, finish my coffee, rinse, and fill the mug with water and ice. I suspected I could use the water later. Gore didn't affect me, but long dead bodies were different. They smelled different, looked different, even felt different. Maybe that was my soul magic coming through, but the fresh dead were fine. Long dead I didn't like being around.

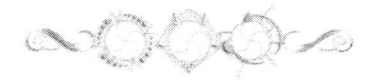

"So Alixant," I said after buckling myself into the car, "now that you own me. How exactly do you expect me to help you, when I don't know a damn thing, have limited offering amounts, and no idea how magic works?" I waved hands bitten to the quick, and hair that barely brushed my chin.

"You're still a Spirit Merlin, and stronger than any we've seen. Spirit is the rarest of the mage classes, at least per the OMO stats."

"They give you stats?" I blurted out the question, staring at him, then I wanted to beat my head. They were a government agency, even if our government didn't control them. They probably had stats for everything and secrets that no one would ever know.

"Yes. They have a website that charts registrations and strengths in every manner you could imagine, and updates darn near real time." He didn't seem annoyed by my question and I made a mental note to go look at the website later. "But you have Soul as one of your areas."

"Sure, as pale," I pointed out.

"Pale is relative. Again, this is stuff you'd learn in your magic classes but your skills are compared to your primary. You are strong in Relativity, which means even if your Soul magic is one percent less, it is considered pale."

I blinked considering that. "I thought Pale meant you could barely use that magic."

"No. That would apply to the one you are not rated in at all. You'll find with a large enough offering, you can use all branches but most mages don't bother. It usually isn't worth the offering. But your Pale areas, Soul and Psychic are almost as strong as your Relativity. That is why I need you. Soul is so rare that I haven't been able to find anyone higher than a six that I could get to come here."

"You mean strong arm," I accused.

"Yes. Strong arm, blackmail, bribe, even threaten. But most people don't get strong in soul, and when it is secondary it is usually very secondary. Those that do exist have jobs that won't let them go or in a few cases their health and age make them frail enough that I hadn't reached the point I was willing to take that risk with them."

The jerk didn't even look ashamed. I didn't know if I was impressed by his willingness to try and stop these murders? Or disgusted by how little he cared about personal freedom and choice?

I suspect it depends on if you're the victim whose death he's trying to solve, or the person he is inconveniencing.

That thought sobered me and I settled into the passenger seat more, not looking at him, but adding mapping where we were to the mental map I'd been building. "That didn't really answer my question."

He heaved a sigh. "I suck as a teacher and I was an arrogant know it all student, but I'll try. I want you to see if you can get any impressions from the victims. As I understand it, if you touch them and make an offering, there's a chance of fleeting impressions, a moment of time and emotion that have impressed on the spirit in the moments before death. It doesn't happen all the time. As you could see from the murder ball there was intense emotions on all sides. That is needed to get that level of impression but since they were about to die, I'm hoping something caught."

"What about ghosts? Can't mages see those?"

"In theory. But contrary to the books and the movies, ghosts take a lot of something to create and we don't know what that something is. There have been verified ghosts of old ladies who died peacefully in their bed remaining for years, and some of children who just never woke up. Then there are people who are brutally murdered who don't leave a trace. We still don't know why. James was researching into it, but if he ever published anything regarding it, I don't know about it."

"James?" I had no idea who he was talking about.

"James Wells. He was the spirit mage that sensed your emergence. Some merlins can feel others emerge and James was huge in the astral walking stuff. Apparently he was on the astral plane when you emerged but it knocked him out to the point he could only remember bits and sounds. He got your name and when, but since the majority of emergences are after puberty – well..." Alixant shrugged as he pulled into a parking lot. "Look, I'll guide you as best I can. I need you to try and we'll see what happens."

Nothing. A whole lot of nothing is going to happen.

Instead of voicing my opinion, I nodded and replied, "Okay," in a voice that hid my doubts. Maybe. We'd been to the morgue once while I worked at Ruby. It was a blocky red brick building that screamed government, but nothing so dark as death. It was almost too cheerful to be where they held dead bodies. It didn't take long to get down to where they stored the bodies. It was full. Having bodies on gurneys as you walked into the morgue made me feel like I was about to star in a zombie movie. It wasn't a pleasant feeling.

"Callister. I'm here. Need access. Which ones have you cleared?" Alixant called out as they cleared the hallway.

"Anything in the long-term storage room next door. Only have about ten of the bodies done so far." The person speaking approached and an older black man with a shock of white hair walked out. Dressed in jeans, a t-shirt and a lab coat, the circles under his dark brown eyes highlighted sharp intelligent eyes. "Why, what are you looking for?" He didn't introduce himself, and Alixant didn't bother.

Men, they are such a pain I swear.

"Got a Spirit merlin, want to see if she can get anything." Alixant nodded at me and I huffed.

"Hi. Cori Munroe. Nice to meet you," I interjected, looking at the man and pointedly ignoring Alixant.

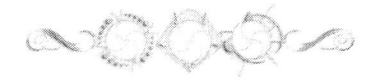

His mouth twitched and he nodded at me. "Topher Callister. Go for it. My Spirit mage couldn't pull anything, but she's only a wizard and pale in Soul, so it can't hurt to try. If you can avoid touching more than their head, with gloves on mind you, you can do the ones in the hall. Don't disturb anything." He nodded once more at us then turned, heading back into the room with more bodies and equipment.

Alixant just reached over and grabbed two pairs of gloves handing one to me. "They've all be sanitized, but no reason to be sloppy. Never know what might need to be checked for after the fact."

I rolled my eyes and pulled them on. I knew the rules of dealing with bodies. Dead didn't mean safe. Blood could still transmit diseases. He headed into a room next to where Callister had gone. I followed and stepping into a body fridge.

Chapter 26

The ability to see what the dead see sounds much more exotic than it is. People don't notice as much as you think, compare eye witness statements sometimes. Even the dead is focused on other things and when you see through their eyes, what you get might not be as revealing as you think.
~Magic Explained

SPIRIT

It was the only way to describe it. Rows of bodies on tables, all sheet draped with tags on toes. They all looked clean, cold, and too much like wax statues. I stood, seeing all the bodies as proof of our failure, my failure, to save them.

They were already dead. There was nothing I could do. I know this.

I did, but they still felt like reminders of my uselessness once again.

"You coming? We don't have all day," Alixant snapped. Force once I was glad of his arrogance. It snapped me out of the frozen state I'd been in and let me move over to the one he stood next to. Late twenties, male, probably Caucasian, was all I could tell and even that might have been wrong. Death leached the color from your skin and made people look disturbingly the same.

"So, what do I do?"

He started to snap, then took a breath and let it out. "As best I understand it, touch the body, the glove shouldn't interfere, if you concentrate, as it works through clothes. Reach out with any amount of offering in mind, two-three thousand molecules should be enough, as you are only looking for emotional imprints or impressions. Then, look to see what you sense on the body. Don't try to make it visible for me, you're not ready to try and do that yet."

"Two-three thousand molecules? What are you talking about?" I looked up at him, confused. He'd completely lost me at that.

"Oh yeah, you haven't had offering classes yet." He paused looking at me, but more like through me. "Assume a strand of hair or two. You shouldn't need more than that."

The memory of the man I swear I saw coming off the body on my first call sprang back into my mind. "Can Spirit mages see ghosts?"

"Maybe. It depends on the situation but if you are talking about seeing a spirit leave the body after death, often yes. If they are in an especially heightened or alert state, they often do it with the offering of almost nothing, as it is two forces as one. We know people have souls and they go somewhere after death. So maybe."

His non-answer helped, and I thought back to the man's expression. Surprise, confusion, but no pain. I could live with that. I still wasn't sure how to follow his instructions and wished I'd focused more on the Spirit magic book instead of Ritual. Oh well, I'd work on it tonight.

Dismissing him from my thoughts, I slowly reached out and not knowing what to do, I asked.

What do you remember?

It probably wasn't the right way to do it, as he was dead, but one of the things the book Alixant had given me stressed was that all magic was more intent on what you wanted than following a formula. The best way to explain it was that you needed to understand that if you mixed ammonia and bleach, you'd make chloride gas. With magic, your intent and your offering meant the difference equivalent between of creating a small cloud of weak, smelly gas, or enough to kill everyone in the room.

A flash of the park, water, and a touch on my shoulder, then nothing. I turned but there was no one behind me, Alixant stood off to the side, watching me but nowhere near me. Unsure, I reached out again and asked. This time there was nothing, as if I'd drained whatever was there.

I stepped back and frowned. It was so similar to my impressions of the park: green grass, trees, and the sound of the burbling water. There wasn't anything in that impression that couldn't have been a fleeting memory, or an impression of my own.

"What is it?"

"I don't know. Nothing probably, maybe?" I didn't want to say anything until I'd been able to make sure I wasn't 'seeing' things because I wanted this to work. I felt nothing, my scalp didn't itch, so I probably hadn't done anything. "Let me try someone else."

Alixant stepped back to the door, blocking it so anyone coming in would need to dislodge him. Nodding at him, I moved over to the next victim, female, middle aged, dark hair. I repeated my motions and asked the same question.

This time there was a glance at a phone, then a touch, turning, then nothing.

I pulled back with a jerk, fighting not to shudder.

That was weird.

Taking deep breaths here brought all sorts of scents that haunted you, and the disinfectant was the least of them. I tried four more times and all I got was vague impressions: the park, walking, fountains, a touch, then nothing. The memory, feeling, impression just ended.

"Well, I got something. Did the ME determine that the majority of the victims all had the same brain damage?"

"Yes. Experts say they would have been alive, possibly even still standing and made to walk via muscle memory. But their awareness, everything that gave them a sense of self was gone. The opinion is it is awfully exact and had to hit three different spots to sever just enough to not kill them instantly. They would have died even without the physical damage in the short term. The bleeds it caused in the brain would be lethal. I could get exactly what was done to each brain. Does it matter or help?"

"I don't think so. I got roughly the same thing from all of them. The park, a touch, then nothing. But always that touch they weren't expecting."

"Why do you say that?"

I had to think about it. "There was a sense of surprise, maybe even being started? It was always the shoulder or back of the arm, so they were turning to look and then it ended. That is the right word, it just cut off, like snipping a ribbon."

Alixant heaved a sigh and stood up straight. "Well, I'm sure magic theorists and research scientists would find this horribly interesting, but all it does it tell me they were lured there and then killed unaware. Merlin blast it. That means we have to get in on the next murder to even have a chance." He yanked open the door and strode down the hall.

"Callister we're gone. Let me know if you find anything."

"You and everyone else," the reply came back from the main room.

I hurried after Alixant, catching up at the elevators. "Now what?"

"Now we keep researching. You study rituals, and I'll trying to figure out what else we know and scour recordings of people entering the park. There has be something."

I had nothing to say, or even offer. We headed back, swinging by to pick up pizza from Fellini's on the way.

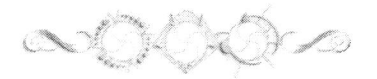

I got back, took my stuff to my new cubicle. D, and didn't that feel weird. I'd never thought I'd be in one of these. I sighed and sat down, trying to figure out what I should do besides be the pet Spirit mage and the next thing to useless.

"Got it!" Chris's shout ripped me out of the rabbit hole I'd fallen in about ritual magic. I figured I'd read that here and focus on the Spirit Magic book at home.

"And what did you get?" Alixant's dry voice came from another cubicle. I couldn't decide if Alixant having the same amount of space as us meant anything. Somehow, I didn't doubt he had a real office somewhere but he didn't have one here.

"I found out why they were all there. I got enough clues form their social media feeds and three different victims had family that were willing to unlock their phones for us." Chris wasn't babbling, he was too reserved for that, but he talked fast and was obviously excited.

He had moved over to the table, laptop in hand and dropped it down as he sat. I cringed, expecting an explosion, but it didn't react at all.

Still feels weird to not have things blow up. Wonder how long getting over that will take.

Having nothing else to do, I followed them, feeling out of place and useless, which is what I had tried so hard not to be. Sitting at the table, I didn't look at anyone, just the image on the screen.

"They had all joined up with a local contest and there was a surprise lunch giveaway where they were guaranteed to be a winner. They were told to come to the fountains and look for the man in the top hat. He would administrate the giveaway."

Images of the emails and the prizes came up, stressing only a limited number had been selected. That they had to show up to collect their prizes. The list was pretty nice, from gift cards, to season tickets to the Fox Theater, to restaurant certificates.

"That might make me show up too," Siab admitted. "The email is well formatted, everything is spelled correctly, and the guaranteed winner phrase makes it seem like something a local radio show would do."

I frowned, looking at it, but I didn't say anything. Alixant did. "Two things. Can we back track who sent the emails and figure out how many were sent? It doesn't make sense to only send twenty-seven. Someone might not have shown up or gotten waylaid. It's too complicated. And how did he know they would be near the park at lunch? This is way too complicated to be that narrow."

"I'm working on that. I can't figure out if he tracked them or if there was something else to get them to come. That is too specific. What if they were late or couldn't get away from work? Nothing has shown up yet."

Niall muttered, poking at stuff. "I'm still trying to figure out how he knew they were mages. None of them seemed to talk about it on their social groups and they didn't belong to many hedge groups. If he's super tech savvy, we might have issues. Can we get geek from the IT Crimes group to take a look at it?"

"Aren't you over thinking this?" I asked looking at them. Did working for the FBI make you paranoid and see Moriarty level complicated schemes everywhere? If so, they really made it much harder than it had to be.

"What do you mean?" Alixant demanded and they all looked at me again which was the last thing I wanted. At this rate I would be looking forward to school, just to get rid of them always giving me looks that were mixes between skepticism and annoyance.

"He probably sent it to a hundred people. He only needed twenty-seven to show up. They'd all be checking their phones and he just needed to touch them. If his spell worked the way you think, then they would just stand there until he got the illusion up." I shrugged and didn't say anything more. That part was obvious.

"But how did he target mages?" Alixant challenged.

"He'd have to have access to the database," Siab said her eyes going wide. "Any chance he hacked the OMO? Can you get records from them of any recent break ins?"

"The OMO doesn't share. Anything," the words were all but growled from his mouth.

"But you're the FBI," I said, a bit confused. Couldn't the FBI do anything or at least get anything they needed?

"The OMO is an independent, international entity that owes fealty to no one. They don't have to share any information with anyone, and they are draconian about protecting their info. They don't give anything away. If there was a hack, they wouldn't tell anyone but I wouldn't expect the hacker to have lived long afterward," Alixant muttered getting up and pacing.

"I can ask. They do have a chat center but they have always been polite but non-helpful," Niall offered looking dubious.

"Wow, you guys don't look at anything simply, do you?" I know my voice had exasperation in it, but really.

"What does that mean?" Niall looked ready to lunge across the desk and strangle me and his voice had nothing but contempt in it.

"That the OMO gives out tons of information without any issue," I spat back.

Niall sneered. " Like what?"

I sighed and walked back, grabbing my computer. Slowly I copied what Alixant had showed me and threw my screen up on the wall. I pulled out my badge. I'd put all my ID on the back of it and I pulled up the OMO website for official use. Then I typed in my id, carefully. It showed me logged in, I then typed in Niall's name. All his information popped up. His driver's license, age, ranking, mages skills, and current draft status.

My bitch side slide out and I smiled at him, a bit smug. "Anyone with official credentials can get access: police, doctors, first responders, schools. Finding out you are a mage with any official access isn't hard. Granted, he might have had to type in a bunch of names, but you can't tell me you couldn't get an automated script to do that or something." I peered back at the screen and saw Options at the top. I clicked it and one of the links invited you to upload a spreadsheet. "Or you could just upload it."

Niall sagged back, Siab smirked, and Alixant just looked at me.

Chapter 27

Don't regard the draft as something evil or even a price you must pay, look at it the same way many people regard the military. Training, a guaranteed job, and if you take the time you can walk out with a career that will provide for the rest of your life.
~OMO Ad

CHAOS

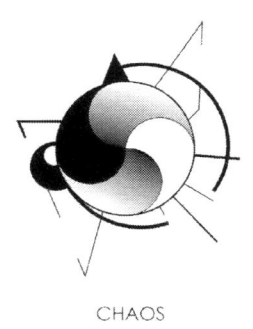

The only thing we verified over the next two days was the identification of all the victims and that they were all hedges. All my reading of ritual still went back to the fact that it meant what the caster wanted it to mean. While there were certain forms and customs, they only had power because people believed they did. That set off a vague idea in the back of my brain but I couldn't figure it out.

Late Thursday afternoon Alixant sighed and handed out badges. "We contacted the con. Here are your badges. Go. Keep your phones on you and make sure that you keep your eyes open. You all have ideas of where the killer might strike. Go and investigate; call out if you see anything at all. The police know you are there, grab them if you need them, and keep your federal ID on you." He paused, then his eyes latched on me. "Cori, come here."

Everyone had drifted away, chattering about the con so I went over to him. "I don't have time to get you a phone and frankly, for this, keeping your personal is better. Here is everyone's contact information. Get it in your phone and use it. Also, download this secure app." He showed me the one he wanted. "I'll set up a chat group with everyone. I expect you to stay in constant contact - say where you are going, and what is going on."

"Not an issue but I don't have any idea what I'll be looking for." I wanted to scream, but nothing would change. I'd read the draft waiver that tied me to him until "my services were no longer critical to resolving this crime".

"None of us do. But from your marks, you had good instincts when working with the police and we don't know how, or if, they will attack here. But, no one can come up with a better idea and since we don't have enough proof to get more help, all we can do is try."

I looked at him and really looked. Mostly I avoided him and never really looked at him, but now I did. His eyes were red and slightly swollen, his circles made him look like he was wearing goth makeup, and even his tie and shirt weren't as pristine as they usually were. He looked like the weight of the world rested on his head.

"I'll see, but don't count on me to make any difference. I don't know what I'm doing ninety percent of the time."

He gave me a tired smile that made him look more approachable than I'd seen. "I'll let you in on a secret: Most of us never know what we are doing. We just keep trying and hoping something will work. That's the key to this job, and most jobs, so don't quit trying. And getting the right people." He nodded. "Go enjoy tonight, tomorrow just show up at the con and go where you think it feels right. Right now, leave the logical stuff to us. You lean on your instincts."

"Will do."

So much for having fun during the con if I was constantly double guessing myself and trying to figure out where I should go. Oh, well, just going would be neat. Maybe next year we could plan on going again if we enjoyed it. I slipped out of the office before anyone could say anything more. I spent the bus ride carefully entering all the data. It was a lot. I got home at almost the same time as Jo. "Hey. So, I get to go to the con, but I gotta work." I held up my badge. "But do you want to go get yours? You can at least enjoy your long weekend before back to school Tuesday?" It was Memorial Day weekend, so Jo had Monday off.

"By Merlin, yes. I need away from this crap. My head is going to explode, or I'm going to fail," her voice had a bitter tinge to it that surprised me.

"Jo? What's wrong?" I touched her shoulder, but she pulled away shaking her head. Her dark hair looked uneven near the bottom where there were a few chunks missing.

"Nothing. Just school stress. Only a month in and I feel like I'm drowning in homework. Yeah, let's go get badges and have a fun weekend. Maybe party a little, drink a little, forget that I have all this school shit on top of me."

That sounded more like Jo, but it was still a bit off. "Well you get to do that. Me, I'll be working and looking for a killer."

She paused in the midst of dropping her stuff. "Do I need to be worried?"

"Yes, no? He or she hasn't gone after any high-ranking mages, but I'd be careful and make sure you don't get isolated. Wander a lot. He's going to want people in a contained area."

"How serious is this?" Her brows knitted together in a frown, watching me.

We had bounced around the idea of shutting down the con but with no proof, and only an idea that it was the killer's target, there was no way we could stop it. Not to mention the financial impact that would have everyone involved. There were enough people that we might not even know it happened until hours afterward.

"A strong hunch? I mean, there will be a lot of people there. It would be an excellent hunting ground, but the odds of him picking anyone one person, if he is there? Well, one in eighty-five thousand."

Jo snorted. "I'll take my chances." She glanced down at her tank top and shorts. "Screw it, I'm ready."

"You look fine," I said, rolling my eyes.

"Ah, I need to look sexy and drool worthy but that is too much work right now."

I dropped off my stuff. My badge hung on a lanyard around my neck and we started walking. The city wrapped hot and stifling around us but I enjoyed being outside. Sitting in the office the last few days made me ache to be outside and moving.

"So we haven't talked much lately. How you handling the whole mage thing?" She gestured at my head.

"It sucks. Everyone looks at me funny and people keep thinking I know how to do things. I don't have the slightest idea and it still doesn't make sense. If I could, I'd just go back to being an EMT."

"Oh, I feel that. I'd love to be back in the shop under a truck right now," the unmistakable desire in her voice made me shoot her a narrowed eyed look.

"What aren't you telling me?" We were at a crosswalk near the Hilton, and the people walking by snagged my attention. Thursday afternoon and already people were in costume.

"Nothing. Sorry. I'm just overwhelmed. It's harder getting into the school flow after being out for a few years. I miss working and knowing I'm earning a paycheck. This stipend stuff is annoying, and I've never been a fan of writing papers."

I laughed a bit. "Which is why I usually did half the writing for you. Your spelling is atrocious."

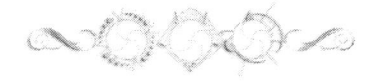

"Yeah. That," she muttered, then straightened up. "Enough. There is a con full of cute women, maybe I'll find someone and we'll hit it off."

"There's a robot track."

She half stumbled, turning back to look at me. "A robot track?"

"Yep, they build them and compete to see which robot can destroy all the others. Robot Wars, I think."

"Oh, now that sounds fascinating. What are we waiting for? There are robots to build and destroy!" Her pace picked up and we followed the stream of people to the Sheraton. It didn't take too long to get the badge, and both of us were more interested in watching the people around us than worrying about the line.

For me, people glanced at my clothes and didn't seem to care about what marked my temples. I saw people with mage symbols on their clothes, a few merlins, some wearing symbols only as jewelry, and some from other countries from the languages they spoke. For the first time since they branded me, I felt like me, not something to fear.

"I think I should get a costume," I blurted out, looking at some of the pretty clothes. I didn't want to wear anything that was barely there, like a few of them, but some outfits looked amazing.

"Oh, you can find a bunch of the more mainstream stuff when the dealer halls open tomorrow. Or if you want to learn to make it yourself find the costuming track. It's a blast." A person walking past us said, winking at both of us and continuing on, her tail swaying back and forth as she moved on.

There was a long pause and Jo swallowed hard enough I heard her over the ambient noise. "I suddenly need to own a tail." Her eyes glued to the ass of the woman turning the corner ahead of us, tail twitching.

I started to giggle. I couldn't help it. "Never change, Jo. I hope you find what you are looking for."

She turned and shot me a look. "I promise you, anyone I fall head over heels for, only makes it if she loves you as much as I do. As far as I'm concerned you are part of my life, always. Ooh, we can be a triad, and you can be the sarcastic, sane one."

That just made me giggle more and I wrapped my arm around her waist leaning my head for a moment against her shoulder. "I love you."

"I know." She said at the same time five other people around us said it. It look a long minute to click and then we began to laugh, tears streaming down our faces. It took us a while to get it back under control, and the looks we received were half wary glances and half winks and grins. I started to see why this con was so popular. It set the mode for the rest of that night. We were amazed at how much of the con had already kicked off. Jo flirted, and laughed, and was happier than I'd seen her in ages. Nothing made me look twice, though I noted a few pop-up things that might have potential over the weekend. But for that night, I ignored everything and just enjoyed having a great evening with my best friend. We drank too much, found out more about things I'd never heard of and that I now wanted to learn about. We were exposed to a world that didn't just weigh your magical ranking or your sexual interests. When we stumbled home at three A.M., I didn't think I had ever had a better day. And tomorrow was only Friday.

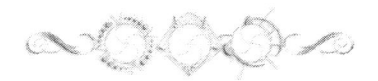

Chapter 28

While the original draft did not require college, after about two decades of service, someone in the Department of Defense noted that those with hard science degrees prior to being drafted tended to survive their draft assignment, while those fresh from high school or blue collar jobs, did not. Further research showed that understanding exactly what you were trying to do, rather than waving your hand and saying 'magic words', reduced the death rate among mages.
~History of Magic

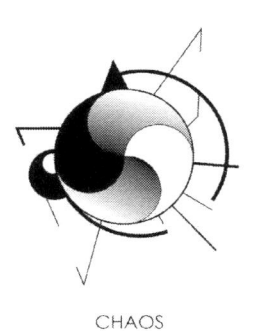

CHAOS

I stood looking at the people collapsed around me. The screaming rebounded off the walls and made it hard to think. My gaze snared on the man lying at my feet and I snapped into triage mode. I'd made sure I kept a mini first-aid kit with me, and I ripped it out with one hand, the other grabbed my phone as I slammed to my knees next to him.

"Call Alixant!" I had to scream over the sounds, but the phone caught my demand and dialed. I pulled out the gloves from the kit, snapping them on and assessing the victim.

Late twenties, breathing, marks on face seared in. Looks like an activated chemical burn.

I patted him down, looking for any other injuries, and saw motion on my phone. The video call had activated, and I didn't waste time figuring out how, instead I looked at it occasionally as I spoke. Well screamed. "Alixant, victims, Centennial Ballroom, I and II. No order to where they fell this time." Again I was all but shouting as people panicked around me, but I ignored them. If you were with it enough to run around and scream, you weren't my concern.

We'd been in the room for a panel, a sci-fi show I enjoyed. I snuck in at the end, wanting to sit for a few minutes because my feet hurt. Saturday had been exhausting, full of people so tight that breathing felt difficult. Friday had been busy, but Saturday the con slammed into you like a physical thing. The crowds of people, the costumes, the sounds, the smells, the atmosphere, they all combined to strike me as hard as a blow. Yet it was addictive and heady and part of me never wanted it to end.

Even though I longed to explore on my own, and only care about my own desires as I drifted from panel to panel, exhibit to dealer room, parade to auctions, I paid attention and looked for something, but nothing had struck me as odd or weird. Or more accurately, everything had struck me as odd and fascinating.

But here, something had flashed across my awareness and people had collapsed like dropped cooked spaghetti. I didn't know what it had been and I didn't have time to track it down. People were dying.

"On our way, do you see anything?"

"No! Focusing on the victims. So many. But can't count." My voice was fading having to shout, but the noise started to lessen, and I could feel my skin crawling as something changed.

"Cori, find the mage. That's more important now. Are there rips? You have to look, see what is around." Someone rushed by me and kicked the phone, it spun away, and I didn't care. This man was in a comatose state, breathing, and the only wound I could see was the blood and ichor seeping from the raw wounds on his face. I didn't know enough to even attempt to use my magic to do anything. Another lay a few feet from me, a female with a man holding her hand and freaking out. I crawled over to them. My body almost vibrating with pain as I felt something but her choking grabbed my attention first.

A bottle of water lay on the floor and I grabbed it, tentatively pouring a little water on the green substance still on her face. It washed away a bit and she wiggled, her body shaking.

It's gotta be an activated paralytic agent. And what else?

"Did she have something on her face? Something that might be blocking this?"

The young man, his hand wrapped around her so tightly I wondered if she'd have broken bones if she lived, nodded. "Heavy sealed base paint. She has bad acne and uses stuff that takes a special face wash to remove."

That might have saved her life.

I handed him a pair of gloves and the water. "Get it off of her as quickly as you can, but don't get any on yourself." I checked her pulse, but other than her obvious distress and pain, I couldn't see any other injuries.

What else is in that stuff? Can you activate magic like that? What is going on?

My skin writhed with phantom sensations and I turned, looking to see what was driving me crazy. With the bright lights flashing red and yellow, the TV showing cartoons in huge screens up near the stage, and the people still milling around, though more and more were streaming in, I couldn't see anything. I shook my head, swallowing to try and chase away the sensation of sharp spider legs crawling up and down my legs and arms. Part of me even thought I could feel the pin pricks of blood seeping from where they landed.

You're imaging this. Focus. People need you.

I crawled to the next person who was older, at least Marisol's age, with similar marks, on the right side, just as if they were tattoos. But where a real tattoo rarely got bigger than a half-dollar coin around the temple, this covered their entire cheek, at least double the normal size. It was no secret they were the three mage symbols, though some were strong in multiple branches, and others empty. What confused me at first glance were the different colors, but as I moved from victim to victim, finding all of them mostly comatose and bleeding, it clicked. Red for chaos, blue for spirit, yellow for order.

Primary colors. Does that mean anything?

A person lying on the floor twitched and caught my attention and I headed that way. Before I reached them, I was yanked to my feet in one fast movement by a hand on my arm. I spun with the movement, ready to attack. My fist froze before it got very far as I looked into Alixant's furious face.

"What the hell are you doing?"

I looked at him, astonished. "What does it look like I'm doing? I'm dealing with the victims. Trying to figure out what happened and how we can stop it. I've already found one person who might survive." I yanked my arm away. "Now let me go. I need to get to them." I turned, intent on getting to the person I saw twitching. Maybe their marks were different. If we could find someone else where it didn't work, or maybe rubbed off.

Before I had gotten more than a step away, my arm got yanked back and I spun, almost falling.

"We don't have time for you to waste. They are either dead or they aren't. Either way, they aren't your problem and you can't do anything."

Shock flashed through me as the screams of pain, fear, worry surround us like hell had reached in and found the sounds that drove me. The sounds I had made the day Stevie died.

"Yes, I can. I can help these people," I started to say more, but he cut me off.

"It doesn't matter. What matters is stopping this idiot, these people are dead and don't matter." His voice was harsh and angry over the sounds and I felt, more than saw people look at him, their eyes wide.

The crawling feet feelings, the eyes on my back (both real and imagined), the sounds that pulled at my heart and soul, and the need to not have more people die on me, more people I couldn't help, all twisted together into a knife made just to hurt me. It sliced in like an arrow to my heart, my soul, my magic and something broke.

It slashed out of me and the world stopped. In perfect clarity I could see every person's shocked eyes, their mouths frozen open. I could feel the three rips between the planes, now so crystal clear, gaping like holes in my mind, the source of the unease. Power I didn't have, or didn't know I had, slammed into them and they sealed even as they spit something out. Time kicked back into gear and people screamed, diving to the floor as every electronic gadget in the place exploded in a shower of sparks.

A warm, wet ball of fur slammed into me and clung, sharp points digging into my skin. The impact was enough it knocked me back, laying on the ground, with something attached to my chest and I could feel blood welling up at the points where the creature had sunk its legs or claws into me. I didn't want to look. I knew it was about to eat me like every alien monster movie ever.

This is not how I thought I'd die.

The frantic thought did nothing to stem my tie of fear as I waited to die.

And waited.

When nothing happened and holding my breath became problematic, I opened my eyes. The ceiling of the hall resolved into a dark gaping maw. I blinked a few times, trying to figure out why it was so dark.

Oh yeah, all the electronics blew.

"What in the magical fuck was that?" Alixant's voice came from my right and I slowly turned my head to see him crawling to his feet, looking rumpled and out of sorts. All around him people were picking themselves up or crawling over to the prone victims.

I watched him, still trying to figure out why I hadn't died. Shock? Maybe I was paralyzed by the creature's venom. Either way Alixant was not the last person I wanted to see before I died. It should have been Jo.

He shook himself and still looked shocky. Weaving a little he staggered over to me and stared down at me. At least I thought he was staring. I couldn't see his face, it was too dark, but doors were being thrown open letting more light in along with the sounds of panicky people coming in.

I felt the creature on my chest twitch and the points of pain went deeper as it began to rumble.

"Oh merlins, it's going to eat me," I whimpered, not realizing it had been out loud until I heard my own voice. I wanted to twitch to shake it off, but I felt like I'd been paralyzed and that any movement would cause it to attack. My own fear combined to make it impossible to do more than hold still.

"Munroe?" Alixan'ts voice had gone strangely flat.

I couldn't answer I just looked at him, almost ready to beg him to save me.

"What is on your chest?"

I blinked. Why wasn't he trying to save me? Or at the least kill it. I knew he was a jerk, but I hadn't thought he'd leave me just die without trying to do anything. A huge light panned over his face and the expression caught me. Not fear, not horror, but amused curiosity. I had to blink twice, wanting to study his face again, but the light had left, leaving me wondering if I'd really seen that.

I swear if I die right here, I'll figure out how to come back and haunt him until he loses all his hair.

Giving in to the inevitable, I slowly lifted my head and peered down to what sat on my chest.

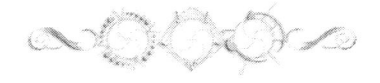

Chapter 29

We still don't know, even after decades of studying the planar rips at Area 51 exactly why the form. There are many theories, but nothing that has stood up to any hypothesis testing. The area 51 rips are stable and have only vanished once that we know of. But other rips can last seconds or years and always they open a gate to another realm with creatures that are no human and do not think or act like humans. Rips should be treated with the greatest caution.
~ Magic Explained

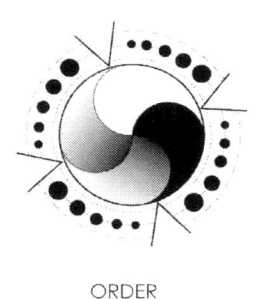

ORDER

Bright green eyes that all but glowed in the dim light, surrounded by red fur met my gaze. *Mine!* rang in my head in a voice that called forth nothing human, but screamed male and possessiveness. It held a timbre, a growl, that reminded me of a tiger's chuffing, and it felt more alien that I could express. Yet it felt right.

"Huh?" I levered up a bit more, looking at the creature on my chest. More lights were brought in, flashlights, spotlights, and all the doors were wide open now as well as the doors between the sections. The light revealed what looked for all the world like a kitten. Ears twitched back and forth even as claws sank deeper into me. From the force it had hit me with, I'd thought a monster sat on my chest but now I realized the weight on my chest was negligible. It was two pounds, maybe three at the most.

Proof that imagination is way worse that reality.

"I would say congratulations are in order but right now I need your ass up and moving. Once we figure this out, I'll follow up with what the hell that was." He fumbled for his phone, pulling out a dead lump of plastic. "Merlin's balls." He threw the useless piece of technology to the floor. I saw it as it bounced and suspected it was worse than what Jo had done to mine when she emerged.

Emerged?

I shied away from that thought. I didn't have time to deal with it but I sat up slowly pulling the kitten into my arms. At least I was pretty sure it was a kitten. I didn't have the time to look. I pulled it into the crook of my arm where it purred loudly enough that I had trouble hearing anything else-at least until Alixant started shouting.

"Niall, Chris, Siab, where in the four planes of magic are you?" The shout had me cringing back, and the kitten uttered a little growl that was so cute I felt part of my heart melt.

"Steven, I'm here. They're coming. What in the world?" Niall's voice grew softer as he approached us and looked around.

"What I think happened can wait until we have time to talk. The perp was here. Spread out and look for him, her, it, whatever!" His frustration leaked through and he ran hands through his hair.

"Gladly, but I have no idea what or who I'm looking for and right now anyone would be lost in the crowd of people rushing out of here, not to mention all the people rushing in." Niall waved his hand at the doors and sure enough more staff, first responders, and even just curious people or con goers that thought they could help were coming in. It was more chaotic than it had been before anyone collapsed.

"Merlin's fuzzy dick," he muttered, and I stared at him. That had to be wrong. Who cursed like that?

"Okay, fine. We'll have to glean what we can from the people. Your phone working?" He snapped out.

"Yes," Niall pulled it from his coat as Chris and Siab came running up.

"Good, most of the victims have their names on their badges, start recording. Siab, you too. Chris, see if you can reconstruct what the hell happened in here. I suspect I know." He turned to give me a meaningful look and an almost envious look at the creature in my arms. "If you can go back far enough to see what made people collapse, do it. Offer as much as you can." He nodded at Chris's rather short hair.

The story Bruce had told us back in college flashed through my mind and I had to fight to prevent a chuckle. No one would understand.

"Will do," Chris said and backed away to the wall, to do what Pattern archies did to recreate the past.

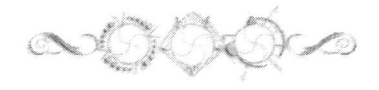

I started to ask a question but heard a whimper and spun, moving to another person on the floor, ignoring anything Alixant might have said. On my knees, I put the kitten between my legs and glanced down at it. "Stay. I need to work."

I don't know what I expected, but I glanced at the people around us and the tiny creature backed up into the vee of my thighs curled up once again in a tight ball. Part of me was amazed by that, but the rest of me focused on the victim. This person was older, male, with the paint mixed into the beard. I paused to looked closer. The gloves were still on my fingers and I touched the red on his cheek, then brought it up to my nose.

What in the world?

"Alixant!" I barked out the word, no doubt he'd be over in a minute. I was right.

"What did you find?" He crouched beside me in less than a minute, looking and sounding interested, whereas before he'd wanted to leave these people to die.

I lifted my finger. "When I was looking at the victims originally, this was a paint that had turned caustic, searing into them and it was oozing blood and ichor. From the reaction of one person I surmised it was a catalyst agent triggered and worked through direct skin contact. But this?" I held the red substance up. "This is ketchup."

"It's what?" He grabbed my finger and sniffed, looking at me with a frown pulling his brows tight together. "It is. What by the merlins?"

"Wait a moment, watch the cat." I ordered as I half crawled, half walked on my hands and feet over to the first victim, the one with yellow on his face. I swiped and sniffed. "And this is mustard. This was the first person I saw. They had either red, yellow, or blue painted on their faces."

He turned and lunged over to someone lying on the ground with blue on their face, or at least it looked blue in the lights that streamed in. Touching it carefully he brought it up to his nose then snorted out a laugh that had no humor in it. "This one is honey."

"Well leave it on. The honey at least is good for the wound." I looked around and to my astonishment and relief people were moving, even the person at my feet.

"I swear they all had some type of caustic chemical when I looked at them," I felt like I had to protest that I hadn't made such a stupid mistake. No one could have mixed up ketchup or mustard with the red and yellow substances that had been on their faces.

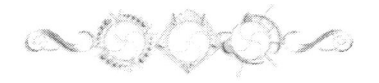

"I believe you. I suspect the power wave transformed them into something else, something less toxic." He turned, watching a few people sitting up, wiping off the stuff. "Interesting, he didn't kill them this time. Does that mean he didn't need to kill them?" For a minute I thought he was going to ask me something then, he spun and barked out, "Siab, Niall, Chris, get over here."

How does that man achieve such volume?

The idle thought made me smirk as I moved over and picked up the ball of fur that hadn't moved. I still wasn't sure about all of this but for right now, I felt better if it was in my arms. That knowledge made me even more uncomfortable, but I pushed it away.

The three agents headed over and looked at him. "Chris, what did you see?"

"Nothing specific. A wave transformed something in the paint to something else. I can sense the wave happening, but other than it being Transform magic, there isn't much else. The person who cast it was at the far side of the room but with so many people moving around, even that is lost. He, and yes, it is a man, hid in the curtains, preventing me from seeing anything, then Cori." Chris turned to look at me, but in the shifting lights I couldn't tell what expression he had. "She pushed something out from her, and everything changed. If you notice her hair is a good two inches shorter across the bottom. The rips snapped closed and the man bolted out the back." He rubbed a hand over his hair, and I noted that there were a few spots where I could see his scalp. "At this point there is too much movement for me to reconstruct without giving blood or more."

"About what I thought, but definitely male?"

"Yes."

"Fine. Chris, Niall - I want full interviews of every victim you can get to talk to you. You know the basics, but ask them about the marks on their faces, why they got them and from whom. See if they are all mages. Ask why they got the marking they did. Collect contact information and then get those wounds treated."

The two men nodded. "On it, boss."

"What about me?" Siab looked at him and she looked a bit annoyed. Dressed in clothes so tight I knew every curve and roll of fat she had, not that she had many. Her braids created a waterfall effect down her back. I envied the look, wishing my hair could be braided like that. She had a notebook out with a messenger bag across her body.

"I want you to get out of the con, at least out of his hotel. You've got sample bottles, right?" She nodded at him but I detected a hint of annoyance in her expression. They'd only gone over her having a collection kit with her three times on Thursday. "Okay, get to the other hotels and look for anyone with this facial paint. There have to be a few that aren't here. Get samples and find out everything you can about where they got it. See why they weren't here and if they had been planning to. Mage rank is important. I want to figure out how they were identified."

Her eyes narrowed but she nodded and spun and headed out of the halls. It was rapidly getting crowded in here with more and more first responders but all I could do was feel an ache. That should be me helping, getting ready to get people to the hospital. The man we had been standing near was in a sitting position, a friend talking to him. Blood trickled down his cheek, but if they had any good nurses or even a doctor with magic, they should be able to prevent it from scaring.

Alixant rotated his body, staring at everything, his eyes scanning, then he stopped and stared at me. The look made me take a step back and I found myself curving my body to protect the small creature in my arms.

"And you," he said, his tone flat but scary at the same time.

"What about me?" I forced myself not to back up. The fact that he intimidated me made me angry. I could feel magic swirling in me, getting ready to lash out. I swallowed and forced it down. Right now having Murphy's Cloak go on a rampage could be catastrophic.

"You are coming with me." He announced it the way I'd have said 'Here's your coffee'. It looked like for a minute he would grab me and drag me out by my arm, but something convinced him not too. Maybe it was my cold stare—I was tired of being manhandled. Or maybe it was the low soft growl from the fuzzy creature I held. Either way he waved at the open doors and we started walking.

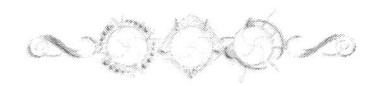

Chapter 30

No one knows where familiars come from. No probes ever sent into the rips have sent back any data and the familiars themselves seem to have a certain level of magic that prevents anything more than basic medical examination. While they are at least as intelligent, as a teenager, they will almost never answer questions about their origin, at least not that anyone has ever shared.
~Magic Explained

SPIRIT

It took us ten minutes to make it out of the hotel and the sound level dropped so fast I almost felt like a weight had been lifted off me. The bright sun seared my eyes after the darkness of the hotel. More lights had gone out than I expected.

"This way," he said, striding down to the corner and flagging down a taxi. I raced to keep up with him, fighting a sudden dizziness. I had to blink to stop from seeing double. All I wanted was a cool place to sit, food, and something cold to drink.

Before I could express this, or even figure out what was going, he pulled me into a taxi. I didn't hear what he said, but a soft, "mrow," pulled my attention down to my arms. For the first time I really looked at the creature in my arms. It had been too dark and too hectic to do more than hold it in the hotel.

Pulling it forward, I sat it on my lap and stared at it. About the size of a guinea pig, it resembled a cat. Two ears were covered with the same red fur flicked back and forth at the noise around us. The claws sank deeper into my thigh as the taxi pulled out, but it didn't leap away or look panicked. Instead, his eyes locked with mine. Bright green eyes with slitted pupils stared back at me. I carefully picked up one of his front paws and frowned at the long paws and thumb instead of the short stubby paws with claws I expected. I squeezed gently and the claw I expected extended - long, sharp, and more than capable of reaching deep into flesh.

"Well, thank you very much for not sinking those in too far," I said, still looking at the creature.

"What?" I sensed Alixant change his focus to me, and I showed him the odd paws. They were more like small hands that curled up into paws and looked normal as soon as I released them, though they looked huge compared to his tiny body. "Huh. I might almost feel sorry for you if it can use them."

I was busy stroking down his body, eliciting a purr as the silky fur went all the way down to a tail as long as he was, and oddly flexible. I hadn't spent much time with cats, or any pets really, but I didn't think their tails could wrap all the way your finger twice. He was also obviously a he.

The fur was thick and soft, reminding me more of the chinchilla I'd petted in the pet store a few times. The rumble of a purr vibrated down through his little body flowing into my legs like I held a small engine.

"Feel sorry?" I managed to drag my eyes away from the cat, because even if the hands and tail weren't exactly cat like, everything else, including the sharp-pointed teeth he exposed when he yawned, were.

"Well, those look like opposable thumbs, and every familiar I've ever met is mischievous and smart. That tail looks prehensile. So, all in all, I think I might have to just start feeling sympathy for you."

I frowned confused then looked back at Alixant. "What am I supposed to do with him? Do I turn him over to someone? I mean, they wouldn't hurt him or something?" Already I felt oddly attached to the little creature, but they'd never let me keep him.

"What?" To my surprise he started to laugh. It started out low a chuckle, but then got louder and deeper. The taxi stopped and he shoved money at the driver, still laughing. He got out of the car and I followed, holding the tiny cat as he leaned up against the wall, laughing so hard that tears were running down his face.

I looked at him, petting the cat to purrs of approval while I wondered who I should call.

Maybe he's having a mental breakdown?

I just stood there, feeling awkward and out of sorts, once again lost with everything that happened. After another minute he slowed down the laughs and straightened, wiping at his face, though another spurt would start as he looked at me.

"I don't understand. What is so funny?"

He had another chuckle but took a big breath of air. I liked this man more than I'd liked the agent he was. This one almost might have been someone I enjoyed talking to. The anger and seriousness fled, leaving in its wake humor and intelligence. The change surprised me.

"Cori, say hello to your familiar. He's yours now and no one is stupid enough to try to take him from you. So have fun with a cat with opposable thumbs."

Shocked, I stared at the bundle of fur I held. It looked up at me, all cute and fuzzy innocence, and repeated that one word in my mind. **Mine.**

The look on my face started him laughing again as he led me into the building.

I went through the stupid test again, and again felt nothing. But I had new objects that called to me and some of my old ones were almost irresistible.

"I get that this is impossible. Why do you think we are here? Because it obviously happened, and your tests prove it." Alixant glared at the tester in the OMO office, while once again, I sat in the tattoo chair, but this time with a bristling cat in my arms.

I didn't know if I wanted to strangle them because I was confused and scared or because they were scaring my familiar.

"There isn't anything recorded like this. We've never had anyone have two emergences. I wish someone had been around to see her first emergence. It would explain a lot. We don't have enough information on trauma based emergence to even guess but at no point has anyone ever emerged twice." The doctor was all but shouting at Alixant. The same guy who'd been at my first test Dr. Lawrence Rendol. Fran was there too, but she kept looking at me with wide eyes that were almost worse than the stares I'd gotten on the bus the first few days.

"Ever emerged, or ever reported to the OMO?" I asked in the lull of the shouting. They all turned and looked at me.

"What?" Alixant said, but his voice had a slowly dawning realization as I looked at him.

"I'm already marked. I'm already registered. Why in the world would I come back and get retested? Do you ever retest anyone? Because believe me, I wouldn't be here, if he hadn't dragged me back." I gave Alixant a sour look, which he ignored.

The two testing officials went white. "What if," the doctor broke off, his voice cracking. "What if you can re-emerge over your lifetime. Gaining new skills. Access to new branches."

"We can see from her she is strong in things she was pale in before. And now has not two strongs as a merlin, but four. Plus one because of her familiar. She has five strongs. No one has ever had that before. This could change everything." Fran sounded like she was so scared she could barely speak.

"I think you're right. This changes everything. This makes some of the more sensational stories over the years snap into reality. What if you can gain more power? Emerge again and be able to do things that no one would ever associate with you." The doctor talked fast and faster as he became more agitated. "This could change everything. I need to call my supervisors. I think we should institute retesting at least once a decade, if not every few years. This changes everything." He was still talking as he yanked open the door and raced out it.

"I don't think there are enough swear words in the English language to cover what I'm feeling right now," Alixant muttered dropping into the chair Dr. RendolX had vacated. "This changes everything. All the files we have could be wrong. Everything could be wrong as to who could do what. Hell, is it restricted only to merlin rank or could it be open to anyone?" He rubbed his temples. "Could hedgies get multiples at their power level?"

His question made my head jerk up and I remembered Kadia's experience at the bank. What if she hadn't just tripped, what if she'd had a second emergence. Nah, I was imagining things, right?

"I'm starting to think this was something I never wanted to know about, Steven. But now that it is here, I can't avoid it." Fran's fists were tight and I still thought everyone was overreacting, but the more I thought about it maybe they were right.

"You know, if the entertainment industry ever gets a hold of this the stories will explode."

"Ugh. If that happens..." she sighed. "Our testing will spike. They will come out with new regs. Oh, I so don't want this to be true." She stared at the objects I'd grabbed this time. Three were different, they'd removed the ones I'd already been strong in. I didn't know how I felt.

"Enough. Cori, your tattoo is getting updated. Talk to the artist." I sighed but figured from the glares they were both giving me I didn't have an option. It annoyed me because it had just almost healed and quit itching.

Thirty minutes later I inspected the work in the mirror. Before I'd been strong in Relativity under Spirit and Time under Chaos, while I was pale in Soul, Psychic, and Earth. Now the pale Psychic had moved to strong, as had Earth and Soul. And I'd added Non-Organic, Transform, and Entropy as pale. I'd chosen purple and green, wanting to pull in more colors and I didn't know if I liked the effect. It looked like a color wheel had exploded on my face with the burgundy and royal blue. But either way it caught attention, not that anyone would know what it meant.

I spun, looking at Alixant and Fran, who were deep in conversation. "Hey." They paused and looked at me. "You get in trouble for altering your tattoos. Am I going to get questioned about this? Or get in trouble?"

"Crap," Fran cussed as she headed out to the main room. "I'll get you a new IDIDnd note the changes on the back."

Alixant just stared at me.

"What?" I protectively clutched the cat to me. He had fallen asleep and I didn't want anything to happen to him.

"I've checked and rechecked. You don't have either a Cloak or Luck attached to you." He said the words with the capitals, so I knew he was referring to the spells. "But you still attract the strange like a lodestone. What are you?"

"Someone who wants to go home. I'm exhausted. I apparently have a pet that will need supplies and I bet food." I didn't mention that I didn't know what something that looked like a cat but wasn't a cat would need to eat. "I also need a new phone because mine is dead and the odds are Jo will be freaking out. And frankly, I'm over all this crap because I have no idea what I'm doing!" The last words were a yell and I realized I was shaking.

The cat looked up at me, with a plaintive meow. **Hungry** registered in my mind and I wanted to cry at the knowledge someone was no dependent on me. I barely felt like I could handle being responsible for myself. But I knew crying wouldn't do anything. I took a deep breath and straightened my back.

"So. I would like my bag back, a new phone, a ride to the grocery store, and then I'd like to go home."

He looked at me for a very long time and I was about to spit out a fine and storm out of there when he nodded. "Yes. I'll see you Tuesday. You have the rest of the weekend off. Come on."

Two hours later I sat at home, the cat eating tuna fish that the lady at the pet store assured me all cat-like familiars liked. Fran had gotten me the new ID with remarks on the back. As Alixant had dropped me off, he said he'd add the familiar note to my file. It meant I'd get a supplement until my schooling was done to afford to feed him. Their diets were a bit more expensive than normal cats in that they rarely would eat the normal cat food, preferring actual food.

I picked up my new phone, glad I'd added all my numbers to my cloud email account. It had popped in as soon as I'd added my email account. And at least ten text messages had popped in from Jo when I'd powered it on. The last one bordering on hysterical worry.

`I swear to all the merlins Cori, you don't fucking respond I'm calling mami and papi and you can deal with them.`

I laughed a little. I hadn't meant to worry her but I also hadn't had much control over anything in my life lately.

`Hey. I'm home. I'm okay. I'll explain when I see you.`

The response was instant. *Thank magic. I'm almost there.*

I smiled and sat, watching the kitten. If his paws were anything to go by, he would be huge but for now he looked like a cute ball of fluff. I just didn't know if I was ready to take care of another being. I guess I'd find out. At least the talking in my head would help. It had to make this easier.

The doorknob turning had me looking up before Jo all but flew into the room. "Cori," she exclaimed as she headed straight in, dropping her bag and keys on the table without taking her eyes off me. Jo pulled me up and scanned me with her eyes, then lingered on my altered tat.

"I'm fine. No injuries."

She blew out a sigh, but her eyes didn't leave my face. "That's new?" Her voice cautious.

I groaned and sat down. "You aren't going to believe everything that has happened. I was there and I'm still not sure I believe it."

"I think we are going to need drinks for this?" It was half a question and half a statement.

"Oh yeah. That would be nice," I agreed.

She turned and came to a sudden halt. From where she was facing, I could tell she'd just seen the cat. I couldn't see him with Jo there, but I knew what she was looking at.

"We seem to have acquired a kitten?" her voice slow and hesitant.

I let out a shaky breath. "Actually I seem to have acquired a familiar." Just saying the words felt odd and scary. Kids dreamed and told stories about being a magician and having a familiar. I never had though I'd found them fascinating. The two I'd met, Dahli and Elsba had captivated me. But one choosing me? I didn't know anything.

That idea set off a spurt of panic. I needed information. What did I know about familiars?

"Yes, drinks are needed." Her voice as shocked as I felt. She headed for the kitchen and I started looking for books to order on familiars.

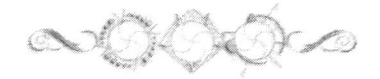

Chapter 31

Fight the power, don't hire mages, hire the normal people they will work harder for you and do it without invoking unnatural abilities.
~Freedom from Magic

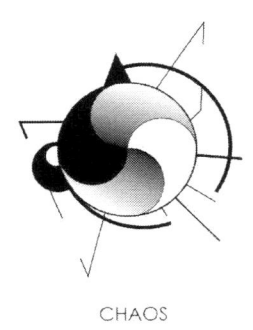

CHAOS

I didn't feel up to public transportation Tuesday, so I splurged on a rideshare to work and brought the kitten with me. I had tried to leave him at home, but cries of "No" in my head were too pitiful. So I brought him.

Sunday Jo had gone back to the con. I'd stayed home, totally exhausted. I played with the kitten but both of us did little but sleep for the next two days. Jo seemed to have fun but was back in the school grind today. I had seemed to have a fog over my brain, but it had started to lift.

I hadn't come up with a name for the kitten. It seemed wrong somehow to just name him, but I also wasn't sure how intelligent he was.

I really need those books to get here. I hate not having any idea what I should do.

One of the things I'd ordered was a cat carrier. He was too small to run around but carrying him in my arms seemed silly. Luckily I'd found one that let the cat ride on my chest in kind of a reverse backpack. It might look silly but it had the advantage of leaving my hands free. That too would arrive Wednesday. For now, I just held him carefully, and stressed the entire ride.

Siab and Chris were there when I walked in.

"Oh, is that your new familiar?" Siab asked as I entered, getting up from her little lab station and coming over. Once again, she made the suit look almost chic, with the sharp cut and the daring see through top under it.

"Yeah." I knelt and let him down. He stretched and began to investigate the office, his long tail a red snake that followed him.

"What's his name?"

"I haven't thought of one yet. I'm still trying to wrap my mind around the idea of having a pet." I watched him, envying the grace as he moved around the office and Chris's bemused expression.

"Um, Cori?" I turned to look at Siab who had a funny expression on her face.

"Yes?" I started to look down to make sure I hadn't spilled coffee on myself.

"You know that they have their own names and you don't really own them, not as much as you think. The law pretty much regards them as eternal children. Your responsibility, but with the understanding they can make their own choices."

"Oh," I muttered. I knew I should have spent the time researching but everything had seen like too much effort. I swallowed, sure my face had flushed. "I just ask him?"

"I think so. I mean, I don't have a familiar, obviously. But the people I know that do have them say they already have names, and personalities. But he is very young. Is he eating?"

"Yes. Though that food budget is going to kill me," I muttered, but I didn't really mind.

"Then ask. The worse he can say is nothing or tell you to choose."

The cat and I hadn't really talked much. I'd been tired, he'd been tired. He'd eaten and slept more than I had. This was the first real activity I'd seen from him. Either way, I felt ridiculous, but I cleared my throat.

"What is your name?"

The cat wasn't paying any attention to me, batting at something under Niall's desk. I was about to go pick him up and let him know I was talking to him, as I had no idea how the telepathy worked. I needed to read that book as soon as I got it.

Carelian, that same rough male rumbling voice in my head. It felt so odd, but so right it caused a shiver down my spine.

"That's your name? Carelian?" I didn't get any response other than a mental purr of affirmation.

"Interesting name. I don't think it is a word in any language I can think of," Siab noted. "But he is adorable."

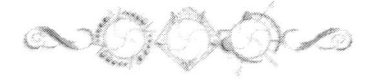

I watched the butt wiggle as he attacked a bug that had the audacity to wander into the area. Already I wanted to make sure he was okay. I didn't have a chance to follow up on that feeling as Alixant walked in followed by Niall. Alixant had a scowl on his face that made him look more like the gargoyles on the churches than an agent.

"I hope you know how many problems you created," he growled, eyes locked on me, then flicking to Carelian.

"What did I do?" I went on the defensive, my arms across my chest and staring at him.

"Your little emergence destroyed any evidence we might have had and gave the perp time to get away. So we have nothing." He all but snarled the words at me.

I snarled back. "Well, so sorry a weird rare thing happened to me. But since I'm pretty damn sure it saved all those people, I'm not very sorry."

"And just how many more people are going to die because we didn't catch him now?"

"I don't know but you probably wouldn't have caught him anyhow. You've got nothing to go on."

"Actually, we might have a few things." Siab interrupted our glare fest and I turned to look at her, almost tripping over Carelian who at sat my feel, tail whipping as he stared at us.

"What?" Alixant sat down at the table and Chris grabbed his notebook.

"Your familiar?" Niall whispered at my shoulder and it took everything I had not to jump. I hadn't noticed him come up behind me. I turned and nodded slowly, somehow expecting an attack. He just looked at the cat for a long moment, something like longing in his gaze and nodded. "Neat." Before I could even figure out how to respond, he'd settled down at the table with a notebook.

Shaking my head, confused by the changing personalities, I walked over. Carelian departed to chase things under the table and Siab headed over, her laptop in hand.

"So, show me." Alixant demanded and I leaned forward, interested in what they had found.

"We talked to other people and some with good memories and minor magic and we created a sketch of the person who did the face painting." A few flicks of his hand and an image appeared on the wall. Older, at least thirty-five, with a low tail of dark hair, wearing glasses and a goatee. Chris gave us all a minute to take it in before he started to talk again. "All the reports had him wearing wild hats with flashing LED lights on it, robes that had swirly things, and dangles. They admitted it was hard to focus on his face."

"Makes sense. Everyone remembered what he wore, not what he looked like," Alixant commented staring at the picture. "Go on."

"He asked them if they wanted to be in a drawing for free prizes at the panel. Nothing needed but they had to be wearing the face paint for their ticket to be valid. He handed out the tickets and painted the face. But here is the interesting part. He usually only offered it to one person, then reluctantly did the other person if they asked. It took us a bit to figure it out, but he always offered to the mage, never to the person with them if they weren't mages. He did have a Chaos tattoo, but no one could remember the strong or pale values which might have helped with tracking him down. Chaos is the highest populated mage class."

"What was the substance placed on their faces?"

It amazed me how he could go from being an irritated jerk to a completely focused person. I couldn't let go of my mad that easily. Or maybe he hadn't really been mad. I played with that thought as I listened.

"At first glance it just looked like a water-based adhesive with colors added. It wasn't until I got back the findings from the two people that died that I think I know what happened."

I couldn't stop the stab of guilt that followed that statement but I didn't know what else I could have done.

Everyone just looked at her and smiled back. "The tox report showed damage from hydrochloric acid and fentanyl caused the few deaths. Though the amounts were small because of the emergence transformation effect."

"That makes no sense, no one should be able to cover up hydrochloric acid on your skin," Niall interjected.

"True. But the powder substance had chloride in it. Here's my theory—we all know that moving molecules is both a high and low cost endeavor. I think this substance was purposefully mixed so that with minimal effort and exact knowledge of the molecules involved, he could change it from one to the other. Breaking the bonds and rearranging them would take a bit of effort but only a small offering, depending on his rank."

"But what good does that do? I mean the acid would sear the skin and fentanyl? That will kill you even being absorbed through the skin." I couldn't keep my mouth shut, but fentanyl was a nasty drug and killed fast. "If that was what he did, they would have all been dead in seconds."

"True, if he did it perfectly. I think he only managed to transform some of it, which was why people were dropping but not dropping dead. Basically sheer luck, and points to him probably being a pale for transform or a low rank mage overall."

"But what does it get him?"

Alixant jerked upright in his chair and glared at me again. "It gets him you."

"What?" I'm pretty sure the other two reacted the same way as I did. But either way, I felt a strange clench of emotions in my stomach.

He rubbed his brow and odd expression on his face. "Have any of you come across the seven grams at death study?"

"Sure," Siab said. I had no idea what he was talking about.

"For the rest of you, they've done studies and shown at the moment of death the body loses seven grams of weight. But what they haven't been publicizing is a few people have died during the magician rank test."

I blanched at that, though Siab just looked interested.

"Oh, nothing sinister. A heart attack, stroke, just odd medical things. But the machine and the merlin monitoring noted a large spike of power being pushed out, similar to what happens during an emergence. So they started asking magicians near death if they were willing to be monitored and they agreed. They have evidence that as you die you bleed out power. What is really interesting is that the slower you die the more power collectively is pushed out. I think this is what that guy was doing. He wanted people to push out power. Whether he figured that out after the ritual magic or something else I don't know."

Chris looked thoughtful. "Okay, I can see where he might be learning from this, even if that is a sharp upwards curve to go from one to three to nine to twenty-seven, then quit caring about numbers at all. So he gets all this power going out, then what?"

Alixant just pointed at me and suddenly it clicked. I thought I might need to throw up. "He wants a second or more likely a third emergence. What if that's it? The first few were to accomplish something else, maybe just to be more powerful. Then after the incident at the park, he realized patterns didn't matter, power did." I turned and looked at Chris. "Do you know if there was a spike in people emerging the day of the park murders?"

Ugh, I'm already sounding like them. This shouldn't be this easy.

But I couldn't help but look for correlations. So much of emergency medicine was if this, then that. It was almost second nature.

Chris shrugged and pulled up something on his computer. "The OMO does show rates and stats."

"But won't tell me a damn thing about second emergences," Alixant grumbled, then shot a glance at me. "You mentioned third. You think you can?"

I shrugged not sure what to say. "I never thought you could emerge more than once, but if everything is about power, maybe you can emerge over and over, getting stronger and more powerful in different branches and classes." I didn't mention my curiosity about Kadia.

"But why you? Why not someone else?" Siab challenged me It wasn't arrogance or disbelief in her tone, more curiosity.

"Something else to consider: I've been following up with the hospital on all the victims. While they won't break HIPPA, they did mention that all the victims had extreme lethargy the next two days, to the point of almost feeling drugged."

"Oh," the word slipped out of my mouth before I could stop it and they all snapped their heads towards me. The desire to join Carelian on the floor spiked but I forced a nonchalant shrug. "I didn't do much the last few days but sleep. I felt completely drained. As to why me? Heck if I know but it might have something to do with emotions. He made me angry." I jerked my head at Alixant, who didn't look repentant at all.

"And your power wasn't being siphoned out…" Alixant trailed off. "I bet that's the key, simple and fast. Magic siphons out, the walls between the planes rips and you grab the power. The perp just wants to grab it, but he missed because you grabbed it first."

"But what? I was more powerful?" I asked in disbelief.

"Maybe? Maybe you needed it more? Anger is a strong emotion and a good motivator."

"And I bet there was a familiar on the other side that liked her better than our perp. Hence Cori being chosen," Siab put in. She had a thoughtful look on her face, but her attention was on Carelian who had decided my chair was where he was going to groom himself.

"You think it matters that much? That magic is sentient?"

She shrugged. "I don't know. Maybe. Or maybe you were closer, younger, prettier, the right combination. No one has ever figured out how or why certain people emerge, and others don't. So it could be nothing or everything."

"Right now, it doesn't matter that Cori grabbed the power. What does matter is her emergence left us with every little evidence." He tossed me an annoyed glare and I resisted sticking my tongue out at him. "Either way, we don't know if he'll try again or not but we have to assume he will. So what do we know?"

"Large event," Chris provided.

"Transformation substance, slow death needed." Siab pointed out.

"No order is needed, as seen from the last thing, so milling crowds would be better for him. It would take longer to stabilize people." Niall had that faraway look on his face, staring at the board.

"Yeah, but why do we think he will stay here?" I asked, feeling like I had to say something.

"To be honest, we don't, but I'm betting on the fact that he has a home base here and Atlanta has more large-scale events," Alixant said. "So, what events are coming up next, Cori?"

Everyone turned and looked at me. "Why do you think I know?" I asked, bewildered, as I looked at all the expectant eyes on me.

"Uh, because you live here, and we don't?" Siab said, her duh clear in the tone.

"No, well yes. I mean, I live here but I just moved here barely a month ago. I have no idea."

"But you knew about DragonWorldCon," she protested.

"It had tens of thousands or people attend! People from all over the world show up! And I knew people that went before. It isn't a small event." They all looked at me with vaguely disappointed expressions.

What? I'm not exactly a social butterfly.

But as I groused, I took over the screen and pulled up the Atlanta Events page. "Here is what is going on in the next couple of weeks."

We all looked at the screen. There were a lot of events. Football games, music events, other conventions, parades, the list went on forever.

"We'll never find him this way. There are too many events and it is too easy to do magic to turn something innocuous into something deadly." For a moment I thought he was going to throw things, but he sighed and sat down. "We're back to the basic tenets of murders. Who are the first people you kill?"

"The ones you know." Chris and Niall said in unison. They grabbed their computers and headed back to their cubicles.

"And that is my cue to get back to looking at the data of the samples I got. I'll keep working on the facial recognition, trying to merge all the sketches and go through the OMO database. Maybe we'll get lucky." She smiled and gave a longing glance towards Carelian, who by this point had curled into a ball and was soundly sleeping in my chair.

I didn't really have anything to do. I'd done all the training and I really wanted to be back at a job that I knew how to do. My insecurity must have shown on my face because Alixant smiled.

"Study. You've got the book I gave you and you might as well look at your college courses. With your AA degrees, you should be starting as a Junior except for one or two classes and your magic courses. If you log on to OMO with your ID, you should see the suggested careers for people with your abilities. Granted, you are strong in so many you should be able to do almost anything." He stood up and moved back over to his area. He paused and turned back to look at me. "Remember, that while the government won't force you to take a certain career path, anything not STEM based and related to your strengths will be denied and if you choose to continue, all classes will be your responsibility to pay for." He gave me one more hard look then sat down.

I looked at the cat sitting on my chair, sighed and went to grab the book and curled back up at the table and started to read.

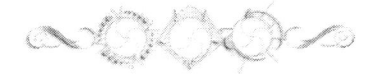

Chapter 32

Each mage visualizes or associates the cost of an offering differently. While molecules are what is taught in most universities, it doesn't me that is how a mage sees it. Often it is an amount of hair or nail or skin, or maybe the time it will take to regrow. There are stories of mages that counted in calories or even one who did it by cell. As always no one knows why they can do this, but test after test shows they are always exact as to the cost.
~Magic Explained

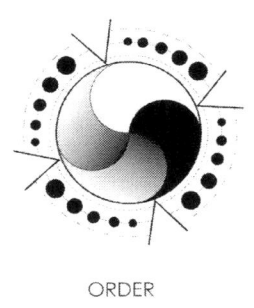

ORDER

The next two days were the same thing with everyone else researching information and I had nothing to do but read. I liked reading and it interested me, but by the time I escaped at four on Thursday, I was ready to scream. Even Carelian seemed bored.

My carrier should show up soon but Siab pointed out I might want a harness and a collar as from his paws and tail he would be a big cat... like dog big.

I still hadn't decided how I felt about that piece of information but either way, it would be a change. In the few days he'd been here he'd already gained what seemed like a pound. I needed to get him to the vet, but familiars apparently didn't need shots or to get fixed, which didn't really surprise me. I mean neutering a sentient creature sounded evil.

Holding him in my arms, I climbed the stairs. So far, outside of Mine, Hungry, and his name, he hadn't spoken to me and I made sure hungry wasn't an issue. The book of familiars should be here today but the online videos I found said he'd learn to use a toilet in the house if I wanted. And I did. The litter box was okay, but it stuck to his paws and annoyed both of us.

I pushed open the door, surprised to see all the lights off. Jo should have been home at least two hours ago. I let Carelian down and he headed right to his food bowl. Of course. I checked my phone. Nothing.

I started to call her when I heard a bottle clinking from her bedroom. I headed back, my steps fast. I was oddly concerned, and I couldn't say why.

"Jo?" I knocked on the door. It was ajar and swung open as I did. She sat on the floor, staring at her computer, the piles of books, and a bottle of whiskey, tapping it with her glass. I stood in the door, frozen for a moment. Her hair, her glorious black hair, hung limp around her face, and her entire body had curled into itself. Gone was the proud, smart, funny woman I knew. Instead, this was someone I don't think I'd ever seen.

"Jo? What's wrong?" I moved in and slid down to sit next to her.

She barked a laugh, bitter and hard. I hurt to hear it. She took a gulp of the liquid in the glass, which by its smell was whiskey from the bottle. "I'm a complete and utter failure. I can't do this. This is why I didn't want to emerge at a high rank. I wanted hedge. I wanted my damn certifications, and I just wanted to work with my *papi*. Maybe someday take over the garage. Now I'll flunk out. I don't even know what they do if you flunk out as a mage. Do they throw you in prison, assign you to grunt work, make you act as a test subject? This will destroy my parents. They'll hate me." On the last words her voice broke and she took another desperate gulp of whiskey as if it would somehow change her feelings.

I had no clue what she was talking about and looked around. Jo had never been the best student, and struggled at English, but then so did lots of people. She'd aced math and we'd never talked about school much. Even the dream of being an engineer was more at the same level you talk about being an astronaut. Not something you think will ever occur.

"Jo, talk to me. What's going on?" I pulled the glass from her and set it away, out of reach, as I moved to sit in front of her. She had to look at me, or her feet. Carelian came in and plopped down between the two of us and began grooming as if there was no place else he'd want to be.

"I can't do it, Cori. I can't. I've been trying. Really, I've been trying. I can't get everything to stay still. They move no matter what I do. My last paper was an F and I have a huge test and I can't figure out what it says." Her voice shook as tears ran down her face.

Confused and scared, I reached out to cup her face, wanting to hold her, needing to comfort her. "I don't understand. What moves? Why doesn't it make sense?" I needed to figure out what was going. This wasn't my Jo, and I'd do anything for her.

"The letters. They change. Every time I look, they're different. There is so much to read and understand and it keeps moving. I like numbers. They don't move or at least they don't move as much. Maybe I should just quit and save them the trouble of expelling me."

I sat there, trying to process her drunken rambling. How much had she drunk already? Then my brain snapped into gear. You read lots of weird case studies with some of the medical assistant classes.

"Jo, are you dyslexic?"

She snorted, scrubbing at her face with her hands. "They said no. Dyslexic kids can't be good at math. Only lazy kids are good at math but can't get their papers right. It got worse after I graduated high school. So I just avoided reading. Didn't need to. All the manuals have pictures and I knew what words went where. 'Sides, math is always the same. Logical. So I'm just stupid."

My mind stutter stopped, and I looked at her. "Who told you that?"

"All the teachers. I was just being lazy. I didn't like English, but since I like math and was good at it, I couldn't be dyslexic. They told *mami* I was just lazy, and she got mad at me. So I tried. I would listen to all the lectures and then get Stinky or you to check my writing. I used a ruler on my words in class and I'd only get marked down for spelling. But while I graduated, it was only because of the science stuff." She gave another one of those raw laughs. "Chemical diagrams don't move, the numbers and lines rarely change or if they do, they don't make sense and I wait for them to move back to what they should say. So see. I'm just stupid. but I swear, I've been trying, and they won't stay still. . . " she broke off in a harsh sob and I was glad the bottle wasn't close to her.

Stupid teachers. Smart queans. The voice sounded in my head. I jumped and looked down at Carelian, who was licking Jo's ankle.

"Did, did he just talk in my head?" Jo had stopped crying and looked at Carelian with wide eyes.

"You heard him?" I knew from what Scott Randolph had told me that they could talk to anyone, but usually didn't bother. I didn't know if I was excited or not about Carelian talking to Jo. Right now, I just felt relieved.

Smart. Mine He fell backwards against me purring eyes closed. **Mine.**

"Carelian, what is a quean?" I petted him as I asked, but he just rumbled a purr and said nothing else.

"Is it a compliment or not when a cat thinks you're smart?" Jo asked, sniffing and wiping her face, her breathing still hard and shaky.

"Well, he's a familiar, so I'd take it as a compliment. Jo, look at me." My voice hard and demanding. This was so important she had to listen. She sighed and looked at me, bracing herself. "You need to listen. You are dyslexic if letters move. There are different types and they affect people differently. Just because numbers don't move, doesn't mean letters don't."

She shrugged but kept petting the small body of Carelian. "So? So what? Doesn't mean I'm not an idiot. I still can't do this."

"Jo, how did you pass your classes in high school?" Her answer wouldn't change what I would say, but I was curious.

"Memorized everything they said in class and did anything I could that was oral for extra credit to make up for my test scores. Lots of tests in English and History were multiple choice and those, if I was careful, I could get it right." Rather than sounding proud she just sounded defeated.

"I have a strong desire to drive back to Rockway and beat all your teachers," I admit I snarled the words. Seeing her like this felt worse than getting hurt myself.

"Huh?" She looked up at me at that, her hand stilling in its stroking motion. Jo seemed calmer. Maybe cat familiars had calming effects?

"Jo, you are dyslexic. That means there are things that will help you, AND," I said, seeing she was about interrupt, "it means you can get assistance from the college."

That stopped her and she looked at me frowning. "Help? Like what?"

I almost laughed. "Like oral tests, audio versions of the textbooks, pass on spelling errors, the ability to get more time to do things. I'm sure all textbooks are set up to be able to be read aloud to you if you get the electronic versions. Plus, they have fonts that are specifically made for dyslexic people and don't move around as much. If you can memorize entire lectures to pass tests, trust me, you're not stupid. And no one who knows you would ever call you lazy."

"Oh." She looked shocked, and just stared at me, a look of bewilderment on her face. "But they won't believe me. They'll say I'm just trying to get special favors," her voice sounded small and revealed a weakness I'd never seen before. Maybe that was why she was always so bold, to hide worry about this? I needed to think about that.

"I'm taking off tomorrow and we're going down there together. You will get the help you need."

"Cori, you can't," she protested, but I could see that odd vulnerability spark back up and I wanted to castigate myself for never noticing. A bunch of things popped into my mind, now that I thought about it. How she'd ask me what looked good on the menu or saw something as we walked in and asked the waitress about it the few times that we went out to eat. Her asking someone to read instructions to her when her hands were full or filthy.

"Yes, I can. Watch me." I pulled out my phone and scrolled to my messages. Jo was the only other person that texted me, so finding Alixant was easy.

Taking tomorrow off. Have to deal with something I hit send and looked up at her. "See. We will get you everything you need. You deserve that doctorate. You're one of the best people I know with machines."

Before she could reply my phone pinged. *Don't think so. You'll be here.*

I frowned feeling my jaw clench. *No I won't. Be back Monday*

Yes you will. You need to be here.

bite me I hit send and powered off the phone just as it started to ring. My smile felt good as I looked at Jo.

"Tomorrow morning you and I are going to get you help."

Jo bit her lip. "You sure? They'll really help."

"Yes, they will. " I didn't know it but I knew I would do everything I could to make sure there was nothing she need.

"Thank you, Cori. I just figured they were right, when everyone else was talking about how easy the course work was, and I was struggling to read the text, much less write the reports. I must be lazy or stupid. I was about ready to run away and quit." Her shoulders hunched.

"Nope. You've been here for me all this time. Now it's time for me to be there for you. So, brace yourself as you may not be happy about this next statement." Jo gave me a funny look as she stood up.

"Do I want to know?"

"Probably not, but you will find out. In an attempt to support you and prove I am always here for you," I stated dramatically as I rose too. "I am cooking you dinner!"

"Oh dear. This isn't going to end well."

It ended up just fine. After my attempt and failure, we ordered pizza. It was delicious.

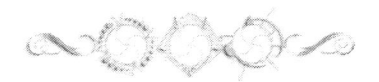

Chapter 33

Being a mage doesn't make you superhuman. The number of people we lose every year who don't understand that is staggering. If you took the draft just as a baseline job, it is the most dangerous one in the world with a death rate of over twenty percent. Mages still get sick, suffer from learning disabilities, get divorced and get fired. Being able to do magic is a skill like painting or playing music. One you can train, but you need that spark to make it work.
~OMO Office Brochure

SPIRIT

I dragged Jo out of bed at five am, even though the resource office didn't open until eight-thirty.

"Cori, not that I mind getting up this early, the sleeping until seven has felt like a luxury. But why are we leaving the apartment at six in the morning?" Jo asked as I dragged her down the apartment steps, a small cup of coffee in each of our hands, and her backpack slipping off her shoulder. I had Carelian in the pack on my front. It felt and looked dorky but having my hands free again was nice. He'd made a few unimpressed sounds but was sitting and looking out as we headed down the stairs. Dawn was just starting to break.

"Because I'm pretty sure the jerk is going to have an issue with me shutting off my phone last night. I bet he'll be here at seven to grab me, and I'm not going. We have stuff to do with you."

"Cori, it's okay. I can do this." Jo muttered, though she looked like she had a headache. She'd had at least two more drinks last night, still asking me if I was sure she wasn't lazy. I reassured her every time and cussed out teachers in my head. Part of it was protectiveness over Jo but most of it was anger at the damage they had done. I think at this point I was more mad at her teachers than myself. I hadn't seen most of it but then not sure I would have realized it as a teen.

So maybe I had a reason to miss it, but I was still not happy that I was that oblivious.

"Nope. He can suck it. He's enough of an ass that I don't really care."

"Won't you get in trouble? *Mami* would kill me if I ruined your life."

I snorted out a laugh as I dragged her out one of the back paths. I didn't put it past him to be in the parking lot already. "I don't care. I haven't been to school yet. If I understand the law, he has a wavier to use my services until I start, but he can't really do anything to me beside yell. I'm tired of being yelled at and tired of not having anything to do but look stupid. I still can't figure out WHY he wants me there. I'm the next thing to useless." I didn't keep the annoyance out of my voice with that last part.

"Ah, so tweaking his tail?" She asked this with a bit more humor as we started toward the college.

"Maybe." I shrugged. "All the stories say there should be sexual tension between us, smoldering and intent. I suspect he's a good man, maybe not a nice one, but there's nothing. I flinch when others call him by name, and I really have to get over that. And he's so driven, he gets upset that I don't jump when he yells. I never wanted this." I tapped the side of my head as I looked around. For some reason I was jumpy and expected him to pull up alongside of us.

"What do you mean?" Jo looked lost and I realized she'd never met him. "He has Stevie's name and I just can't call him Alixant all the time. I don't want to associate him with Stevie."

"Ah. Makes sense." We walked in silence for a while, enjoying the sounds of the city waking up around us. "Are you going to be okay there, Cori? I mean, I know you don't want to go back to school."

"I can't get away and I want to stop this guy. I think he's going to kill more, but I feel out of place. This isn't where I should be, but I don't know where I should be." I kicked at a stone on the ground and Carelian complained at I jostled him.

"Sorry, Car." I said as I scritched his ears. He wrinkled up his nose and hissed at me, the meaning clear. "No Car huh? Lian? Ian?" At Ian, he paused and nodded, but I felt a word in my head.

Still Carelian

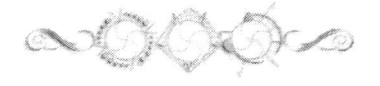

How you could purr or roll the sound of letters like that I didn't know. But I shrugged and scratched. "Carelian or Ian it is. " I pronounced it as Ean, because of how he said his name.

"Do you like having a familiar?" Jo asked as we approached the admin building and I shrugged.

"That's like asking me if I like having my hair growing. I haven't had enough of it to know one way or the other yet."

"Point." We stood looking up at the building, then at our watches; only six-thirty. "Coffee shop? I could do with some food."

"Sure." We turned and headed towards the nearest place, which was already bustling. We ordered and found a table in the corner, while people talked and chattered around us. I made sure my hair covered most of my tattoo. Maybe I needed to move to someplace cold, so I could wear hats all the time.

"What exactly are you going to do?" Jo didn't look at me, just fiddled with her drink. The coffee was okay, not as good as at Grind Down, but okay.

"About?" Her comment pulled me out of the focus on the coffee.

"Well, both. Your schooling, the resource office, this job that isn't a job?"

"Oof, you want me to make decisions this early?" I muttered, staring at her, but I smiled. Carelian was in another chair nibbling on a dog treat. He hadn't seemed to care it was aimed at dogs.

"You're the one who dragged me out this early, so yes." Jo had the audacity to smirk at me over her coffee but I could still see the odd fear in her eyes. I'd never realized how much she hid from me, and it hurt. Almost as much as realizing how much I hadn't seen.

Some friend I was, to not notice your BFF has issues reading.

"School first. We deal with the administration. I figure this might as well come in handy." I tapped the side of my head. I had the marks mostly hidden at the moment, but for all the misery they had caused me, they might as well do me some good now. "You need the testing, the assistance. Asking for help shouldn't be an issue and anyone who knows you knows you're smart."

Jo didn't look convinced, but I ignored her. All the medical assistant stuff about how to support and recognize people with disabilities might actually come in helpful.

See, education is never useless. I need to keep reminding myself of that, because the one thing this degree gets me, is access to more information. Maybe I can figure out what killed Stevie. Maybe I could even become a doctor.

That idea tugged at me but didn't feel right. I needed to take the time to sit down and go over the degrees, but the problem with being a merlin was there were so many options, and Carelian just added to them as with him I was strong in not two but three fields. That was unheard of as far I knew and it made me uneasy.

"After that, I'll deal with the FBI. The lead jerk is mostly taking out his anger on me, though I don't know why. I get they may need someone to help with the planar rips and even untrained, I might be the best person available. But sitting there all day and feeling stupid is a waste of time, though they are paying me, which helps. But still, I'd rather work and I have four months before I can start school. I'd like to be an EMT. It's what I trained for." I gave a helpless shrug. I enjoyed being an EMT, so it was an option.

"Are they going to accept that?" Jo asked, arching her brows.

"I'll have to figure out how to make them. I know the draft can put me anywhere, but I want it to be something that will lead to a long term job and future. So that means me thinking about it. Right now, I just want this case over with so maybe I can work and deal with college, something I thought I was done with." My tone wry as I glanced at the clock on the wall. "It's after eight, lets head that way and get you taken care of."

Jo heaved herself up, looking like the weight of the world rested on her. "I still feel deep down I'm just being lazy, or not trying hard enough, or something."

"Yes, cause not having letters move around is something you can control?" I gave her an arch glance and she flashed a smile.

"You trying to tell me letters aren't like men and they don't react to my awesome rack?" She waved at her chest and I saw at least two men follow her motion with their eyes.

"Exactly. So come on." I grabbed Carelian and put him back in the carry thing, feeling more than one person eye me. I did feel ridiculous. The odd looks I got just increased my discomfort.

Mine his voice rumbled through my mind and I couldn't stop a smile.

"So I'm your servant, am I?"

Jo glanced at me, then the cat and grinned.

Yes, the voice said smugly in my mind and I laughed.

"I take it he responded?" Jo asked once we were out.

"Yes. He agrees I'm his servant. He might need an attitude adjustment." His purrs were loud and rumbling as he rested his head on the edge of the bag.

"Uh huh. Somehow I think he's right." Her smirk made me roll my eyes, but I couldn't disagree too much.

We continued our walk to the services building. Jo's steps came slower and slower as we approached.

"Nope, come on. You're doing this." I all but dragged her into the building and to the desk where an older woman sat. "Hi. My friend here needs testing and resource assignment, plus considerations for a learning disability."

The woman, her hair shot with gray and tied back in a tight bun with glasses perched on her nose, squinted at us, mouth pursed. "You do? And what does your friend say?"

I elbowed Jo, giving her my best "I mean business" look. She sighed and muttered out, "I'd like to get tested to see if I qualify." Her voice was audible only because at this time of the morning the area was mostly empty.

"Fine, take a seat," she waved us to a chair, and I heard her muttering, "Young people always thinking because it isn't all video games, they need special assistance. Humph, I could show them what hard classes were like."

I almost spun around and let her have it right there. Standing up for myself was hard, standing up for Jo I'd do in a heartbeat. But she seemed to be placing a call, so I let it go; for now.

We sat in the uncomfortable chairs, and I let Carelian out to explore.

"Hey, no pets are allowed in here," the woman snapped out.

Carelian froze, and affronted look on his furry face, whiskers and ears laid back.

"Familiar," I replied, my voice saccharine sweet.

She hmphed and Carelian lashed his tail at her, then continued his exploring. We'd been there a half hour and Carelian slept in the chair next to me, when a woman came out. Older, probably only late thirties to the wench at the desk's sixties. She walked over, a smile and a tablet computer in her hand.

"Hi, I'm Beth. So, what's up?"

Jo swallowed hard, but with my shoulder bump began to speak, extra low, probably because of the wench and the few students passing by. While you could see the edges of my tattoo from my hair style, it wasn't on display like Jo's in her ponytail. Most people ignored us, though Carelian did get a few extra glances. He was a gorgeous kitten. His red fur was almost truly red instead of the russet brown of most cats. He almost looked like I'd painted him red. While it was an odd color, it also screamed not normal, cementing him as a familiar.

"I'm having problems in my classes. I've always had the issue, but after being out of school the last few years it got worse. Cori here says it's dyslexia, but I was told it couldn't be because numbers don't move on me?"

Beth shrugged. "Everyone is different. Why don't you describe what is going on?"

"It's the reading and the tests and the papers. Every time I read a sentence the letters move and create different words, or words that make no sense. I'm having to read sentences five or six times to guess at what it says. And when I type, I think I know what I'm typing, I mean I know where the letters are on the keyboard, but I can't read it to make sure it's right." Her voice shook, but she kept her head up.

"But you don't have this problem with numbers?" She didn't sound disbelieving, which made me feel better. I never wanted to see Jo that down again.

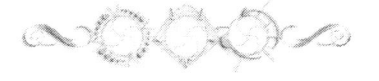

"Not really. Most of the time, especially with engineering, the numbers stand alone or there are only one or two of them, and if they move the math doesn't work, so it's easy to correct them."

"You can do the math in your head?"

"Sure, a calculator takes too long and most of the time my hands are covered with grease." Jo shrugged, still looking unsure about everything.

I hadn't known that. I mean, I knew she could calculate everything without trying, but advanced math in her head? I always needed to write it out. I felt absurdly proud of her, which was ridiculous as I had nothing to do with that ability.

"Interesting. Well, I have everything set up if you want to come take the assessment." She turned to me with a smile. "This may take a while. Do you want to wait?"

"Is there someplace with how to transfer credits so I can see where I will come in with an Associates degree?"

"You mean three Associates," Jo said giving me the same shoulder bump I'd given her earlier.

I saw Joanne flick to my temple and frown, but she nodded. "Sure. If you want to log into that kiosk over there, you can apply for admission. You need your OMO registration number, then enter all your information. It should tell you what will transfer and what you may need to take in the lower classes." She stood and gestured for Jo to follow her, and the two of them headed down the hall.

"Well, Carelian, let's go see what my options are."

He only flicked an ear at me, so I sighed and left him there. Cats, really. Soon enough I lost myself in the maze of school forms, applications, and transferring information.

Chapter 34

Familiars don't follow any rhyme or reason that has been validated. They usually resemble Earth creatures, but not always. They are always intelligent and it seems like they can speak telepathically with whomever they wish. But though people long for them they don't seem to know why one person gets them and another doesn't. There have been merlins that were executed because of the evil they did with their magic that had familiars as well as hedgemages that never did anything except simple spells.
~History of Magic

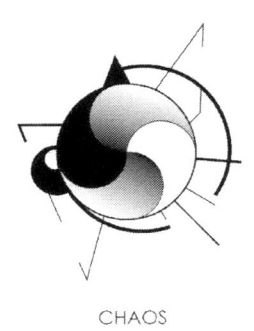

CHAOS

I was so lost in my search through the Byzantine maze of academia that until Jo called my name and pulled me out of my haze, I had no idea how much time passed. I saved my information and turned to look at her, and she had a huge smile on her face.

"What?" But I couldn't help but smile also. Carelian made his way over, twining between our legs.

"They said I have one of the worst cases they've ever seen. Normally this is addressed in grade school or high school and there were things I could do to help with it. But they said absolutely I qualify for assistance." She all but glowed. I don't think I'd ever seen anyone so glad they were diagnosed with a learning disability before.

"This mean I don't need to kick some butt? Beat up on people until they treat you right?" I made punching motions with my hands.

She let loose a peal of laugher and pulled me into a one-armed hug. Her hug was tight enough I ignored the need to breathe until she released me.

"No. They are sending out notes to my professors to allow me oral testing most anything except math, and then I am allowed to verify what the tests say. They are providing me with a software that will let me talk into the computer and do all my reports orally, as well as access to all the books via audio. Plus, they are giving me licensed versions of some fonts that are supposed to be better for people with dyslexia. And spelling and word use? As long as it sounds correct, it won't be counted against me in my classes."

"See! I knew you could get what you needed." I picked up Carelian slipped him into the carrier, still a bit surprised he didn't complain or fight, not that I would ignore my good luck and we began walking out.

"That just leaves you dealing with the FBI people."

"I want to work as an EMT," I blurted out, the words surprising me. "I still need some money as I won't ask your parents to support me in addition to you." I'd read up on financial support. While the government paid tuition and housing, it didn't cover the incidentals like books, supplies, or food. That meant I still needed some sort of job. Most kids had their parents sending them a few hundred a month, or work study. Jo saved her money while she worked full time for her dad and her parents were giving her three hundred a month for other things. But I didn't have that, and my savings would disappear rapidly. Plus, I was tired of being broke all the time.

Jo was about to respond when a woman stepped out of a hallway and we collided with her, sending her to the ground as even I was larger than she was.

"Oh Merlin, I am so sorry," Jo gushed, dropping to her knees to help her up. I moved back a bit to get out of the way. She was tiny, with long dark hair that hung in an intricate net of braids down her back and brushed the top of her butt. As she rose, I took in the bright colored sari styled top over jeans. But what really grabbed my attention was the merlin tattoo on her temple - Entropy/Non-organic/Time. I didn't think I'd ever seen that.

"Are you okay, please tell me you're okay?" Jo was still talking, but I watched the beauty of the woman register with her and she changed subtly. She was standing straighter and doing the little pose she always did when she thought someone was cute. I rolled my eyes.

"No worries, I should watch where I'm going more. I know they say don't text and drive, I obviously need to not text and walk." She held up her phone, smiling, and it transformed her into stunning. I could see why anyone would be captivated by her, and her voice, low and melodic, only amplified her beauty.

"But you're sure I didn't damage you?" Jo bite her lips looking worried and I knew damn well she was making them redder as neither of us had put on any makeup, not that I almost ever did. But Jo loved to dress up and be fancy. Heels and dresses were fine with her, if she had someone to wear them for.

"It takes more than a little tumble to damage me." Her bright brown eyes turned to me and before I had a chance to react, she moved towards me in a fast gliding motion that reminded me of the acrobatic martial arts movies I'd seen. She reached up and brushed my hair away from my temple, revealing all of my crazy tattoo.

Unnerved, I stepped back out of her reach, uncomfortable with anyone being that close into my personal space, especially when I didn't know them.

She however didn't move. She tilted her head and smiled more, adding something I recognized as a sultry smile because of Jo practicing in the mirror. A very practiced sultry smile.

"How lucky for me I didn't run into you two young ladies." This time she shared the smile with Jo, who was much more affected than I was by it, at least from the way her eyes lit up. "Everyone in the Merlin circles has been chattering about your double emergence. Though the reactions are mixed. I know Steven keep bragging about finding you, but I don't know if that is a good thing or a bad thing. Are you attending classes here, Cori?"

Her familiar use of my name made me even more uncomfortable, as did the knowledge anyone was talking about me. I shifted back another half step, oddly wary of this woman. "Next semester, I think."

"Ah, well then I will hope to see you around." Her eyes dropped to my chest, and for a split second I thought she was checking me out, but then she smiled and reached out her hand. "This must be the familiar you acquired in such a dramatic fashion." Before she could touch him, Carelian who had been watching all of this with what I associated with fascination, pulled his head down and hid from her.

Smart cat.

"Ah, he is still shy. Don't worry, he'll get over that." She turned and started away, her ass swaying so hard I thought she might have a limp. With a sudden whirl she spun back around and smiled. "I forgot to introduce myself. I'm Indira Humbert, one of the three merlins on staff. Remember, you'll need a advisor when you start Cori. All merlin students do. I'd be delighted to work with you." Again she gave a smile that I was sure was meant to get my heart racing and libido up. And all it did was make me think about snakes hiding in the grass.

"I'll look forward to seeing you again," Jo said, not quite drooling, but I resisted the temptation to elbow her, hard.

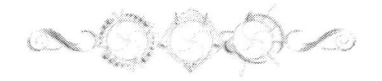

"Oh, I do hope so. Both of you," she all but purred as she sashayed away, the phone going in her pocket.

We stood there watching her go. "Wow, she is something. Why can't I find someone like that? Smart, sexy, and not afraid to show it."

"I agree with those adjectives, but I'm not sure I'd want you to find someone like her." I didn't know how to explain it, but I thought the entire thing had been staged, and I didn't know why. To meet me? Why?

I pushed it away. When it came to my advisor, I'd worry about that later. Much later. Like in January when I'd actually start.

"Where to?" I asked as we got out into the open. The packets I'd been working on still had more to do, and I needed to decide on a major now, but that meant more thinking. It was looking like I might come in as a junior, but I still needed to take some lower level classes, like everything to do with magic, though every single credit had a 'pending approval' note on it.

Jo glanced at her phone. "I've got class in an hour, and a paper to hand the teacher, but I'd like to hit the campus store first. Joanne said I could ask for talking software and a headset, and the font CD. I've got time. Besides, maybe..." She trailed off and laughed.

"What?" I knew I was missing something.

"I really am a horrible person. First lusting after that woman, who was clearly trying to get you to bite her hook and now getting excited about maybe running into Sable."

"Ah, is Sable the one you had hoped would be at that disaster dinner at the Varsity."

Jo blushed, a subtle red going up her cheek. "Yes. And I am still feeling horrible about that, though you know they would probably fawn all over you now."

"That doesn't make it any better. Worse even. You need better friends."

"I have better friends. You. But I don't think Sable would have done that, and you're also right. I haven't been hanging with them as much. And you were right. They think being a mage is something special and even denigrate hedgies."

I cast her a look. "Denigrate?"

"I can listen. I just apparently need to listen to more audio books. It is reading the stuff that is hard." She came to a halt. "Do you know that is a huge weight lifted off my shoulders? I almost feel lighter. I kept thinking I just wasn't trying hard enough, and mom would get so upset at my grades in English. She loved those courses, though math was always her favorite. Now maybe I can explain to her why."

"I think you should. Why don't you head up there this weekend, just you, and spend some time with your parents? I think they would like that."

"She shot a questioning look at me. "But what about you?"

"I think I'll spend time reading up on familiars and seeing about on call weekend work as an EMT. I'm not willing to give that up, not right away. If I do that, maybe I can find a balance with all this. But if it helps, it looks like my entire first semester will be on magic classes and nothing else, but then I'll be in as a junior."

"Oh awesome. Maybe if this dyslexia stuff helps, I'll be able to catch up in my classes."

"You can't be that far behind, you're barely a month in," I pointed out.

"In reading I am. It was taking everything I had to keep up. Being able to listen to it, I can crank it up to a faster speed. Plus, I can listen while I walk, or," she grinned slyly at me, "we work out."

I groaned, but I knew I needed to. "Then see, everything is good." We walked into the bookstore and I watched Jo's head pivot as she looked, then locked on someone. "I take it she's here?"

Jo snapped her glance back at me, ducking her head. Watching the flush rise up her cheek amused me. "You must really like her. Normally you aren't so avoidy. You tend to go in, ask her out, and let the chips lay."

Jo groaned even as she headed over to customer service. "I know. I just can't. Heck, I don't know if she likes girls. But she's smart, funny, has talents, and wow, is she something else." We reached the desk, and Jo turned to get the extra aids she needed while I backtracked her gaze to find who was the object of her affections.

I can see why she caught Jo's eye.

Her skin was the same color Jo's would get when we spent all our weekends at the lake. Jo turned a pretty dark brown like a medium roast, while I went lobster red, then a pale peach. The girl, well woman as she had to be roughly the same as us, had a lithe build that implied she went to the gym. It was yet another reminder that I really needed to work out. Her hair was stunning though. While most mages had long hair and braids, making it easier to do offerings, hers seemed to be twisted around itself in little corkscrews that she had tossed together to form designs. All in all I was jealous. From here I couldn't see much else, other than vaguely pretty and I didn't want to stare.

"I can see the attraction," I said my voice dry when she came back up. She looked at me, a bit panicked, but must have realized I hadn't gone anywhere.

"Yes, she's pretty. But she's also wicked smart and funny. I think she said she was an Army brat. Dad retired, I think."

"So are you going to ask her out?" I was tempted to introduce myself but figured Jo had been through enough for one day.

"Maybe, after I get caught up. Not until." She cast one last look at the girl who I noticed had seen her from the flash of a smile I caught.

Carelian rumbled a loud purr then a whine and wriggled. "Oops, I think I need to let him out for a bit." Outside there were lots of grassy areas. It was the MageTech campus, which meant there were at least some familiars. We headed over that way and I let him down, watching carefully. He looked so tiny compared to everything and everyone, it made me nervous.

Huh, I didn't realize how much him being in that bag, purring, calmed me down.

"Well," Jo started, dragging out the word so I glanced at her. "We have me all sorted out. I almost feel hopeful, though I'll need to spend some time tonight installing all this stuff, and maybe your help if the instructions get a bit wonky."

"Always," I said, having gone back to watching Carelian. He acted like a cat, at least in grooming and bathroom habits. I needed to follow up on the idea that I could teach him to use a toilet. That would make things much nicer.

"That means you need to deal with your mess; the one you created to help me." She shoulder bumped me a little and I groaned.

"The temptation to run away is strong. But, you're right. Can't hide or avoid it forever. " Carelian was still investigating and I pulled out my phone and powered it on, cringing back like I expected it to shout at me.

Beep, beep, ding, ding.

The sound of alerts and messages continued for a full minute before they stopped. "Huh. Fifty-six text messages, ten voicemails. I really don't know if I care." I looked anyhow. A few from Siab, one each from Niall and Chris, and one verifying my registration code for the MageTech admissions process, the rest from Alixant. His name of Steven burned on my screen. I needed to change it.

I glanced at the other messages, they were along the lines of Alixant was really mad, though Siab asked if I was okay. I sighed and scrolled through his. Anger, frustration, and demands, all came through the list of texts and I didn't care. I wasn't a slave, not really, and even with a waiver I still got to take personal time. He would just deal.

I froze when I got to the last text message, locked on the words.

"Cori? What's wrong?" Jo asked. Carelian had finished his investigations and was rubbing against our legs, but his tail flicked back and forth. I could tell he wanted to chase something.

I need to take him to a park so he can chase squirrels or something.

It was an idle thought and I didn't take my eyes off my phone.

"Cori?" Jo prompted leaning over to see if she could read my screen.

"He says he apologizes and asks me to come in Monday morning. To enjoy my weekend, but that we need to talk." I said all of it in a flat voice, hardly able to fathom the words.

"Huh. Well, I guess if you're going to get executed Monday, we should party this weekend?"

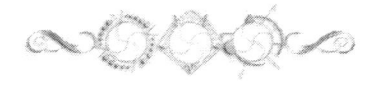

Her irreverent comment made me laugh. "No. You're going to see your parents Sunday and explain all this And I'm going to take Carelian to the park." His ears perked up. "And we are going to spend Saturday getting you all ready to rock the academic world. But," I wiggled my phone in front of her. "Don't you have a class to get to?"

"Oh, crap." Jo was up and gone before I finished laughing. Trying not to think about the Monday ahead, I went home to look up nearby parks that didn't have dead bodies in them.

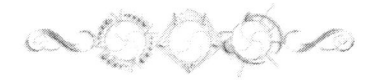

Chapter 35

The Egyptian government has announced they are extending their mandatory service for all magicians. The Middle East already has the severest restrictions on magicians. This extension of a decade for all magicians to twenty years is unexpected. Already the Middle East is one of the few areas where even hedgemages are required to be marked. They also use branding instead of tattoos like every other country under the OMO.
~History of Magic

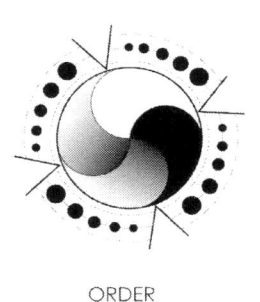

ORDER

The weekend went just as planned. Jo and I fought through updating her computer with new fonts, the audio translation for class texts, the headphones, and the computer software. But once we finished, in one hour she had read, well heard, two chapters and passed the quiz. Something she admitted had taken her three hours before and she couldn't pass because she didn't know which word answers were which. She headed up Sunday and Carelian and I went to the park. He still rarely said anything, but I suspected it was something that wouldn't last. Either way, he chased squirrels but let them go each time, did flips over blowing pieces of paper, and charmed at least three teenage girls.

Jo came home glowing and she had a lightness about her that made her all but radiant. I just hugged her tight and we got ready for Monday.

I'd achieved a strange state of apathy regarding Monday. It wasn't that I didn't care but more that nothing else would shatter my balance now. I knew what I wanted, and what I would no longer give up.

Too bad my stomach didn't listen to my mind as I walked up to the office with Carelian in his pack. I walked in at seven-thirty and the others were already there but what caught my nose was the smell. Fresh coffee and pastries, not donuts but turnovers if my nose was correct, enveloped the room, making it more welcoming than any day prior. Siab and Chris were at the table with coffee in cups, and Niall was standing at the wall display with Alixant. They all turned as I stepped through, making me feel like I had a spotlight on me.

"Good morning, Cori. Grab some food and take a seat. We'll start in a minute."

I blinked at Alixant. His tone was polite almost friendly - more than he'd been since this whole thing started. Thrown off kilter, I let Carelian out, stroking his back as I did so. He gave a soft purr then headed over to my chair. I'd woken him from his nap after chasing things under my bed all night. He jumped right, curled into a red ball of fur, and fell asleep in a way I envied.

Oh sure, keep me up all night, but you get to sleep all day.

I mentally glared at him and got back the feeling of amused agreement. Shaking myself, I walked over to refill my coffee and grabbed a turnover. My nose had been right, apple and peach. With coffee and turnover in hand I approached the table and sat, feeling unsure.

I sat and worked on the turnover. I had a habit of peeling them apart. They lasted longer that way and it gave me something to do with my hands. It took another minute, but Niall sat down and nodded at me, with another half smile.

Okay, have I entered the twilight zone? This is starting to creep me out.

"I owe everyone an apology, and especially Cori," Alixant stated. His voice was matter of fact, but you could tell he was forcing himself to say the words. The question was why.

Regardless of the reason, all of us snapped our attention to him. Part of me wanted to watch the others to see if they had expected this, but I couldn't pull my eyes off of him. His shoulders slightly hunched and hands in his trouser pockets, ruining the line of his suit. He reminded me of a boy having to apologize for something.

"As my agents know, we'd just come off a hard case with a Fire Wizard. All of us had offered up more than usual. We'd seen too many people die and needed a break. They called me in because I'm one of the few merlins in the FBI with any experience with murders."

All of this was new to me. Somehow I'd thought there were hundreds running around but if I thought about how few people were merlins, why would you waste them all in law enforcement?

"I went because I figured it would give me a chance to visit my kid sister. She was distraught because her best friend was missing." I felt the coffee in my stomach start to churn. "Jane Tanner." He sighed and sat down. "I hadn't recognized her from the pictures because of the damage, and the fact that I had only met her a few times. My sister Rebecca is eight years younger than me, and it had been at least two-three years since I'd seen Jane. Plus, you add in the fact that her fingerprints had been removed, well until they told me the name, I didn't realize it was the same case."

He took a swig of coffee and I continued to crumble my turnover into small pieces, unable to work up the energy to put any in my mouth.

"What all of this means is I've been a bit of an ass lately. Between the stress here, my sister and her grief, and then you, the unexpected magic user who seemed somehow involved, yet you weren't." He grimaced like this hurt but continued. "I was less than professional about this entire thing, especially to you, Cori. I was so sure it involved you, you not being involved made it worse. I should not have treated you the way I did, and I've had a talk with the team. I think they have a better understanding of my fears and why I wanted you here. Granted, at first it was to keep an eye on you, but you aren't a suspect. You just seem to end up in the worst possible place, at the worst or best possible moment, depending on how you look at it."

Alixant cleared his throat and took another drink, then looked at me. "I promise more professionalism and a better understanding of each other."

All the decisions I'd made all weekend, rose up. It would be so easy to just give in, duck my head, and be a good little girl. So very easy.

I grabbed on to the resolutions I'd made. "Thank you. I was having issues with all this. But none of that changes the fact that I am useless here. I get that as a mage, I have rules I have to follow, including education and the draft, but I haven't started yet and I don't know anything. Not really. So why am I here? And why did I have to give up my job?" That last statement may have been a bit plaintive. I saw Carelian lift his head and look at me, then tuck it back into his paws.

Alixant rubbed the back of his neck and sighed. "Because I wanted to punish you, since I didn't have anyone else to lash out at."

His brutal honestly took me aback, and from the tiny squeak from Siab, I got the feeling she was just as surprised.

"I don't think I can get your job back and when this asshole strikes again, I will need you. I hoped the pay was enough to at least make up a little bit for all of this."

"Oh, it helps. But still, once this is over, I have at least four months until school starts and I don't have a family supporting me. I really don't want to take out loans. The Mage Draft only covers tuition and housing, not food, clothes, etc. Heck, even after school starts and for the next few years, I'm going to need to be able to work just so I can feed myself."

"Point. I'll see what I can do. But until then, will you help us? Work with us?"

Like I could say no. What? I'm going to let some insane lunatic run around killing people and not try to help?

I didn't say that, but I did say the other part. "That's fine, but I don't know what I'm doing. I know nothing about how to use my abilities. I don't have any magic that is going to help you find him."

"No, but you can help with the planes and stop them from ripping and pouring into the world. We are seeing a spike already. If it happens again, we may start getting repeat emergences." He looked like he was about to say something else but flicked his hand as if tossing it away. "I'll see about getting you some training on the planes. A head start on schooling if you will."

Before I could reply, Chris spoke up. "With that said, we think we have a lead on who the perp is."

The reaction was like an electric current going through the room as we all snapped our attention to Chris, who had a little self-satisfied smirk on his face.

"Spill," the polite voice was gone, the hard, demanding man I knew was back.

"I spent all day Sunday with your sister Rebecca, going over Jane's planner, her emails, and her phone bill. Her phone is still missing but we have her phone bill. Unfortunately, like most users, she did everything via her apps. We can see data usage, but not much else. The only text messages were between her and Rebecca."

He typed and images appeared on screen. "Per Rebecca, she had headed down to Savannah for a long weekend before coming back to Atlanta. It was just a break from everything as her mage draft assignment began September 1st. She'd talked to Jane on the drive down, and had mentioned maybe going out that weekend but nothing specific. She received two texts from Jane while she was in Savannah, way less than normal, but they seemed like things she would say."

Up on the screen an image resolved of a phone text message screen. "The green is Rebecca, the gray Jane."

Green: Got in, talk tomorrow.
Gray: Hey, busy day today, will be out of pocket – ttfn
Green: still out running around?
Gray: sorry, have a date later. Truby's tonight.
Green: I know him?
Gray: Tell you all about later – ta

Chris started up after we had time to absorb the words. "The problem is, we figure Jane was killed about two hours after Rebecca hung up with her. She said she didn't remember Jane mentioning meeting anyone, just heading out for dinner, but not a date. The text messages here were all sent after Jane had been dead for a day or more."

The way he said it made my spine crawl.

"He used her phone to send texts?" I asked. I knew the answer, but that level of creepiness was more disturbing than any body I'd found. Even if you added crabs.

"Yes. We got pings off of towers for those messages, but they were both in places where the MARTA goes by, so there isn't much we can glean from there."

Alixant seemed to sag as he glowered at Chris. "Then how is this a lead? Other than we know he has, or at least had, her phone."

The smile the crossed Chris's face made him look like a wolf who has cornered his prey. "Because I went through every person Jane had mentioned to Rebecca in the past year and scrutinized all her social media. Then I pulled up everything about the people on the boat. Jane was probably the first, but if they are the same killer, then they should have something in common. And we found it." This created a repeat of the electricity that went through the room.

Another image appeared on the wall. A man in his late twenties, nice enough looking I guessed, but he seemed a bit nerdy and even in this picture, taken by the OMO for his ID, he seemed desperate.

"Who is he?" Alixant asked. He wasn't asking the name, which was clear on the idea that had appeared next to the picture, but what mattered. Who was this person?

"Meet Paul Goins. He is a Fire Wizard, age twenty-eight, just finished his draft service about six months ago, where he was assigned to the fire jumpers emergency response squad." I blinked and looked at the man. It might be biased, but most fire jumpers I'd seen interviewed were people who got a kick out of an adrenalin rush. This guy, with his skinny frame, pale complexion, and down turned mouth, didn't look like he'd want to do anything that required physical effort.

"How was he assigned that?" Alixant must have had the same reaction I did.

"Reading through the notes in the file, sheer need. His reviews all had the same phrase 'Does exactly what is required' and I can't find that he made any friends while there."

"Four years is a long time to stay at a job you're where ill suited."

"Well, the last year they got another mage, and moved him over to the R&D people doing vulcanology experiments. From what I can intuit, he hated it there as much as he had at the jumper school, but what was interesting was what happened there."

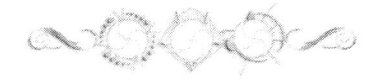

Chapter 36

The draft is usually regarded as a good thing, but not all personalities or choices work well. But then that can be said of any profession. In the end, you get out of it what you put into it, both good and bad.
~OMO Interview

SPIRIT

Chris drew out his words out like an expert storyteller, and even recognizing that, I leaned forward a bit, wanting to hear the rest. "They were in Hawaii, studying the erupting volcano Kilauea. Now Paul is not an earth mage. The best vulcanologists are merlins with both Fire and Earth, though they're rare."

My mind flashed to Shay. I knew he was Earth, but what was his second? It took me a second, before I remembered it was Time. So the odds were, he wouldn't have known Paul but I still couldn't get away from the idea of pinging Shay about this guy. I pulled out my phone and made a note, then turned my attention back to Chris.

"He was supposed to warn them when lava started moving so they could get people and equipment moved out in time. From the notes in the file, the volcano had an unexpected mini-eruption that caught everyone off guard and lava trapped three team members. They couldn't get to them. From all accounts it was a slow death as they were cooked alive. A side note mentioned that three planar rips appeared, small but real, though no one took much notice of them. They collapsed soon after the three died. There was a strange burst of energy that emerged right before the rips collapsed that cooled the lava to stone, but not in time. They had a Psychic that spent most of her time between screaming and sobbing as she felt them die." His tone had lost the storyteller vibe, instead had a grimness to it that made my heart ache. "His service debt ended three months later. What caught my attention was this note in his file." Another image appeared on the screen of a report with big red letters stamped across the top - "Service Fulfilled".

It felt odd to see the personal details of another person's draft service, but then I knew intimate details of many people at this point, so maybe it was just the way it was.

"This was what his supervisor noted as he left," Chris said, then read aloud the comment, which helped as the supervisors handwriting was atrocious. "Paul did an adequate job, and the findings of the investigation into the volcano accident verified he had no prior knowledge. I still find it odd however, that in the last few months, he has been more energetic and been more willing to make offerings to help our mission than before. If anything, he seemed gleeful after the tragedy. This disturbs me but I can't find anything else in his actions to indicate anything untoward besides an idiosyncratic reaction to the deaths of his coworkers."

Chris looked up at us, and I knew he'd made the same conclusions I had. "It is my belief that Paul Goins had a second emergence in the presence of the planar rips that boosted his power and he is seeking to replicate it."

I followed the logic and it made my blood crawl in my veins.

"He realized the slow death of mages would rip the planes. He tried first with Jane, but her solo death wasn't enough. He then tried again with three and what? It didn't work? He wanted more power? Then he jumped to nine?"

"Do they record planar rips anywhere?" I asked, suddenly curious.

Siab tilted her head. "I don't know. The only stable ones are the ones at Area 51. The OMO monitors them 24 hours a day. But I've never heard of anything that can detect or monitor rips in real time or even after the fact." She had already started typing before she finished speaking.

"What if it did work?" I asked and managed not to flinch when Alixant looked at me.

"What do you mean? If it did work, why would he still be trying to replicate it? I could feel the magic pouring out of those people, but they were all hedgies." He caught his voice and cussed. "Anyone drafted would be a magician or higher. Chris, what were the ranks of the three people that died?"

It took Chris a minute, and while he looked, I went to see if I could find contact information for Shay. I didn't have any but I shot Laurel Amosen a note, asking her if she could ask him to call or text me. I was positive she had his info.

"Got it. Two were archmages, the third was a wizard."

"Relatively high ranking. But if it is the amount of power that matters, he may have originally played with ritual to see about amplifying the amount of power, then decided to go with volume over ritual? We already know it works but what happened at the park?" Alixant looked at me. "Did the rips occur there?"

I started to snap back with a retort, but I paused and thought back, comparing the sensations between the oddness at the park that day and the scene in the convention.

"No. They were there, but they didn't tear. They felt," I struggled to come up with an explanation of what I had felt now that I had something to compare it with. "Like balloons that were being filled with water and about to burst, but they weren't there yet. At the convention they hit it and exploded, but I didn't really notice until after going over what happened." I hated to admit it, but him making us sit down that Tuesday and write out every detail, what we felt or sensed, even if we weren't sure, had helped.

He nodded. He had a faraway look in his eyes as he obviously wasn't seeing us. "Let's make a lot of assumptions. Three mages, two arch and one wiz, were enough to create planar rips. One hedge wasn't. Chris, the nine on the boat, were they related to Paul? How?"

"That took a bit, but it turns out they were all members of the same society at college. Not noted as friends but they were all there." Chris raised his hand before Alixant could say anything. "And before you ask, some were, some weren't. Three hedges, four non-magic, two wizards."

"Huh." Alixant leaned back. "We don't know if that worked or not but the supposition is not. So he went for quantity, but why target specifically hedges? Did we ever figure out how?"

"Yes," Siab said with a grin. "A contest and a lot more than just the twenty-seven showed up but only those were pulled into the illusion. The rest kept looking for the contest. We got the notifications off a few phones. Fingerprint access really makes hacking phones easy." She shrugged. "As to the hedges, apparently that was what the contest was geared towards."

"Most hedges don't flaunt their magic. And they might not have enough power to stop him. Maybe it was easier to get them than an archmage, remembering they needed to die slowly," I pointed out, even as icy prickles ran up my spine at how easily I talked about people dying slowly.

"True. I guess that part doesn't really matter. But we know twenty-seven hedgies wasn't enough, but the number in the ballroom was."

I tugged at my hair, thinking as he talked.

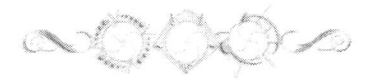

"That means he might try again as we're pretty sure only Cori emerged there, even though it may have triggered more people to emerge. Siab, can you make sure to get a memo to the OMO with all our recordings and information and point out that planar rips can encourage emergences. That is their problem, not mine, and I'm not wasting my time tracking that down." She nodded as he kept talking, scribbling a note to herself. "Okay next step?"

"Waiting for the warrant to toss his place. I put in for it this morning once I received the final bit of information. I'm hoping to get it approved by sometime after lunch. The judge has been prepped by Detective Stone." Niall said, flipping through information. "He has a team on standby to go with us. They have techs to tear the place apart."

I wrinkled my nose at the name. He hadn't impressed me.

"Excellent. Then we have a plan and suspect. Keep double checking, just in case it is someone else, but right now we have a good path forward."

An aura of suffused excitement filled the room, but I felt strangely excluded by it. I had nothing to do with tossing this guy's place, and I hated feeling like a dead weight. I turned my gaze on Alixant and waited.

He must have felt my eyes on him as he looked up and half smirked. It made me wonder how many women fell for that self-deprecating look. Even I softened a bit, but not enough to go away. No longer would I be passive in my own life.

He got up and dropped in the seat next to me.

"So what now, Alixant? The warrant isn't anything that involves me and I'm spinning my wheels here."

I expected attitude, but he'd apparently been sincere in his statement. "You can call me Steve or Steven you know."

I mutely shook my head. Stupid, but I still had issues calling anyone that. With luck I'd never really care or get involved with anyone named that. It would be uncomfortable.

"Ah, I see. Very well. You're right, I don't want you anywhere near that apartment but I do need you to think about planar rips and how to seal them."

"Which would be how?" I didn't keep the stress or exasperation out of my voice, didn't even try.

"Well by closing them. But I'm well aware that is easier said than done, so I've asked someone in to help."

I shrugged. "Okay. But you know I haven't heard anything about how to catch this guy. He sounds dangerous but how do we catch him."

"People have patterns and go to what they know unconsciously. If we are lucky, we'll find something that will give us a clue. Otherwise," His jaw clenched as he gave me a level stare. "We wait until people start dropping and react. Which is why I must ask, even if I am being an ass, please don't kill your phone again. We have the police on alert to grab team members as soon as we have an idea. So please stay relatively available. As to the rest of what you mentioned. I'll remove the waiver on you as soon as we catch this guy. I'll warn you, trying to work while going to school is difficult, especially as mage.

It's why the government covers so much and expects the families to fill in the rest. Don't you have any support?"

I looked him dead in the eye. "No. So I need to work. If I have four months, the more I work, the more I'll be able to save and lessen what I need to do once I start. We do get summers off, right?" I hadn't thought to ask Jo that as she had started just this fall.

"Technically you can, though most take some classes to try and get through sooner. Every program and school is slightly different. You'll need to talk it over with admissions."

I nodded. "We need to catch this guy soon then. Wait." I thought about the money and gave a bitter laugher. "I just dawned on me, I'm making more sitting here doing nothing than working as an EMT."

Alixant blew out a breath. "Let's get this guy first, then we'll talk. But about your planar rips? I've asked an expert to come in and work with you. While Spirit can seal, Chaos can open rips, at least small ones. I'd like you to get some experience learning how to close them." His phone chimed and he pulled it up. "Oh good, my expert is here. Hopefully she'll be able to let you practice on a small scale and then maybe you'll have a chance at the larger ones if it comes to that." He rose as he spoke and headed to the door. "I'll be right back."

I sat there, staring at nothing as I tried to wrap my head around it. I needed to do some budgeting and figure out how much I needed. And here I thought I'd been past that. It had a lot to do with my reluctance. Another four to five years of scrimping and scraping didn't sound fun at all.

"Come on in, I'm sure Cori will be delighted to meet you." I heard Alixant talking and I turned in my chair and froze as I saw the woman we'd run into Friday smiling at me, like she'd won the lottery.

"Oh, we've met, but I'm delighted for the opportunity to get to know her better," Indira all but purred.

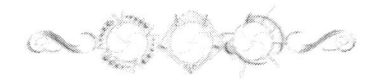

Chapter 37

China's emperor is a merlin, proof he is the son of heaven. Their society is still feudal in structure, though very technically advanced, and has one of the few known non-earth familiars. The Dragon of China is the familiar of the Qin Dynasty Emperor and when it comes time for him to die or is dying, the familiar selects the successor from the available merlins from that family. Oddly it has worked without flaw for the last five hundred years.
~History of Magic

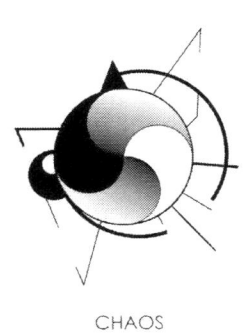

CHAOS

"One of the skills Chaos mages have under Entropy is the creation of planar rips, though to do more than make a micro-rip you need usually to be at least an archmage," Indira's soft silky voice purred. It was driving me nuts. I suspected that it was supposed to turn me on, make me interested, or captivate me. In all honesty it made my skin crawl.

"Okay, but what is the purpose of making the planar tears?" I asked. We were outside the office building in a nice patio like area that was rather big and spacious. It made we wish we had an area like this in the apartment complex. Carelian was trying to climb a tree and I kept glancing at him. I was worried if he got too far up he'd get trapped and I'd have to go rescue him. Since they were Bartlett Pears, they would not hold my weight.

"Practical? None that I know of," Indira admitted. Her full name was Indira Amira Humbert, a widow, and full-time professor at the college. The way she had announced she was a widow unfortunately made me think of black widow spiders, and I worried she had me on the menu for her next romantic meal. "We often do it in laboratory settings to measure and run experiments. We compare most of those against readings at Area 51 to see if anything can be gleaned."

When she wasn't trying the vamp act, she had a lot to say and I suspect made an interesting lecturer.

"All of this I'll learn in class?"

She pursed her lips and shrugged. "Maybe. It depends on what you study. But since you have a touch of Chaos," Her hand drifted up towards my temple and I pulled back, more out of instinct than anything else. "You may find that you are interested in what you can do with that ability."

A meow caught my attention and I looked up to find Carelian staring at us, blazing green eyes watching us from the leaves of the tree. "Don't get stuck up there. I don't want to have to try and rescue you."

I never get stuck, the offended comment rang in my mind and I blinked, looking up at him, my eyes narrowing.

He's smarter than we think. I'm going to have to watch him.

"You've never been around familiars much, have you?" Indira's comment pulled my attention away. I looked at her, taking in her pose, more artful and less obvious than Jo, but still a pose.

"No. Have you?" I was curious, and maybe she'd relax a little. Anything to quit this weird game I didn't know how to play.

"My husband. He had a familiar, an avian." She glanced up at Carelian and smiled. "Yours is very young, truly the kitten it appears. Don't be worried if it seems young or rather quiet. As he gets older, though he won't age quite as fast as a real animal, I suspect you'll wish he would be quiet more."

Humph, Carelian muttered. I looked up, but he was already moving away, tail twitching as he stalked something I couldn't see.

"Back to planar rips. While we proved that magic came into this world by the rips, and they have a tendency to appear and disappear, the three at Area 51 are the only know semi- permanent ones and one of the few where rips to all three planes are present."

The way she said that had me grabbing my phone and texting Chris a question. `What were the classes of the mages?` I had a niggling theory that scrabbled at the back of my mind. Nothing concrete yet, but it would be interesting. `and the counts of mages at the park, I mean how many of each class?`

"But they monitor those constantly. Can't you just research on those?"

"They are researching them. The OMO doesn't share easily, but some information is available. They also don't let scientists in often." She shrugged an elegant movement that called to mind Elsba. It was just as fluid and somehow more discomfiting.

"So back to me. You're going to create rips and I'm going to seal them?"

"Essentially. The rips I'll create are small and only to one plane at a time." She lowered her eye lids, peering up at me through her long dark lashes. "Then, you seal them closed with your magic," she purred out the words while making a languid snap of her fingers. The motion had her leaning forward to provide a view of her generous cleavage, and hints of a candy red bra.

I didn't have any issue with undergarments. I wore my own and preferred the pretty lacy ones. But other than doing the laundry and pulling out what Jo wore, which were either plain and practical or fancy and barely there, looking at other women's bras held no attraction for me. I mean, I wasn't disgusted, I just didn't care.

But I did. Her actions were making my skin crawl.

"Just think, I open, you close." Her purr and innuendo laden voice made me snap.

Figuratively and literally.

"Okay, enough. You are creeping me the hell out. Stop it or I'm gone." I had pulled back and was about to leave as her whole attitude made me just more uncomfortable than being kissed by Danny Lane as a freshman.

She sat up, blinking at me, then in what seemed like magic, her whole body changed. She straightened, her shoulders firming, becoming stronger, the softness of her face hardening, and her gaze became more direct, losing its sensual nature. I stared at the woman sitting in front of me. While still dressed in the same clothes, but she came across as a completely different person.

"Not into women or just me?" her voice was frank and remotely curious. Gone was the soft sensual tilt of words or the hint of innuendo.

"Both? Either?" I stammered out, still trying to figure out what I'd seen.

"Oh well. The information was you were living with a known lesbian, so we figured you were probably lesbian or bi." Indira tilted her head looking at me. "But you really are just friends, aren't you?"

"Yes. Why?" Now I had no idea what was going on. Who was this woman? I glanced around for Carelian and tried to decide if I should run. I should have spent more time practicing magic, and not just reading about it. My hair had been growing like crazy, but I hadn't thought of using any of it.

She gave me a wry smile and settled back on the bench. "Merlins are a small group. We talk about each other a lot, but you are of particular interest. I was asked if I could seduce you since they thought you preferred women. Obviously that didn't work. I'm sure someone will ask Steven to try his hand at some point." Her half shrug didn't bug me this time, it looked like a shrug, not a sexual movement.

"Why would someone want you to seduce me?" I felt like I was asking stupid questions, but none of this made sense. "And why think I was a lesbian?" I was oddly insulted on Jo's behalf. She could do much better than me and the idea of Alixant trying to be sexy with me made me want to gag. I might be able to tolerate him but like him? I still didn't know.

"To control you, get you to bend to various groups' interests more easily. But mostly to encourage you to give us access to the mansion." She rolled her shoulders. "Oh well. You really aren't my type anyhow. Your roommate prompted the preference speculation, that and no one had reported you drooling over Steven or Niall." Her smile was quick and full of white teeth. "I would love Steven to put through the paces. I bet he's very good." Her voice seemed more real this time and even while the idea did nothing for me, I could at least quirk a smile.

"And which mansion?" something vague stuck in my mind but I couldn't pull it forward.

She shook her head. "Never mind. Just be aware you are of great interest to very many people. For now though, planar rips." Indira spoke in a clear voice with a hint of a smile and all the posturing disappeared. I relaxed and even Carelian decided to show up and learn.

I opened my mouth to protest. I needed to know which interest group she represented but before I could ask her about that, she snapped her fingers and I felt reality tear. I'd felt it before, I'd just not realized what those sensations meant. But now, seeing a tear in the reality of space, time so close to me and Carelian went almost statue still. Now I could associate the feeling with what it meant. The ripple of ice and the jab of pain my skull. Quick, transient, I'd never paid that much attention before. Now I knew to pay very close attention.

While I still wanted, needed, to follow up on all the questions her comments had raised, the little tear in reality demanded all my attention.

"What do you feel?" She asked, in a normal voice, thank the merlins.

"An icy feeling with a sharp stab that went away." I knew that was the sensations, but it didn't make much sense.

"That sounds similar. Once you identify the feeling, you then link it to planar rips opening. Have you felt it before?"

I barely had to think about that. "Sure, I always assumed it was a headache. Swift stab of pain and then nothing. As long as I can remember."

Or since I emerged at twelve.

That thought was bleak.

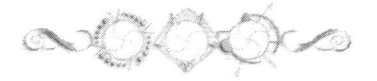

"Then you've been feeling planar rips appear for a long time. As far as anyone has reported, there is not any difference in sensation level between a tiny rip like that," she pointed at the rip in air between us, "and a major tear like what is at Area 51. Which is good. If the sensations were comparable, anyone alive when those ripped open would have died on the spot."

A strange thought flitted across my mind: Maybe most spirit mages had this awareness, which is why we were so rare. I let the thought go, in favor of another one.

"You've seen them?"

She nodded, a shudder rippling through her body. "Yes. They feel like looking into gaping maws of hell, but-" Indira broke off and shook her head. "But it doesn't matter. Some day you can travel there yourself and decide what they mean. Now I want you to try and close that rip in space."

I had so many questions I wanted to ask. What happened if it stayed open? What was on the other side? Could I touch it? Reach through and experience the other planes?

Instead I went with what we seemed to be focused on—the here and now. "How do I do that?"

She gave a wry smile. "I was afraid you would ask that. Here is what I've been told, reach out and feel the rip, feel the breadth and size of it, then you'll know what it will involve to seal it; how much your offering will be."

I lifted up my hand to touch it. Indira grabbed my wrist hard in a hard, tight grip even as Carelian growled. I didn't know if he growled at me or her.

"Touch it with your mind. Feel it. Touching it physically can have unforeseen side effects."

I swallowed and pulled my hand away. Then I stared at the rip, trying to figure out how to touch something with my mind.

I swear, if everything at college is this much mumbo jumbo, I'm going to go insane. At least the certification training was all concrete and nothing fuzzy wuzzy.

I couldn't feel it, not really, but the longer I stared at it, the more I could sense a hole. Kinda like when your tooth falls out. No matter what, your tongue gets drawn to the hole. I realized there was the same sort of sensation in my mind, to the right, where the stab of pain had come from. Something I wanted to seal up.

I started to ask how I would seal it, but I could see how. Well not really, but more sense it. There was a zipper, at least that was how my mind interpreted it. I found the tab of the zipper and pulled. I expected resistance, but instead there was a question of an offer. It felt like a question or a trade and I knew without having to think about it, it would cost me 4,321 molecules. Which would be about a quarter inch of a single strand of hair.

How in the world?

My stunned thought held me frozen and confused. But I remembered a question, this same feeling, asking me for the cost with the man up the ladder. Then I'd shoved it away, agreeing without thought, without paying attention to the feeling, to the question. I'd just given. Same thing with the murder ball. It had asked, but I'd batted it away, agreeing without paying attention.

My skin crawled, trying to figure out how could I have not paid attention. The feeling was so subtle, so shallow, that if I wasn't paying attention to the sensation, I'm not sure I would have even noticed. The cost was so low I would still just dismiss it.

I pulled my attention outward, my mental fingers still on the zipper of the portal and looked at Indira. "Is the agreement of the offering more noticeable the higher the cost?"

She gave me a half smile. "Good job. Most don't think about that until their senior year. Yes and no. If you have yards of hair and it will cost you half of it, a huge offering. It won't be as demanding, as if you have hair like yours and it will cost you a finger. When you offer living body parts you'll learn to agree to the offering and then direct it. There is an entire year in college about nothing more than how to offer and choose the offering."

"Huh," I muttered and pulled my attention back to that zipper. I sent an assent, and the zipper flowed with my thought, sealing the rip. It was so easy and I'd expected to have to struggle.

I opened my eyes and the weird rip in the sky was gone. I poked at it mentally, then with my hand. Indira didn't stop me and when I was sure it was gone, I turned to look at her. "Can you make bigger ones? And do you control what plane they open up to?"

Her elegant eyebrow arched up at me and she shrugged. "Usually I just let which ever plane is closest to us open, but I keep them very small. Otherwise, there is the chance of something that isn't a familiar coming out."

"What? Does that happen? Things come out like that?"

Indira smirked at me - half amused and half pitying. "Where do you think unicorns and dragons come from?"

Chapter 38

While no mage can hold an elected office, they are often the advisor's and temporary fill ins for those offices, working around the law. With many mages staying in public service after their draft term is met, there is a disproportionate numbers of mages to non in the government halls. This is concerning to many and something OMO is taking seriously.
~OMO Interview

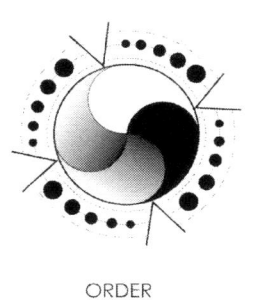

ORDER

Try as I might, she avoided every attempt to find out more about who wanted hooks into me. Instead she made me recognize, locate, and tell her the plane of every rip she created. We'd been at it for two hours when a noise made me look up as Alixant headed our way.

He gave Indira a warm smile, and the siren appeared just for a second, smiling a sultry smile at him, then he turned to me. "We got the warrant approved but go home. I'll call if they find anything but somehow I don't think it will be that easy."

With that, he was gone. And it wasn't that easy.

For the rest of the week nothing changed. They found nothing conclusive, no journal, no social media accounts gloating about his new power, but he had left in a hurry. That left me once again twiddling my thumbs. Well, not quite as much. Alixant apparently thought the world of Indira and had me meeting with her Tuesday and Thursday, practicing the portal closing. I was getting better quickly and even the largest they dared to open, about six inches wide, didn't cost more than a single strand of hair. I didn't think I'd get why most people were so stingy with their magic.

Mondays I spent in the office and got caught up on their progress, which wasn't much, though Chris verified one thing for me. The three mages had each had a different class. When we looked at the park, only two of them had been spirit mages, the rest almost split between Chaos and Order. From the interviews it looked like there had been about twenty percent Spirit at the convention.

My thoughts were that you needed all three to be dying, which is why it worked. It wasn't the number of people; it was the power and balance of the classes. No one disagreed, which didn't mean I was right but it didn't mean I was wrong either.

The next two weeks went by with me either practicing, or fighting with the school. Jo was doing much better and I hadn't realized how depressed she'd been until she wasn't. Mostly I tried to not feel like an idiot. Niall was at the point he was almost friendly and Siab was a kick. I'd actually miss seeing her every day. Other than that, I enjoyed collecting pay for not doing a damn thing but since I had so much free time, Jo made me use our gym membership and work out. Which I hated.

Friday evening we were at the gym and I almost wanted to beg to go out with her friends, but I needed to build muscle. I'd been putting on weight and had curves, but I wanted to be able to lug all the books around I'd need next year without dying. So I was here. Under protest.

"Hey," Jo puffed. "You have plans Sunday?" She was on the Stairmaster, going up them faster than I could have done with zombies chasing me. I was greatly regretting my desire to get more in shape as I slogged through my time on the elliptical. Evil machine.

"Uh," I tried to remember my schedule through the haze of exhaustion. "Yeah. The funeral for Jane." I had to go. I needed to put closure to this one and maybe the nightmares would stop. Odd that out of all the deaths I'd seen, this was the one that still haunted me. The look her face, the face they had to do reconstruction on to match to identification photos. Anything to try to help wipe it away from my memories.

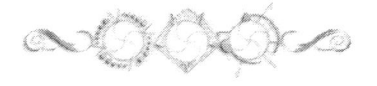

"Oh well. *Papi* won tickets to the SEC game this weekend. He's got six. *Mami*, Stinky, and Paolo are going. Marco had other plans." I could hear the wicked smile in her voice. "If he isn't careful, *mami* is going to start wedding plans. He's taking his girlfriend away for a weekend in Helen." Helen, Georgia was a town north of Atlanta that was all in a Bavarian style from the buildings to the stuff they sold. It was a fun getaway but living there would have driven me crazy. Cute scalloped eaves and everything else was not my personal design taste. I might still be working on exactly what styles I liked, but I knew for sure that wasn't it.

I had to laugh. "Yes, she will be. Good for him. But nah, you go. I've got the funeral, then I wanted to work on more school stuff. I'm trying to get out of some classes and I need to write an argument as to why I should be excluded. You'd think my degrees and certifications would be enough of a reason." I was still annoyed at that but because people so rarely went from one to the other, they were balking. That was something else I'd talk to Alixant about if it didn't quit being a pain. I'd have time Sunday. "Why don't you ask Sable?"

I heard the muffled sound from her and didn't even try to hide my smile as I kept on elipticalling. Was that even a word?

"You think she'd come?"

"I think you've been talking about her non-stop, that you text her most evenings, and that since she responds at least as fast as you do, she might be interested. Introducing her to your family as a first date might be extreme but if she's a keeper you might as well throw her into the deep end."

"Hmm. I'll think about it."

Ha, I bet she is texting her before we even make it to the locker rooms.

I won that mental bet thirty minutes later as I dragged my wet noodle body back to the locker room.

"She said she'd love to but to be aware she was wearing orange."

"And what color will you be wearing?"

"Neither. I don't like yellow and refuse to wear orange. *Papi* however will be decked out in yellow, which means *mami* will be. All them." She rolled her eyes as she grabbed her stuff out of the locker. We headed home to our own showers and a half hour later I was in bed, sound asleep while she finished listening to some of her texts.

Sunday morning I got dressed in funeral clothes while Jo tried to decide what to wear to be sexy, comfortable, parents appropriate, and the right attire for a football game.

Her room looked like a tornado had gone through it. "You are a clothes horse, you know that."

"Of course I am. With this body I need to display it properly. Make men weep at what they can't have and make women drool." Her comeback lacked its normal zest as she dug through another set of clothes.

"You're over stressing. She's seen you most days. Wear cute jeans, boots, hair in a ponytail, and one of your favorite t-shirts, one with a v-neck. You'll look awesome, you always do."

She paused and lifted her head, looking at me for reassurance. "You sure?"

"Dang, you must really like her. I've never seen you this freaked out. Yes, I'm sure." My phone beeped at me. "And I have to go. Let me know who wins." I grabbed a big purse I'd bought. It was almost nice, but bigger than anything I'd have normally gotten but Carelian fit in it nicely, for now. At three weeks, he'd almost doubled in size and I was starting to worry he'd be the size of a German Shepherd before he quit growing. While he still fit in the carry bag on my chest, I refused to wear that to a funeral.

"Come on. We have a funeral to go to."

He still didn't talk much, but all the books I read backed up what Indira had mentioned. If you got a baby familiar, and he had been barely past the milk stage, they started out relatively quiet, but soon talked much more. I thought it was odd that even young he'd seemed much older than his equivalent human age, but I wouldn't argue. We'd already started on the toilet training - or more accurately, using the toilet instead of the litter box. But he needed to get bigger before it was easy for him.

The rideshare waited outside for me and the day was already heating up. Fall didn't really start in Georgia until late October, if then. So the day, at ten A.M., was already at ninety and getting warmer.

The driver looked askance at Carelian then glanced at my face and got even more pale. I never could figure out if it was that I was a merlin, or that my tattoo looked altered, which had heavy penalties for both the mage and tattoo artist. Either way, it wasn't anything a driver needed to worry about.

I arrived at the funeral home early. That driver had treated every yellow as a reason to accelerate leaving me closing my eyes for most of the ride. Funeral homes were all depressingly similar. I made my way in and stayed in the background as people milled around. Thinking about everything we'd talked about in the meetings, I people watched, keeping an eye out for our unsub. Even the language they used put you at a distance and it made me uncomfortable.

Now that is an interesting thought. Why does unsub make me feel uncomfortable, but patient or victim doesn't?

Carelian lay at my feet while I turned over the concepts in my head. I'd been there about fifteen minutes when Alixant walked in, Niall and Siab with him, and a young woman I didn't know. They headed my way, so I didn't worry about getting up and heading towards them.

Does the man have radar to know where I am at all times? I mean really.

It was a valid thought. The place wasn't packed, but there had to be about fifty people there already and I was against the wall wearing a dark blue blouse, black slacks, my quietly professional black shoes, and a bright maroon bag. It was the only color they had.

"Cori," he said as he walked up, the woman with them. "I wanted to introduce you to my sister, Becca. Becca this is Cori Munroe, the Spirit Merlin I mentioned."

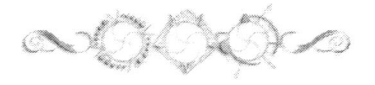

"Ah, you're the one that found Jane? The one that is going to help them catch the asshole that killed her?" The venom in her voice was actually refreshing compared to the studied calmness from all the agents. Her hair was the same dark brown as Alixant's and her widow's peak looked better on her than on him, giving her an aristocratic elegance I could never hope to achieve. With dark brown eyes and a long, burgundy dress, she looked like someone who had stepped down from a painting, she was so regal. Her tattoo, brown and dark blue, indicated she was an Earth mage but the grief in the lines around the corners of her mouth and eyes, made her human.

I stood and shook her hand. "Hi. Yes, I found Jane. I'm so sorry. I don't know about the stopping the guy, but I will help if I can."

"That is good enough. And thank you. I hate the idea of her dying with no one there." Her grip was tight, almost painful, but I could tell it was from emotions, not anger or anything else.

"Come on, the service is beginning," Niall said, turning as people streamed into the main area.

We headed that way, Carelian jumped into the bag and I lifted it. He was still too small to walk with this many people. Getting trampled would not be fun. The idea of him getting hurt at all made my stomach twist. As a group we went in and listened to the story of a girl's life cut short before she had a chance to be anything, and all I could do was thinking of Jo being the one nailed against that tree.

Chapter 39

While religions and faith still exist, America holds little resemblance to the world of pilgrims started. Magic made too many miracles the recourse of men, and being able to talk to the dead shattered many of the beliefs of heaven and hell. While there is a resurgence in Wicca and other religions, for the most part Rome is now a figurehead of a religion that many give only lip service too.
~History of Magic

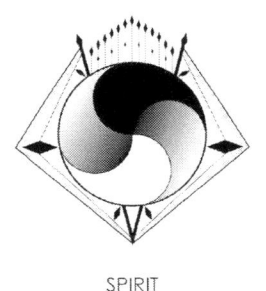

SPIRIT

No one spoke on the drive to the burial site. I rode with Alixant and Rebecca. I slipped into the backseat before anyone could protest and I occupied myself with petting Carelian, who purred loud enough Rebecca glanced back at him and smiled. It was the first smile I'd seen it on her all day. I got the feeling she was a fierce friend, as fierce as Jo. I hated the fact that my mind immediately went to imagining how Jo would react if someone killed me. My hand tightened on Carelian at that thought. I needed to make sure she never had to face that. The thought of her face as lined with grief as Becca's made me ill.

The funeral was somber. From here I could see her family, while during the service itself I couldn't, though I heard a few people muttering about no viewing.

They don't know how glad they should be. None of her family should have their last view of her like that.

I watched Rebecca hug Jane's parents as tears wet her cheeks and I glanced at Alixant. What I saw erased the remainder of my resentment. Pain, grief, sorrow, and a determination that made his profile seem chiseled in stone. Right then he could have modeled for a bust and driven the artist world crazy with the emotions it would have held.

She walked back and joined us. Chris had another commitment, but from what they had said, no one expected Paul Goins to attend. It was doubtful Jane meant, or had meant, much to him. She was a means to an end, and his goal must be more power. It was the only thing that made sense.

It made me wonder what his family history was. I knew I was running from my parents. While my desired profession, EMT, was in direct correlation to all the people I found hurt or dying, it also helped that being an EMT nothing to do with their careers, not even close. Avoiding them still drove me even when fighting with the choices of classes for the next few years and trying to decide what degree I wanted.

"Would it be against your ethics if I asked for a favor from the FBI merlin?" I asked as we walked back towards the waiting cars.

"OOh, hear that Stevie? You are famous," his sister teased, even though her face still was damp from tears.

I flinched at the nickname but kept a half smile on my face, shifting my bag with Carelian in it from one hand to the other.

"I don't know what you could want from me, Cori. But ask." He seemed both amused and curious.

"I'm having issues with MageTech. They are saying my job experience and previous classes don't count for much. I've given them transcripts and it was a fully accredited college. As they have told me repeatedly, mages don't come in with college credits, or if they do, it is only a few. Not me with a triple AA."

Rebecca looked at me, lifting a brow. It pulled her tattoo up, changing it in a way that caught my attention for a moment. "You have a triple AA? I didn't think that was possible. What did you get them in?"

Her tone seemed interested, so I answered without the defensiveness that Alixant seemed to kick off in me. "A new program at the community college. You get your degree and or certifications in Medical Assistant, Criminal Justice, and Emergency Medical Tech. I then got my paramedics certification. So I was working as an EMT when your brother decided to interrupt my life." I managed to only keep the comment wry instead of aggressive. I would take that as a win.

"They what? No. Everything you have should count. I'll call. Yes, you should be going in as a junior though there will be a few lower level mage courses you need to take."

Becca looked at me, a frown creasing her brow. "You didn't think you'd emerge?"

I gave a laugh that was only slightly bitter. "I knew I wouldn't emerge. Except apparently, I already had, a decade ago."

"What?" Her shock caused real laughter, and people walking by frowned at us. I cut it off quickly.

"Yeah. So Alixant? You help?"

"Yes. I'll get on the phone this week, if I can find time. We know people sometimes emerge when they don't expect to, they should be adept at handling just about anything. And not accept work experience?" He got a funny look in his eye. "I'll bet I can get you some college credits for this. It might not count towards your bachelors, but I bet it would towards your masters, depending on what you major in."

The hint wasn't subtle, but I just nodded. "Thanks." We had just reached the car when all of our phones went off. I grimaced and heard Carelian whine at the cacophony. Pulling out my phone I noted the time, just after one, as I answered the call from Chris.

We all must have answered at the same time as the feedback between our phones was crazy. I hung up and moved closer to Siab.

"We're all here. What's up, Chris. I thought you were at Quantico this weekend?" Niall asked, speaking loudly as Siab set her phone to speaker.

"He's struck, and it's worse than we feared."

"What?" Alixant's voice was sharp. "How can you know?"

"He hit the SEC game. They have over three hundred 911 calls already, the system is crashing, and our seers are foretelling the rips opening so large other things will get in. Things we can't fight against."

His words made my blood run cold. Indira had mentioned things coming into our world via the rips, but what could be worse than a dragon? Not that I'd ever seen one. Then the rest of what he said registered.

"The SEC football game? Here in Atlanta?" I clarified, because even I knew there were multiple games on weekends, or at least I thought they were. Maybe it was in some other city.

"Yes, at the Mercedes Benz stadium. The place is becoming a ground zero for terrified people, mages and non, alike. You need to get there and stop him."

Aliant broke into a run towards the cars. "Everyone with me, we don't have time for multiple vehicles. Niall passenger, get us linked in and start collecting details."

I followed, running as fast as I could, holding Carelian tight in my arms as terror washed through me. I had never felt fear like this before. Jo was there. All the Guzman's were there. I might lose them all. I didn't know how to help. What would I do if I lost Jo?

I slid into the car, Becca squeezed in the middle and Siab on the other side. I held Carelian in my lap, trying not to crush him as I buckled the seat belt and kept my panic at bay.

Jo, dear merlin Jo, please be all right.

A purr and Carelian rubbing his face against mine broke my thoughts even as the car slammed into reverse and then into drive. Chris' voice came through the speakers as lights and siren began to strobe out.

"Here's what we know. End of first quarter, calls started coming in. That people had collapsed. It ramped up as time went on, last count was over two hundred." Chris' voice bobbled up and down as Alixant ramped onto the freeway, lights and siren blaring. I braced myself with my legs and held Carelian tight. At least the three of us were wedged into the back tight enough that I only needed to worry about keeping my head from slamming into the window.

"Any verdict? Do we have verification of any rips forming?" Alixant snapped out the questions as he went into the emergency lane to avoid traffic. I closed my eyes.

The second I did, the image of Jo, laying there lifeless, the greyness of death around her lips appeared in front of me. My eyes snapped back open. I had to fight not to cry, the image was so real. I took deep breaths, trying to clear my mind. I didn't want to take the risk that just thinking something could have it happen.

"ETA eight minutes. Take the next off ramp," Niall spoke before Chris could answer Alixant's questions.

"Right now, they think it is some sort of poison. No reports of death. A few are writhing in apparent agony. The current personnel can't find any wounds, so no one knows what is going on. If it is a transformation, how the hell can he affect that many people?" His voice sounded frustrated, upset, and perversely, it made me feel a bit better. Knowing it did matter to them helped when they kept a distance from everything. I leaned back in the seat as Alixant stepped harder on the gas. I almost shut my eyes again as Carelian let loose a plaintive meow and wiggled into the corner of my arm.

"Revised ETA, three minutes," Niall said, his voice calm as Alixant raced up a one-way street the wrong way. I felt like I was in a video game, but knowing we were getting to Jo faster helped.

"Back in the bag, Carelian. I'm going to need to run." I pulled up my phone as he crawled into the bag with a sad, worried meow as he did what I asked. She'd sent me a pic of the tickets as they went through, and I could clearly see the section and seats. I knew where to go. Blue lights caught my attention and I looked up to see us pulling into a parking lot already full of flashing light from cops, firetrucks, and ambulances.

"Get out and head in, spread out and see if you can figure out what the vehicle is. Make sure you have your phones," he shouted the orders even as the car slammed to a halt, rocking me back in the seat. I undid the seatbelt, grabbed Carelian's bag, and leapt out of the car. I didn't even worry about the fact there was nothing to identify me as an agent. I just ran.

Either I looked intimidating, or no one had time to mess with someone who was ambulatory and not begging for help from them. I got past the entrance and paused to read the section labels. I'd never been here so I had no idea where to go.

There, section 115 is that way, and she's in row 20.

People might have yelled for me but I didn't pay any attention. I held Carelian tight to my chest and I ran. Jo dead or dying. Her parents. Stinky. Fear lent speed to my feet but it did nothing for my energy or stamina as I raced up the stairs.

If she lives, I promise I'll never whine about working out again.

I was puffing by the time I reached that section, and I swore Carelian had doubled in weight. At any other time I would have stood there panting, trying to catch my breath. Instead, I lumbered towards that section, looking for anything familiar. While I was racing through the passageways to the seats and even up the stairs, it had been loud with people crying and running around, both first responders and fans. But up here it was like the convention times a hundred. People were screaming and begging but no one looked at the field. I glanced at it, to see people milling around down there, but no one laying on the ground.

So something only the fans would get?

As I moved towards where they should be, I tried to parse what I was seeing. Lots of people were yelling and screaming, but I didn't smell blood or anything caustic, so what could it be?

I found the right spot and started trotting down the stairs, heading to row 20. Then I saw the familiar shaved heads of Henri and Stinky, the glorious mane of Jo's hair, and Marisol luxuriant black shot with silver. But they weren't moving, and Jo was leaning down over her chair. My heart caught in my throat as tears welled into my eyes and I stumbled down the last few steps.

"Jo?"

Chapter 40

What lays on the other side of the rips to other planes is anyone's guess. But given that no one has ever come back alive, the odds are it is nothing friendly to humans.
~Magic Explained

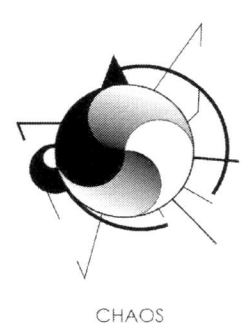

CHAOS

H<small>ER</small> name was barely more than a croak and I got ready to have my heart broken for all eternity. Her head jerked up and she spun. "CORI!" She leapt off the seat and grabbed me in a hug that almost cracked my back and narrowly missed crushing Carelian. I responded by wrapping my arms just as tight around her, my relief almost making me sob.

"Oh, thank the merlins you're alive." I had to reach up and touch her face to reassure myself as she pulled away.

"I am, but Stinky and Sable aren't doing well." Her voice hoarse with something, screaming? She stepped back, and I saw what she had been hovering over. Stinky lay slumped in his chair, and the girl I'd seen in the bookstore was silent, almost looking dead, except I saw her chest rising and falling, barely. Henri and Marisol were trying to rouse Sanchez, while Paolo stood back, his arms clenched across his chest, and shoulders so tight I could see the line of his muscles through his shirt.

"Move," I said as I pulled gloves out of the side compartment of the bag. Carelian had crawled out and sat on the back of one seat, peering around. I worried, but only a teeny bit. He was a smart cat and knew more than you would think.

Henri moved, though Marisol stayed on his other side. I went through his vitals, looking at him, trying to figure it out. His breathing was slow, skin clammy, but his pupils weren't fixed or dilated. I crawled over Marisol to check on Sable, who had Jo perched next to her. Her condition was the same.

They were exposed to something, but what? Why aren't all of them affected?

That removed it being aerosol. That left ingestion or skin. I started to ask questions, but then the smear of color on her face caught my eye. Bright yellow, it looked like someone had wiped it off. I glanced at Jo. She didn't have any colors and neither did Marisol, but Henri and Paolo had bright orange streaks on their faces. I moved back over to Sanchez and looked. Sure enough there were traces of yellow on his face, though mostly smeared.

"What is the paint from?"

They all looked at me blankly, though Marisol's grip on Stinky's hand tightened to make both of their fingers go white.

I touched my face. "Henri and Paolo have orange, Sable and Stinky have yellow. Where did you get the paints?"

"Oh," Henri's voice cracked a bit but he cleared it and pulled out two jars. One had a label from a local craft store, the other was unmarked and in a disposable plastic jar. "They were handing them out. I already had the orange from our local high school. Same colors but Sable and Sanchez wanted to root for the other team. Mostly to tease us, I think." I knew the orange team was Henri's alma mater, so that made sense.

I reached out and grabbed the small jar of paint. It just looked like something you'd do at home, simple and not at all dangerous. I opened it and sniffed it, but I couldn't tell anything. The last thing I wanted to do was touch it. I grabbed my phone and called Alixant.

"Where in the four fucking planes are you?"

"Take a look at the victims. I think they all have paint on their faces. They may have jars near them or on them that look like homemade disposable jars. The one I have is yellow."

"They had orange also," Henri interjected.

"They apparently had both colors." As I spoke, I moved over to across the row, giving Carelian a quick glance to make sure he was safe. He hadn't moved from his vantage point on the back of the seat. I bent over to look at a teenager whose father was in a panic, holding and rocking. The kid had the face paint, but it was yellow. The father had none. "See if all victims have the paint on them. Look close as people might have wiped it off trying to get them to respond."

I paused and turned back to the Guzman's, watching me anxiously. "What did you wipe the paint on their faces off with?" My worry spiked, as the idea of that getting on their hands, if that was what caused it, hammered into me.

Marisol wordlessly held up the corner of her shirt. She'd worn a tank top, it was hot still, and a light over shirt. That was what she had used to wipe off the paint.

"And Sable?" I looked at Jo, knowing she'd been bouncing between the two of them worried and frantic.

"I used napkins from the hotdogs we'd gotten. I didn't touch it."

"Good. You hear all that, Alixant?" I hadn't moved the phone from my ear as I'd talked, looking around.

"Yes. We are collecting samples now." His voice was gruff but he didn't waste any more time trying to get me to obey him.

I turned slowly, looking at the hundreds, if not thousands of people laying slumped in chairs, on the stairs, on the landing areas. I didn't know how many were dying or already dead. That thought spurred me forward and I checked the pulse of both Sanchez and Sable. It was becoming erratic.

"Alixant. Could this be another transformation? Where it was changed to something else?" I couldn't even see distinct people on the other side of the dome. This place was huge. How could it be?

"Doubt it. If they were that powerful, they wouldn't need to be doing this." He stated it slowly and I clenched my hand so tight on the phone the edge hurt. "Is it working, are the rips forming?"

"I can feel the rips forming. They are almost fully made," I admitted. "They're huge. About a third of the field."

"Damn it. Cori," he said urgently. "Can you close them?"

I swallowed and forced out the words. "Maybe. But from what Indira told me and the other specialists I worked with, if we don't stop the flow of magical energy, it would be me putting my strength against all of theirs." All the thousands dying with their magic streaming out to rend the veil between worlds. There was no way I could compete. No merlin, no matter how strong would be able to.

"Fuck," his curse was low and vicious, and I pulled the phone away from my ear. "We're working on it, but we don't know how long it will take to identify." He clicked off, saying nothing more and I stood there frozen, feeling helpless. I HATED feeling helpless.

Fuck this, I am not letting Stinky die. I'm not letting any of them die. I am so tired of letting people die.

I dropped the phone back into the bag and headed over to Henri. He and Marisol were hovering over Stinky, while Jo bounced between Stinky and Sable.

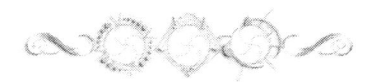

"Give me the paint," I ordered, holding out my hand. Henri said nothing just put the small bottle into my hand.

I'd been studying like crazy and still didn't know how to even begin to use my abilities, but I was a Spirit Merlin dammit. With my gloved finger I opened it and took out a small smear. It lay against my blue clad fingers. I tried to sense it like I did the rips but it slipped through my mind. I didn't know enough. From everything I had read since I had a pale Non-Organic, I should be able to identify and even do things with this. But I hadn't played with enough compounds to recognize anything. Once more I was going to be a failure.

Stinky choked and began to seize. I could hear others scream as it seemed to be spreading. I moved over to him. "Get them both flat so they don't hurt each other. We need to wait."

"You can't help? Neither of you?" Marisol's voice broke as she looked up at me, her face pale, eyes red.

I fought down a scream. "I'm trying. Really." I looked at the bottle and brought it up to sniff it. The faint smell of oranges and lemons, with a dark hint of something tainted and bad under it. "They used essential oils to cover up the smell. What would they need to cover up?"

There were so many things that could kill people, how was I supposed to figure it out?

My phone rang and I dove for it, pulled it out. "You figure it out?"

"Yes. That son of a fucking demonspawn used nicotine. We already have people dying. It's an easy molecule structure and I have people here shattering it as fast as possible, but the strongest I have is a wizard. We don't have anyone who can do mass amounts."

My throat had gone tight. Nicotine, an easy poison to make and it killed with so little. "What do you mean you are shattering it?"

"We have transform mages breaking it, but the strongest I have can only do an area about ten meters across and we are running out of offering fast." His voice sounded weary and defeated.

"Send the picture of the molecule to me," I snapped hanging up. I looked up at Jo crouched near Sable. "I need you. We all need you."

"What?" She climbed over the others and moved over to me. More and more people were succumbing, and I saw more than a few that looked at their hands and were shaking and wiping them at their pants.

"How much are you willing to offer?"

"For what?" Jo looked at me blankly.

"To save as many as you can. To save Sanchez and Sable?"

"My life if I need to," her voice held no doubt. I watched her sink into herself, changing becoming older in a way I couldn't define. "What do I need to do?"

I showed her the picture of the molecule. "I need you to break it. Shatter the molecular bonds. It's hydrogen and nitrogen. The body can handle those as free atoms. Can you do it?"

She closed her eyes, and focused. I knew that they had just gotten into how to transform... well barely. Merlin. For all I knew she didn't have enough training or skill to do it. Time seemed to stand still and rush by as I waited, hoping that she could find, recognize, and be able to break the chains. And while I waited that interminable amount of time, I heard the screams and wails of despair as people started to die, convulsing, and their heartbeats slowing. Plus, I felt the rips snap into existence. So huge and powerful. I fought to grasp how much they opened our world onto theirs. And worse, I could feel things on the other side, noting the access to our world.

Where do you think unicorns and dragons come from?

Indira's idle comment floated in my mind and I shot another worried look at the rips. I didn't know why everyone wasn't staring at them. They had to be visible to everyone. Didn't they?

"I got it." Jo's comment took a second to register as I dragged my attention back to her.

"You do?"

She nodded her face pale and her mouth flattened into a line. "I can do it, but it will take everything."

I paused, then looked at her my stomach curdling. "What do you mean everything?"

Jo swallowed but her shoulders stayed squared. "The place is drenched in it. It is almost everywhere. It will take more than I have to break them. There isn't any way for me to separate what is in the paints versus what is in the cigarettes and cigars, and even vapes in people's pockets. So I have to break them all. And there are lots. More than I have, using every trick I've learned or even heard of."

Left unspoken was the knowledge that she didn't know enough, that there wasn't anything she could do to learn what she hadn't had time to learn.

"Jo, I - " the words died in my throat as she looked at me.

"Would you not offer yourself to save Stinky? To save me? How can I do less to save them?" Her hand wave didn't encompass just Stinky and Sable, but the entire stadium.

The urge, the need to protest, to tell her not to do it, that I had no right to ask, died in my throat as I looked at her and the sounds of the dying filled the air worse than any cheer ever had.

"Okay. I love you," I blurted, needing to make sure she knew past any shadow of a doubt.

"I know."

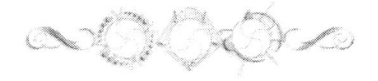

I fought not to cry as I watched my best friend get ready to sacrifice herself for her family and strangers.

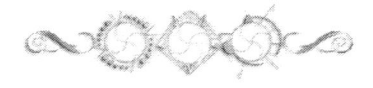

Chapter 41

Heroes exist. But you'll find the ones people idolize, rarely think of themselves as heroes.
~Scott Randolph

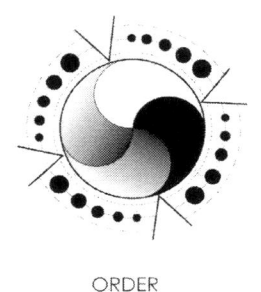

ORDER

I'll aid. Carelian's strong, clear voice shocked me as it cut through my haze of grief and fear. He leapt up next to us, pressing into Jo's legs.

Jo rocked back on her heels blinking at the cat, as if coming out of a dream. Carelian headed butted her and her hand fell to bury into his fur. "You'll what?" Her voice broke as she looked at him. I realized he was talking to both of us. She could hear him, and he offered to help. I had to fight not to fall to my knees and worship the red fur clad body.

I'll help. Reduce the cost. His voice had a firmness to it that sounded so much older than his kitten frame suggested. His long tail wrapped around my leg as he pressed into Jo. ***Will let my magic boost. Make very powerful.***

"Anything," I said. "But remember I must close the rips also. But first, can we do it?" I felt like ethereal claws were running down my back as the rips became more solid and I knew things were coming to the holes in reality. Maybe even slipping in.

Easy. Seek, find the offering amount. His voice so calm and assured. Jo kept her eyes closed, but her hand stayed buried in his fur while her other reached out to me. I clutched it bruisingly hard, but neither of us cared. This was too important.

"Got it," she whispered, the rest of the world disappeared from my awareness. Only Jo and the rips existed.

Offer, Carelian murmured.

I felt the magic explode out of her, crossing across the stadium, shattering the molecular bonds of that specific structure. It took less than fifteen seconds, but it felt like eternity before her offering was accepted and reality became fluid.

Reality blinked back into place around me as Jo sagged to the stairs. Her hair, her long gorgeous hair, had vaporized to stubble on her skull and she was pale and shaking, but she was alive. I quickly counted all her digits. I could see her nails were gone to the quick, but she had all her fingers.

"The cost?" I asked as I supported her to sag to the ground. Carelian curled up next to her purring loud enough he sounded like a buzz saw.

"Worth it. Stinky? Sable?" she asked, her voice weak and shaky. I wondered what else she had offered up, but I didn't press. Instead I rose and headed over to where the Guzman's sat, their faces as pale as Jo's.

"What did she do?" Marisol's voice was the highest a higher pitch than I'd ever heard.

"Saved everyone, I think," I said it absently as I knelt in the seat next to Sanchez. His pulse beat in a steady rhythm and his breathing had become regular. Color was returning to his face and I couldn't see anything else other than unconsciousness that looked or felt wrong.

"Go to her, honey," Henri encouraged. "I've got Sanchez."

Marisol gave a jerky nod and got up to go to Jo as I moved over to Sable. She had a trace of bloody foam at the corners of her mouth. I checked and it looked like she'd bitten her tongue while seizing, but she, like Stinky, breathed normally and her heart rate was good.

Let's hope that worked. And I didn't miscalculate and sentence them all to being living vegetables.

My phone rang as I worried about what might be worse. I answered the call, but before I could say anything Alixant was yelling. "What just happened? What did you do? We felt the wave wash through. My Transform wizard says it was stronger than anything he's ever felt. All the molecules have shattered. They say they can't find any nicotine anywhere."

"Oh good, it worked," I sighed out the words. "Are people okay? Did it create anymore issues?"

"Cori! What. Did. You. DO?" He was almost shouting the words. And oddly, I sensed a bit of fear in the question. That made no sense. I looked at the rips in the air and stood.

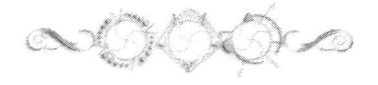

"I'll explain later. I have to get those rips closed." I noticed movement on the field. It was the first I'd seen in a while as all the players had disappeared by the time I got to Jo and her family. Not even the cheerleaders had still been there. All movement had been in the stands as people frantically worked on the afflicted.

I also realized the sound, the feel of the stadium had changed. When I got up here it had been unrelenting panic and fear. Now, there was confusion, almost relief, as the noise changed from screams and pleading. Now I heard laughter, sobs of relief, evening crying.

"Something is going on at the field. I have to get down there. I feel things coming and the rips are closer to the field." And they were, which made me panic. When I'd felt them earlier, they'd been high in the air. Now they had moved or reformed or something, much, much closer to the ground and I just knew I could close them easier if they were closer to me.

"Dammit. Okay, I'll get people headed that way." I didn't hear if he said anything else as I hung up on him and grabbed my bag.

"Come on, Carelian. We need to get down there. I have to close those rips." He stood stretched with a cat's nonchalance and walked over. I scooped him up and set him in the bag. "You okay Jo?"

"I'll be fine. Just exhausted. Go." Her eyes locked on mine and she nodded.

I turned and ran. At least this time I was going down the stairs, so I moved faster than I did going up. But the place was a maze and the path to the field seemed purposefully barred. I stood in the main thoroughfare, trying to read how to get there but I didn't see anything that gave me a hint as to which way to go.

"Cori!" The shout made me turn, and I saw Niall sticking his head out of a door. "Down here!"

Relief made my knees go weak as I sprinted towards him. I would never refuse going to the gym again. When I got close enough to speak without yelling, people were still rushing about, though with less stress. "Can we get to the field this way?"

"Yes, follow." He turned and the door almost hit me in the face before I managed to grab it. I went through, then tried to keep up. I failed. His annoyance was clear as he had to wait at each door for me, they were all card key locked.

Bite me. This isn't the life I had in mind.

The stitch in my side had reappeared with Carelian had tripling in weight before light at the end of a tunnel greeted me. I tried to step up my pace, but we were moving at a steady jog and even imagining blood thirsty monsters behind me didn't get more than a step or two at a greater speed. Sunlight, hot and almost searing after all that time in the tunnels, speared into my eyes and I closed them in reflex, but I kept moving forward. The second I was out from under the weight of earth and metal above me, the presence of the tears were like an ice pick slamming into my mind.

"Ow," I muttered. A quick glance around showed almost no one, so I let Carelian out. He bounded out with way too much energy. "Next time you're walking," I muttered, but I knew he was still too small and too young to take that risk. But out here he should be safe.

"Cori!" Alixant's voice from my left pulled my attention away from the tears hanging what felt like ten feet from the ground.

"Yeah?" I glanced and saw him coming my way, then I turned back to look at the tears and the man that looked like he was in the middle of them.

"What's going on?" He demanded and I felt his glare burning into me, but I didn't bother to look at him.

"You see the same thing I do. Is that the guy? The one that did all this?"

"We think so. My mages tell me they can feel the power flowing towards him. Can't you feel it?"

I frowned, none of this made sense. I hadn't played with my abilities enough yet but after he said that, I realized the odd breeze that I had been feeling wasn't a breeze. I should have realized that running through the maze, but I had dismissed it as air conditioning or my rushing. It was magic flowing out of the openings, swirling around, then being pulled back towards the figure, though I could almost sense it swirling around the other mages. That made me take a few more steps closer and I turned and looked up at the stands. Then it hit me.

"Oh crap."

"What?" He was next to me, so close I could smell his cologne, definitely not a scent I favored, too much woodsmoke.

"Can you see the magic swirling around people?. Since most of them have quit dying," I paused and shot him a glance. "They have quit dying, right? What she did worked?"

"Yes, they have, and you will explain this later," he growled out but he motioned me to proceed.

"So now the magic is flowing into them, but there is so much it is making them emerge. Expect a wave of things to start hitting." I didn't know how to explain it. It was like I had a weird set of glasses on my face, letting me see the magic like currents of water and some people were pulling it in and starting to glow with magic like a bomb in a video game, close to exploding. Dismissing that, I turned and looked at the man in the center of the rips and went cold, so cold I wanted a coat. I knew it was above ninety out, but my fear was so great I was shivering.

"Cori? What is it?" He must have seen something on my face, because he sounded worried.

"He's about to emerge and there is so much power." I saw the man began to pulse and I just reacted. "CARELIAN! Jo, down!" I put everything into that scream, my eyes locked on the section she was in. There was no way she could have heard me, none. But I saw a figure wearing the colors Jo wore, with a bald head, jerk upwards and then grab others and pull them down.

Red fur streaked towards me and I grabbed him and fell to the ground, wrapping around him, my back to the man about to emerge at levels I suspected no one had ever witnessed before.

"Everyone, take cover now," Alixant bellowed as he hit the ground next to me. I curled up tighter, then gasped in pain as I felt the rips react to the building power in the man on the field.

Oh, this is so going to suck.

Chapter 42

Gods exists, or at least powerful monsters. Do you really want to use anything associated with them? Turn your back on magic and the corruption it brings.
~Freedom from Magic

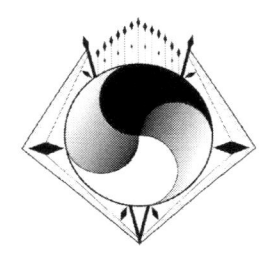

SPIRIT

Curled tight, I thought about how bad Jo's emergence had been and wondered if this would kill us all.

And I waited.

And waited.

Had I been wrong? Was he not about to emerge? I thought back to the image of him all but pulsing with power and clenched tighter around Carelian. I hadn't been wrong.

"Cor-" I heard Alixant say, when the bubble of power popped with a sound I sensed but didn't feel, at least not until the wave of power slammed into me. I felt my clothes ripple around me, and Carelian burrowed deeper into me.

Air, heat, and sound, all blasted into me with physical force. Then it vanished as if it had never been there. I listened, scared for a minute. I'd seen what Jo's emergence did. If this one had changed the material of the stadium, we might all be at risk. But after lying there, frozen for an eternal moment, nothing more happened. No creaking of material no longer steel, no screams of terror, just ambient noise that didn't set off alarms. I lifted my head slowly and looked at Carelian. His green eyes met mine and when he licked my nose.

Am fine. Go. His voice sounded shaky, but not hurt, so I looked at myself next. This time my dress, my only decent dress, had changed to black leather that clung to what curves I had. I was already starting to bake in the sun. My shoes, previously black flats, were now so heavy I almost couldn't lift my feet. I didn't waste time trying to figure out what they had changed into, I just slipped my feet out and stood, tugging down the dress awkwardly. If I had to guess, my undergarments were now something much less supportive and comfortable.

I saw Alixant standing and gaped at him for a second. His nice suit jacket changed to crepe paper, if I wasn't mistaken, and already started to tear as he moved.

"I hate Transform emergences," he growled out, pulling the jacket away. His shirt looked like it was now silk instead of cotton clinging to his torso in a way I'd seen on romance covers. His slacks had turned to leather and all in all he'd make a good model for anything using sex as a marketing technique

Realizing how bad this could have been, I counted myself lucky. Being naked in front of all these people would have just been the capper on this day.

The intent of magic indeed. This could have been so bad, but it isn't.

I needed to follow that train of thought at some point, research paper maybe, the sentience of magic. The crunch of grass turned into paper caught my attention and I turned and stared at the man walking towards us. Arrogance in every step.

Out of the corner of my eye, I glimpsed Alixant reaching for his gun then growl as it crumbled in his grip, making the sound of aluminum crackling. He let it go and narrowed his eyes at the mage, who stopped about ten feet from us and grinned, a wide smile, full of malice.

"Don't bother. There isn't anything you can do to me. I'm the first triple merlin in the world. Did you know if you plan for this, you can combine powers to make yourself shields? The elements combine nicely together. Even if you had a mage here who knew exactly what veins in my skull to rupture, I could kill him before even one of them broke. It helps when you can set your magic to monitor your every cell. Years on that damn fire jump team gave me lots of time to research, to read. That volcano killing those morons answered all my questions about the things hinted to in the books. I am now a god!"

He roared the last part of the monologue and tilted his head back and laughed.

Oh Merlin, we're all going to die. The people he's killed will just be the beginning.

The realization we had failed, and not only had we not stopped the guy, but now he was more powerful that ever tasted like bitter ash on my tongue.

I knew almost nothing. Could I stop him? In theory I should be able to, but with what? I knew how to close rips in the fabric of reality, not much else.

As if my thinking of them woke them up, the rips rippled. Where they had looked like tears in fabric, gaping a little where our reality was pealed back and revealing another existence, they now looked like mouths that were gaping open, ready to spill things out. If they hadn't already.

Indira had told me not to look into them, that you could get enraptured by what you couldn't quite see but I stared. I didn't see how you couldn't. Colors I didn't have names for, colors I shouldn't be able to see sparkled on the other side. Things moved in there - creatures that were dark, wondrous, immense, ethereal, and yet they were all of these, some of these, and none of these at the same time. I felt my grasp on reality start to slip when pain blossomed from my thigh. It hurt bad enough I looked down to see what had stabbed me.

Carelian stared up at me, his claws in the exposed skin of my thigh. *Dangerous, seductive, not for you.*

Blinking, I snapped out my hand at Alixant. I hit him hard in the arm, the silk shirt absorbing none of the sting.

He turned his head slowly at first then, moving faster once his gaze left the rips. "What the hell, Munroe?" He demanded, rubbing at his arm.

"You were getting entranced," I said, my voice bleak. "We need to snap the others out of it."

Me! Carelian's voice had way too much delight to it as he scampered behind people, needle sharp claws swiping at calves, and in at least one case, a rear end. Muted exclamations of pain, then sharp indrawn breaths followed his path of bloodletting.

I turned back to look at the man, Paul, laughing and staring at one of the rips.

"Maybe we can grab him now? You think he's entranced?" Alixant muttered starting to move forward, head tilted down slightly.

"I can hear you. No. I am no longer subject to the weakness of mortal minds." He waved his hand behind him and Alixant few back toward the benches lining the field. He hit with a crash that made me wince. A sound emanated from the rips and I found I couldn't look away, but I wasn't entranced, this time I couldn't look away from sheer fear. Things were stepping out of their own realities into ours.

Niall had somehow ended up next me. His clothes had come out better than Alixant, wearing cotton jersey and denim, and I could see Siab making her way towards us, though I had no idea what they thought we could do. Maybe they had a sniper somewhere that could kill him or another archmage or merlin that could explode his brain.

Paul turned his eyes on me, and I realized he was crazy. Not just wired crazy, but the snap and kill everyone type of crazy.

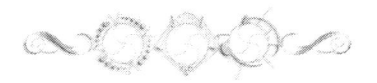

"No, silly woman. There is no one that can stop me. Reading all your thoughts is laughably easy but killing you would ruin all my fun. I want you to see what you couldn't stop." A sound of grass, or what had been grass, crunching as one of the beings stepped onto the ground grabbed my attention. A smile spread across Paul's face as he turned away. "And look, my familiars are coming to me. With them I'll have everything I ever wanted."

I heard his rambling but at this point I was trying to watch three things at once. A hoof, silver and delicate stepped out of the plane that felt like Order to me. A long, snakey tail had slithered out of the opening to Spirit. Then something, something black, oily, and writhing, oozed out of the portal to Chaos, and it was attached to something larger on the other side.

Fur brushed by my naked legs and I bent down to pick up Carelian, not glancing away as a unicorn stepped out of the Order rip. It gleamed silvery white, its horn at least three feet long and a pearly silver that hurt to look at. I wanted to go pet it and that scared me even more. I'd never been into horses I'd always liked cats, but horses never called to me and I wanted to go pet this one? It nickered, a long musical sound, and revealed a mouth full of fangs.

Paul twisted to face the unicorn. I looked at his back and for a moment I wished I had the ability or knowledge to kill him, but before it could complete into a real thought, much less an action, I snared on the creature coming out of Spirit. A long snakelike body that coiled and twisted, in hues of green and blue that seemed restful. I let my eyes wander up the perfect torso, muscular and tanned to breasts that even air brushed models never had. Her face was classic, clear beauty, with not a flaw or wrinkle on it, full lips, high cheekbones, and the snakes that formed her hair seemed to match perfectly.

But for all that, I was sure people were supposed to turn into stone if she looked at us. No one did as her gaze ran over all of us, though I couldn't turn to see anything else. Siab had made it next to me. She stood on one side while Niall stood on the other. I didn't know if Alixant had managed to get back up or if Paul had killed him. We had to do something, and I had no idea what we could even begin to do.

"See what comes to serve me?" He laughed with his arms spread wide. I didn't. Neither the gorgon nor the unicorn looked remotely servile. Without really wanting to, I turned my attention to Chaos and the things oozing out of it. It formed on the field, the earth cracking under it and I couldn't see it. I mean I saw it, but it shifted and twisted and wasn't there even while it was there. I could comprehend a mass of writhing shapes with an oily feeling that made no sense.

With a sense of desperation I ripped my eyes away to focus on the unicorn, if unicorns ate meat, and the gorgon. Turning to stone might have been the easy way out, but while she looked around with an aura of supreme disinterest, nothing turned to stone.

"What do we do?" whispered Siab.

I gave her an incredulous look. I had no idea, then I realized she was asking Niall. The flush of stupidity didn't have a chance to last long. Paul walked up to the three of them and crossed his arms; I could still see power leaking out of his body. Even though I couldn't see him, I knew he was smiling a smile that made me want to smack it off his face. His words confirmed it.

"See.? I get three monsters to serve me. I will have every person on Earth kneeling before me. Everything I have ever wanted will be mine."

Me? Serve you? The gorgon looked at him and laughed. *Did you hear that, Salistra? The mortal thinks we would serve it.*

Her words rang in my mind and ears, though what my ears heard was a string of syllables that meant nothing while my mind filled with her words.

The unicorn shook its head, and matching laughter filled my mind. *As if. I think I shall pass. I prefer mine more innocent, if not an actual virgin. He is already so corrupt that what little he has left to fall would be of no interest to me.* This time I heard nothing, but the words in my mind sounded like crystal bells and I shuddered with revulsion as the sexual over tone of corruption seeped into my mind.

You and your virgins. Just because they've never had sex doesn't mean they are innocent. There have been a few that even turned my stomach. Somehow I knew it was the gorgon talking and my eyes kept drifting back to her. She was fascinating and less scary than the overly perfect unicorn with lavender eyes and teeth made to rend and tear. I had zero doubt she was just as deadly.

"Excuse me?" Paul Goins sounded surprised and insulted. "I'm the most powerful mage Earth has ever seen. You will serve me." The black ooze from Chaos had reached his leg and started climbing up around it. His leg jerked as if stung. "Get off. You are mine to command, do you understand?"

We know you are the most powerful mortal in centuries. Why do you think we are here? We wanted a new toy. The gorgons voice held contemptuous amusement as she slithered around him, circling him as if he was her prey.

Viriginity just ensures there is something for me to model to my desires. I prefer those I can twist and bend. He is already too tarnished to enjoy. After all, look at what he was willing to do just for more power. So simplistic, so wasteful. The musical horsey sound of the unicorn filled my head and I didn't know if I wanted to cry or scream at the sound.

Mineeee, a voice, dark, oily, twisted, hissed through my mind and I moaned a bit in pain. Niall screamed.

A dark tentacle, except it changed width and length and twisted as it moved, slithered forward and started to glide around Paul Goins.

A sound that I couldn't hear in my mind assaulted my ears. It was followed by the gorgon's voice midway through a sentence, making me think that horrible sound was the Chaos thing's name. *You never did have any patience. Why are you claiming this one? You took one last century. We should get him. What if I want him?* Affront and amusement coated the voice, but no true anger. It worried me how I could tell the feelings of these creatures.

Out of the corner of my eye I saw Siab with both hands over her ears, tears running down her face.

Still jealous, Tiriane? Lovecraft did so enjoy my company. I broke him too soon. I need another to tell stories of me. Merlins tell the best stories.

The voice drew blood from my mind, and I screamed, hitting my knees, tears streaking down my face as I fought to deal with the pain. Siab lay next to me on the ground, her hands over her ears, sobbing.

"What are you doing? You are mine. You will obey me," Paul shrieked that last part as the oily darkness wrapped around his leg and started to climb up.

Why would I be jealous? I prefer the solitude. Go, take your toy. I think they would be glad to be rid of him.

Her words didn't stop the pain, but like a salve they coated over the wounds left by Chaos'that voice, easing the ripples of agony.

Quit being so dramatic, again that sound that made me shudder in pain, *take the mageling and leave. If we destroy this world they would be most annoyed at us.* The unicorn's crystal bell voice added another layer of ease and I managed to look up when Paul started to scream.

"I will destroy you!"

Laughter from the three of them brought me curling around my knees as joy, pain, amusement, and contempt were all expressed at the same time.

Humans. Always so arrogant. That is why I do love to keep them as pets. Oh well, maybe next time, the gorgon murmured slithering backwards a little.

Paul thrashed as the black living ropes wound around him. Fire and lightning slammed down at the thing that gripped him. The earth began to shake and wind rose fast and vicious. We were in the middle of the field, but I saw a tornado starting to form, something I didn't even know was possible for a mage to do.

Oh Merlin, if a tornado forms, thousands will die.

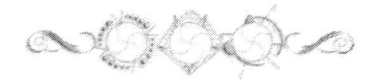

Chapter 43

That which men do, be it for greed or power, has little to do with if they are mages or not. Some people will always use others for their own gain regardless of the cost. Do not confuse magic with the ability to do harm. All people have that ability, the difference lies in their choices, not if they have magic or not.
~OMO Interview

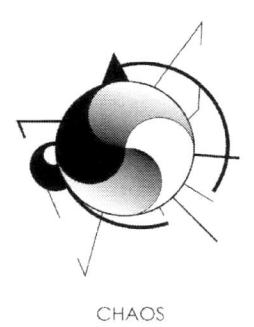

CHAOS

Even if Jo had broken the poison, people were still in need of medical care, there were people milling around, and this stadium held over sixty thousand people and it had been almost full. That meant tens of thousands could get killed. My stress ratcheted up as I tried to think of something, anything.

Really, I don't need my girls pouting for a week, the gorgon sighed with a sound that made me want to weep with sorrow. I raised my head to watch her. She moved over to where Paul was thrashing and lashing out with magic I'd never seen, even at the movies. Her face changed. Where she had been perfectly beautiful, something any woman would have longed to look like, a monster emerged. It was so horrid that I choked, unable to breathe as her snakes rose up around her head creating a corona of horror around her. My mind kept trying to figure out how incomparable beauty could change, then it was gone. As was the magic. I looked at Paul and he had frozen. A statue of stone? Marble? Something hard and elegant.

There. It will wear off in a few hours, I only glanced at him. He annoyed me.

A burble of something, then the black oozed over Paul's statue and pulled him into the gaping rip. I relaxed, so glad to have that awful dark thing gone. I saw all the openings were still rippling and burbling at the edges, unlike the which the ones Indira had created never did.

Until next time, Tiriane. Don't linger too long, their mundanity might leak in, and that takes forever to cleanse out of the soil. The unicorn turned and stepped through, though it seemed to me the hooves stepped over something. Once fully in it, she turned, I'd had ample proof from the hind view it wasn't a male, at least not how we identified males, and swung her horn from one side of the tear to the other, and it sealed behind the glowing silver spike until it disappeared.

Oh that creature can never close doors. Tiriane sighed like a wash of cooling water through my mind, and grasped the rip with both hands and pulled it together.

I blinked and waved my hand outward, mimicking her actions. That made no sense. I'd never been told you could pull them close, besides I'd assumed she was six, maybe seven feet tall but to reach that wide easily, she would have been close to twenty feet tall. It snapped closed like magnets pulled it, leaving a ripple that faded into nothing. Then she turned and looked at me. Well, at us, I supposed. Niall, Siab, myself, and from the crunch and breathing behind me, I assumed Alixant.

I guess he didn't die. He might not be so lucky in a minute.

Now what should I do with all you humans?

I swallowed. Or at least I tried to. The lump in my throat didn't want to move. The gorgons gaze swept over all of us as she moved forward, the length of her serpentine body cracking the former grass as she moved towards us.

What had the grass turned into?

I dismissed the thought as she got closer. She was taller than I thought, at least seven feet, but not the monstrous twenty feet she'd had to have been to grab the tears like that.

"Who are you?"

I jerked, not at the words but more at the aggressive tone in Alixant's voice. I wanted to turn around and slap him. Hadn't he seen everything that happened? This creature, woman, whatever was not something to annoy, much less piss off. Siab's hissed intake of breath told me she had the same reaction.

Laughter boomed like thunder and I winced. *Mortals are so amusing, thinking they have power when in all reality their little slice of existence is nothing more than fodder for our dreams. But I have no desire to deal with your posturing at the moment.*

Her face changed, just for a split second, looking behind me. Then she was back to beautiful. The lump of fear that rested in my throat might never ever go away as I turned to see Alixant standing behind me, frozen like a statue. I could see his pulse beating in his neck, so I turned back to look at the most dangerous being I'd ever heard of.

She caught me in her gaze, and I couldn't escape, look away, or even close my eyes. This close I could see her eyes were the green of pale jade but her pupils were slitted like a snake, yet rather than black, they were white slits that seemed impossibly deep and bright.

You are interesting though. I suspect I may see you again some day. But your lives are so fleeting. Ah, I know.

Her words sounded like musings out loud, but none of us made a peep. At this point I figured we were all dead anyhow, so I just stood there, waiting.

She leaned in close, her face filling my vision and I heard Siab whimper even as Niall made a sound somewhere between a growl and a cry.

Yes, that will work well. One of her snakes, one with red and blue diamonds on it, lashed out and sank fangs into my left arm about two inches below my wrist.

"Ow!" I yelped, but the snake had pulled back before the words died in the air. I dragged my gaze away from her beautiful and deadly visage. My wrist burned where two drops of blood oozed out of my arm. I wiped them away and saw two holes, with dark blue outlining them like a tattoo.

It will serve to remind anyone that I have a prior claim. Though I do not believe you shall follow the path of the other one.

"What will happen to him?" I hadn't really meant to ask, but the words were out. Once again my speaking to authority without thinking issue with authority came to the forefront.

A shrug of shoulders made her breasts rise and fall, and my eyes snapped to them. While I didn't want to touch them, they commanded attention. She spoke, that name that caused pain and we almost whimpered in unison.

… will play with and use that mageling until bored or the mageling dies. Then either let other toys play with it or dispose. Do you really care?

I didn't have an answer to that and glanced over at Niall and Siab.

"Not really. The sentence was death for what he did, if we could have done it." It sounded like the words were dragged out of Niall, but he was correct. Paul had been terrifyingly powerful, and no mage could really be locked up.

Then worry not. I should go. She smiled, both unsettling and beautiful. *You will have other things to occupy you until we meet again.* She turned and slithered, though it came across as an elegant movement.

"What things?" Siab's voice quavered but she spoke, having risen to a kneeling position on the grass, though tears still stained her face. "And is Steve dead?" She waved back at Alixant, still frozen there. A perfect statute.

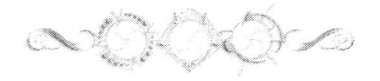

Tiriane glance back, at the edge of the tear. *No, killing him would be counterproductive. He will regain mobility soon enough.* She started to slip through the tear, then speared us with her eyes, the pale jade green glowing. *You may want to track down some of the denizens of the planes that slipped out into your world. While not all of them are deadly, neither are all of them familiars. They may not be what you want roaming around your existence, though I could be wrong.* She smiled, showing black obsidian like teeth with long fangs. *Some people enjoy having dragons and Salistra's children roaming around.*

With that comment she slipped into the fissure and turned to face us.

"There are dragons loose on Earth? But I didn't see anything come out." The words had an unsettling level of squeak in them and I clamped my mouth shut with a hand over it, the other still clutching Carelian.

Do you not think any creature from our existences could not manage invisibility? Silly mortals, you see everything as if you are the only ones that can think. I wonder how long your world will last before you are forced to choose? Her snakes writhed outward creating a halo of serpentine bodies and she waved at me.

Reacting on automatic I waved back. As I did so the opening began to shrink. I stood there watching her until with one last fang filled smile, the tear sealed.

Sound rushed in. I hadn't realized how much the rips had dampened the sound until they disappeared. Voices spoke over the speaker system, people were still yelling and screaming, and even more people streamed towards us. I turned around and looked at everything. Siab and Niall were checking on Alixant, who looked like something that should be in Madame Tussards Wax Museum. But even as I watched, I saw him blink.

If everything around us was this active, people should have reached us while we were dealing with the monsters.

Time stop. A bubble.

I looked down at the cat in my arms, his fur all fluffed and his ears laid back. Since I felt freaked out, I understood completely.

"Why?"

Siab looked at me funny, then saw I was looking at Carelian and just shook her head, turning back to Alixant, who managed to swallow.

The great ones don't like to explain themselves. Tiriane likes you. He licked my wrist where the two blue punctures sat. I stared at them.

"Why do you say that, and what do they mean?"

Must like you, or you dead. His voice was amused as he licked the punctures once more. Then he wiggled to get out of my hold. I let him go and ignored the people that had almost reached us, football fields were big.

"He going to live?" I nodded at Alixant as I spoke to Siab.

"Yes, thank you," he replied, his voice a bit stiff. I watched him roll his shoulders and stretch. "Did everyone hear what I did about Lovecraft and toys, and finding Cori interesting?"

"Yes," Niall and Siab responded together and all of them focused their attention on me. I squirmed.

"Then you heard what I did," my voice defensive.

Alixant signed and looked around. "Our unsub is taken care of and in a way we can't be held responsible for. Which is oddly nice. Writing up the report will be a bitch and a half but must better than trying to pull in a merlin. One that is insane on top of it all." He paused, people reached us and started to clamor, demanding explanations, wanting updates, giving reports. "Cori, go grab a first responder and have them put you to work. Be in the office Tuesday," he stopped for a second and gave me sharp look, "with your friend. I'll want to know everything, and I'll decide where we are going from here."

I started to protest, but the need to help people decided it. "You want to go stay with Jo?"

Rather than answer, he jumped into the bag and looked at me. I grabbed it and bent over to grab my shoes, then stopped. They looked like solid obsidian. Felt like it too. I blinked then shrugged. Barefoot it was. Wearing those wasn't an option. I turned, holding Carelian in his bag and ran, my heart singing at the idea of being useful and not stuck in a job I couldn't do. Maybe they'd even have a spare jumpsuit and booties for me.

Epilogue

While we think we know everything about magic, we don't. Magic changes as we do, and how we use it in the future may change everything we know about it now.
~Entropy Merlin Rasputin

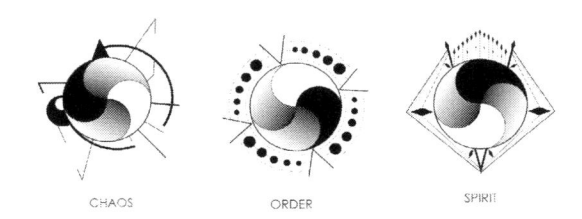

CHAOS   ORDER   SPIRIT

I didn't leave the stadium until two A.M. Monday morning. Jo had left with her family, and they were keeping Sable overnight. Sanchez was fine and , but Sable needed supervision and the hospitals were full. I thought they would go back to Rockway, but when I opened the door, the lights blazed out and I saw Jo, sleeping with her feet on the couch while a dark haired figured snored softly under a blanket.

Jo jerked up as I closed the door, her all but bald head looking wrong after years of hair to her butt.

"You okay?" The first words she said to me. She stood, stretched and moved towards me as I set down my bag. Carelian was sound asleep and was about as tired as me.

"Tired. Hungry," I admitted, my nose twitching at the scent of Mexican rice and beans.

She pulled me to into a hug and I just wrapped my arms around her, leaning in for a long minute, trying to let her love erase a day of hell.

"Go change. I'll get some food ready."

"Sable okay?" I asked as I headed back to the hall.

"I'm fine. Still a bit sick to my stomach, but I'm fine. Thank you." Her voice was soothing and had traces of the south in it, but not enough that I could tell from where.

I didn't respond, just headed to peel out of the borrowed suit and shoes, shower, and get some food.

The three of us talked until four am, then we all crashed again. Jo and I had our meeting tomorrow with the FBI, though I'd already sent him a text that we wouldn't be there until well after ten.

Sable had quickly fallen back asleep so I didn't' get much chance to talk to her, but what little I did, I liked.

On Tuesday we left her sleeping there on the couch when we headed to meet with the FBI people. Oddly, Carelian wanted to stay so I left him sleeping on my bed after making sure his food and water were filled.

Jo drove me there on her bike, though she had to run back up to get a scarf, her helmet wouldn't fit without all her hair.

We made it to the office about ten-thirty and I stood outside, not wanting to go in yet. My phone buzzed and I jumped, then looked at Jo. She texted me more than anyone else. I pulled it out and looked at the text message.

`Laurel gave me your number. Knew him. Whiney mage. Hated doing anything he didn't have to do. Good riddance. BTW - good job with the gorgon. Shay.`

"Huh, Shay got back to me a day late and dollar short. But what does he mean, good job? And how did he know about the gorgon?"

"It's Shay. Do you expect him to make sense?"

"Point." I grinned and I walked her in, feeling myself tensing at every step. I still didn't know how to deal with Alixant.

"Ladies, come on in."

I stared at Alixant. He was dressed in jeans and a t-shirt that clung to his body. I dragged my eyes to the others and they were all in similar casual apparel, nothing like the almost formal stuff offor the last few weeks.

Jo looked at him, then at me. "And you aren't chasing that?" Her voice carried and I thought about turning and walking back out of the room, though the blush that tinted his cheeks made me laugh.

"That is my boss, so no."

Jo just rolled her eyes and walked in, holding out her hand. "I'm Jo Guzman."

Alixant rose from his chair and gave her a narrow look. His eyes focused on her nude skull, then at me. "Steven Alixant. Come on in. I think you both have a story to tell."

We got everyone introduced and I noticed that Niall gave her one or two interested looks. We took seats and Jo started talking first about the paint. There had been five to ten people handing it out. They had painted it on once they got seated. So it took a while before anything happened.

"Honestly, at first I just thought Stinky was hitting the beer harder than he should have in that heat."

"We had a few jars of it away from the stadium when the transformation happened, so we discovered he mixed it with the wax in the paint. Once it melted it started to absorb into the skin. A few other chemicals made it last for a while, but once it was in a victim's system the results couldn't be stopped," he paused and looked at us. "Except they were. Would you like to explain how?"

I looked at Jo, this was her tale to tell, not mine.

She reached up to push hair back, hair that wasn't there and her hand fell awkwardly to her lap. "I'm a Transform mage, archmage rank. Cori showed me the molecule and I could sense it floating through people, the air, everywhere." Jo didn't look at me, her hands made abortive gestures to twist her hair. "I could do it, but it would cost everything."

"Wait? Cori asked you to-" Siab broke off and stared at me. I shifted back uncomfortably, but Jo continued.

"No. She didn't ask, but it was my brother, my friend. It was people. Was my life so precious that I was willing to let them all die so I could live?" She shrugged. "I'd figured it out, the offering clear in my mind, when Carelian said he'd help."

Alixant jerked up as it hit with a jolt of electricity, staring at Jo. "Cori's familiar offered to help you? Spoke to you?"

Jo looked at me, frowning, and I shrugged, confused about his intensity.

"Sure. He talks to me occasionally. Not much, but he likes having his ears scratched." I watched, and all of them seemed shocked and surprised at what she was saying.

"You're only a freshman, right? Just emerged? And you two aren't lovers?"

I almost snapped at Alixant's question but he didn't seem curious about our sex life, just verifying facts.

"Freshman, and no, Cori and I have never been sexual partners, but I do love her. Possibly more than I love anyone." Jo's back had gone rigid and her hands tightened into fists.

Alixant opened his mouth but Siab stepped in. "The shock is because familiars almost never interact with anyone other than their mage. Occasionally a spouse but even then, that is rare, to the point there have been divorces over it. So Carelian freely working with Jo is surprising."

"Oh," I muttered, and I saw the tension go out of Jo's body.

"So your hair was enough to pay the price?" Niall asked.

Jo did something that struck me as odd, her head ducking down, then she rubbed her face with her hands. I didn't know why it bugged me, but that wasn't her normal mannerism.

"Hair, nails, top layer of skin, a bit of blood. I bit my tongue for that, and a few other things. It was enough. Barely."

He leaned back, looking at the two of us, and I wanted to hide and poke Jo.

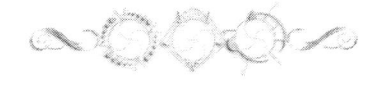

"I'd like you both to fill out detailed reports, for record keeping if nothing else. We got Goins phone from his car and it had the information we'd been searching for. He'd been passed over for a few better placements due to his ranking, and he'd lost his fiance' to an archmage not two months before the volcano incident. His ramblings all focused on how fate hated him because he'd been born as a wizard, not a merlin. It ramped up after a bad fire jump where they lost two jumpers. Odds are that was what drove his fiance' away. He talked a lot about failing and then needing power. From his notes he had an emergence at the volcano and came out with the Air skill. He thought it was the slow death and that if he made it last longer it would let him emerge again. The ritual magic stuff was a first attempt. He used it with Jane." Alixant swallowed. "It took her a full day to die, but her power wasn't enough. So he switched to more victims, and used the ritual magic again, but it didn't matter. He still couldn't emerge again."

"We verified the start of planar rips in both Savannah and Valdosta. I also found verification for what we sensed at Centennial park. There are sensors that can note rips but until now it has been a curiosity. What happened to you will change a lot of how those rips are handled," Chris said looking up from this computer.

"Great. More things to lay at my feet," I muttered, sinking down into my chair. I just asked the question. I didn't cause the issue.

Alixant looked around. "If I may continue?"

I saw Siab roll her eyes and I snickered a bit.

"Goins focused on more at the park but because everyone was hedgies, his notes said he focused on them because no one would notice their deaths, while real mages dying would create a panic. As far as his notes mention, he realized the amount of energy released was higher but not due to the symbols, just the quantity. That was when he started to figure out the numbers, it was all about volume. He didn't seem to register that it was the power of the mage dying that was the key. Or maybe he did. The notes on his phone implied he suspected it but figured most hedgies wouldn't have the power or the training to strike back and hurt him, at least in the beginning. But," Alixant sighed. "We'll probably never know for sure all the thoughts that went into his choices and his crazy actions."

He looked at all of us, waiting for a question.

"Did he get access to the database?" I was curious about that.

"Yes. He had access while working with the volcanologists. It was enough. He downloaded a list of all mages, and determined Atlanta had the most at the hedgemage rank, which is why he started here. Anything else?" No one said anything. "Very well, there are a few other things. We are not writing down anywhere that the slow deaths of mages releasing magical power creates rips in the planes. Large rips. While people like Indira can create them, the largest created rip has never measured more than a few feet in width. We are also not mentioning that the release of that much magic can spur multiple emergences in people. While my supervisors know, we all agree that letting the public know they can become more powerful mages, or even that a mage can emerge, given the number of people reporting in the last few days here in Atlanta, would not be good for the general public."

I hated the idea of hiding information, but letting people know that to get magical power all they had to do was kill people? I wanted to protest that people wouldn't do that, but the last month had proved all too well that people, at least some people, would do that.

"Okay. I don't like it, but I'll keep that to myself," I said, a touch reluctantly. Jo nodded her agreement.

"Excellent. Cori, there are a few things you should know." He cleared his throat, and I looked at him, brows furrowed. Was he nervous? That seemed odd. "While the players left the field, the video cameras recording the game for the teams were left running. They were turned over to the press," he almost snarled that part. "They show you and Paul and the three creatures from the planes. Because of the angle, they also show the fact that you remained standing during it, while everyone else crumpled, plus they have the last part of interaction with the snake lady-"

"Gorgon. I'm pretty sure Tiriane is a gorgon."

"Gorgon then, though I expect the details of that conversation leaked out. While I was, immobilized, I didn't hear what she said. But as I was saying, from the way it was filmed and your gestures, it looks like you stood up to her and you closed the portals. The media figured out your identity, so I'd expect lots of attention here shortly."

Oh shit. That's what Shay meant. Why me?

"Great, and I can't tell them what really happened?" I could see all the ways this was going to go wrong.

"No. Just smile, accept the credit and the blame. Better you than people starting to go on murder sprees to summon creatures from other realms." Alixant's voice was dry.

"You did catch that some got out, right?" I asked suddenly. Everyone's attention snapped towards me.

"They what?" I had no idea who said that, as the jumble of conversation made it hard to tell but I just answered.

"The rips were open for so long Tiriane said many creatures had come over, and not all of them were familiar types."

"You are telling me we have monsters roaming around?"

I shrugged. "I'm telling you what she said." I thought about it. "Yes, you have monsters. Did you see that unicorn's teeth?"

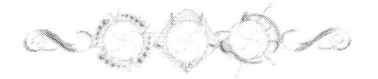

Alixant sighed. "Great. Another thing to worry about. As for you." He gave me a direct look and I braced myself. He never had good news for me, and it frustrated me. "I have arranged for you to be on retainer until your classes start. I'm not expecting anything, but we will pay you a thousand a month to be ready to come assist. And I made sure all blocks on you doing fill in shifts for the local agencies are gone. Your housing is taken care of with the stipend for familiar care. That should help."

I sagged in relief. "Yes. If I can work until school starts, I should be good then with working on the weekends."

Alixant smiled. "Good. But be aware, I have a definite interest in your degree choices." There was something about his smile that made me wrinkle my nose.

I glanced at Jo and she smirked. "I still love you."

"Good. I'm starting to think I'll need it."

She laughed and wrapped an arm around me. "BFF. It's on my skin."

I'd make it. With Jo and now Carelian, I'd make it.

Appendix: Magic Symbols

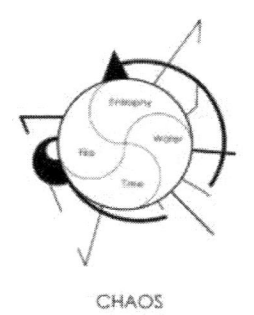

Chaos:
- Entropy
- Fire
- Water
- Time

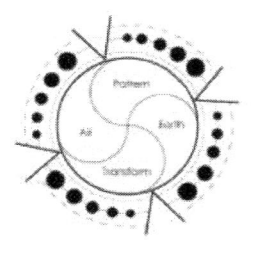

CHAOS

Order:
- Pattern
- Air
- Earth
- Transform

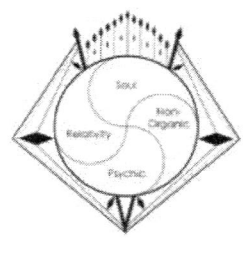

ORDER

Spirit:
- Soul
- Relativity
- Non-Organic
- Psychic

SPIRIT

Author Notes

The Ternion universe is here and Twisted Luck is just the first series in what is a complicated and fascinating world. If you enjoyed Cori getting a taste of what life holds in store for her, wait until you see where she ends up. This is a long series and I hope you enjoy this world as much as I do.

If you loved this novel, please take the time to leave a review, you will be amazed at the difference it makes.

If you'd like to stay in touch, you can follow me on social media at the following places:

Website: https://badashpublishing.com/
Facebook: https://www.facebook.com/badashbooks/
Twitter: https://twitter.com/badashbooks
Instagram: https://www.instagram.com/badashbooks/
Bookbub: https://www.bookbub.com/profile/mel-todd

If you're interested in free books, keeping up with what is going on in my life, as well as sales and launch announcements you can sign up for my newsletter at my website. You never know what freebies might be in it.

Take care!

Mel Todd

Author Bio

Mel Todd has over 20 stories out, her urban science fiction Kaylid Chronicles, the Blood War series, and the new Twisted Luck series. Owner of Bad Ash Publishing she is working to create a place for excellent stories and great authors. With over a million words published, she is aiming for another million in the next two years. Bad Ash Publishing specializes in stories that will grab you and make you hunger for more. With one co-author, and more books in the works, her stories can be found on Amazon and other retailers.